SCALES AND STINGERS

SCALES AND STINGERS

HEROES OF AVOCH
BOOK ONE

K. M. WARFIELD

This is a work of fiction. All of the characters, organizations, and events portrayed in this novel are the products of the author's imagination or are used fictitiously.

Published in the United States by Creative James Media.

SCALES AND STINGES. Copyright © 2023 by K. M. Warfield. All rights reserved. Printed in the United States of America. For information, address 9150 Fort Smallwood Road, Pasadena, MD 21122.

www.creativejamesmedia.com

978-1-956183-72-6 (trade paperback)

978-1-956183-73-3 (eBook)

Cover Design by Diana TC Triumph Covers

First U. S. Edition 2023

Dedicated to The Murder Hobos

May the dice always be kind,
The alchemy jug always be full,
And the enemy be dumber than the paladin

PROLOGUE

Thia cleared the dishes as Papa and Father Philip talked. The priest had visited before, and she liked him. Something was different today, though.

"I'm sorry, Bran," the cleric kept his voice low. "I did all I could, but they wouldn't let me speak. Drogon's got the entire village worked up. I fear it's only a matter of time before he convinces them to use force against her. This has been a haven, the one village in all of Avoch where you could keep her hidden. It was only a matter of time before travelers began to ask questions. You knew this, before she was born. The only safe place for her now in the entire kingdom is under the protection of Keroys."

Thia heard the men shift in their chairs, looking her way. She kept her head down and began to wash the dishes. Something to distract her from their gazes. Plunging her dark-skinned hands into the cold water, she sighed. She knew she looked like her mother. Where Bran was fair skinned, with brown hair and eyes, her curly hair was blonde and her eyes a pale lilac. It was the one feature that announced to the world she was part Fallen, though.

She heard Papa sigh. Thia knew the sound. He'd made a decision, but not the one he wanted. Honor, justice, and obedience were important to him. If she looked like her mother, her personality was all from him. "Tonight?" he asked the priest.

"It may be for the best." She heard the chairs scrape against the floor as the men rose. "I'll come an hour before sunset. They already know I'm heading back to Almair. I won't be missed, and my departure will be accepted."

"Bran Tannersson!" A deep voice bellowed from outside. "I know who you really are! And what you hide in your house!"

Thia whipped her head around, eyes wide. She knew the voice that echoed through the small home. Drogon had visited them several times. Each time, her father had turned him away, refusing to make the item he requested. The plate she held slipped from her fingers, crashing into bits on the wide-planked floor.

"I'm sorry, Papa," she muttered as she bent down to pick up the pieces.

Bran motioned to her. "Thia, come here." He knelt as she got closer, taking both of her hands in his. "I need you to take Father Philip into your room. Lock the door behind you and show him the tunnel under your bed. Stay with him, and I'll know you'll be safe."

"What about you, Papa?"

He shook his head. "I've got to stay here, Thia. Drogon isn't going to go away quietly. Not this time. Here," he said as he rose and walked over to his workbench. The back was full of drawers and cubbyholes. Thia knew better than to explore them. Most were hidden behind neat stacks of leather and forms he used to repair boots. Pushing a pile aside, he opened a small door. He placed a cloth packet on the wooden tabletop. It rolled open, and she caught sight of small, intricate instruments. Ones that were too delicate for repairing leather, and probably cost more than the simple three-bedroom house they lived in. Two locks of hair, one blonde and one brown, rested in the center of the kit. Bran pulled something else out. Turning around, he knelt in front of her and placed a small, carefully wrapped item in her hands. "I made this for you. Keep it with you, always, and I will be there. Trust in the law, and in Keroys, my daughter." He kissed her on the top of her head, then rose. "Now, take Father Philip and show him how to leave here safely."

"Bran!" Drogon's voice screamed out again. "Give us the Fallen spawn and we'll leave."

"I'll keep her safe. This is my vow to you and Keroys both." Father Philip whispered, "Come, my child. Show me our escape."

Thia ran for her small bedroom, fear driving her forward. As soon as they were both in the room, she slammed an iron nail into the hasp. "Under my bed," she stammered at the priest.

Together, they slid the bed aside enough to lift the hidden panel. "You first, child," the priest instructed. "I'll put the bed back as best I can."

Dropping down into the tunnel, Thia clutched her father's parting gift. Footsteps echoed from above them. Dozens of muffled voices filtered down, all angry and demanding. Thia couldn't make out what they were saying. Loose bits of dirt and dust sprayed on her with each stomp.

"Which way?" Father Philip whispered. Thia jumped at the sound.

Pointing, she led him through the dark, damp tunnel. The smell of smoke filled the passage. Tears stung her eyes, but she kept moving. "We're almost to the end." She dared to look back at the priest. Even though the tunnel was pitch black, she could make him out clearly.

"Good. My horse is there, and I left her saddled. We'll use her to get to safety."

Thia scrambled forward, willing her small body to keep going. *They're not going to hurt Papa,* she told herself. *The villagers like him.*

They used to like her, too. Then Drogon started to visit, and Papa said no to him. That's when Papa told her she couldn't go to school anymore. Father Philip came, about once a month, and gave her lessons.

This is all my fault. If I didn't look like her, they wouldn't care!

The tunnel stopped and she stood up in the small space. Pushing aside the wooden toggle, she opened the hatch. "We're here," she said as she climbed up out of the hole.

The barn was much older than Thia's ten years. Papa had said it was barely standing when he first moved in. He didn't keep horses, so they'd never bothered to fix it up much beyond the tunnel. As far as Thia knew, it was as old as the barn. But Papa always made sure it was clear, just in case.

Father Philip climbed out, closing the trap door behind them before looking at her. "This way, my child. Quickly. We don't want them to see you."

Following him to his horse, she caught sight of their home through a large gap in the boards. Thia stopped, drawn to it. Thick, black smoke curled from under the thatched roof. A reddish glow backlit the few windows set with glass. Villagers were running out, carrying things that had been hers or Papa's. As they ran, they stepped on a body laying across the threshold.

"Papa!" she screamed.

"Thia." Arms grabbed hers, spinning her around. Father Philip looked at her, his face full of compassion and grief. "I can't help him. His soul is with Keroys now. But I can save you." He picked her up and placed her at the front of his saddle. Mounting the horse behind her, he took hold of the reins. "Hold on," he told her.

She felt his legs urge the horse forward and it took off at a gallop. She held onto the pommel of the saddle with one hand. The other clenched Bran's last gift tightly.

CHAPTER ONE

Thia forced herself to keep a steady pace as she walked toward Father Philip's office. Running wasn't going to help her nerves, and it might hurt someone who got in her way. *It's nothing*, she told herself. *Probably nothing more serious than a change in the class schedule that I have to correct and post.*

The knot in her stomach didn't go away, though.

Fifteen years spent within the walls of the cloister, in the center of Almair, and Thia had learned more than she ever would have in the village of River Run. She had excelled at her classes and won praise from her teachers. Yet most of the students saw her as one of the Fallen. They either feared or mocked her. Her innate abilities earned her the title of priestess years ahead of the acolytes she had started classes with. Keroys himself blessed her with his presence when she was raised up. That hadn't made things easier.

"Fallen witch," a voice hissed at her from the shadows as she passed.

Thia didn't miss a step. She kept her head down,

ignoring the taunt as she had for years. It stung, but she'd learned how to hide the pain. As long as Keroys and Father Philip wanted her here, she would stay. No matter how much the other residents tried to drive her away.

She felt the hood begin to slide from her head. Stopping, she reached up and adjusted it. *They know it's me. But I can pretend not to see them if it's up. Pretend I won't get beaten if I lose my way in the catacombs under the cloister. Pretend I'm not the one they'll blame if something, anything, goes wrong.* If it wasn't for Father Philip's protection, she knew she would have been sent to some remote village by now. Someplace where she could be forgotten by everyone else connected with the church. He took the vow he made to her, and to her father, seriously. Punishment had been swift after the first attacks by the other acolytes. That just made them more careful not to be caught. It taught Thia an important lesson. Trust no one who can't prove they don't want to hurt her.

As she rounded the last corner, she slowed down. Armed men lingered in the area in front of the door. Their heads snapped up as she approached, studying her. Each wore the same medallion around their neck, the silver sword and shield of Garret. Paladins? What business would they have with Father Philip? While it was true that those in service to Garret often worked with Keroys's priests and priestesses, seeing them here made her heart race. *It's nothing*, she whispered to herself. *I'm probably needed to do a blessing for some mission they're on.*

The churning in her stomach said something different. She was a full priestess now and would go wherever and do whatever Keroys demanded of her. Without question or hesitation. At least, not one she would say out loud.

She kept her eyes down, her face hidden. Her hands

were swallowed by the flowing fabric of her golden yellow robe. Maybe none of them would notice. Stopping at the door, she glanced at one of the acolytes standing guard. "I've been summoned," she said.

"He's not alone," the man whispered as he opened the door for her.

Thia slid through the small opening. In the center of the room, Father Philip sat at his desk. Two men she didn't know rose from their seats in front of the priest. "Ah, Thia. Come here."

Thia walked across the thick, woven rug toward one corner of the desk, trying not to stare at the strangers. The familiar warmth of the room was gone. The knot in her stomach tightened. "What did you require, Father?"

"Thia, this is Drakkus Heath. He's the head of Garret's Paladins from Dragonspire." He pointed to the man closest to her. "And this is Jinaari Althir. Gentlemen, this is Thia Bransdottir."

"Hello," she said, trying not to stare. Drakkus was the shorter of the two but carried himself with a sense of command. Jinaari was almost a head taller. While she was used to being scrutinized, there was something in his dark eyes that was unsettling. He was sizing her up in some way. She nodded at each of them, then turned her attention back to the priest. Maybe that would change his focus.

"Sit down, Thia. This may take a few moments."

She took a seat. They sat again, once she was settled, and turned their attention back to the priest. "She's the one?" Drakkus asked.

Father Philip nodded. "Thia's excelled at every class she's ever taken. She's talented, one that Keroys favors with his grace. She took her vows before any in her group. Don't let her demeanor fool you. She'll do what needs to be done."

Drakkus nodded. "Good. I must return to our chapterhouse." Rising, he looked at the other man. "Althir, you know what needs to happen. Follow the law, stay true to your vows, and may Garret grant you strength in combat."

"Milord Commander," the other man replied as he rose, grasping his arm briefly. "I will not fail."

Drakkus glanced Thia's way. "He's arrogant, and sometimes insufferable, but Jinaari's the best I've ever met with a sword." With a bow to Father Philip, he left the room. The remaining paladin sat down again. Thia felt his eyes on her but couldn't find the courage to meet them.

She sat, her hands in her lap, and waited for Father Philip to say something. Anything. Was this Jinaari person on a quest of some kind? Was she supposed to bless his endeavors? "Father Philip, I don't understand . . ." she started to speak.

"Thia," he turned his attention to her, "the time has come for you to leave here. Word has reached us, and Jinaari's Order, of a problem to the south. In what remains of Tanisal."

Her mind reeled from his words. Leave the cloister? "I don't . . ." she stammered. "I don't understand, Father. Have I done something wrong?"

He smiled at her. "No. Quite the opposite. You're the best we have, Thia. Jinaari is the best that Drakkus has."

"Priestess," Jinaari interrupted, his deep voice made her jump slightly. "Garret himself reached out to my Order. Tanisal's been taken over by something evil. We think a mage by the name of Drogon is behind it."

Thia's pulse raced. "Drogon?" she asked Father Philip.

"You know the name?" Jinaari asked.

She turned her attention back to him, nodding. She felt the hood slide off her head at the motion. Jinaari's eyes widened slightly as he saw her face, but he didn't flinch. "He is responsible for my father's death." She glanced back at the priest. "Are you certain?"

Father Philip nodded. "Keroys confirmed it just before Drakkus and Jinaari arrived. He specifically commanded that you join the effort to cleanse Tanisal before the contagion spreads."

She lowered her head obediently. "If this is the will of Keroys, so be it." Rising, she was startled when the paladin did the same. "When do we leave? And is it to be just the two of us?"

"There's a ship in the harbor. We'll catch a ride with them, be put ashore about a mile or so from the city wall. Others are heading that way. We'll join them before we go into the city itself," Jinaari said.

"Then I should go pack." She looked at the priest. "May I be excused?"

Father Philip walked around his desk. "In a moment. Jinaari, please ask one of the acolytes outside to lead you to the kitchens. I've already sent word. We will not send you on your way without food for the journey."

Jinaari bowed. "It's appreciated." The tall man strode from the room, closing the door behind him. She watched him leave, still confused.

Turning back to the priest, Thia asked, "Have I done something wrong, Father? There's plenty of other priests and priestesses here that can heal, fight, or do what it is that Keroys requires. Why me? I haven't left here in over a dozen years."

"Which is why it should be you. Beyond that our God

has said so. I've kept you here far too long, thinking it was the best way to keep you safe. It's not. Too many cannot see beyond what their eyes show them. They do not see you, Thia. They only see the reflection of who your mother was."

"Do you think it's the same Drogon?" She wasn't sure she wanted to hear the answer. Memories of that night still haunted her.

Father Philip leaned on the edge of his desk. "I can't be certain, but it's possible. Rumors are strange beasts. You know this. If it is, he's harnessed a type of magic that few have even tried to summon since Tanisal fell."

"Is he one of the Forsaken?" Her eyes grew wide at the thought.

"If he is, you'll need all the help Keroys can give you." He pushed off from the desk and took her by the elbow, leading her toward the door. "Remember his teachings, his laws. Hold to all you know to be true, Thia. Jinaari's the best at what he does. The others are, as well. I'm certain of it. If this is the same Drogon, you'll be safe."

"Are you sure?"

"He's a paladin, Thia. One of the best fighters ever to come out of Garret's Order. Trust in that. The rest will come in time." He opened the door and waited for her to leave.

She reached for the hood, instinctively placing it over her head. She was leaving the only home she'd had for fifteen years; with no guarantee she'd be back. *Keroys, I will do as you request of me. But what if I can't remember the spells and someone dies? Or I do?* Ignoring the tears that threatened to spill from her eyes, she kept her head down and kept walking. *It's a test. I can't, no, I won't fail.* A familiar sense of duty chased away the self-doubt. *Papa wouldn't want me to be scared.*

Reaching her small room, she pulled off the robe and

hung it on a hook. Her trunk didn't hold much, but there was an old backpack buried at the bottom. Tossing it on her bed, she opened the wardrobe doors. Outside of the ritual robes she'd been issued, she didn't have much beyond the simple tunic and breeches she wore daily. A few spare outfits went into the bag, along with a repair kit for her boots. She laid her best cloak across the bed. *It's warm and I can hide my hands in the sleeves. I hope it's enough. I don't know what else...*

Popping a panel in the base of the cabinet, she pulled out two pouches. The small, worn bag held the few coins she possessed. *It should be safe there*, she thought as she buried it between the clothing. Sitting on the edge of the bed, she took the time to open the other pouch. Resting within, wrapped in a scrap of tanned leather, sat an oblong box. She pulled it out, her fingers finding the three hidden copper acorns in the design. Pressing all of them at once, the box opened silently. Inside, a small assortment of items she'd need to perform some of her spells sat on a bed of gold velvet. Her father had made the box for her, and it had been years before she learned the secret to open it. Even longer to discover that whatever she put within would never run out.

"You ready?" Jinaari said from the doorway.

Thia looked up, startled. The paladin leaned against the framework, looking at her expectantly.

"Almost." She shut the box and rewrapped it before placing it back into the pouch. Securing it to her belt, she rose from the bed. "What about you?"

"Always. What's with the box?"

"My father made it for me." She secured the top of her pack. Throwing her cloak on, she fixed the clasp and went to pick up the bag, but he grabbed it first.

"Come on," he said, slinging her bag onto one of his shoulders. "The captain's waiting for us."

"I can carry my own bag."

"I know that. And you will. Once we get closer to Tanisal. The wind's picked up though, and the hood on your cloak isn't going to keep your face hidden without you holding in place. If I carry your bag, you can do that."

"Don't you have a bag?" She adjusted the hood, trying to read his face. Was he saying that because he thought she should be hidden?

"I sent it to the ship before coming here." He moved aside, waving his arm. "Ladies first."

She hesitated, then went through the door. "You'll have to lead once we leave the building," she told him. "I've not spent much time at the port. I have no idea which ship is ours."

"That's fine," he said, falling into step next to her. "I talked Drakkus into giving me some things for you. They're on the ship."

"Like what?"

"A chain shirt, for one. A dagger or two as well. Your order isn't a militant one, so I thought you wouldn't have those." He shrugged the shoulder that carried her pack. "Judging from the weight of this, I was right."

"Do I need those? Do you think we'll be fighting anything?" she asked.

They reached the gate leading out of the compound. Father Philip stood there, waiting. "May Keroys guide you, Thia. Keep his teachings in your heart during your travels."

The massive wooden gate swung open, exposing them to the bustling chaos of Almair. A gust of wind flew into her face and her hands grabbed at the hood of her cloak. "Like I said, it's windy out here."

She skipped a few steps, trying to keep up to the paladin's long stride. "Stay close," he cautioned her. "The city's big, but not everyone is welcoming."

"I know that," she replied.

He stopped, looking back at her. "You do. But not to the extent I do." He gave her a direct look. "I'll keep you safe, but I'd prefer if you didn't make that harder than it needs to be. So, listen. Do what I say. When we're alone on the ship, or when we reach the others, you won't have to hide. If we're anywhere else, keep the cloak on. Now, let's move. The faster I get you on the ship and below deck, the better I'll feel." He grasped her elbow and led her through the crowded streets.

Thia worked to keep the hood up, her mind trying to make sense of it all. This was happening so fast. It had not even been an hour since she got the summons and here she was, being escorted through the city to a ship that would take her to a ghost town. And, together, they were supposed to cleanse the ruins? Of what? How? The questions she didn't ask earlier formed in her mind. *Next time*, she chided herself, *ask them before you agree!*

"In here," Jinaari whispered, shoving her into a building. He eased the door closed behind them and held a finger to his lips as he pressed his head to the door. "This way," he said, taking her elbow again.

"What's going on?" she asked.

"I saw someone. He wasn't thrilled when Drakkus chose me for this assignment. He's also notorious for killing any Fallen he finds." He led her through a maze of hallways.

"I'm not Fallen. I'm human."

He looked at her. "I see it. It doesn't matter to me. Garret said you're coming, as did Keroys. When two Gods talk to me, I listen. However," he moved his head around, scanning the junction, and then moved her forward, "Alesso isn't as flexible. His family was taken by the Fallen when he was a child. He'd see your eyes and reach for his sword, regardless of orders."

They reached the end of the hallway. Two windows, covered in heavy fabric, flanked the exit. Jinaari moved the curtain aside, peering out. "Good," he said as the fabric moved back into place, "we're within sight of the ship. The storm's gotten worse, though." He stared at her cloak. "There's no time to fix it here. We move fast and you stay with me. The goal is to get on our ship. I know the captain. He's not going to let anyone on board that isn't part of the crew, or a paid passenger. Which is just you and me." He moved the curtain again, waving her closer. "It's the last ship at the end of this dock, the Ninaa. See the man at the end of the ramp? Lots of feathers in his hat?"

Thia peered outside and located who Jinaari described. "Yes. What's his name?"

"Sylver Stone. If I tell you to run, head to him. I'll take care of any pursuit."

A knot of fear formed in Thia's stomach. "Why would anyone be chasing us?"

"That's a question for another time. Something feels off. Just do what I said, okay?"

She nodded. "Stay with you unless you say different, then go to the captain and get on the ship."

"Here," he said as he slid her pack off his shoulder. "If I have to fight, I can't have this."

She put her arms through the straps and settled it on her back. Jinaari reached out, adjusting the hood slightly. "Ready?"

Grasping the fabric of her cloak under her chin, she nodded. He eased open the door, peering outside, before entering the busy street. "Come on." He motioned to her urgently.

She moved quickly, keeping pace with him as he strode toward the pier. Their captain caught sight of them, shouting orders to his crew while watching them approach.

Thia let out a scream as an arm circled her waist, lifting her off the ground momentarily. Her hood fell back, her pale blonde hair blowing in the stiff wind. "Consorting with the Fallen now, Althir? I didn't think you were this kind of 'honorable'." A male voice sounded in her ear.

She twisted her body, struggling to free herself. Whoever held her tightened his grip, forcing her closer to him.

"Let her go, Potiri. This is bigger than any grudge you have. The Gods are involved." Thia snapped her head up at Jinaari's voice. His sword was out, his eyes looking at her captor.

Thia's heart hammered in her chest as fear set in. "Where were the Gods when my family was taken, Althir? Maybe this witch knows how to find them. I won't know until I ask." Alesso's body shifted as he changed his stance.

"She's part of my task. You were there when it was given to me. Put revenge aside long enough to obey Garret's will."

What did Father Phillip teach me? After one of the acolytes tried to grab me that first week after Papa died? Pushing down her fear, Thia slammed her foot onto Alesso's. He screamed in surprise; his arm relaxing. Breaking free, she ran toward the captain. The captain gestured toward her as the sound of swords meeting rang out. She stopped as she got to him, turning to see Jinaari and Alesso fighting.

"Get on board, Milady," Sylver Stone commanded. "Jack! Take her to my cabin when she's onboard."

Thia ran up the ramp. A woman stood at the rail. "Jack?"

The brunette nodded, "Follow me."

"Jinaari?"

"He's on his way. We won't leave him behind. Come on. We must get you out of sight." Jack grabbed her arm and led her toward a small door nestled under the wheel.

"Stay here. When we're underway, we'll show you where you'll sleep." Jack left the room, closing the door behind her.

Thia fell into a chair, her hands cradling her face. All sense of security and normalcy evaporated. What had she gotten herself into? The motion of the ship changed. Raising her head, she looked out the closest window and saw the ship at the next dock begin to retreat. *We're leaving? What about Jinaari?* Standing up, she grabbed a low beam on the ceiling to keep on her feet. Orders were shouted out on the deck. The door opened again, and Jinaari came in. A red blotch spread down the ragged edges of the torn sleeve of his shirt. Thia shrugged off her pack and unclasped her cloak, tossing both onto the bed resting under a window. Walking over to him, she said, "You're hurt."

"It's a scratch. He got a lucky shot in."

"Sit down," she told him. "I can take care of it."

"It's nothing," he protested, but he did as she asked.

Moving aside the ripped portion of his shirt, she located the wound. It was small, but his blood kept seeping out. Not wanting to explain what she was doing, she tapped into the place of her soul where her magic resided and drew a finger across the wound. It closed beneath her touch. "There," she said as she moved away.

He looked at his arm, then back at her. "So, that's why."

"Why what?"

"I was told you would be necessary, but not why. You're a healer, aren't you?"

"I have a small amount of proficiency in that, yes."

"I think, Thia, that it's time you and I get to know each other better." He nodded toward the other chair. "Take a seat."

Nervously, she did what he suggested. She kept her head down and waited. This was how it always started. First, they'd be happy she could help them. But then they'd want to know who her parents were, why she didn't live in Byd Cudd with the rest of 'her kind'.

"I'm not going to hurt you, priestess." His voice was soft and without fear. "I swore an oath to Garret to protect you. I also don't judge people based on how they look. Your actions today, on the dock . . .healing me just now . . .they tell me more about you than anything my eyes see. I do have questions, though. If I ask them, will you answer truthfully?"

"You doubt me because I'm half Fallen," she whispered. It wasn't a question but a statement.

"No. I prefer to start out with the truth." He leaned forward, resting his arm on the table between them. "I have to trust the people I travel with. And you have to trust me in return. Most of that is earned, and you've given me enough so far for me to learn a few things."

"Like what?"

"You're a healer, and a good one based on how whole my arm is. You've spent a number of years behind the walls of your cloister, hiding from the world. But how did you go from living in Byd Cudd to being a priestess of Keroys? There's never been any worship beyond that of Lolc Aon allowed in that city."

"I never lived there. I lived with my father, in River Run.

When I was ten, the villagers turned against us. Father Philip saved me, but Papa was killed. I began my studies at the cloister because I had nowhere else to go." She looked up at him, trying to keep her voice even. "I devoted myself to lessons because books didn't taunt me. They didn't laugh at me, point fingers, or blame me for their own mistakes. Every other acolyte I trained with called me 'Fallen witch'. One went as far as trying to poison a stable hand and say it was my doing. You talk about needing to trust me? Keroys ordered me to be here, and I am, but every part of me is waiting for you and these friends of yours to do exactly what every other person has. As much as you say I need to earn your trust, the same can be said about you."

He leaned back and looked at her. She couldn't read his face. "Your father was human? And he raised you?"

She nodded.

"Do you know who your mother was?"

"No. Papa never told me her name."

Jinaari nodded. Standing up, he looked at her. "That's enough for me. No matter who your parents were, Thia, it's your actions that matter. And I've seen enough to know you won't run from a fight." Without another word, he turned and left the room, closing the door behind him.

CHAPTER TWO

"Thia?" Jinaari called from outside the door.

"It's open." She swung her legs off the wide bunk. Captain Stone had insisted she take his cabin for their voyage. Jinaari slept in a hammock belowdecks with the crew. She felt guilty, but everyone said it was the best option.

The door swung open and Jinaari entered, carrying a canvas sack. He dropped it on the table, and she heard the chink of metal on metal. "What's in there?" she asked.

"Your armor," he replied as he kicked the door shut. Opening the bag, he put two sheathed daggers on the table, followed by a chainmail shirt. "Come here," he said, holding it up. "You need to get used to the weight."

Thia walked to him and reached out, fingering the garment. The smooth, steel rings had a fluidity that mesmerized her.

"It's not a toy, Thia. This is going to keep you from dying."

She shot him a dirty look. "I know that," she muttered.

He held out a padded coif. "Put that on first. It'll keep your hair from snagging on the rings." He watched as she twisted her curls, securing them with a pin before putting it on. "Good. Now, raise your arms," he commanded.

She did, and he slid the shirt over her hands and head. It settled on her shoulders and fell almost to her knees. It was heavy, but not overly restrictive. "Turn around," he said.

She moved slowly, making sure he saw whatever it was he was looking for. Facing him again, she asked, "Well? Do I pass inspection?"

"It'll work. How does it feel? Too heavy?"

"No. I know it's there, but it's not bad."

"When you get up tomorrow, put this on first." He pulled out a heavily padded shirt and tossed it on the bunk. "Then the chain shirt, followed by your tunic. That's going to keep the armor from chafing your skin, but you don't want to advertise you're wearing it, either."

Thia nodded her understanding. "What are these for?" She reached for one of the daggers resting on the table. She started to pull it out of the hard leather sheath when Jinaari's hand landed on top of it.

"Are you planning on cutting something?"

Puzzled, she looked at him. "No. I just wanted to look at it."

"These are weapons, Thia. Never take it out unless you're ready to use it." He removed his hand and leaned against the wall. "They're for you, both of them. Once we're off the ship, I'll give you some basic training in how to defend yourself."

"I have magic for that."

He nodded. "You do. That's not limitless, though. If it's

been a hard day, you may not have the stores left to use it. It makes my job easier if I know you can hold someone off until I can get to you."

She looked at him. "What is that? Your job, I mean. You've asked me a lot about what I can do but you've shared very little about yourself."

"It's to find out who this Drogon is and what he's doing to Tanisal. Put an end to it somehow. And keep you and the others safe. Pretty straight forward." He narrowed his eyes. "You might want to talk to Jack, find out how she puts her hair up. Leaving it loose is going to give anyone you're fighting something else to grab onto."

"I'm not a child," she snapped at him. "I know how to do that."

"No, you're not," he shot back. "But you've spent almost your entire life hidden in a church. Even there, you hid. It's second nature to you, Thia. Hide from everyone, including yourself. I get it. Your mother was some Fallen witch. I don't care. The Gods don't care. Neither will Adam and Caelynn. I have to know you're not going to run in a panic the first time you're faced with a serious injury. Or a skeleton that's coming after you. Hide your face if it makes you feel better, but not what you're capable of. I need to trust that you have my back in battle."

The motion of the ship changed. "Stay here," Jinaari ordered. He walked to the door and left, slamming it shut behind him.

Thia moved to one of the small windows. "Arrogant . . . insufferable . . . your commander had you pegged!" she muttered. The summer dawn illuminated the large rocks jutting out of the water. A sandy beach and lush, green forest, barely discernible in the fog, lay beyond the crags.

The door swung open. "Get your gear. We're being put ashore here," Jinaari said. "I'll meet you up on deck."

She grabbed at the daggers and padded shirt. "Is something wrong?"

"I'll tell you more when we're on land." He closed the door.

Thia shoved the shirt into her pack, then sat down to put on her boots. The sheaths for the daggers had loops, so she threaded her belt through each one before tying it around her waist. Throwing her cloak over her back and working the clasp, she found the middle of the hood. She had attached a small comb underneath it, making so she could secure it to her hair. It was not perfect, but it would keep the hood in place.

Grabbing her pack, her other hand touched the pouch on her hip. Her box was still there. Her eyes scanned the room, mentally checking for anything she might have left behind. "Thia!" Jinaari's voice called out.

"I'm coming!" she shouted, dashing out the door. Running up the short ladder, she stepped out onto the main deck of the ship.

A wave of warm air hit her as she emerged from the cabin. To the south, where she knew Tanisal would be, an inky black cloud sat in the sky. "That's not natural," she breathed.

"No," Jinaari said. "That's why we're getting off. Stone doesn't want to risk getting any closer. Come on."

She followed him to the ships' rail. A small rowboat, hanging from thick ropes, sat alongside. "Get in."

Thia moved quickly, settling onto one of two benches. Jinaari tossed in a bag, and she grasped the edges of the craft as it swayed. The paladin sat opposite of her, followed by a crew member.

"He's going to take us ashore. After that, we're on our own." Jinaari opened the bag that rested between them and started to pull out smaller pieces of armor, buckling them into place as the dinghy was lowered.

She didn't try asking any questions. Her gaze was drawn to the ominous cloud above the ruined city. They were still miles away, yet a chill ran down her spine. Whatever created it was hiding something evil.

Something hit her leg and she pulled her eyes off the cloud. Jinaari was looking at her. "What is it?"

"A feeling . . . I don't know how to explain it. Whatever made that cloud is hiding something."

He nodded. "I feel it, too."

The bosun raised the oars. "I can't get her any closer. 'Fraid you'll need to get wet."

"No worries, my friend," Jinaari said as he rose. He held out a hand to Thia. Gratefully, she used his strength to find her balance as the craft gently rocked beneath her feet. "Wait," he told her. He grabbed her around the waist, lifting her easily over the edge and into the water. "You good?" he asked.

Water seeped over the top of her boots, but the waves were small and weren't going to knock her over. "Yeah. Thanks." Taking her pack from him, she asked, "Can I take anything else?"

"I've got it," he replied as he climbed out. "Get to the beach."

Thia waded through the water and onto the shore. She watched Jinaari do the same as she slid her arms through her pack and adjusted her cloak beneath it. The temperature was rising. *The forest will be cooler*, she reasoned. *I should keep it on as long as I can.* "Where now?"

"Let's go that way." He motioned toward the tree line.

"I've got to get the rest of my armor on, but we're too exposed here. I want to give us some cover."

Tiny bits of sand, churned up from the waves, had washed into her boots and wormed their way between her toes as she walked. Her socks were soaked, but she refused to say anything. *He already thinks of me as a child*, she thought. *I'm not going to change his mind if I complain.* Either her feet would dry as they walked, or she'd take care of them when they stopped for the night.

"Here's good," he said, dropping the large sack on the ground. "This is going to take a few minutes. You've got time to get your feet dry, change boots if you have them." He began to lift a breastplate out of the bag.

"I'm fine."

"Suit yourself. I personally hate walking around in wet socks." He buckled the front and back pieces together at one shoulder, then went to lift it over his head.

"Do you need help?"

"I'm fine." He gave her a direct look, mimicking her tone.

She let out a deep breath. "Fine. I'll change my socks. But only if you let me help you."

"It's just the one buckle, up there." He pointed to his shoulder. "Part of it is under the shoulder piece and I can't reach it."

Thia walked over to him and found the piece he was looking for. "How tight do you want it?" she asked, threading the leather strap into the buckle.

"Third hole, please."

She found the right one and secured the strap. Stepping back, she shrugged off her pack.

"Thank you."

"You're welcome," she said, rummaging into the bag.

Finding some thick, wool socks and a small towel, she sat on the ground and pulled off her boots. Sea water dribbled onto the forest floor. "Where do we go next? Is this where we were supposed to meet the others?"

"No, but we aren't far from the rendezvous point." He wound a wide leather belt around his waist twice before buckling it. His sword rested in the scabbard on his hip. "If we keep a good pace, we'll make it there before dark."

She finished drying off her feet and got the larger damp spots out of her boots. The dry socks made a difference. She put her boots back on and tied the wet socks and towel to the outside of her pack. Shouldering it again, she looked at him. "Ready when you are."

He nodded, putting his hand into a gauntlet. His helm hung from a strap on his pack.

"You're not wearing that?" she asked.

"I need to be able to see where we're going, what might be coming at us. It restricts my vision too much. If we get into a fight, I can get it on easily. Let's go."

They walked through the forest, heading south. Thia had to push herself to keep the pace he set. Three hours into the journey, she finally spoke up. "I need a minute." Leaning against a tree, she closed her eyes against the throbbing in her legs. Sweat trickled down her back. The canopy of trees helped keep the sun off her, but it was still hot. Adding the cloak, pack, armor, and keeping pace with Jinaari wasn't helping.

"I'm impressed."

She opened her eyes. "At what?"

"I figured you would've been complaining hours ago. I'll slow down. We've covered a lot of ground. Finding them before nightfall's a real possibility now."

"Don't do that," she said.

"Do what?"

She pushed off from the tree. "Slow down. I may not be as strong as you are, but I can keep up." She moved past him, heading the way he'd been going when she stopped.

"Thia," she heard him call out, but didn't turn around. "Hey, Thia!" His hand landed on her shoulder, and he spun her around to face him. "Look, I'm not trying to—"

She stared at him. "Be an arrogant prick?" The words left her mouth before she could stop them. "I get it. You're supposed to keep me safe. From what, I have no idea. You haven't shared that with me. But I won't be treated like I'm some pampered noblewoman who faints when she stubs her toe!"

"No, you're not. But you've been sheltered. Admit it, Thia." He gestured to the area around them. "I know more about this, than you do. You're wearing armor, carrying knives, for the first time in your life. If a bear came charging at us right now, you'd probably drop both daggers on the ground just trying to get one out. Not because you're weak. Because you've never had to fight before. Not this way, anyway. If I thought you weren't strong enough to do this, I would've said so back in Almair. But our Gods, both of them, say you can do this. That's enough for me. You don't have to push yourself to exhaustion to prove a damn thing. Got it?"

She clenched her jaw, trying not to let her anger show. Something moved in the forest beyond Jinaari. A cold sensation began to creep up her spine. "We're not alone," she whispered.

He raised his head, searching the area. "They're trying to surround us. Keep your back to mine. And don't cut yourself."

Thia turned around, throwing her cloak back so her

hands were free. She caught sight of the creatures as one darted between trees. Stringy hair hung from the skull. An emaciated body, with arms too long for the torso. The fingers ended in claws. "Dangreth," she said.

"A pack of them. Might be as many as a dozen. If they rush you, head up a tree. They can't climb worth a damn."

She smiled. "That's not going to happen." Her fingers began to trace the sigil in the air as she tapped into her stores. When the spell was ready, she launched it toward the advancing creatures.

Four of them let out a high-pitched scream before disintegrating into dust. Two more advanced on her, snarling.

She heard Jinaari's sword slash through another one. "We don't have time for this," she muttered. Quickly, she changed the sigil and let loose another barrage of energy. Dirt and leaves blew across the forest floor as the force of her spell expanded out from her. The two coming at her collapsed. Turning, she saw most of the Dangreth that had advanced on Jinaari fall. Only one remained.

"He's mine," Jinaari growled, charging. The creature slashed at the paladin. Dodging the attack, he swung his sword across its belly. It dropped to its knees. Moments later, Jinaari severed its head.

"Will there be more of them where we're going?" Thia pointed at the corpse at Jinaari's feet. Her heart thudded in her chest, and she felt alive from the adrenaline coursing through her.

"More Dangreth?" He shrugged.

"More undead," she said.

"Probably. If Drogon's become Forsaken, it's highly likely. Why?"

She smiled. For the first time since she'd been

summoned to Father Philip's office, she felt excited about this journey. "Because they need to die." She raised her head and looked the paladin in the eye.

He nodded. "Yes, they do."

CHAPTER
THREE

Thia kept her focus on Jinaari's back. Night had started to creep through the forest, though it would be an hour before the sun set. The dense woods created a canopy that made the light fade faster.

The paladin held up one hand and she stopped. He whistled out three distinctive notes. "What are you doing?" she asked.

He turned around and looked at her, one finger against his lips. Instantly, she started scanning the area. Was something about to attack them?

From the path in front of them, the same three notes echoed back at them. Jinaari nodded. "Come on," he said, "they're here." He raised his voice, calling out. "In the camp!"

"Come to the fire and eat something," a male voice retorted.

He led her around a large boulder, and she saw the campsite. A small fire, sheltered by the rocks, burned in the center. A pair of tents sat to one side. Two people, a man and woman, both rose to greet them. Instinctively, Thia checked to make sure her hood was up. "About time you got here," the man said, clasping Jinaari's arm in greeting. "Caelynn was getting worried." He inclined his head to the pink-haired woman.

"I was not," the woman shot back. Her face, curious, looked past Jinaari to Thia. "I thought you were going to bring Kathra?"

"That's another story," he replied. "Adam, Caelynn, this is Thia Bransdottir. She's a priestess of Keroys. She'll be joining us."

Thia muttered a greeting, keeping her hands covered. Her hood was still up, and she stayed out of the firelight. If they didn't see her until the morning, she might live through the night.

"These are the two we're going to work with," Jinaari whispered. "Try relaxing a little sometime."

Adam looked at her, his head cocked to one side. "Welcome, Thia. If you travel with Jinaari, you're welcome to join us. Are you hungry?" he pointed at the pot suspended above the fire.

"Any trouble so far?" Jinaari asked as Caelynn handed Thia a steaming bowl of stew.

Thia took the bowl, watching the elf to see if she reacted to her dark skin. The woman simply smiled and moved to where she'd been sitting earlier. *That's a good sign*, she thought. *Stop being paranoid. Keroys sent me here. He wouldn't have done so if they would shun me immediately.* The warmth of the stew seeped through the bowl, making her realize how cold her hands had gotten. Turning slightly, she found a nearby rock big enough to sit on. She kept her head down and began to eat.

"No, which bothers me," Adam said. "Whatever's taken

over Tanisal is not friendly. We're not going to encounter a warm welcome."

Jinaari nodded. "We saw the cloud from the ship. Whatever Drogon's doing, it's not natural."

Thia ate in silence, listening to the others talk. It was obvious they knew each other well, and it made her feel even more out of place. "Who's Kathra?" she asked.

Adam turned to her. "An old friend of ours. She'd traveled on things like this with us before. When we decided to come here, I sent word to Jinaari. I was hoping he could talk her into joining us."

She lowered her head. Even if Keroys had decided she was the one to come, she wasn't who they wanted.

"Kathra refused, Adam. She's done. She blames herself for Flink's death. Won't set foot outside of her convent now. I went back to the chapterhouse and dismounted in the courtyard when Drakkus and about a dozen others came over." He took a deep breath before saying, "Next thing I know, Garret and Keroys both appeared, flanking Drakkus. Garret tells me to go by the cloister in Almair, pick up a priestess of Keroys. I'm not arguing with the will of two Gods. It would be stupid," Jinaari snorted. "That's Alesso's job."

"Alesso? What'd that jackass do this time?"

"Tried to force his way into the job, for starters. Then tried to attack Thia at the docks. I chastised him."

Adam looked at her, then back at Jinaari. "Why would he attack her?"

Jinaari put his bowl down. "Thia, show them."

She hesitated, then removed the hood from her head.

Caelynn smiled. "I love your eyes!"

Adam's gaze was more calculating, and she fought the urge to hide again. "I get it now," was all he said.

She noticed his hand move as he reached for something and stopped himself. Shifting her gaze, she saw the staff lying on the ground next to him. *A warlock? They hardly ever leave Helmshouse!* Swallowing her fear, she shifted how she sat, hoping he'd stop looking at her. The cloud was ominous; knowing a warlock had been sent to help deal with it told her it was even worse than she'd imagined.

"I don't know about you gentlemen, but I'm exhausted. Thia? There's space in my tent for you. I even have an extra bedroll." Caelynn gestured toward one of the tents.

"Thank you," she muttered. She wasn't really tired, but she did want to get out from under Adam's scrutiny. It was obvious Jinaari trusted them both, so she was fairly certain she wouldn't wake up and find she'd been left behind. But would they trust her?

Once inside the tent, she shrugged out of the chain shirt and laid down. Her pack was soft enough for a pillow, and the cloak would keep her warm enough. Caelynn looked at her. "Get some sleep," she said. "We're likely to make it into Tanisal tomorrow. That's when things will get interesting." The woman closed her eyes.

Thia looked up, trying to get comfortable. The pad was thin, and she could feel every pebble underneath.

"Are you sure about her?" Adam's voice was low, but she could hear him easily.

"Garret and Keroys both are. The priest said she was the best they had. She healed me at one point."

"What happened?"

"Alesso got a cheap shot."

"I don't know, Jinaari. She's Fallen. They're not known for holding to laws or vows."

"She's also human, Adam. On our way here, we got jumped by a pack of Dangreth. She turned them into ash faster than I could blink." There was admiration in his voice. "I only took out two . . . she took out ten. Keroys instilled his hatred of the undead in her. She asked if we'd be encountering more in Tanisal. I think she's looking forward to wiping the city clean of anything evil."

"Where's she from? Humans and the Fallen rarely interact, let alone mate."

"Ask her."

"Don't you know?" Adam asked.

"I do," Jinaari paused, "and she trusted me enough to give me an answer. I'm not going to betray that. I don't think she told me everything, not yet. Her life this far hasn't been easy, even at the cloister. Trust isn't something that she blindly gives. You gotta earn it. Garret said I had to keep her safe. From what, I don't know. But I made a vow to him and Keroys to do that." He paused. "She's not like what Alesso and his kind think, Adam. She takes after her human side. As long as you show you're okay with her heritage, trust her, she'll come around. And she's damn good at magic."

"I can do that. I wasn't expecting what I saw. That's all. If you trust her . . . if the Gods do . . . then I can." He chuckled. "Caelynn won't care. She's just happy to have another woman with us. I wouldn't be surprised if she was telling her stories about our bad habits before we hit the gates of the city."

"Speaking of the city," Jinaari said, "what are we looking at?"

Their voices dropped too low for Thia to hear anything else. She shifted on her pallet and drifted off to sleep. Whatever was coming, she'd find out soon enough.

CHAPTER FOUR

The ruined battlements of Tanisal lay in piles of rubble. Thick fog blanketed the areas that still stood, masking any activity. A chill spread through Thia's veins as she spotted the blackened bricks. *Keroys, give me strength*, she silently prayed.

"Which way are we going?" Adam asked.

Jinaari pointed to an overgrowth of thornstalk bushes near a wall. "Over there. There's a passage in the brambles. It leads to a tunnel that'll take us under the wall. The exit's in a mausoleum."

Thia's head snapped toward him. "How far underground?"

He looked at her, his face serious. "Not that far, Thia. The Fallen have shunned this place as much as the rest of the world has."

Using his staff to knock aside a tree branch, Adam said, "I think I read somewhere that one of the Fallen even helped a Daughter of Hauk escape the city. It was that act that led to Nannan waking up and destroying Tanisal."

"There was a lot that went on between the two events,

Adam," Caelynn said. "You need to get better history books."

Thia drew her cloak around her, trying to find some warmth. She couldn't shake the cold sense of dread that shrouded the ruined city.

"Hey, Thia?" Jinaari's voice startled her, and she jumped.

"Huh? I'm sorry, I didn't hear you."

"You okay? We're heading in." He pointed to where Caelynn's back disappeared into the brambles.

Shrugging her shoulder to adjust her pack, she nodded. "I'm fine. It's just..." her voice trailed off.

"Just what?"

"I can't explain it. It's a feeling. Like I'm about to walk a path that will change me, but not the way I expect it to."

"I think we all felt that way when we went on our first adventure. Adam won't admit to it, but I know he was scared that first trip out from his tower." He stopped her. "You aren't thinking of going back, are you?"

She shook her head. "No. Father Philip has never lied to me. If Keroys said I am to walk this path, then I will do so. It's not my place to question his will." She looked up at the wall again. "The cloister wasn't perfect. Most thought as your friend Alesso still does. I'm just feeling as if I have no real home in Avoch." She saw a shadow pass over his face. "It'll go away, I'm certain. You said there'd be more Dangreth inside. Let's find them so I can earn my keep."

Walking quickly, she forced herself to move into the tunnel under the thistles before she lost her courage.

A small bit of light filtered through the canopy of branches and leaves, and she made out an opening ahead. Caelynn stood in it, waiting. "Keep moving," she told her.

"Adam's that way." She pointed to a small light that moved away from them.

"What about you?" Thia asked.

"I'll bring up the rear." She pushed Thia forward. "Move. The tunnel's narrow, and Jinaari can't get in there until you do."

Taking a deep breath, Thia moved into the dark, damp tunnel. The smell of earth and decay surrounded her. Blinking once, her eyesight adjusted, and she was able to make out Adam as he moved through the passageway. One of the things she had inherited from her mother was to see better than most in the dark. When she first arrived at the cloister with Father Philip, it served her well. There were plenty of nights when she used it to hide from her fellow acolytes.

She heard the paladin mutter something to Caelynn. *Focus*, she chided herself. *The tunnel's been deserted for centuries. He said the Fallen abandoned it along with the rest of the world. You won't find anyone here.* Taking another deep breath, she walked faster trying catch the warlock. The crystal on top of his staff glowed enough that she knew he could see where he was going. Hopefully, it was where they needed to be.

She lost track of time. Keeping her eyes focused on Adam's staff, she tried to remain calm. She felt the weight of the rock and earth around her, pressing down. The walls seemed to close in, creeping ever closer, even though she never saw them move. Her breathing became more difficult to regulate as the edges of panic began to crack through.

"There's a door," Adam called out. "The handle's rusted shut, though."

"Need my help?" Jinaari's deep voice sounded close, and she jumped.

"No, I can get it," he responded. "We don't care if the door works when I'm done, do we?"

"I don't plan to leave this way, if that's what you're wondering," Jinaari said.

"Good. You might want to cover your eyes. It could get a little bright."

Thia turned toward the wall instead of looking at Adam. From the corner of her vision, she saw a bright red line sear into the door. As it grew in intensity, she heard the metal begin to pop and crack. "Almost there," Adam reassured the group.

A loud bang echoed in the passageway, and then the light faded. Thia turned her head. The door now had a sizeable hole where the lock had been. With a gentle push, it swung open.

"What's out there?"

"It's a mausoleum. The bodies look undisturbed." Adam disappeared through the opening.

"Thia?"

She looked at the paladin. "What?"

"I've seen what you can do. Don't hesitate. If something in there moves, blast it into dust."

Thia nodded. Adjusting her pack, she pushed back the sleeves of her cloak enough that her hands were free. Walking through the ruined door, she looked around.

The light from Adam's staff bounced off the marble. The white stone was yellow in several places. Two sarcophagi rested on top of long platforms, making the carved tops at the height of her chest. Dust covered both. She looked intently at the edges of each one, without touching them, trying to discern if the lids had been disturbed.

Adam had already walked to the door leading out of the tomb. The hinges screamed in protest as he tugged it open.

The small of her back grew cold. Without thinking, she spun to face the crypt on her left. The lid slid to the side.

"They're awake," she whispered.

Jinaari moved behind her, drawing his sword. "Not for long."

She drew in a deep breath, steadying her nerves. This, at least, she knew how to deal with. Four skeletal fingers crept out from the narrow opening between the sarcophagus and the lid pushed it aside. Deftly, Thia wove the sigil in the air in front of her and cast her spell. An unnatural shriek rose from within, dying away quickly. The sound of stone crashing to the ground made her spin around.

A figure rose from the other niche. No flesh was left on its frame, just some bits of cloth that hadn't rotted away. Empty eye sockets stared blindly at the paladin as it pushed itself upright. "Jinaari," Thia said as she raised her hands.

"I've got this one," he replied, his voice even. With a single swing of his sword, he sliced through the creature's neck. The animated bones collapsed into a heap as the head bounced across the floor.

"We're not done yet," Adam said from the doorway.

Thia looked his way. In the fading light, she could see dozens of skeletons rising from the earth. "Out of my way," she commanded as she pushed past the warlock. Stopping on the cracked slab at the front of the door, her feet brushed aside the dead leaves covering it.

"Thia," Adam asked, "what are you doing?" There was an edge of panic in his voice. "Get back inside where it's safe!"

"This is what I trained for," she said. She threw back the hood of her cloak and raised her arms. For a moment, she closed her eyes to help her visualize the sigil she needed. The moans and cries of the undead grew as more of the creatures climbed from their graves. Her lilac eyes snapped open as her fingers weaved the intricate spell. "Life is the balance to death. Love is the balance to hate. Keroys's Justice is my voice. Hear it and embrace the balance again." Thia screamed the words as loud as she could, sending a wave of magic forth. The creatures screeched in pain as the ripples hit them, disintegrating into nothingness.

The world spun and her legs threatened to buckle. Exhausted, she leaned against the wall of the mausoleum. Her heart pounded in her chest. The rush from using that much power was exhilarating.

"Thia?"

She opened her eyes. Jinaari stood near her, concern on his face. "I'm fine," she lied.

"No, you're not," he said. "You need to pace yourself better. We can't stop for a breather every time we fight something."

"It worked, didn't it?" She looked around the graveyard.

"This time, yes. But I can tell you're running low on your magic now. Start small, reserve the big spells for when we really need them."

"Hey!" Adam called out from a gate, waving at them. Caelynn was at his side, watching.

"We have to keep moving." Jinaari grabbed her elbow, urging her to walk. "We don't know what all is here. I don't know about you, but I'd like to find somewhere defensible for us to rest tonight." Irritation worked into his tone.

Thia jerked her arm away angrily. "I don't need your help. I can walk." Picking up her pace, she tried to put some distance between herself and the paladin.

"Thia," he called out. "Wait."

She stopped. "What?" she asked as she placed the hood back over her pale blonde hair.

"I didn't mean to make you upset. There's a lot at stake here, including their lives," he gestured to the pair waiting at the gate. "I'm responsible for that. I can do some magic, so I have an understanding of what it costs you to do this. I've also done castings in the middle of combat. That, at least, is new to you. Am I right?"

She nodded, crossing her arms.

"We don't have time to ease you into that. Your God said you had to be here, but we've got to trust each other. And that starts with knowing what each of us can and can't do." He started walking again. "When we make camp tonight, we'll talk about this. As a group. Adam and Caelynn might know some tricks to keep you from overextending yourself."

She nodded again but kept silent. He was right, at least about being open with what she was capable of. And, if she was the only one that could heal wounds, she'd need to know that. Learning their strengths and weaknesses would help keep her stores from draining.

The rush from the one spell faded. At least, the adrenaline had finished coursing through her veins. Up until the last twenty-four hours, almost everything she'd done with spells had been theoretical. To see it work, to know she had the ability to lay waste to so many creatures at one time, that was something she wanted to experience again.

An hour later, she stood in the center of what had been an inn as Jinaari and Caelynn searched it top to bottom, making sure there wasn't anyone in the building. A crispness to the night air made pull her cloak around her a little tighter. *It shouldn't be this cool*, she thought. *We're just past midsummer*. Adam checked the shutters, making sure they were locked. The windows were already covered which was why the building had been selected. If anyone was watching, they wouldn't see them move around inside.

"I think we're good," Caelynn said as she came back downstairs. "Though I wouldn't trust lighting a fire."

"Adam, how's the kitchen?" Jinaari asked.

"It's clear. Back door is barred from the inside, and the cellar door now has a pile of stuff on top of it. If anyone comes in, we'll hear it."

The paladin nodded. "I still want a watch. No more than three hours. I'll take first."

"Second for me," Caelynn said.

"That puts me on third."

"When do I go on watch?" Thia asked quietly.

Jinaari sat in a chair, laying his sword on the table. "You sleep. You don't get a watch." She opened her mouth, ready to protest, but stopped at the look he gave her. "Adam and I don't need much rest to restore our magic stores. Caelynn's an elf. She sneezes and gets replenished." He shot a teasing look at the other woman, who laughed. "You, though" he continued, "you're the mystery. How much rest does someone who's half-human need to regain her magic?"

She blinked, taken aback by his choice of words. He focused on her human traits, not her Fallen ones. "I," she hesitated, "I'm not certain. I was never pushed at the cloister to the point of draining it all. And we had set times for everything, including sleeping." Her voice faltered. *Jinaari was right*, she chided herself. *I don't have a clue how to pace myself!*

"We know you can heal, Thia. Jinaari and I both can too, even if it's not as well as you. Your Order's magic is different than mine. Yours comes from within, is innate. Mine is learned, and I need this to give it focus." Adam held up his staff briefly before leaning it against the wall. He sat down and put his feet onto a chair he'd placed in front of him. "Though, I gotta admit, what you did in the graveyard was impressive. I can blast stuff. But clearing out that much at once? Not something I can do."

"Where'd you learn that?" Caelynn asked. She sat at the foot of what had been a stage and pulled out a small harp. "I thought Keroys didn't train his followers to fight."

"Mostly it's theoretical teaching," Thia responded. "We learn the sigils in one class, the words in another. And you're right. Few of us ever have to put anything beyond healing into practice. Today was the second time I'd ever used them in tandem. Honestly, I wasn't sure what to expect. Each spell is different." She sank into a chair across the table from Jinaari. The tall man pushed a small bundle over to her. Unwrapping it, she saw some food and gratefully began to eat.

A few notes from the harp rose in the silence of the room. "Not too loud, Caelynn," Jinaari said.

"Of course not"

"You're a bard?" Thia asked.

Caelynn smiled. "Most of the time. That," she nodded toward the rapier laying at her feet, "isn't just for show, though."

Adam yawned. "Do you want us to stay down here, or are there beds up there?" He pointed toward the staircase.

"Might as well use the beds," Jinaari said. "They're old, probably lumpy, but they'll be more comfortable than the floor. And who knows when we'll get any sort of comfort for a while."

The warlock nodded. Rising, he grabbed his staff and pack before disappearing up the stairs.

Thia sat, absently tearing bits of bread off a roll,

listening to Caelynn's song. Next thing she knew, Jinaari tapped her leg.

"Thia?"

"Huh?" she asked, blinking.

"You dozed off. Go up and find a bed. We'll wake you when it's time to move out in the morning."

Rising, she grabbed her pack and stumbled up the stairs. She went into the first open door and dropped the pack on the floor. Her weary body fell asleep as soon as she laid down.

CHAPTER
FIVE

"Hey, Thia."

She rolled over at the sound. Opening her eyes, she saw Caelynn standing at the foot of the bed. "What?" she asked, still half asleep.

"Jinaari wants to get moving. You need to get up." The pink haired woman placed Thia's pack onto the bed near her feet.

Tossing her cloak aside, Thia sat up. "What time is it?"

"Early. The sun's barely over the horizon. It's going to be a long day, so we need to take advantage of the daylight."

Looking down, she took in the wrinkled fabric of her tunic. There was a rip and the chain shirt showed through. *Next time*, she thought, *take that off before you go to sleep.* She considered changing but ruled against it. Her cloak should hide the tear, and she'd try to mend it when they stopped tonight. "Any idea where we're going next?" Her hands busied themselves with reworking her hair. The braids had come loose from the pins as she slept, and she wanted to get them secured again.

"We're looking for Drogon," Jinaari said as he entered the room, "or clues about where he is, what he's doing here. And we're going to do whatever it takes to get that cloud to go away." He paused. "What do you remember of him, Thia?"

"You've met him?" Caelynn asked.

Thia shook her head. "Not really. He came to visit us, but Papa sent me to my room every time. I know he could do magic, but not what kind. He wanted Papa to make him a box, but he wouldn't."

"What kind of box?" Adam asked.

Jinaari looked at her. "Like the one you have?"

She nodded, "I think so."

"Show them," Jinaari commanded her.

Reaching for the pouch on her belt, Thia pulled it out. Removing the leather, she held it out for them to see.

"It's pretty and well-made, but I don't understand why Drogon would need one. Or why your father would refuse him," Adam said.

Bringing it back close to her, Thia spoke as her fingers sought out the right places. "It's designed to hold spell components, Adam. There are three acorns in copper in the design. The only way to open it is to touch them in sequence." The lid popped open. "Once I put one thing inside, it stays there no matter how many times I cast the spell. And I don't have to open it to get it out." She closed the lid and began to rewrap it. "One of the acolytes said I stole it, refused to believe my father made it."

Adam let out a low whistle. "I can see where that could come in handy. But why wouldn't he make one for Drogon?"

"I really don't know the reason. I overheard them talking once. It sounded like they were both part of a group that went to Byd Cudd as part of a trade delegation. Drogon said it'd taken him years to realize the Bran in River Run was the same one he knew from that journey. The same one who used to make them for a living. My box is the last one he made, and it was finished before I was born." She placed it back in the pouch and wound the belt around her waist.

"Thia, I don't want to pry," Caelynn's voice hesitated, "but how did you come to live on the surface with your father?"

She glanced at Jinaari. He nodded his head once. Rising from the cot, she reached for her cloak. "All I know," she said as she fastened the clasp, "is that my mother was Fallen. That she abandoned me on the surface when I was born. Somehow, a message got to Papa that she was going to leave me out in the cold for wolves to feast on. He got there before the pack did." She kept her tone even. The feeling of being thrown out had been one she'd grown used to, even if she rarely spoke of it. Father Philip had been the one that told her after they'd reached the safety of the cloister. "I don't even know her name," she whispered.

"Let's move," Jinaari said, breaking the silence in the room. "We have to find out where he's at, and what he's up to before we can stop him. Whatever it is, it's not good."

Thia grabbed her pack and pushed her arms through the straps as she followed everyone else out of the room and down the stairs.

"But where are we going to start?" Adam asked.

"I've got two ideas," Jinaari replied. "Either the city center or the remains of the Paladins of Silas Chapterhouse."

"I thought they were full of Corrupted? They'd turned against Silas and embraced Corse?"

Thia saw the paladin's head nod curtly. "They did.

Nannan targeted the chapterhouse when she laid waste to the city. Which is why it's a possibility. The entire compound became a focal point of evil. And Drogon's certainly attracted to that."

"Do we know why he's doing this? Or even what it is he's doing?" Caelynn asked.

The paladin stopped, shaking his head. Thia turned to Caelynn. "You mean we don't know anything?"

"Shhh!" Jinaari snapped at her.

Thia stared at him in shock. She blinked a few times, then stood still. His ear pressed against the door. "It's clear," he said, looking at them. "Adam, take up the rear. Thia, follow Caelynn. Keep close, stay to the shadows if you can. Back to the buildings. If we get separated, head to the fountain at the center of the city. We'll reconnect there." He pulled the door open and slid out into the city.

Thia focused on Caelynn's back, trying to keep pace with the elf. She moved so fast, though! Within minutes, she was out of breath. "Can we stop for a minute?"

Caelynn glanced back, studying her. "Okay, but not long. I don't want to lose sight of Jinaari."

"Keep moving, Caelynn," Adam said. Thia turned, looking at him. "I'll stay with her. We'll catch you guys at the fountain."

The bard nodded once and sprinted after the paladin.

Thia leaned against the wall, trying to catch her breath. "I'm sorry," she muttered.

"For what? Jinaari can keep a fast pace when he wants to. Sometimes he forgets he's got people behind him."

"I'm not used to any of this," she admitted. "I don't even know why I'm here."

"Jinaari does, and I trust him. You'll get used to the pace. How often did you leave your cloister? I mean, you've gone shopping, right? To an arena to watch some games? Horseback riding with friends?"

She shook her head, "I don't have friends." Reaching up, she adjusted the comb inside the hood of her cloak. "Father Philip thought it best that I stay within the walls, for my own safety. Almair isn't always kind to anyone that looks like I do." She refused to meet his eyes as he studied her. She knew the look. He was evaluating her, trying to figure out if she was human or Fallen.

"That'll change, Thia. We're all here because we've been told to deal with this, even if we don't understand why. I trust Jinaari and Caelynn with my life. We'll do the same for you." He pointed toward a side street. "Come on. Let's get moving."

Pushing away from the wall, she ran down the street Adam had pointed to. The sound of her chainmail clinking as she moved echoed off the buildings. Only the lower floors remained. The rest was a mass of charred wood and soot covered stone. The ruins bore testament to the fury of the attack that had leveled the city ages ago.

The wind picked up and she noticed the temperature drop. Looking up, she saw the clouds darken. "The storm's getting worse," she shouted at Adam above the roar.

"I noticed," he said. "Stay close. I can't tell if this is natural. It could be Drogon trying to discourage us."

A clap of thunder echoed above her head, making her wince in pain. Bright white lightning struck the building next to her. Adam's arms circled her waist, pulling her away as the wall tumbled down onto the spot where she'd stood moments earlier. When the dust settled, the entire alley was blocked.

"Well, that's not good," he said.

"What do we do now?"

The blonde-haired man looked around the rubble strewn area. "There's a door over there," he pointed at the next building down. "Let's go before there's another strike."

He shoved her and she ran for cover. Hail bombarded them; large balls of ice bounced off the shattered pieces of stone and scattered across the path they had to navigate. She winced in pain as several found places on her where the armor didn't cover. Reaching the doorway, she twisted the handle, but the door wouldn't open. "It's stuck!" she screamed over the raging storm.

"Not for long," Adam shouted. He pointed his staff at the door, and it exploded inward. The warlock pushed her through the opening and out of the storm.

Thia stopped in the center of the room, staring through the doorway as another bolt of lightning struck. Her hands flew to her ears as the thunder roared. Adam stood in front of her, saying something, but her ears rang too much for her to make out the words. He grabbed her arm, leading her deeper into the house.

He stopped in what used to be a workspace of some kind. Two long tables dominated the room. Bundles of dead plants hung from hooks that lined the walls. Adam sat her in a chair and searched the room. The ringing in her ears began to subside. The storm still raged outside, and she could hear it, but it wasn't as loud here. "What is this place?"

Adam looked up from the cupboard he was rummaging through. "I think this was an apothecary's shop," he said. "We'll ride out the storm, then find the other two. Aha!" he exclaimed, pulling a small box out and placing it on one of the tables.

"Do you think they're caught in the storm?" she asked.

"They've probably found cover. That storm came up

fast." He drew out a dagger and pried open the lid. Dust erupted in a cloud. "Then again, with the cloud that's over the city, the weather's bound to be strange."

Thia pulled back one of the sleeves of her cloak. A couple of bruises formed on her skin. They were tender, but not something to worry about. "What did you find?"

"Every apothecary I've ever met kept a box like this," he explained, pulling small jars out and looking at them carefully before replacing them. "It was designed to safely transport some of the more volatile components they'd deal with. Separately, they're inert. Mix them together, not so much."

"Can we still use any of that? It looks ancient."

Adam smiled. "Oh, yes. They're still sealed, so the contents are protected." He closed the lid. "Caelynn can use a lot of what's in here. What she can't, I can. We got lucky . . ." His voice trailed off and his gaze shifted behind her. "Thia," he spoke slowly and carefully. "Don't move a muscle. Stay perfectly still."

The hair on the back of her neck began to rise as she felt something brush against the hood of her cloak. Her heart racing, she watched Adam grasp his staff with one hand. A beam of light erupted from the crystal at the tip, flying toward her. As it hit the air above her, she ducked and tumbled out of the chair, landing on the floor. Her eyes flew wide in horror as the giant spider dropped to the floor behind where she'd been sitting; the legs curled inward. A single, high pitch scream escaped it as it died.

She twisted her head, looking at Adam. "What was that?"

"I'm not certain," he said, "but I'd rather take my chances in the storm. What about you?" Thia nodded, scrambling up from the floor. Adam shoved the case into his bag, then slung the long strap over his head. He held out his free hand to her. Grasping it tightly, she followed him back out of the house.

The hail had stopped, replaced with a driving rain. The cobblestone road was slick and wet. Thia tightened her grip on Adam's hand, desperate not to fall. He led her through another door different than the original one. "Come on," he urged her, "keep your eyes on where you're stepping." He glanced back at her and his jaw hardened. "Don't look back, whatever you do. We're not far from the fountain."

He led her around a corner. Her foot slipped and she thrust her hand against a wall to steady herself. As her body twisted with the motion, she caught sight of the building they'd left. Thick, white strands glistened in the windows above the apothecary sign. The entire top floor was a giant web.

"Adam! Thia! Over here!" Jinaari called out. Thia turned toward the voice and saw the paladin standing on the other side of a large courtyard. In the center, what was once a fountain was nothing but rubble.

She felt Adam pull her forward and she stopped staring. Dashing toward the building where Jinaari stood in the doorway, she ran past him and inside. Caelynn was wiping blood off her rapier. "You two okay?" Thia let go of the warlock's hand and looked around the room.

"Yeah," he said. "Here, found something you might find useful." He pulled the box out of his bag and handed it to the bard.

The room was practically empty. A few broken chairs and other debris sat in a single corner. "Any trouble?" Jinaari asked.

"I took us into the wrong house," Adam replied. "Lightning destroyed a wall, blocking the way, and then the hail started. I didn't look up before we went in." He leaned his staff against a wall and removed his cloak, shaking water from it as he spoke. "I mean, we found the apothecary box. That's great. But we had to leave pretty quick."

The paladin looked at her closely before glancing back at Adam. "Why?"

"It was occupied."

Thia shuddered. "That's one way to put it."

"Giant spider nest," Adam said. "I didn't catch the signs and one almost reached Thia. I took it out and we ran."

Jinaari glanced outside between two boards that'd been nailed across the window. "Just the one?"

"That's all I saw. Top floor was nothing but webs, though."

Thia stared at the two men. "Isn't one enough?" While she hadn't intended to be funny, she caught the fleeting smiles of her companions.

"Was it an adult or juvenile?" Jinaari asked, his fingers flexing around the hilt of his sword.

"It was young." There was a catch to Adam's voice that worried her.

"They get bigger?" she asked, her heart dropping in fear.

The dark-haired man didn't look at her but nodded once. "Depending on how young that one was, an adult could be two to three times as large." He looked back at her and the others. "Caelynn, check the back door. Look for any hidden ways in or out of here. We may need them once the weather clears."

"What's going on?" Thia asked, her voice wavering with fear.

"The adults won't come out when it's raining, so we

have time. When the storm clears, though, they'll come hunting."

"Hunting?"

Jinaari turned, his face a stony mask. "They're carnivores, Thia. To them, we're food."

CHAPTER SIX

Jinaari looked at Thia, gauging the impact of his words. She was visibly shaken but held her ground. *Good*, he thought, *she's not going to run. Not without cause, anyway.*

"Adam, see if there's a way to prevent them from coming downstairs. I want to keep them up there as long as we can." He turned back toward the gap he'd been watching through. The rain was beginning to slow down. The storm was weakening.

"On it." His friend said as he turned and bounded up the stairs.

Thia's voice was faint as she asked, "What can I do to help?"

He turned back to her. She hid beneath the voluminous cloak and hood. If it wasn't for her eyes, she'd pass as human, maybe a half elf. The lilac color, though. That marked her as part Fallen. Hiding was probably so ingrained in her she didn't know she did it anymore. "How are your magic stores? Used anything today?"

She shook her head. "No. Adam took care of the spider earlier, not me."

"Stay out of reach if they come close. Your job's not to fight. It's to keep the three of us alive. Caelynn and I will do most of it. Adam's better from a distance. Stay aware of your stores. If you've got plenty, and there's an opening to kill it, then do it. But only if you've got the magic to spare. Got it?"

"Yes."

A staccato sound echoed in the room, and he jerked his head up. They'd been found already.

"What's that?" Thia asked.

"They're here. At least the first scouts." He walked toward her. "Grab the packs, carry as many as you can and keep your hands free. Caelynn and I need to be able to fight."

"Here, I'll take Jinaari's." Adam ran over to them. "I sealed the door at the top, inscribed a few runes. It won't hold them long, though. I could hear them breaking through the roof while I worked."

"Can you do something with the front door? I don't want it sealed in case we need to retreat that way, but a delay tactic would be good."

Adam nodded. "There're a few vials in the case I found that'll be deadly to the spiders, if we have time to mix them."

A high-pitched scream came from above them, and Jinaari looked at the stairs. "There's not enough time. One is already through."

"Jinaari!" Caelynn called out. His head snapped toward the sound. She stood inside a doorway. "In here. There's a waste pipe leading to the sewers."

He gestured to the others and headed over. Above them, wood cracked and split from the weight of the spiders converging on the roof. "Is it big enough?"

She looked him up and down, a teasing smile on her face. "For us, yes. You might get that shiny metal suit you wear scraped a little." Caelynn grabbed her pack from Thia and slung it across her back. Her face grew serious. "It's going to be tight for you, Jinaari. How do you want to do this?"

"You first, then Adam. Thia, you're next." He motioned toward the door. "Let's go. The faster we get down there and close the hatch, the less likely they'll find us."

He pushed them through the doorway, keeping his gaze on the staircase. Judging from the noise, there could be close to a dozen adults coming after them. *That's too many. A nesting pair, sure, but they wouldn't swarm like this unless they were being directed to.* As soon as Thia was past him, he crossed the threshold after her and closed the door.

The kitchen was dirty. Moldy lumps dotted the counters, covered with dead maggots. Caelynn's pink head disappeared into the floor, and Adam began to climb after her. "There's a ladder," Adam said to Thia, "but watch your step and grip. The wood could be rotten."

Jinaari saw Thia nod as she adjusted her pack. Adam disappeard down the hold as she knelt next to it. A high-pitched chittering erupted above them. Both of their heads snapped up at the sound. "They've got our scent and Adam's ward won't keep them at bay much longer," Jinaari said. "Go!" he commanded as he drew his sword and turned toward the door.

"What about you?"

"I'll be right behind you," he scanned the room. A pile of

rags sat near what could be an old oil lamp. If he set the place on fire, that'd buy them some extra time. He ran to the table, shoving his weapon back into the scabbard. He took out the cork stopper and grabbed at the closest rag. A dozen bugs ran across the table as he shoved it into the neck of the bottle. "Ignis," he whispered. Smoke began to rise from the cloth. Jinaari laid the bottle on the rest of the pile, then ran back to the hole.

Caelynn wasn't joking. It was narrow, and he'd have to work to fit. Hopefully, it opened up as he went down. He found the handle on the bottom of the trap door and closed it as he began his descent.

His armor scraped against the walls of the tunnel. He kept one arm raised, dropping the shoulder on the opposite side, and waited. It was pitch black, and he could barely make out the rung in front of his face. "Adam?" He kept his voice low. "Any chance at some light?"

A soft glow began to illuminate the tunnel. "You're not getting old on me, are you? I remember when you could see in the dark!" Adam's voice rose from below.

"Not old, but there's no stars down here, either," Jinaari shot back. Glancing down, he saw Thia making her descent. He'd have to wait, let her get farther down before he started. "How far down is it?"

"About fifty feet. Thia's almost here. It opens up in the last ten feet," Caelynn answered.

Smoke began to filter through the cracks between the boards above him. Coughing, he twisted his shoulders to try to minimize the damage to his armor as he climbed down the ladder. The crackle and pop of the fire grew louder as it began to gain momentum. He could see the flames eating away at the dried wood above him. He shoved his shoulder down as his feet moved. It was taking too long. "Is everyone clear?"

"Yes. What is it?" Adam said.

"I'm doing this the fast way," he answered. Leaning back, he found his balance before letting go with his hands. He pulled both arms into his chest, making himself as small as possible. He drew in a deep breath, readying himself for the impact, and pushed his torso forward as he moved his feet off of the ladder. He dropped quickly, landing in a heap at the bottom. Sitting up, he waived off Thia. "I'm fine."

She studied him before speaking. "You told me my job was to heal you three so that means I decide who's fine and who isn't."

"I won't lie to you, Thia. That's not who I am."

Her lilac eyes softened slightly. "You'll live," she said as she moved away from him.

Was that a hint of trust in her eyes? He shook off the thought. Gaining her trust would make keeping her safe easier, but it wasn't the biggest issue right now. Rising, he looked around. "Where's the tunnel go?" he asked, pointing down a dark archway.

"That's the thing, I'm not certain. It should be the city sewers, but that's not what this is." Caelynn was quiet. She turned to one of the walls of the chamber. In the dim light, Jinaari made out the outline of a bricked off tunnel. "They closed it off. Recently, too." She pointed to the wall. "See? The mortar's not that old. It's not crumbling like the archway."

"Adam? What do you see?"

"It's warded. If we'd come through on the other side, we wouldn't have known this passage existed. We got lucky."

"Looks like we found the way to Drogon's hiding place. Let's go pay him a visit."

"You don't think he'll just let us walk up and say hello, do you?" Thia asked.

Jinaari smiled. "I'm counting on him doing his best to keep us from getting to him. We still don't know what he's doing down here, so we'll want to look for anything that's out of place or unnatural."

"Like giant spiders?" she shot back.

"Actually, those aren't that odd. The amount that came after us, though . . . they normally stay in small groups. A mated pair and the younglings. Once they leave the web, the female either eats the male or they mate again. I've never seen that many adults swarm onto one location before. Even when food was scarce. They're just as likely to eat each other." He kept his tone casual as he took his pack from Adam. No point in scaring Thia any more than she already was. Taking a closer look at the area, he frowned. Something wasn't right. This was too obvious. "Caelynn, did you actually touch that wall?"

"You're not thinking it's an illusion, are you?"

"I'm thinking," he gestured down the opening, "that it's way too obvious which way we're supposed to go." A charred piece of wood, flames still eating away at it, dropped from the tunnel they'd come through. The fire was growing. They couldn't stay here all day, debating. He walked over to the wall, removing one of his steel gauntlets, and placed his hand against the bricks. "Everyone, take a section," he told them. "Let's make sure there's no levers or hidden doors."

As they began to examine the wall, he glanced back. The fire would have engulfed the building by now. Going up wasn't an option but going the wrong way could prove more dangerous than the fire.

"I think I found something," Thia said. Jinaari turned to

look at her. She knelt near the base of the wall. Her hand hovered over one brick. "This one's loose."

"Wait, Thia, don't—" he said, stopping as the floor beneath her gave way. Dropping to the ground, he grabbed for her as she fell, screaming. His hand closed around a fist full of cloth. *I have to calm her down.* "I've got you," he told her. "Can you reach my arm?"

"I think so," she replied. She reached above her head. He saw her hands slip off the metal bracer encasing his forearm.

The unmistakable sound of tearing cloth reached his ears. If they didn't hurry, the weight of her body would slide her right out of her chain mail, tunic, and cloak. "Thia, don't move." He kept his sights on her. She looked up at him, the hood of her cloak falling back, terror all over her face. "Cross your arms and grab your upper arm with each hand. Don't move them until I tell you to." The sound of hundreds of creatures moving echoed up from the inky blackness. "Adam, I need your staff."

"On your left," he said.

Jinaari reached out, his hand searching. "Thia, when you see the staff, grab it. Don't look down. Just keep your eyes on me or the staff." Slowly, he lowered it down past her head. The light from the crystal illuminated the space. The floor was covered with scorpions, some of which were starting to form a tower to get to her. "Get a good grip."

She wrapped both of her arms around the wood. "Got it. Please hurry." Her voice waivered on the edge of panic. "They're coming closer."

"Hey, look at me. Not down there," he commanded. Her head snapped back up. "Adam, Caelynn, I need you to keep me steady while I pull her up." He waited until he felt them grab his legs and waist. "Okay, Thia. This is the hard part. I'm going to let go of you so I can put both hands on the staff and pull you out." Her eyes widened in terror. "Trust me," he said calmly, trying to mask his own fears for her sake.

She nodded, took a deep breath, and closed her eyes. His arms and back hurt, but he wasn't about to drop her. Not now. Quickly, he released his grip on her cloak and grasped the staff with both hands. "Hold on." Gritting his teeth, he began to pull the staff, and Thia, out of reach of the scorpions.

When she was level with him, he glanced back at the others. "Pull us out." His body scraped against the floor, the chest plate of his armor absorbing the damage, but it got her close enough to the edge. Caelynn appeared next to him and helped her onto solid ground.

Rolling over, he stared at the ceiling. "Let's try the open tunnel."

He pushed himself off the ground, taking another look down into the pit. The scorpions were swarming. Not enough to reach the lip, but more than he'd ever seen at once. *First, the giant spiders. Now, scorpions. What was going on?* He looked at Thia as she leaned against a wall, catching her breath. "Adam, anything in that case you found that you can drop down there?"

"There should be."

He waited while Adam and Caelynn took care of the scorpions. Potions weren't his specialty. He looked back at Thia. Her eyes were still wide, but her body wasn't shaking any more. The only person he knew of that was powerful enough to command both spiders and scorpions was Lolc Aon. Did Drogon make a deal with the Scorpion Queen? If so, what could he have offered that she'd be interested in? The Goddess was known to keep a watch on all the Fallen. But Thia was also part human and devoted her life to Keroys.

Gods, what's really going on? Am I here to stop a mage gone mad? Or protect a priestess from something even worse?

CHAPTER SEVEN

"You need any more light up there, old man?" Adam called from behind her.

"No," Jinaari replied without turning around. "You done playing with that stick of yours?"

Thia smiled at the banter. It was obvious the two were old friends, with stories that no one beyond them would fully understand. She took a deep breath, releasing it slowly. While it was fun to listen to them talk, it was a reminder of something she'd never had in her life. Friends.

"I wouldn't worry about what they say," Caelynn said as she walked next to her. "Those two have more private jokes than most I've known."

"I'm not worried," she said. "It's actually fun to listen to. I rarely stayed near any of the other acolytes long enough to hear what they told each other when we weren't in class."

"Didn't you talk with friends?"

Thia shook her head. "I didn't have any, not beyond Father Philip. The few times I tried to make friends; it didn't end well."

"That's horrible!" Caelynn said. "Everyone should have at least one friend growing up."

Shrugging, she kept walking. "Most people look at me and only see that I've got Fallen blood. They don't see the human part of me. They turn away. Out of fear, hatred, ignorance. I went about my studies, practiced." She kept her voice even, factual. "I became better at magic than they did, mastering skills and spells faster than the rest. It didn't endear me to them, but they stopped laughing when I walked by." The whispers were worse. The stares, how they'd go quiet when she got near in the hallways. It was only her connection with Father Philip that kept her from being spat on. Or worse.

"Well, you've got friends now." Caelynn smiled at her.

Thia smiled back but didn't look at her. She barely knew these people. She stared at Jinaari's back. *I can trust him*, she thought. *If he wanted to be rid of me, I'd be back in the pit with the scorpions. And he didn't tell the others anything I told him on the boat.* Adam was a maybe. He'd kept that spider from doing whatever it would've done to her, back in the house. Caelynn . . . she was still unsure. It was always the women and girls back at the cloister who'd been the biggest bullies. Their words cut the deepest.

Suddenly, Jinaari's hand flew up, signaling them to stop. Her heart began to beat faster. What had he heard?

"Thia," he turned and looked at her, his voice barely above a whisper, "do you understand Olc?"

She nodded. "Yes. They made me learn it. Something about my heritage making it important."

"Come up here, as quietly as you can."

Walking toward him, she cringed as the chain mail seemed to rattle loudly. "Over here," Jinaari said as he motioned to a section of the wall in front of him. There was a bend within arm's length. "I heard someone talking. I think they're Fallen. They were speaking Olc, anyway. See if you can hear what they're saying."

"I'll try," she said, "but everything I learned was out of a book. I've never spoken the language."

"Just give me the best translation you can."

Putting her back to the wall, she inched forward, listening for the voices he'd heard. Closing her eyes, she concentrated on her breathing. Three voices, two women and a man. It was hard at first to distinguish the voices from each other. What they were saying made no real sense. Then, her name was mentioned. What followed made her sink to the floor in shock and fear.

"Thia?" Jinaari knelt next to her.

Her breathing was uneven as she fought against the wave of panic. She slammed her eyes closed, trying to prevent tears from falling. A hand grasped her upper arm, and her eyes flew open in fear. "Get up," Jinaari said, his voice barely above a whisper. "We need to move away from here before you tell us what's going on."

She nodded, grateful for his help, and stood up. Her entire body shook. Adam and Caelynn stood several feet away, concern on their faces. The panic was subsiding, but fear sat heavy in her stomach.

"What were they saying?"

Taking a deep breath, Thia kept her focus on the paladin. "There's three of them. Two women and a man. There could be more. But that's all I heard talking." She stared at him. "They're looking for us. For me." The last words were barely a whisper.

"How do you know?"

"One of them, the man, said 'Herasta wants Thia. We can't hurt her, no matter what'."

"Jinaari, we don't have time. They're getting closer." Caelynn said, glancing toward the junction.

"Caelynn, get to the other side of the hallway. I'll stay on this side. Wait for my signal. Adam," he pushed her toward the warlock, "stay with Thia. If they get through us, get her to safety. We'll try to keep one alive so we can ask questions. Thia." He glanced at her.

"I know. Stay out of the way and keep everyone alive."

He nodded. "That and keep close to Adam. Until we learn why they're looking for you, you're not going to be left alone. If he tells you to run, do it. Understand?"

Not a chance, she thought. But she nodded in agreement. She wasn't about to run and let either of them die, or worse. She'd grown up hearing stories about the Fallen, what happened to those who they took prisoner.

In that, Alesso's hatred of the race was well founded.

That's not me, though. Papa told me all the time that I looked like my mother but my manners, personality, all came from him. And he was kind, peaceful, a good person.

"Thia, over here." Adam pulled on her sleeve. She moved back a few more feet, keeping her eyes on the other two. She watched as both of them flattened themselves against the wall and drew their weapons. Thia's heart pounded as adrenaline mixed with the fear. It wasn't until the first foe rounded the corner and stared at her that she realized Adam had made her stand in the center of the hallway.

His skin was pitch black. The long hair, so white it practically glowed, was pulled back into a single braid. But it was his eyes that caused a fresh wave of fear to wash over her. The same pale lilac of her own. "Hello, sister," he said, a malicious grin on his face. He reached out a hand as he started to walk toward her.

She took a few steps back. Without warning, Jinaari swung his sword at the man's back. He swore, spun, and parried the blow. Four more Fallen, all women, came through the opening and joined the fight.

Adam appeared at her side, sending a blast from his staff that bathed the corridor in bright light. The Fallen noticeably cringed but recovered quickly. Caelynn used the distraction to thrust her rapier through the body of one of the women. The fighter hadn't hit the ground before another one stepped up to engage the bard. Jinaari had two opponents, deftly moving between them.

Thia tapped into her stores and drew a sigil, sending some healing to Caelynn. As soon as it hit, she saw the man shove his sword in between the plates of armor, plunging it into Jinaari's side. Without thinking, she drew a new figure in the air.

Her insides twisted in pain so intense that sweat began to form on her forehead. The palms of her hands slammed against the ground as her legs gave way.

"Thia?" she heard Adam call out to her through the agony. "Jinaari!"

Struggling, she waved off Adam's arm. "I'm fine," she said weakly. The flashes of light faded from her eyes, but the pain remained as she struggled to stand.

"No, you're not," he insisted.

By the time she was standing again, Jinaari was in front of her. His dark eyes studied her. "Caelynn," he called out, his gaze never leaving her, "what's over your way?"

"There's a room. Looks empty."

"Make sure." Pausing, he glanced at Adam. "Get her in there. I'll make sure we're not followed."

"I can walk," she protested, shrugging off Adam's supportive arm.

"Either he helps you," Jinaari pointed behind her, "or I'll put you over my shoulder and carry you. Got it?"

She stared back at him. He didn't flinch. Nodding, she agreed and felt Adam's hand on her elbow.

"Caelynn?"

"It's safe."

Jinaari moved aside, pointing down the hallway. The pain was fading quickly. Stepping over the bodies, she counted four. All female. Where had the man gone to? The one whose eyes were the same as hers?

Adam ushered her into the room. A small wooden table and chair were off to one side, but nothing else. Caelynn lit a candle and placed it in a lantern, illuminating the room in a soft glow.

She shrugged the pack off her back and sat it on the ground before sitting in the chair. Jinaari leaned against the wall opposite of her. "What happened?"

"I did my job," she replied. He scowled at her, but she didn't back down. "I saw the blade sink into your side, Jinaari. That's never a good thing if you want to live. The spell I used is designed, in theory, so that the caster 'feels' the wound they've healed. That's all."

"No, it's not. If it was, Adam wouldn't have shouted at me."

She leaned forward, resting her arms on her legs. "I was fine. I'm almost recovered now. The level of magic I'm working down here . . . in the cloister, it was all theoretical. We weren't permitted to do all the elements of a spell together, experience the outcome. Priests and priestesses of Keroys serve in churches. We stay in our homes, tend to our parishioners and the occasional group that comes through that needs our help. Or we stay in the larger cities and teach. When I say I'm fine, I mean it. I'm not lying. The more I cast, the faster I'll get used to the effects. Next time I use that spell, I won't react the same. I'll know what's coming, I can prepare for it. I've been learning and adapting since I got on the ship. If I'd cast that spell a week ago, I would've been screaming in agony. I saw the blow, Jinaari. If I didn't do my job, the one you gave me, you'd be on the floor out there with the other corpses. You've asked me to trust you. Now, I'm asking you to trust me. There's only one way for me to minimize the toll my body takes when I use magic. And that's to use it. I don't need a babysitter." She looked at him, waiting.

After a moment, he nodded. "One more thing. When you heard the conversation, you fell apart. Why?"

Thia looked at her hands for a moment, gathering her thoughts. "I was raised to fear the Fallen, like everyone else. I heard all the stories about how they brutal they are, the," she coughed, trying to distract from the flush she felt on her cheeks, "way the women treat the men. Some of it was thrown in my face. No matter how much I came across as human, people around me only saw the Fallen in me. Outside of Olc, I've turned my back on every part of the culture. I am human. I am my father's child, not my mother's. What I could understand was that they were looking for me specifically. Someone named Herasta sent them to bring me to her, alive." She looked at Jinaari. "There is nothing good that would come of such a summons, nor is it one I will answer willingly."

"It's my job to make sure that doesn't happen," he said.

Thia relaxed slightly. *Keroys trusted him enough to send him to protect me. He's saved my life; never said I was anything but human after the time on the ship. He's demanding, arrogant . . . but he'll keep his word.*

"Are you hurt?" Caelynn asked

Thia looked at her arm. The skin had turned a sickly yellow and purple.

"Show me." Jinaari said.

"It's just a bruise," she said, holding it out. "I probably hit it on the edge of the pit when I fell."

Jinaari traced a sigil similar to one she used. It faded some, but not completely.

"Why didn't it work?" Adam asked.

Jinaari shook his head. "I don't know. That bruise should be gone."

"Show me where you were stabbed," Thia demanded.

"We don't have the time. I've got to find the one that ran."

"If healing spells aren't working right, I need to know you're not going to bleed out. Now, show me."

He shifted, allowing her to see the gap where he'd been stabbed. Carefully, she found the hole in his tunic and examined the skin. It was whole, no bruising. "You'll live," she said. As he stepped away from her, she frowned. "I don't understand, though. Why did my spell work and yours didn't?"

"The cloud."

She looked at Adam. "What about it?"

"It's the energy I felt coming from it. I couldn't place it but now it makes sense. Whatever's creating that storm is affecting how we can heal. Thia's a stronger caster than you are, Jinaari. Her magic's going to work. Yours won't be as effective, and mine will be completely ineffective. It could also be why she's feeling such extreme effects from her castings. If that were to spread . . ." his voice trailed off.

Thia's mind reeled from the implications. If the entire world was robbed of healing, disease would run rampant. And healers, like herself, would be blamed.

"You three stay put, get some rest. I'm going to find the man, bring him back here. We need some answers." Jinaari headed toward the door. "He was limping pretty bad when he ran. He won't have gotten far." Adam walked with him, the two talking quietly. It was about her. She knew that from the way both men looked back at her. Jinaari left, closing the door behind him.

"We'll be here for a while," Adam said. "Might as well catch some sleep while we can. Caelynn and I'll take turns on watch."

Thia didn't argue. She was tired. The adrenaline from the day's events was leaving her system. *Don't think about it. I survived, that's all that matters. Nobody died. Nobody I'm responsible for, that is.* Rising from the chair, she grabbed her pack from the floor and moved away from the table. Caelynn moved the chair closer to the door while Thia unrolled the thin sleeping pad. "How long do you think it'll be before he's back?"

"Not long," Adam replied. "He's fine, thanks to you. The one he's hunting isn't."

The door to the room flew open, banging loudly against the wall. Thia's head jerked toward the sound. Someone stood in the doorway, but there was no way it was Jinaari. Caelynn and Adam took defensive stances in front of her as the figure started to remove his helm.

"Let's talk," Alesso said as he kicked the door shut.

Rising slowly, Thia kept her eyes on Alesso. "About what?" Adam asked.

The man unsheathed a sword and dagger, then laid both on the table before stepping away. "I'm not here to kill the mongrel." Thia felt his gaze settle on her. "I've been told not to. I'm actually here to protect her."

"How about you stay over there and wait for Jinaari to come back? Then we'll talk about who's doing what."

"Not going to happen." The brown-haired man leaned against the wall near the door.

"What's not happening?"

"Althir. He's not coming back. Not for a while, anyway."

"Dunno about that," Adam countered. "He's going to walk through that door within the next few minutes. I'm pretty sure he's not going to be thrilled to see you. Not after the stunt you pulled at the docks."

Alesso snorted, muttering something Thia couldn't understand. "Let's get this over with," he said. Reaching over his shoulder, he pulled a large shield free and placed it on the ground. Picking up his weapons again, he put them on the shield, pointing at him. He then knelt on the ground. "By Garret's Grace do I, Alesso Potiri, offer myself as Champion to Thia Bransdottir. My blades are yours to command. I will tell you no lie. I will do you no harm. I will protect you from all foes. This do I swear, until such time as Jinaari Althir returns, you dismiss me, Garret recalls me, or my life is spent." He raised his head, staring at her.

Thia took a few steps forward, sliding between Adam and Caelynn. That vow was not one he would've made lightly. Her own vow, when she became a priestess, was similarly worded. If he broke any of it, the consequences would be dire. Deadly, even. It was on her to accept or reject him. She glanced at Adam, whispering, "We need a sword until Jinaari returns. And we won't get him to tell us where he went until this is done."

He nodded in agreement.

She walked forward, stopping at the pointed bottom of the shield. "I accept you as my Champion, under the conditions you have stated. May Keroys guide me as Garret guides you." She stepped back as he rose, collecting his weapons. "Now, where's Jinaari and why are you here?"

Alesso leaned his shield against the leg of the table. "Garret called him home for special training. I was sent to take his place, help you three do whatever it is you're doing down here, and keep you," he pointed at Thia, "safe." The sword slid into its sheath at his hip.

"Safe from what?" Adam asked.

Alesso stared at him but didn't answer.

"He asked you a question, Alesso." Thia said.

The paladin grinned. "He did. My vow was to you. If you command me to answer," he shrugged. "I can't disagree with your, ahem, wisdom."

Thia took a deep breath. She'd have to talk with Adam, get advice on how to handle Alesso. It was obvious he would hold to his vow . . . and only that. "Please answer Adam's question."

"Seems Lolc Aon wants to meet you. The entire city of Byd Cudd is awash with teams of Fallen plotting against each other to be the one to bring you before the Scorpion Queen. They reestablished a colony near Tanisal in case you came this way. Probably several others. I've heard whoever brings you to Lolc Aon, alive, will be given quite the reward." His eyes narrowed as he spoke. "I personally don't care if they slaughter themselves by the hundreds to find you. And I'm not going to pull back from letting my blade feast on their blood. But I will keep my vow."

"What happens when one of the conditions you listed is met?" Thia stared back at the brown-haired man.

The cold smile never reached his blue eyes. "You'd best hope you can run damn fast, witch."

Drawing back from his gaze, she raised her chin. Striving to put some sense of command into her voice, she said, "Adam will set a watch schedule. You'll follow it. You and Caelynn are the fighters here. I'll keep you healed. If they get through you---"

"Not likely," he interrupted her.

"If they get through," she continued, "Adam will get me out of there. Understood?" It was the same plan Jinaari had outlined less than an hour earlier. She waited for him to nod, then kept on. "There was a Fallen man that Jinaari was chasing. He was planning to bring him back so we could get some answers. Do you know what happened to him? I don't want to wake up and find him standing over me."

"Don't know where he went. Garret didn't fill me in on that. But he's not coming in here. Not on my watch, anyway."

Adam cleared his throat. "Thia, get some rest. I'll take first watch. Caelynn, you're on second. Alesso, you'll be third."

She walked back to her bedroll. and felt Alesso watching her. Caelynn moved her blankets closer to hers. "Snug up to the wall, Thia," she told her. "Let's make it where he can't come near you without waking me up."

"It doesn't make sense. Why would Jinaari's God take him away? He was told to do this, by both Garret and Keroys."

"Do you think Alesso's lying about where he went?"

Thia laid down, shifting part of her pack under her head. "I don't know," she whispered. "His vow was specific. One of the only ways he can get out of it is if Jinaari returns. That tells me he's still alive. But there's no way I'll trust everything Alesso says."

"He said he couldn't lie to you, though."

"He can't, no," she drew a deep breath, "but that doesn't mean he's going to tell me every detail he knows.

He'll stick to what I ask him and nothing more. Even if he knows it, he won't tell me unless I can ask the right question." She looked past Caelynn. She could see Alesso but wasn't sure what he was doing. Adam leaned against the door; his staff cradled in his arms. She caught his gaze and he nodded at her once.

"Get some sleep," Caelynn yawned. "Who knows what tomorrow will be like."

"Caelynn?"

"Yeah?"

"Wake me up when Adam has you start your watch. I need to talk to him without Alesso overhearing." She closed her eyes, but sleep didn't come quickly. Too many thoughts screamed for attention. Why would the Gods need Jinaari? What happened to the man who called her 'sister'?

And why would Lolc Aon want her?

CHAPTER EIGHT

Jinaari caught sight of his foe as he rounded a corner. The Fallen man's hand was pressed to his side and his leg dragged along the floor. "Why not stop? I'm going to catch you," he called out. Honestly, he didn't expect the man to give up that easily. But he had to give him the option.

The man glanced back, a sneer on his face. "I'm not going anywhere."

The hair on Jinaari's arm rose. Directly behind the man, the air began to shimmer and swirl as a portal opened up. *Damn it!* Jinaari sprinted, intent on grabbing him before he could escape. He tackled him, the momentum pushing them both through the gateway.

They landed with a thud on the ground. Rolling to his left, Jinaari looked at his prey. He was unconscious but breathing. A dozen young men came running, swords drawn. Blinking, Jinaari sat up and took stock of his surroundings. He knew this place well. Too well.

It was the training arena at his chapterhouse back in Dragonspire. That ruled out the Fallen man from casting it.

Who did, then? And why here? "I'm fine," he waived off the closest initiate. "This one should be taken to the infirmary. Keep him restrained and under guard at all times." Standing, he sheathed his sword and watched them carry off the Fallen man.

"Sir?" a small voice called.

Looking down, he addressed the small child. "Where's the Commander?"

"In his chamber, Sir. He said you should go there as soon as you arrived." The boy ran off before Jinaari could ask another question.

This didn't make sense! Why would Drakkus bring him back here? He had a mission. Storming through the stone hallway, he kept his anger in check. *I should be there, with them! Not here! Drakkus, you'd better have a good reason!*

Torches flickered wildly in their sconces as he strode past. Strange. The chapterhouse shouldn't be deserted. Outside of the courtyard, though, he'd not seen another soul.

The commander's door, situated at the end of the corridor, stood slightly ajar. Another warning sign; Drakkus never left it that way. Either it was open, or it was shut. Jinaari slowed down, one hand easing his sword from its scabbard. He steadied his breathing and stopped, listening before moving forward.

"Althir. Come in. We've been waiting for you." A voice, commanding in a way that couldn't be disobeyed, came from the room.

Jinaari put away his weapon but kept a hand on the hilt. The voice was familiar, but he couldn't place it. He'd heard it before, but where?

It wasn't Drakkus. He knew that much.

Stopping in the doorway, his gaze was drawn to the

fireplace to the left. The logs burned with an unnatural yellow hue. Three chairs sat in front of it, the center one unoccupied. A pair of cloaked figures sat in the other two.

"Sit," the figure on the right commanded, pointing to the empty chair. "We have much to discuss."

"I mean no disrespect, but I have a task that needs completing. I need to know why I've been summoned, and by who, before I'll enter. Or you can just send me back where I was."

The figure on the right rose, hands moving the hood off his head as he turned. "I summoned you because it is my right, Althir."

Jinaari's eyes grew wide, and he dropped to a knee. "My Lord Garret. I am yours to command."

"Then get your ass in this chair as I told you to do." The God commanded, irritation evident in his voice.

Without hesitation, Jinaari moved into the room and sat down. He kept his focus on the fire in front of him and not the cloaked figures. If Garret's here, the odds that the other was Keroys, or another God, were high.

"We have a problem, Althir. My brother has a priestess. One that you've met." Garret began.

"Thia?"

"Don't interrupt." Garret snapped. "But yes. Thia herself is not the problem. Rather, it's her parentage."

"My daughter has come to the attention of Lolc Aon." Keroys's deep voice was tinged with sadness. "I grew complacent. When Thia was raised to priestess, I thought it would help by personally accepting her vows. The blessing I gave alerted our sister to Thia's potential. She knew, eventually, I would send Thia out into the world. Lolc Aon would use her skills to the detriment of all. The surface world as you know it would not survive such an invasion."

Jinaari couldn't help the low whistle that escaped his lips. "I know Thia. She detests that part of her heritage. You have nothing to fear, My Lord. She would not willingly go to Byd Cudd. Her devotion to you is absolute."

"The problem isn't that she'd do so willingly, but that Lolc Aon would manipulate her into doing so under the guise of saving others. Thia has a good heart. Too good, I fear." Keroys sighed. "Can you tell me that Thia would not sacrifice her life, her soul, if she felt it was for the greater good?"

Jinaari stared at the fire. Keroys was right. Thia would do exactly that.

Garret spoke up. "Lolc Aon has commanded all her followers to bring Thia to Byd Cudd to be converted to the Scorpion Queen's service. One attempt has already been made, as you know."

"If this is the case, then send me back!" Jinaari insisted. "I cannot protect her from here! What of Drogon? Adam figured out what the cloud's doing. It's got to be stopped before it spreads across all of Avoch. Why bring me here to talk when I should be there, fulfilling my vows? The task you yourself gave me?"

"The group is well suited for the task at hand. I sent Potiri to guard them for now."

"Alesso? He hates the Fallen! He's already attacked Thia once!"

"Thia has a purpose, Althir," Keroys said. "She doesn't know what it is, not yet, but she needs to start on that path. Potiri is necessary for her to begin her journey."

Garret sighed. "I also threatened to end his life if he so much as allows her to stub a toe. I need you to learn additional skills. To defeat Lolc Aon will not be easy. I will not let you fail, Althir. Stay here. Training will be provided. When you are ready, I will send you back."

"How long will I be here?"

"That depends on how fast you learn."

Jinaari shook his head. "I do not like this. I should be there."

"I don't care if you like it or not, Althir. Your choice is simple. Stay and take the training I require of you or leave my service." Garret's voice cut through any resistance Jinaari still held onto.

Lowering his head, he replied, "Let's get on with this."

The Gods rose, and he followed quickly. "Drakkus will get you started in the morning. Get some sleep. You're going to need it when you meet your training partner."

Jinaari nodded, realizing he was being dismissed. "May I ask who it'll be?"

"His name's Aust. You brought him with you. Drakkus will explain the rules and the consequences if he doesn't abide by them."

"The Fallen that I was chasing? Why him?"

"Two reasons. One, his race doesn't fight the same as you do. You have to learn how your foe moves in order to defeat them."

Jinaari headed to the door. Resting his hand on the latch, he looked back at his God. "What's the second reason?"

"We need information that he can provide. You can't kill him, Althir. Not yet. But making him talk is allowed."

He pushed the latch down and opened the door. The hallway was still deserted. A wave of exhaustion hit him as he walked toward his room. He fished the key out of a small pouch he kept under his armor. Inserting it into the lock, he whispered the password that deactivated the magical wards.

This may be home, but Alesso lived here as well. And Jinaari's family connections made the ward prudent.

The room was cool. Simply furnished, it suited him. His bed beckoned, and he knew there were enough blankets in the chest at the foot that he could forego a fire tonight. First things first, though. He walked to the armor stand. He removed the shield from his back, placing it against the wall. Unbuckling his belt, he left the sword in the scabbard and laid it across the table, then shrugged off his pack. With deliberate movements, he removed the armor, reverently placing each piece on the form. The breastplate was covered with gouges. First from the pipe and then keeping Thia from falling into the pit. They weren't deep and could be buffed out. *I'll take it to Henry tomorrow.* The blacksmith had made it originally, at his mother's request, and would be the best one to repair it.

He finished and walked over to the bed. Sitting on the edge, he pulled off his boots and placed them near the trunk. Quickly, he pulled out two more thick, wool blankets and draped them across the bed. *They're in a maze, and the cold's going to seep through the blankets while they sleep. And I'm here, comfortable. This doesn't make sense.*

He climbed under the blankets and passed a hand over his weary eyes. *I have to do what I do best. Train. Learn. And get back there before Alesso screws everything up.*

Jinaari spun, ducking underneath the blunted axe, and swept the legs out from underneath his opponent. The man grunted as his body hit the stone floor. With a smooth motion, he positioned the tip of his sword at the creature's throat. "Do you yield?"

Hatred glared back at him, but the Fallen nodded. Jinaari moved the weapon aside but didn't relax. "Take a break," Drakkus commanded. "You're slowing down, Althir. He almost had you that time."

Jinaari crossed to the barrel of water that sat in the corner and splashed some on his face. "You've had us sparring for over an hour, Drakkus. Even you'd be tired by now."

"My kin will not let up simply so you can rest, paladin." The man's words were full of contempt. "We are many. There's only one of you. Eventually, we will overwhelm you. Herasta's daughter will be rescued. You can't hide her forever. Lolc Aon will have her prize."

Jinaari clenched his jaw, refusing to respond to the taunt. He rested his hands on the windowsill, looking out to the courtyard below. Despite what Garret and Keroys told him, he still wanted to be with his companions. That's where he should be, where he'd be of use. Not stuck in a small room, sparring.

"The Gods are not without compassion, Althir. They sent help to your friends. Thia will be kept safe." Drakkus stood next to him, keeping his voice low.

"For how long? I know you trained Alesso, same as me, but he's not your best. He's got too many prejudices."

"Agreed. He's not who I would've sent. In my opinion, the last person to be guarding Thia is someone who cannot see beyond her lineage. But that's not what Garret wanted, and we all serve him." He tapped the back of Jinaari's shoulder, "I was there when Garret made his wishes clear. He imposed broad constrictions on him and spelled out the consequences."

Jinaari blinked, "He's under a *geas*, then?"

Drakkus nodded. "Potiri won't risk breaking it. He knows what'll happen to him if he lets anything happen to Thia."

A dry laugh came from behind them. Jinaari turned, glaring.

"You sent Alesso Potiri? My kin will not hesitate to slaughter him to get to my sister. He might as well escort her to Lolc Aon's temple now. We do not fear him." He secured his white hair into a ponytail, snickering.

Turning, Jinaari looked at him, his eyes narrowed, "What do you mean, 'sister'?"

Aust leaned against the wall, his arms crossed against his chest, "What do you think that word means?" His lilac eyes stared at him. "Are you so dense you cannot see what's right in front of you? There's only four of us that have this color," he pointed to his face, "in all of Byd Cudd. Herasta has birthed a dozen children in Lolc Aon's name. Three of us take after our mother and bear the favor of Lolc Aon."

"I've never heard of a God Marking so many in a generation," Jinaari said.

"It's not a true Mark. We aren't bestowed with abilities like a Son or Daughter of hers would be. But it lets all Fallen know not to move against us, lest the Scorpion Queen's wrath descend on them. In that alone, Thia will be granted safe passage." He grinned. "Her return to the city will be celebrated. Lolc Aon has been planning the ceremony for almost a decade. Colonies we abandoned are alive again, full of both Fallen and Barren, with one purpose: find Thia and bring her home. Her ascension will result in many children born. Every woman will take as many men as they can find into their bed, hoping to bear one that will rise up and take Thia's place one day. Before the day is done, my sister will lose all of what she is now and embrace what Lolc Aon requires of her. Perhaps she'll even bless me with the opportunity to lay with her."

Jinaari lunged at him, one hand circling his throat, and slammed him hard against the stone wall. For the first time, he saw fear flicker in his eyes. "You'll be dead before that happens. I guarantee it."

Aust laughed. "Try it."

"Althir. Stand down." Drakkus commanded.

Releasing his grip, Jinaari took a step back. He'd heard the stories about life among the Fallen and knew what Aust said to be true. The damage that would do to her soul made him cringe.

"What's wrong?" Aust mocked him. "Are you afraid that she might like that life? She's Fallen. Even she can't deny that forever. It's in her blood."

Without hesitating, Jinaari turned. His right fist connected hard with the other man's jaw, sending him to the floor. A thin trickle of blood ran from the corner of his mouth. "Blood isn't all that makes a person who they are," he said. He glanced at Drakkus. "I need some air." Without another word, he threw open the door and stormed out.

The parapet surrounded the chapterhouse. He kept a scowl on his face as he passed the guards, guaranteeing they'd give him an open path. There was one small tower at the southeast corner. From there, he could see the palace. A constant reminder of what his life would be if he hadn't chosen this one instead. The one that always loomed over him as what may still come to pass. What Aust had described . . . that wasn't Thia. He knew that. It'd only been a week or so since they'd met, but he knew her well enough to be certain about that.

"That was one hell of a punch," Drakkus said.

Jinaari didn't turn around. The royal banner, a blue eagle against a yellow field, flew above the city. "Is that what you had in mind?"

"More or less. He's confused, which is good. He knows he said too much, but he thinks he has the advantage. I was impressed. I honestly thought he'd gotten under your skin."

Jinaari smiled, "Not even close." *Believe me*, he thought. The last thing he wanted was for his commander to learn it hadn't all been an act. The idea of leaving Thia to the fate Aust described turned his stomach.

The commander came closer, leaning against the stone wall next to him. "You broke his jaw."

"Good," he said. "Has there been any news?"

"Of Adam and the rest? No, nothing's reached me yet. The cloud is still over Tanisal, but it's stopped growing. They've at least got Drogon's attention."

Jinaari felt the frustration rise. A small pebble rested on the rock near him. Picking it up, he threw it into the forest below them. "I should be there," he muttered. "I just got her to trust me, Drakkus. There's no way she'll trust Alesso. If Garret hadn't put the *geas* on him, he'd kill her at the first chance he got."

"That's why he did it, Althir. Potiri needs to learn not to judge someone based on how they look. By forcing him to keep Thia safe, he'll realize that. I hope."

Turning his head, he snorted. "You hope? You have more faith in Alesso than I do."

Drakkus grinned, "That's why I'm the commander and you're not, Althir. The world isn't always black and white. Sometimes hope is the best thing you have." His eyes narrowed, and Jinaari followed his gaze. "That's not right." He pointed toward the castle. The banner was slowly being taken down. "Did your mother send you word about any change in the royal progress?"

"No," he said. "I haven't heard from her in months."

"Come on," Drakkus tapped his arm. "If they're heading out, I'll need your help getting the detachment ready. If they aren't, you might be needed elsewhere."

Jinaari took one more look at the palace, then followed Drakkus down the stairs. Whatever was going on, it wasn't good. *Drakkus said that hope was all you had sometimes*, he thought. *I hope Adam's keeping them safe. If that banner doesn't go back up, I may be here even longer than Garret planned.*

CHAPTER NINE

"There's a staircase over here." Alesso held his torch out into the darkness, then pulled it back. A malicious grin sat on his face. "But you saw it already, didn't you?"

Thia drew a deep breath, a retort ready to leave her mouth. "He's not worth it," Adam whispered in her ear. Nodding, she ignored the taunt.

"Wait here," Caelynn said. She disappeared into the inky blackness. Thia waited, trying to stay calm. Alesso had been leading them around the maze for days now. Somehow, he managed to find every dead end in the place. This was the first indication they'd found that it went deeper underground.

"I know it seems like we're taking too much time, Thia," Adam kept his voice low, "but there's a method to this. Better to make sure there's no enemies lurking behind a door than have them sneak up behind us."

"What could be down here? Besides Drogon, that is."

"Lots of things, none of which I'll say. They'd just make

you jump at every noise. Better that you trust us to take care of those things."

"You, yes. Alesso? Never."

His face changed. "I'm glad to hear that I've earned your trust. Jinaari told me it doesn't come easy for you."

She leaned against the wall, "It doesn't. Jinaari trusts you, though. And you kept me from becoming spider food." She shuddered at the thought. "I'm not sure what's worse. Worrying about what's around the next corner, or what Jinaari's going through."

"The next corner is your main concern. Jinaari's a survivor, in more ways than you know. He'll do whatever it is his God demands of him as fast as possible. If there's one thing he hates, it's being taken away from a task before he can complete it."

"It spirals down," Caelynn said, emerging from the opening. "It's narrow, so we have to move single file. And I heard noises. We won't be alone for long."

Alesso turned to her. "Well? What's your decision?"

I'd like to smack that smug look off your face, that's my decision! She glared at him, "You lead, Caelynn will follow. Adam will bring up the rear. I'd like to avoid a fight if possible. We don't know if they're evil yet."

"Are you telling me not to kill them if they're Fallen?" Disgust dripped from his voice.

She shook her head. "No. If they're Fallen, they're here for a reason. But it could be slaves that we can set free, or some animal that's lost."

"Gods, you're naïve. We're in a godsforsaken dungeon, *priestess*! This isn't some pretty church! Anyone down here, besides those two," he gestured at Adam and Caelynn, "is going to want to hurt you!"

"You included yourself in that, Alesso." Caelynn stepped closer to her and Adam.

"Just because I want to doesn't mean I will. I know what I promised, and I'll stick to it. Just keep that witch out of my way. I'd hate to have a swing go wide and slice her open . . . on accident." Without another word, he stormed toward the staircase opening and disappeared into the darkness. Caelynn nodded at them before following him.

"He's right about one thing, Thia," Adam said. "The likelihood of anything beyond us being friendly down here is slim. Better to anticipate a fight than be caught by surprise."

She placed a hand on the wall and started to descend. They were right. Drogon wouldn't be welcoming them with open arms, ready to simply stop whatever he was planning because they asked nicely. The Fallen were chasing her, as well. *Wake up*, she thought. *I've already been chased by giant spiders and almost fell into a pit of scorpions. The threats are bound to get bigger, not smaller.*

"Get down here!" Caelynn screamed from the darkness ahead of her. Thia glanced back at Adam as the sound of something hitting metal rose up to them.

"Go!" Adam encouraged her.

Without much thought, she ran down the stairs. Rounding the corner, she stared at the sight. A giant scorpion filled the hallway. The curved black and red tail, the tip glowing with an ugly green slime, danced as the creature's pincers snapped at Caelynn and Alesso.

Blood ran down the elf's arm. Drawing the sigil, Thia sent some healing to her. At the moment it hit, the scorpion's tail lashed out and struck Alesso. The razor-sharp point pierced his chest plate and the creature lifted him off the ground, throwing him toward Thia and Adam. His body skidded to a halt at her feet.

She knelt at his shoulder. His breathing was shallow. "I can stabilize him," she said, "but I can't heal him here."

"Do what you can," Adam replied. A blast of energy flew from his staff, hitting the scorpion. The creature screamed in pain.

She pulled off his helm and placed both of her hands on each side of his head. Closing her eyes, she whispered a spell that halted the spread of the venom. She looked at his chest again. It rose with a steady rhythm now. Staring at the creature, her hands drew a sigil she had never tried. A wave of black energy surged from her fingers and tore into the scorpion. It shuddered, dazed, and Caelynn thrust her rapier through one of its eyes. One final spasm as the legs gave out, and it collapsed to the ground, dead.

Thia lowered her head, waiting for the wave of dizziness to pass. At least she'd been sitting down when she'd cast the spell.

"Thia?"

"I'll be fine, Adam," she didn't look up. "He's stable, but it's going to take a lot for me to purge the poison from him. And he's not going to wake up for hours afterward. Ideas?"

"Do you think we can move him back upstairs?"

"We could, but that staircase was awfully narrow. I'm not sure how you and Caelynn can manage it. I'm not going to be much help. What's left in my stores has to be used on him."

"I found something," Caelynn called out.

Thia raised her head at the sound of Caelynn's voice. The bard stood on the other side of the scorpion's corpse, pointing to a wall. "Looks like an abandoned room. There's a couple of beds."

"Come back here, help me carry Alesso. Thia" Adam's hand appeared in front of her. "Can you walk?"

Taking his hand, she rose. Swaying slightly, she used the stone wall to steady herself. "I have to," she said. Taking one step at a time, she hugged the wall, keeping her gaze on the dead scorpion as she forced herself not to sprint to the room Caelynn had found.

In addition to two cots, there was a pair of chairs, a table, and a small chest. Thia slumped into a chair, letting her pack slide off her back and onto the floor. *Eat something*, she thought. *It's going to help. I can't help him unless I've got the energy to move.* Rummaging in the bag, she found the last bit of cheese that Father Phillip had sent with her.

By the time the others brought Alesso, her head was clear. They placed him on the cot and Adam turned to her. The crystal in his staff began to glow, bathing the room in a soft light. "What now?"

"Take off his armor, then his shirt. I need to see the wound." Rising, she took off her belt and chain shirt, throwing her tunic back on over the padded undershirt. For this to work, she couldn't have that much metal on her. Carefully, she removed her box from its pouch and unwrapped it. This, she would need.

"Caelynn, get my pack. There's some rope in there. Let's tie him down once we get his armor off."

Thia blinked, "Why?"

The blond man looked at her. "I'm guessing this could be painful?" She nodded. "Then I'd rather tie him down than have him thrash around and break your jaw with his fist." Working quickly, they secured him to the bed. Adam stood up, looking at Thia, "I'm going to bar the door. Anything else you need when I finish?"

"Keep out of my way and stay quiet. Please. And can I

borrow your cloak? It looks warmer than mine, and I'm likely to get cold while I'm doing this."

Without a word, he unclasped it and draped it over her shoulders. Grabbing at the heavy red fabric, she said, "Thank you," as she moved the chair next to the cot. Placing the ornate box near her feet, she looked at her patient.

"There's a bolt. We'll be safe for a while." Adam said from behind her. The sound of the metal sliding into the hasp reassured Thia.

Alesso's skin was pale. Angry red lines spread out like a web from the entry wound. The strike was just above his heart; an inch farther down and he would've been dead before the scorpion raised him off the ground. She placed one hand on his abdomen, feeling the rhythm of his breathing. With her right hand, she chose one of the veins filled with poison at random. "Caelynn?"

"I'm here. How can I help?"

"Get a rag ready, something clean that we can burn." Thia instructed her. She heard Caelynn rummaging around but kept her focus on Alesso. *I have to get this right!*

"Found one," the bard said as she came up next to Thia.

"Watch the wound. You'll see the poison start to exit as I heal him. I don't know what it'll look like, but it should be pretty obvious." *I hope!* "Use the cloth, gather as much as you can. Keep your gloves on, though. You don't want it on your skin."

She heard cloth being ripped behind her. "I'll get more rags ready," Adam said. "And find something we can throw the used ones in."

Thia nodded. "Are you ready?"

"Whenever you are," Caelynn said.

She inhaled, letting the air fill her lungs. Her index finger traced the closest line. As she moved it along his skin, she drew on her magic to pull the poison from his body, back out the way it'd entered him.

A thick, viscous green liquid bubbled up from his chest, followed by the stench of rotting flesh. Thia kept her finger on her patient but moved her arm so Caelynn could mop up the poison. One by one, she unraveled the web of lines on his chest. Her body shivered as it reacted to the spell. About halfway through, she felt someone drape a blanket across her back. Sweat broke out on her forehead, dripping into her eyes but she refused to wipe away the stinging moisture. Only when the last line was cleared and the wound on his chest closed, did she take her hands off of him.

She looked at his face. The pain she'd seen earlier was gone. His breathing was deep, rising at even intervals. "He'll be fine now." She rose from the chair and felt her body sway dangerously.

"I've got you," Adam said. She felt his hands on her elbow and back, steadying her. "You need to sleep, Thia."

She didn't resist as he guided her toward the other cot. Her entire body ached, and a fresh wave of cold crashed over her as she laid down. "Caelynn, do we have any more blankets?" she heard Adam talking as her teeth rattled from the spasms.

Gradually, the warmth began to chase away the aftereffects of her spell work. Adam sat in a chair he'd pulled near her head. "You look exhausted."

"I'm fine," she protested.

Adam smiled, "I believe that about as much as Jinaari would. Get some rest. We'll go back to saving the world tomorrow."

Stifling a yawn, she drew the blankets closer to her chin. "How can you even tell if it's morning or night down here? We haven't seen the outside since the spiders chased us into the house."

"You have your spells. I have mine. Get some sleep, Thia. Caelynn and I will keep watch. You won't do him any good if you can't stand up. And Jinaari will yell at us for letting you get that low." He reached out and passed a hand over her eyes. She closed them, drifting off to sleep.

Slowly, she began to wake up. She kept her eyes closed, trying to gauge how her magic was. It felt normal, no lingering effects from the night before. Her stomach growled loudly. Okay, so maybe one side effect.

Opening her eyes, she sat up. Adam slept on the other bed, while Caelynn had made herself a bed, with their packs lined up beneath her. Alesso sat in a chair positioned in front of the door.

His head turned to her, watching.

Thia pushed the blankets off and sat on the edge. Her belt, chain shirt, and daggers still rested on the table. Someone had moved her box and put it next to the rest of her gear. "How are you feeling?"

"Alive."

She cradled her face in her hands, rubbing at her temples. A headache was forming. Maybe she wasn't as recovered as she thought.

She heard him get up and walk her way. "Here," he said.

Looking up, she saw him standing in front of her, holding out a waterskin. "Thank you," she said as she took it. She raised it to her lips. The liquid slid down her throat and some of the pain began to subside.

"You need to drink more," Alesso said. "Dehydration's a problem when you use too much magic at one time."

She tested the weight of the bag. "Do you think we'll find a water source down here? There's not much left."

"Drink. You need it now. I'm sure Garret will provide more before we need it."

She took another swig. *I can't argue with him all the time*, she thought. *It's not going to change anything.* Closing the lid, she handed it back to him.

Scowling, he said, "Keep it," and went back to the chair.

"Because I've tainted it somehow?" She couldn't resist taunting him.

"Something like that."

Sighing, she rose. He'd never change his mind about her. To him, she was nothing more than a reminder about what happened to his family. Even if she had nothing to do with that, had never been in Byd Cudd. She was Fallen. For him, that was enough.

Placing the waterskin on the table, she carefully wrapped her box in its coverings. "Who'd you steal the box from?"

She stared at him. "No one. My father made it for me."

He snorted. "You expect me to believe that? I know the work. My mother had one she prized." She started to open her mouth and stopped as he raised his hand. "I know it's not that one. The acorns aren't in the same place. Still, I know the craftsman was human. There's no way you're related."

"My father's name was Bran, and he was human. He raised me on the surface. My mother was Fallen, yes, but I don't even know her name." She finished wrapping the box and slid it into the belt pouch. Removing her tunic, she picked up the chain shirt. "I don't know what happened to your family, Alesso. I only know what happened to mine. He was the only family I had, and Drogon turned our village against me. Against him. The last time I saw my father, he was lying dead across the threshold of our home after the looters set it on fire." She let the weight settle on her shoulders, then reached for the tunic. "I know you don't like me. The feeling's mutual. But you're the one who asked me to accept you as my Champion."

"You didn't have to accept, witch," he growled at her.

"Yes, she did." Adam's voice cut in.

Thia turned her head, pulling her tunic down across her hips. The warlock sat on the edge of his bed, his staff in hand. "Without Jinaari, we're dead down here. Drogon wins. Garret knows this. We're stuck with each other, Alesso. You're here, breathing, because of Thia," he pointed at her, "so try being grateful instead of a jackass." He stood and walked to her. "Feeling better?"

"Yeah," she said. "A little bit of food would be nice if you have any. I'm out. Jinaari insisted on carrying most of the food we were given at the cloister."

"Absolutely." He tossed his pack on the table and started to dig through it. "Alesso?"

"I'm good."

Thia wound her belt around her waist, making sure the daggers rested someplace she could grab them quickly if she needed them. "How long did I sleep?" she asked Adam, her voice low.

"As long as you needed. That was one thing I told him." He nodded at Alesso, "We weren't moving again until you woke up and were ready. What you did yesterday . . . he doesn't understand how much that took out of you. I've never seen someone draw on that much magic and not collapse before they finished. How deep are your stores?"

"I'm not sure," she said. "I've never tried to reach the bottom. And this place," leaning against the table, she took the chunk of bread he offered her, "it's affecting my spells. Add to the mix that most of my spells I've never done completely. I don't know how to test my limit other than by casting. What I did, though, it took a lot."

Something behind her banged against the floor. Turning, she saw Alesso pushing aside the chair. His face was stony. "Can we all agree that it happened and get moving now? The witch is recovered. We've got a job to do." He strode over to the pile of armor and began to strap it on.

When he got to the breastplate, he turned and stared at Thia. The hole from the scorpion's stinger hadn't been mended.

"He did some mending while you slept, but kept it there on purpose," Adam whispered. "Said he needed the reminder of how close he came to failing at his task."

"What task?" she asked.

"Protecting you."

CHAPTER
TEN

Jinaari lowered himself into the large copper tub. It sat close enough to the fireplace to keep the water at the perfect temperature for his sore muscles. Leaning back, he closed his eyes. Drakkus was relentless in his training, but with reason. Every day, he was getting faster at anticipating Aust's attacks. The Fallen had been sent to the infirmary for healing after both sessions today.

And he was taking fewer hits from his opponent. The soreness he felt today wasn't from bruises but because of how long Drakkus had kept them sparring.

He was close. He knew it. When he could take down Aust every single time, without being hit, that's when he thought Garret would send him back. Being here at the chapterhouse full of comforts, like this bath, when they had none grated at his mind.

Grabbing at the cake of soap, he washed up. Drakkus hadn't been able to tell him anything new beyond Thia and the rest were still alive. The Fallen search parties hadn't found them yet. But the cloud remained over Tanisal, as well. Whatever Drogon had at his disposal, it wouldn't be friendly.

Frustration gnawed at him. *Tomorrow*, he decided. *Tomorrow, I'll avoid all blows and make him wish he'd never left Byd Cudd. Then Garret will send me back, and I can finish this.* Rising from the water, he stepped out and grabbed a towel. As he finished drying off, he heard someone pound on his door.

"Althir! You have a visitor," Drakkus called out.

"Just a minute," he replied, grabbing at his pants and shoving his legs into them. His hands worked the laces as he headed to the door.

It flew open before he could reach it. "You were taking too long," the brunette woman said as she strode into the room.

"Hello, Mother," Jinaari said, tossing the towel to one side. He walked to the chair where he'd left his clean shirt and started to put it on. "What brings you here?"

A single bell began to peal, loud enough to echo through his room. His jaw tightened at the sound.

"Your grandfather has passed away."

Bowing stiffly, he said, "Your Majesty. Long may Queen Agrana reign."

"Enough of that," she snapped. "I've been surrounded by courtiers and sycophants my entire life. I didn't raise you to be among them." She sat in a chair. "I have things that must be declared, and soon. You'll continue as Lord Defender of Avoch, of course." She sighed. "You earned the shield, and title, many times over. No one would question that."

"That's not why you came here, though."

"Too many already feel I'm unfit simply because I'm a woman, want to have me abdicate in favor of another.

Those whispers have been around since your father died. I must declare my heir before they try and change the succession."

"What are you saying?" He sank into the chair opposite of her.

"You will be announced as my successor tomorrow." She held up a hand, silencing his protest. "I need you to swear your allegiance to me. I need those vows, from the Lord Defender, next in line, and my son."

"What about Amara? Or Stijyn? Either one of them is a better choice. And more comfortable with the politics that court requires. My vows to Garret cannot be put aside that easily. You know this." *Not now!*

"Down the road, when my rule is secure, I may change my mind. The second reading of the marriage banns between your sister and Duke Tomil will be done after the funeral, when the Almair delegation comes to court. I need that alliance. As to your brother," she paused, "I have thought of him. But not yet. He's too wild. He doesn't have the sense of duty that you do." She reached out, taking his hand. "I know this is the life you are best suited for. You are a warrior, not a politician. Sometimes we must do what is needed, not what we want. If the Gods are with us, you will keep to this one and not have to return to mine. That is up to the needs of Avoch, though. Please, I need you to promise me this. Now."

"There's a task that Garret and Keroys have set me to. One that is vital to more than just Avoch. I cannot stay here and play at being a Prince."

"You only need to say the words. Drakkus," she nodded to the commander, "will be the official witness. When the declaration is read tomorrow, we'll word it to include your absence in the days—"

"This could take weeks. Months even."

She gave him a direct look. "Don't make me wish I'd given into your father's wish that you become a barrister. It will say enough, in the right language, for the populace to know you are loyal to me. To Avoch. And that you'll answer any summons of either the Crown Prince or Lord Defender. You *will* answer such a call, won't you?"

He sighed, knowing the answer before he said it. "Yes. Should Queen Agrana summon me as the Lord Defender, I shall answer. Should the council require The Crown Prince, I will answer. If my mother needs me, I will answer." He looked at her, his head tilted to one side. "Does that satisfy the requirements?"

"It'll do," she rose, and Jinaari stood with her. "I hope, one day, you'll grow to love us as much as you do this life. Not everyone who was born to privilege wants to do evil. Some do want what is best for others to come first."

He didn't respond. Too much of his youth was spent seeing his grandfather say one thing while doing another. Being raised by others, because his parents were gone. When word came, less than a year into his training at the chapterhouse, that his father had died, he had trouble remembering his face. To Jinaari, he was someone to avoid.

She sighed and headed to the door. "I encourage you to attend the funeral if you're still here. It would be good for everyone to see the man you've become."

"Good for me or good for you?"

"Don't be rude." She waited as Drakkus opened the door. "May Garret keep you safe, my son." Without another word, she left, followed by the commander.

He dropped back into the chair, cradling his head in his hands. This wasn't supposed to happen. Not yet. He should have had years to be true to himself. Time for Stijyn to grow up and into the role he was born to. This was Jinaari's life. A suit of armor sat well on him. A crown didn't.

Desperate to find some sense of peace, he rose and walked to the window that overlooked the main courtyard. There was still a light burning in the smithy. Grabbing an apple off a tray, he shoved his feet into his boots and headed downstairs. Henry had asked for five days to fix his armor. It'd been seven. If it was done, he'd feel better about what was going on in the palace.

Steam rose from the forge as he neared. They were busy, even at this hour. Several workers moved about the area. Jinaari scanned the space as he approached, looking for Henry. He spotted him near the largest forge, supervising one of his apprentices as they hammered on a glowing piece of metal.

"Evening, friend," he called out as he ducked under the low hanging awning.

"Your Royal Highness." Henry bowed slightly. Jinaari frowned. How could he know? Was word spreading that fast? "I didn't expect you. Is the armor not fitting well?" He picked up a rag and wiped his hands with it.

"I'm here to pick it up now. I haven't seen it yet."

Henry looked at him, concern on his face. "I finished it two days ago, as promised. One of the new recruits came, said he was to bring the armor to you. Commanders' orders. Perhaps it's being blessed?"

"I'm sure it's a simple misunderstanding. I'll go find him and get this straightened out." Curiosity ran through his mind as he left the smithy. Why would Drakkus pick up his armor and not tell him?

"Prince Jinaari!" A young boy ran toward him. "The commander says you're to meet him. I was sent to show you the way."

"Is there a problem?"

"No, not that I know of. But he said you had to come with me right now." The boy darted ahead then turned back around, waving his arm. "He's this way."

Something wasn't right. Too many people addressing him by a title that he'd never used within the chapterhouse before, the armor had been collected but not returned to him. "Let's go back to my quarters first. I need my sword."

The boy's eyes widened. "No, you can't. You have to come. Now. That's what the commander said." He pulled on Jinaari's hand.

First, no armor. Now, no weapon. It wasn't ideal, but the boy was insistent. Sighing, Jinaari tousled the boy's hair. "Fine. We'll do it your way. Lead me to him."

The boy led him through a few familiar tunnels, then veered down a seldom used passage. "Where are we going?"

"It's not far. I promise." The boy reached for a torch burning in a wall sconce. "The staircase is this way."

They rounded another turn and came to a dead end. "Lad, there's nothing here."

"Are you certain, Althir?" Garret's voice sounded from behind him.

Jinaari spun around and lowered his head. "My Lord."

"Look again."

Turning, there was now a sturdy wooden door, bound with iron, in the wall. Torches flanked it, flickering with an unnatural green light. His shield leaned against the door.

"Aust has escaped. He attacked one of the healers and ran. Your brothers were able to maneuver him into the maze. Find him, destroy him before he can get to the portal in the center. Do this, and you will be allowed to return to your companions."

He picked up the shield, fastening the straps as he spoke. "I need my armor and sword, as well."

"Everything you need is in that labyrinth."

"That's the test, then? Kill one Fallen, find my gear?"

"He's held back, restrained himself from using all of his tricks. We limited his ability to cast, as well. Those restraints are gone. He won't hold back from killing you. He wants to leave as much as you do. More so, as going back to Byd Cudd without Thia would be a death sentence for him."

Jinaari looked back over his shoulder. "I will do this."

"For Thia's sake, I hope you do. You will get no help from me or Keroys once you enter. If you don't succeed, death will not be swift or merciful. If Aust wins, so does Lolc Aon."

Squaring his shoulders, he took a deep breath. Reaching out, he tugged at the large iron ring and swung the door open. He grabbed at one of the torches and crossed the threshold.

The door closed behind him on silent hinges. The sound of the bolt sliding into the lock, however, echoed down the stone corridor in front of Jinaari. The light from the torch in his hand only illuminated so much. It was also the only thing he had to defend himself.

He had no other armor or weapon beyond the shield, but he would find Aust. One of them wasn't leaving this place alive. And it was going to be the Fallen. For the last week, he'd described things that would happen to Thia if she returned to Byd Cudd. Half of Jinaari's desire to kill him was based off those horrors.

He'd promised two Gods, and Thia herself, to keep her safe. Which meant making sure this brother of hers never came near her.

Jinaari crept down the hallway, holding the torch in

front of him. It would give him away, yes, but couldn't be helped. After a week on the surface, Aust's eyes had adjusted as well. He'd be almost as blind in the dark as he was. The difference was that he'd adapt faster.

As he followed a curve in the wall, the light bounced off a glint of metal. Settled into an alcove sat a suit of armor. He breathed a sigh of relief. He rested the torch against the wall and took a closer look. It appeared to be his. Not only had Henry buffed out the scratches, but he'd repaired a couple of straps. Removing the shield, he put it on, taking his time to buckle each piece securely.

Reaching back, he positioned the shield on the small hook before picking up the torch. He'd found his armor, but not his sword. With slow, deliberate motions he inspected the wall in front of him. Just above eye level, a small hole in the rock drew his attention. *What's this?* Reaching inside, his hand touched a hilt. *I found my armor here. It makes sense that my sword would be, as well.* Pulling it free of the niche, he stared at it, puzzled. The supple leather belt and scabbard held a longsword, yes, but the hilt and grip were caked with rust and grime. The layers of age and neglect crumbled away from his touch. Drawing the weapon, a soft blue light shone from the blade itself. The steel was smooth and sharp, despite the condition.

"You won't catch me, Althir!" Aust's voice echoed through the corridor. "Thia will be brought before Lolc Aon and turned to her service. And I will be rewarded for it."

"Over my dead body," Jinaari muttered back. With sword in hand, he left the torch behind. He didn't need it to hunt.

CHAPTER ELEVEN

"Thia! Watch out!" She turned around at the sound of Adam's voice. The high ceiling of the cavern was crumbling down on top of them. Before she could react, Alesso shoved her to the ground. He stood over her, his shield raised to deflect any rocks from hitting her.

"We have to run!" Caelynn screamed above the deafening roar of the collapse.

"Get up," Alesso commanded her, grasping her arm.

Thia scrambled to her feet, her hands flying up to protect her head. Adam and Caelynn stood a few yards away, in what looked to be an exit. As she ran, an arm encircled her waist and pulled her off her feet. "Let me go!" she screamed, her fingers trying to pry Alesso's arm from her.

Her body slammed to the ground. Snapping her head around, she gasped in horror. Quickly she pulled her body into a ball as the paladin dove on top of her, his shield held high to deflect the torrent of rocks and dirt that pummeled down on them.

Thia coughed, the dust from the cave in engulfing them both. Pain shot up from the arm pinned beneath her. Alesso's armor-clad body forced the air from her lungs as the rocks continued to fall. The deafening roar finally slowed and stopped.

She felt him roll off her. "Are you okay?" he asked.

Stretching, she moved off the arm. She opened her eyes. They were in a small pocket of clear space, surrounded by earth and rock. Smaller pebbles, mixed with dust and dirt, tumbled down the walls. She sat up, cradling her left arm close to her body. "I think it's broken," she said. "Where's Adam and Caelynn?"

"On the other side of that wall," he pointed behind her. Tossing aside the dented shield, he knelt in front of her. "Let me see," he demanded.

She sucked in her breath at the pain but held it out. The wrist sat at an odd angle. "This will hurt, but I need to try to move your fingers to see how bad it is."

Nodding, Thia took a deep breath as he grasped her hand. For all his gruffness, Alesso's touch was surprisingly light and gentle. Carefully, he moved each of her fingers. "How's that?" he asked.

"It hurts, but just at the wrist. I think the fingers are fine."

Nodding, he sat back. "That's good, right? You need the fingers to do whatever it is you do."

"Yes and no," she said. "The wrist is pretty important on some sigils. Like healing." She pulled the arm back near her chest and leaned back, resting against the rock. "I don't know that I'll be able to heal myself. Not for a while, anyway."

"Why not?"

"Pain is a distractor. I can't concentrate. There's a first

aid kit in my pack, I can splint it. There's a potion in there, too, to help with the pain. Once I stabilize it and numb myself, I can cast the spell. With how healing doesn't work right down here, though, it won't be as easy."

He leaned forward. "Hand me your pack," he said, "and tell me where to find this kit."

She leaned forward and shrugged the bag off her back. "Side pouch on your left should have a hard leather case. There are three small bottles in there. I only need one of them. The splint and bandages are in a bundle on the top of the main pocket." She watched him as he dug around in her bag.

"I could fix it. Garret does make us learn basic healing spells," he looked at her briefly.

"It won't work. Jinaari already tried on a bruise. He was able to halt the damage but not get rid of it completely. Adam's theory is it's the cloud above the city. Drogon's found a way to prevent basic heals from happening. If that gets stronger or spreads out over Avoch, there'll be panic. If he then attacks with an army that doesn't need healing . . ."

"Everyone on the surface would die. Is that why you're down here? To stop that from happening?" He tore at the wax surrounding the top of the small bottle and removed the cork before handing it to her. "You're sure that's the right one?"

Holding it beneath her nose, she inhaled. "Yes," she said. Quickly, she raised the bottle to her lips and drank the bitter liquid inside. She scrunched up her face. "Water," she said. Dropping the empty bottle, she reached out toward him.

He handed her a waterskin and she drank enough to wash the taste out of her mouth. "How long before it kicks in?"

She cringed as it flared again. "Not soon enough for me, but it really won't take long." She sighed. "I may need your help to get it into position for the splint."

"Whatever you need, priestess." For the first time, he didn't say that last word with disgust or sarcasm.

"What happened?" she asked him. "With your family?"

He sat against the opposite wall. "I only know what I was told. I was at the chapterhouse, training. The commander called me into his office, told me that the caravan they'd been traveling with had been attacked on the way to Dragonspire. The few survivors said the Fallen had taken the rest back into the mountain's base. The ones that hadn't been killed or escaped. A search party was dispatched. My family wasn't among the dead, and they never sent word to me that they escaped. The only other option is that they'd been enslaved by the Fallen." He stared at her, the familiar hatred back in his eyes. "When I found out, I swore an oath to find them, rid Avoch of the filth that stole my family. My sister was only seven years old. If she lives, she'd be twenty now. And who knows what they've turned her into. Your race isn't known for being kind or compassionate masters."

"I'm as human as you are, Alesso. It was my father that raised me, not my mother. I know the stories. I've heard them, over and over. I've been ignored, whispered about, and spat at. Simply because of people like you. It wasn't until Jinaari brought me to Tanisal that I started to understand that not everyone is that way. Humanity isn't exactly brimming with acceptance and tolerance. You only see what you want to see; someone who is Fallen. You don't see what's important." She closed her eyes as the first wave of drowsiness set in. The medicine was working. "I accepted your help. I didn't want to, any more than you wanted to give me that vow, but the Gods have decided we need to work together. Right now, that means putting the splint on." She held out her arm again. "Can you do it, or do you need me to walk you through it?"

"I know how," he said. Scooting closer, he picked up the short pieces of smooth bone that made the splint and the bandage roll. He laid them out across his lap before reaching for her hand. "It's going to hurt when I put it into place."

"I know that. Just do it." She took a deep breath. Her right hand grabbed onto the fabric of her cloak, balling it up in her fist.

Pain flared through her arm, arching into her shoulder, when he moved the wrist into place. She bit her lip to keep from crying out. He stared at her. "Don't stop," she told him. "If it's in place, you have to secure it before it moves again."

The medication began to dull the sharpness, eating away at the edges enough where she didn't have to blink back tears. She watched him secure the splint and wind the bandages around it, making sure it was snug against her skin. "What's next?" he asked.

"We wait. We figure out how to get out of here, find Adam and Caelynn. It'll be a few minutes before I'll even try to cast."

He rose, looking around their area. "There's a gap at the top," he told her. "We might be able to worm through there, get close enough to the exit where we only have to move a few rocks to get out. You planning on burying your friends someplace besides here?"

"What are you talking about?"

"They're likely dead, crushed under this," he smacked

his palm against the rock. "And digging them out isn't within the scope of what Garret charged me with."

"First, they're not dead. I don't believe that, so don't bring it up again. They were in the tunnel when the cave-in happened. They could've easily escaped. Second, I want to know exactly what it was your God said. Especially if you split hairs like that."

"You know already. I can't lie to you, I have to keep you safe, and I'll fight whatever you tell me to fight."

"No, that's not what I'm asking. What I need to know is why you were sent, and what did your God promise you to get you to be the champion of someone you hate?"

"I was sent because Althir," he spat at the ground, "needed his hand held. Again. Like everything else in his life. If you think for a minute that he's who he is only because he's good at it, you're deceiving yourself. He was born into privilege and uses it every chance he can. He didn't want you to come with them. He wanted someone else. And the minute he could escape, go back to his comfortable life, he did.

"As to the rest," he took a breath, "Garret said that, as long as you didn't come to any harm . . . as long as I didn't cause you pain of any kind . . . He would talk with Lolc Aon about freeing my family. The ones that are still alive, at least." He glared at her. "Yes, that's why I'm here. Not for you, priestess. Certainly not because of the other two. But being your babysitter until Althir decides to remove whatever stick went up his ass this time is the best chance I've had in thirteen years to gain their freedom. So, if you would be so kind as to heal yourself so we can get on with this? Because this isn't fun for either of us."

She rose, keeping her eyes on him. "I hope you get what you want, Alesso. I think you're wrong about Jinaari and the others. I know you're wrong about me. After so much time in Byd Cudd, your family may not be able to come back. Not the way you remember them, anyway. For your sake, I hope that's not the case." *I'll never change his mind,* she thought, *so why try so hard? Concentrate on the others, keep them alive. He's wrong. Jinaari's arrogant, sure, but he wouldn't be doing this if he wasn't capable. Alesso would've let me fall into that pit. Jinaari pulled me out of it.*

She was as numb as she'd ever get without being asleep. Carefully, she started to test her finger movement on her injured hand. *I can do this! I have to do this!*

"You sure you should do that?"

"Why don't you worry about finding the best way to climb that wall and leave the healing to me?" she shot back. Spending any more time with him, alone and trapped, wasn't going to work. They had to get out, find the others. And that meant getting herself healed.

With slow, deliberate movements, she started to draw the sigil while muttering the words under her breath. She winced once or twice but was able to complete the spell without stopping. The energy she summoned wormed its way under the bandages and into her skin, fusing the broken bone. It was the first time she'd healed herself, and the sensation surprised her. She could feel her body mend itself, becoming whole again. *Is this what Jinaari felt when I healed him?* She was drugged, he wasn't. Even with her pulling the pain from him as she did, he should've felt something. *Had he even flinched?* She couldn't remember. *Probably because I was on my knees, gasping for breath.*

"If you're done, priestess," Alesso said. "I found our way out." He pointed to an area above her head.

Looking up, she saw what he did. The rocks had fallen in such a way that there was a shallow dent in the line. It was still going to take time, but they'd make it. She picked up her pack with her right hand and put her arms through the straps.

"You leaving that on? I thought you healed yourself." He pointed at the splint.

"The healing's done, but the bone's still weak. The splint will keep it stable until it's stronger." She reached out, grasping at one of the rocks and testing her grip. She'd have to take it slow, but she'd do this. Without Alesso's help.

He moved alongside her, keeping at her pace. It took longer than she liked, and her wrist throbbed by the time her head came even with the opening. Alesso was already there, crouched down in the small space. "Here," he said, holding out his hand.

"I'm fine," she said, ignoring his offer. Laying her hands flat on the opening, she sucked in her breath as a fresh wave of pain shot up her arm. She shifted her weight from it and pushed herself up onto the ledge.

"You're as stubborn as he is arrogant." Without warning, he grabbed at her cloak and pulled her the rest of the way into the opening.

She tore herself from his hand. "I didn't need your help."

"Yeah, right," he snorted. "If you're done, priestess, I recommend we go that way." He pointed down a long, narrow channel in the rock. "You lead. That way, I can't accidentally leave you behind."

Jinaari was arrogant, and insufferable, but at least he didn't hate her. *I hope you come back, and soon,* she thought. *Otherwise, I may have to kill him myself.*

She inched her way down the tunnel. It wasn't tall enough for her to stand up in. Rubble dug into her knees.

Her backpack scraped against the ceiling in places. The end came into her vision within minutes. It wasn't solid. Small slits of dim light showed between the rocks; if she turned around and kicked at them hard enough, they should fall away. "We're at the end," she said.

"Do you see a way out?" Alesso asked.

"Yes. I'm going to turn around," she told him, moving at the same time. "If I kick hard enough, the rocks will move, and we can get out."

"Why not just blast them?"

"My wrist is still in the splint. I don't have the mobility to make the correct sigil." She replied. Scooting forward, she positioned herself close enough to strike at the rocks with maximum strength. She took a deep breath, pulled back, and started to kick.

The rocks started to shift after her third strike. "They're moving," she told him. She drew her legs back again and hit them with as much strength as she could muster. The boulder she'd been striking fell forward, and a dozen or more around it followed. When the dust cleared, she saw out a large cavern before them.

Thia crawled forward, twisting her body around, and began to find a place for her feet. "Be careful," Alesso said.

She took her time, making sure her feet and grip was secure before moving down to the floor. It wasn't as far as the climb up had been. Once her feet touched the ground, she stepped off to the side and looked around.

A single torch burned off to one side, and she could see two people sitting on the ground. "Adam?" she called out. "Is that you?"

One of them raised their head but didn't answer. Something was wrong. Alesso reached the ground, pulling out his sword as he turned around. "Show yourselves!" he demanded.

From the surrounding darkness, several armed Fallen moved forward, weapons at the ready. The two on the ground were jerked up and brought into the light. Adam and Caelynn were both gagged; their hands tied behind their backs.

"Hello, Potiri. It's a pleasure to meet you." One of the Fallen women spoke. "I've heard so much about you. Why don't you put the sword away? There's no reason why the negotiations have to be unpleasant."

"What negotiations?" he said, moving in front of Thia. "How fast can you climb back into the tunnel?" he whispered.

"Not fast enough," she said.

"We have something you've been looking for. And you have something that interests Lolc Aon. A trade may be beneficial to both of us." The Fallen snapped her fingers. Thia saw movement behind them. There were more? Her heart raced with fear, and she backed up against the wall.

"What? The warlock and bard? I don't care. I already thought they were dead." Alesso said.

The Fallen smiled, though her bright orange eyes remained cold. "They're coming with us, don't worry. I have something unique. Give me Thia," she paused, reaching behind her. A young woman with brown hair was thrown forward. Her clothes were dirty and torn. A gold chain ran from the belt around her waist to another Fallen. "And I'll leave this one with you. With the key to her chain."

The woman on the ground looked up. Her face was pale and thin. Her blue eyes filled with tears. "Alesso?" she said, her voice weak.

"Ashynn?" Thia heard his voice break. She looked closer at the woman; there was a resemblance.

"This is your choice, Potiri." The leader stepped forward, drawing a dagger. She yanked the slave's head up by her hair, placing the blade against her throat. "Give us who we want. I give you your sister. If you decline our generous offer, I slit her throat. We attack. We take Thia and your name dies in this cave. So? Do we have a deal?"

CHAPTER
TWELVE

Jinaari ran down the passage. Aust was in front of him, running scared. He'd caught up to him, had a clear shot, when the earth beneath them began to shake. Jinaari's blow was deflected by a rock falling from the ceiling, but he'd still drawn blood.

Aust's hand was pressed against his side. Ahead of them, at the end of the tunnel, was a blue glow. The portal! He had to get to the Fallen before he could reach it. A low growl rumbled from his throat as he charged at the man. He turned and tried to parry Jinaari's blow. He wasn't fast enough, not this time. Jinaari's sword slid into his chest, pinning him against the wall.

"You're too late, Althir." The man taunted him. "All that armor may protect you, but it doesn't do my sister any good. You may as well give up. You can't keep her from her fate." He coughed, and blood trickled out of the corner of his mouth.

He twisted the sword. "I don't give up."

Aust's body went limp as he died. Jinaari pulled his sword free, watching the man fall to the ground. Grabbing at the fabric of his cloak, he wiped his sword clean of blood before sliding it back into the scabbard. He nudged the corpse once with his foot, making sure he was dead. His lilac eyes stared back, empty of life. *Now to get back*, he thought, *and make sure Thia's don't look like that.*

He moved closer to the light, his ears alert for any sound. A light shuffle of feet made him stop. He flattened his back against a wall. Someone, or something, was ahead. The sword left his scabbard with a steely hiss. One way or another, this game was going to end.

"Come forward, Your Royal Highness. There is nothing left for you to slay in this maze." The deep voice had an ethereal quality to it. He knew it wasn't Garret. That left only one other possibility that made any sense.

Keroys.

Jinaari shoved the weapon home and walked out. The portal shimmered in the center of the circular room, casting a warm blue light around the chamber. Five other tunnels led off it, back into the maze.

Keroys stood, his hands hidden within the sleeves of his robe, watching him. His eternal face was tinted with a sadness that made Jinaari's heart sink.

"Did something happen?"

The God shook his head, "No, not yet. You've done what was asked of you. My brother is proud of you, and we both feel that you are ready to return to your companions. There is nothing left we could teach you to succeed at the task given you."

He wasn't sure how, but he knew Keroys wasn't saying everything. There was something more that he would ask. "But?"

The God drew a breath. "You're perceptive, which is necessary. There is a favor I would ask of you." He held up his hand, and Jinaari remained silent. "Do not answer me aloud, or even right now. You've earned the right to return, no matter your decision on my request. I only ask that you consider it carefully."

Jinaari nodded, "I will."

"Let me see the sword."

He drew the weapon and rested the blade against his forearm.

Keroys reached out a hand but didn't try to take the blade. Instead, he brushed his fingertips along the channel running down the center of the sword. A golden glow followed his touch, disappearing into the blade itself. "It is as I hoped. Garret gifted you with a weapon uniquely suited to aid you in bringing down Lolc Aon." He let out a sigh. "It may be necessary, however, to use it on someone else." He took a step back.

"Who?" Jinaari asked as he put the weapon away.

"Thia has a purpose in this life. I have nurtured her gifts. Garret knows what her destiny is. So does Lolc Aon. We cannot allow that abomination to have sway over my Daughter. If ever you think that she has turned away from the path she was meant to walk, that she has embraced the evil that is Lolc Aon, I ask that you use this weapon to end her life. In doing so, her soul will come to me and not that vile Goddess. It's not about her life, but her very essence. If my sister were to corrupt Thia, have access to all she is capable of, the world would know darkness. Do this for me, please. I cannot bear the thought of Thia serving Lolc Aon in both this life and the next."

"You can't mean that?" he stared at Keroys; his eyes wide. "Why would you ask that I murder someone who's totally devoted to you? That makes no sense!"

"Tell him, brother," Garret's deep voice came from

behind him. Jinaari turned, watching as the other God entered the area. "Althir is bound to my service, not yours. If you're going to make a request that goes against everything I've taught him, everything he holds to, he deserves to know why."

Jinaari looked back at Thia's God. "Thia bears my Mark, Althir. She is unaware of it, but Lolc Aon is not. She is capable of more than any other priest or priestess that walks Avoch right now. When she is ready, she will have access to all of her power. But she must reject everything that is her mother's heritage. And accept that, despite what she's experienced so far, there are those who see her as more than just half Fallen. If she doesn't, and Lolc Aon turns her to her service, that power will be our sisters to control. The undead will rise, and Thia will be there to guide them. Avoch as you know it would be no more."

"Why not just tell Thia? Let her know about the Mark? She's not evil, Keroys. She's terrified of the Fallen, of Lolc Aon. When she heard them talking about bringing her to Byd Cudd, she fell apart. If you tell her, she'd understand." Jinaari pressed his case. The thought of having to kill her, in cold blood, chilled his soul.

"She has to find her own Path to grow into her power. If she tries to tap into it before her mind and soul are ready, the consequences could be deadly."

He turned toward his own God, "I am your servant, Garret. Not his," he gestured behind him at Keroys. "I am not betraying a vow I made to you unless you direct me to do so."

"As my brother said, Althir, the decision is yours. I understand his logic. Lolc Aon having access to what Thia is capable of would be devastating. Avoch may never recover. But I will not command you to do this. If you think you know her well enough that she'd handle knowing she's Marked, then tell her. If that's something you believe will keep her from turning away from Keroys, then do it. I see her death as a last resort if all other options are expended. Not the first solution you must do." He leaned against the archway. "Enough talk. You did what I required of you, and more. Events are moving quickly. Drogon needs to be dealt with, and Thia needs your sword to protect her while she figures out who she is." He nodded toward the portal. "Whatever your decision on this matter, Althir, I know it will be the right one."

Jinaari took a deep breath, knowing he was being dismissed. Turning to the portal, he saw his pack sitting at the base. Grabbing it, he stepped through.

When he emerged, his hand flew to his sword. The cave was full of shadows and movement; a single torch illuminated an area. Slowly, he put the pack on the ground and surveyed the scene. His arrival had gone unnoticed. Thia was pressed against a solid rock wall, her eyes wide with fear. Alesso stood in front of her, but his attention was on someone or something Jinaari couldn't see. Fallen were scattered around the cavern, all focused on Thia and Alesso.

Glancing to his left, he saw Adam and Caelynn on their knees. They were bound and gagged, but no one guarded them. Adam's staff rested against a wall. He slid a dagger out of his pack before sneaking toward his friends. "What's going on?" he whispered in Adam's ear as he pulled the gag off his mouth. Using his dagger, he began to cut at the ropes around the warlock's wrists.

"The Fallen have Alesso's sister. They're trying to trade her for Thia. Where's my staff?"

"Against the wall, on your left. Think you can distract

them, maybe take a few out, when I get Caelynn free? I'll head to Thia."

"On one condition."

"What's that?" Jinaari asked as the dagger sliced through the last bit of rope. He shifted to Caelynn.

"If Alesso resists at all, punch him for me. The jackass needs a lesson in manners."

Jinaari looked past the bard, watching Alesso. He was hesitating, considering the Fallen's offer. "Gladly," he whispered.

"Well, Potiri?" the leader said. "What's your choice? Will you leave here, alive and with your sister? Or shall we take you back to Byd Cudd with a collar around your waist?"

"Caelynn?" Jinaari whispered.

"Get to Thia," she said.

He nodded, putting the dagger on the ground near Caelynn's hand. There were three warriors between him and the leader. If that really was Alesso's sister on the ground, he had to keep her alive as well.

A bright red beam of light shot out from behind him, exploding in a hail of fire over the majority of the Fallen. Jinaari took off running, his sword swinging wide, toward Thia. He caught Alesso's gaze. It was full of shock and disgust at seeing Jinaari. Snarling, Alesso charged at the leader. Jinaari finished off the second warrior as Adam sent another blast through the cavern. The slave girl was on the ground; her hands clutched around her throat as blood flowed between her fingers. "Thia!" he yelled. "Help her!"

He parried a blow from the third warrior, then drove his elbow into the woman's face. Blood ran from her broken nose. Twisting, he sliced through the gap in her armor, and she fell back, dying.

Thia knelt in front of the young woman, and he noticed the splint on her arm. Alesso's fury had made the leader drop the end of the chain. Kicking it away from the combatants, he said, "Can she move? You two need to get away from the fight." He heard Thia say something to the girl and they darted toward a wall. He moved behind the leader; his sword ready to swing.

Adam let loose with another blast, illuminating the cavern. The floor was littered with bodies. Turning his head, he watched as Alesso ran the leader through. The tip of his blade appeared in the Fallen's back. Keeping his focus on the field, he backed up closer to Thia. The fight was over, but he didn't trust that more weren't on the way.

"Alesso threatened to kill Thia when you came back," Adam said, moving alongside of him.

"Move, Althir!" Alesso demanded. His hand moved nervously on the hilt of his sword, making the weapon turn in his hand.

"Not until you put that away," he pointed at his sword. "Thia?" he didn't shift his focus away from his fellow paladin. "How's the girl?"

"She'll be fine. Caelynn's working on the lock now." Her voice was pained, and tired.

"Get away from my sister, witch!" Alesso growled, stepping closer. Jinaari raised his sword, shaking his head slowly.

"What happened to your arm?" Jinaari kept his voice even but didn't shift his gaze. Alesso paced in front of them and hadn't sheathed his sword. "Brother, put your sword away. I'm not going to fight you unless you try something stupid."

"I broke my wrist." He heard her get up and walk closer to him. "There was a cave-in. I've healed it, but it needed the support for us to get out of the rubble." She stood beside him now, but he kept his focus on Alesso.

"Go with Adam. You too, Caelynn. Now." He waited as the two women moved away with the warlock. "Thia didn't hurt her. See for yourself." Carefully, he stepped aside.

Alesso ran past him, dropping his sword to the ground. Jinaari felt the tension between them dissipate. The younger man's focus was on his sister now, where it belonged. Sheathing his sword, he joined his friends. "So," he said, "what did I miss?"

Adam held out his hand, and he took it. "Too much to explain in five minutes. Or five years."

"Did you find Drogon yet?"

The warlock shook his head. "No. We've had a few run ins with giant scorpions, some other nasty things. This was the first time Fallen have shown up since you left. Did you catch the one you were chasing?"

"You could say that," he said.

"I'm glad you came when you did, Jinaari. I think he was about to take them up on their offer." Caelynn's face was hard. "The collapse separated us. Adam and I were trying to figure out the best way to blast through the wall when they attacked. We didn't have much of a chance against that many."

"You did fine. Even with Adam's big stick, you couldn't have held them off for long." He looked around the cavern for an exit. "It makes me think Drogon's got a deal in place. It doesn't make sense that he'd give the Fallen free passage otherwise." He watched Thia in the dim light. She leaned against a wall, looking like she wanted nothing more than to fade into the rock and disappear. "They're going to have to stay with us for a time, until we can find a way out for them. Caelynn, why don't you and Adam see if you can get her to eat or drink something? Maybe give her a spare cloak? He's not going to want either Thia or myself near them. Not yet anyway."

"Good idea," Adam said.

Jinaari found his pack. Grabbing it, he moved to a boulder not far from Thia and sat down, watching Alesso and his sister. *I hope that's her, my brother.* If it wasn't, Alesso would slide even deeper into his obsession. "What about you?" he asked. "Hungry at all?"

"Not really," her voice was quiet. The pain he'd heard earlier was gone, but something else had replaced it. "Did you finish whatever task you had?"

"You could say that," he said. "So, Thia. How are things with you?"

She shrugged, "I've got a Goddess sending Fallen after me. Ones that are intent on killing both of them," she waved a hand toward Adam and Caelynn, "and hauling me to Byd Cudd and someone named Herasta. Alive, as I understand it. How do you think I'm doing?"

"If it was me, I'd be pissed. And ready to fight back at the drop of a pin."

"Pissed, angry, scared. More than a little scared, to be honest." Her voice shook slightly. "The fear is constant. Every door we open, each hallway we find, I expect to see Fallen behind it. I don't like living this way, Jinaari."

He looked at her. "Hold onto that fear. It's important. I don't know what Alesso told you but leaving wasn't my idea. Both Garret and Keroys know what Lolc Aon is trying to do. They trained me, gave me insight into how to defeat her. Eventually, we're going to have to go into Byd Cudd. The only way to get her to stop chasing you is if I kill her. Don't ever think we can do this any other way. As long as you're scared, you'll survive. I won't let them take you, Thia. Ever." He paused. "You still trust me, right?"

She nodded, taking a few deep breaths. "You, yes. Alesso was about to let them have me when you showed up. I don't trust him, no matter what vow he gave me."

"What?"

"After you left, he came into the room. Put his shield and weapons on the ground and offered his service as my champion. He told us you were gone, and that Garret had sent him to help us until you came back. I didn't have much choice but to accept his offer. You returning was one of the conditions he set to release himself from the vow." She glanced at him, "You're not going to make me do some sort of ceremony or anything, right?"

"No. I gave my word, and that's more binding in my mind than any sort of rite. For him, though," he pointed at Alesso, "I'm betting Garret forced him to make a specific vow to you. Without loopholes he could use."

"I'm glad to be rid of them, though. I don't know what's been worse. Knowing the Fallen were hunting me or having to listen to him question everything I said. Even after I saved his life."

"What happened?" He dug into the pack and pulled out some jerky, handing it to her. She may have said she wasn't hungry, but she didn't look right.

She took it and gestured, "See the big hole in his chest plate?" She asked as she ate.

"Yeah."

"A giant scorpion hit him in the chest, flung him across the floor. I was able to pull the poison out of him before it reached his brain."

Jinaari studied her face in the dim light. Was she

coming into her magic? And where had Keroys put his Mark on her that she didn't know? "I'm impressed."

"It needed to happen," she shrugged. "I'd rather not do it again, to be honest, so please don't get stung."

He laughed, "I'm not planning on it." He looked back at the rest of them. Adam was coming their way.

"Ashynn says there's a freshwater pool an hour or so from here. They stopped there last night. She says there's a path there that leads to the surface. We rest at the pool, clean up. Tomorrow, the four of us go after Drogon, let Alesso take her out of here. Does that work for you?"

"It'll have to. We need the rest, and the water wouldn't hurt. I don't care what he says, Adam. One of us is on watch at all times, normal rotation between the three of us."

"I can take a turn," Thia said.

"Not with that splint on, you're not," he shook his head. "Make sure either Adam or Caelynn's between you and Alesso while we walk. He's probably going to stay with his sister, but let's be cautious."

"You really don't trust him, do you?" she asked.

"With my life, yes. Not with yours." He rose, picking up his pack and settling it on his back. "Come on. The sooner we get to this place, the faster they'll be gone."

CHAPTER
THIRTEEN

Thia yawned, trying to keep her eyes open. The cave-in, her injury, and digging out only to be surrounded by Fallen had her running on adrenaline for too long, and it was fading fast. As much as she didn't want to admit it, she was glad Jinaari handed her the jerky earlier. She needed the food, even if she didn't feel hungry.

She watched the two paladins walking side by side in front of her. She hadn't realized how tall Jinaari was, not until he stood next to Alesso. Hopefully, this area of Ashynn's was close. Thia dearly wanted to rest.

Her hand moved behind her neck, scratching at the itch she'd felt for the last hour. Dust and dirt had slid into every possible gap in her clothing, and her body found new levels of being uncomfortable. Fill the waterskins, then maybe she could get some of the dirt off her. Anything would be better than nothing.

Besides, she thought, *the last thing I want to do is try and take a full bath with him watching!*

Her ears perked up at the slow, gentle sound of falling water. "Are we close?"

Alesso turned around, glaring at her. "What do you think, witch?" Jinaari reached out and slapped him in the chest. He turned back around, going silent.

"Ignore Alesso. He's leaving us by morning. I doubt you'll ever see him again," Adam commented. "Jinaari will keep him away from you tonight. He wants to be gone from us as much as we want him out of here. I wouldn't be surprised if they're on the road before you wake up tomorrow."

She let out a sigh. "I hope so. Ashynn needs to get out of here." Pausing, she glanced at the blond man. "Can I ask you a question?"

"Sure," he replied, smiling.

"Why did you leave Helmshouse? I thought only mages left, not full warlocks."

"You're partially right. Mages are trained in the towers, but never go beyond the basics because they either can't handle the lessons or don't have the magic stores. Even with these," he nodded at the staff in his hand, "we need the mental strength to remember our spells. And no, warlocks don't normally leave. But sometimes The Solar, that's our leader, sends us out into the world. She doesn't always share her reasons, either."

"Does that mean Drogon was trained in Helmshouse?"

"Probably. When we get back to Almair, I'll visit an old friend. He's a historian of sorts. How old were you when your father was killed?"

"Ten. Why?"

Adam shrugged. "It's probably nothing important. A moot point if we're successful down here, really. But I'm wondering what Drogon did between then and now. If all the Gods have shunned him, if he's really Forsaken, I'd like to know what happened to put him on that path." He chuckled. "That's one of the prerequisites of becoming a warlock. Insatiable curiosity about the why of things. Hamish is the worst of us, but his library's the best outside of Helmshouse. And I'm getting extremely curious as to why Drogon ended up down here."

Thia nodded. That made sense. "Do you think there's going to be enough water for me to wash my face?" The dust and dirt were caked on it so thick she could feel it crack and flake away.

"I've got a bar of soap," Caelynn offered, "and a towel. It's not much but you're welcome to use them."

Muttering her thanks, Thia focused on the path in front of her. The sound was getting louder, and she could make out some of what was beyond the tunnel. "It's getting lighter," she commented.

"There's some quartz veins in the walls," Ashynn's voice was quiet, but Thia could hear her. "At the top, there's a tunnel where the sunlight can come into the cave. It reflects on the quartz, making it light. That's what my mistress said, anyway."

"You're free, Ashynn. I don't want to hear that word again. Understand?" Alesso's voice was gentle, but insistent. Thia drew a deep breath but stayed silent. *It's not going to be that easy,* she thought. *The woman's been a slave for most of her life. You can't just forget that. I really hope he's patient with you. You'll need it from him.*

The tunnel opened into a good-sized cavern. A small waterfall trickled down one wall, feeding the wide pool at the base. The water had eroded a narrow channel through the floor; the slow-moving stream disappeared through the rock wall on the other side of the cavern. A plank of wood served as a bridge over the water, and several boulders sat near the pool's edge.

"Adam, Alesso, let's make sure we're alone. Caelynn, you and Thia stay with Ashynn. Once we give the all-clear, you ladies can clean up. We'll worry about camp and dinner, switch off once you're done." Jinaari said.

Thia didn't even try to argue. The water was probably cold, but the need to get clean was strong. She walked over to a sheltered part of the water's edge and shrugged off her pack. Draping her cloak across a rock, she sat down and began to pick at the knot Alesso had put in the bandage around her splint.

"May I help, priestess?" Ashynn asked quietly.

"If you'd like to. I appreciate it." She held out her arm.

The woman kept her head down as she worked. "My brother says you saved his life."

"It's not in me to let others die if I can prevent it."

She pulled the ends free and began to unwind the bandage. "He says you're not all that you seem and I shouldn't fear you, even if you're Fallen."

Thia coughed in surprise, and Ashynn stopped. "I'm fine," she reassured her. "Just some dust in my lungs." *Alesso told her that? It doesn't make any sense! He hates me!*

"He wants to stay, to make sure you're safe, but knows he needs to get me to the surface first. He doesn't trust the other one." She finished unwrapping Thia's arm and the splint pieces fell away. She looked at her intently. "Alesso says Althir has another reason for being here, but he doesn't know what it is."

Twisting it slowly, she tested the wrist. Nothing hurt. It was stiff, but she expected that. Smiling, she looked at Ashynn. "I wouldn't worry about it. Those two don't get along. I think they've competed against each other for too long. Jinaari has saved my life a few times, without hesitation." She glanced around and caught sight of him and Caelynn talking. He looked at her briefly, but she couldn't read his face. The elf started to walk toward them. "I think we're clear," she said as she reached for her boot lacings. "I don't know about you, but a bath sounds wonderful right now. No matter how frigid the water is."

Ten minutes later, her teeth chattering from the cold, Thia waded out of the water. Quickly, she grabbed at the rough towel Caelynn had left and dried herself off before finding some clean clothes in her bag. The first ones she'd worn in a week or more. "Do you want me to wait for the two of you?" she asked as she shoved her feet into her boots and began to tighten the laces.

"They've got a fire going already," Caelynn replied. "Go get something hot to eat. We'll be out in a few minutes."

Thia stood up and slung her pack over one shoulder. The chain shirt and cloak she draped across her arm. She'd grown used to wearing the armor, but tonight she didn't want to sleep in it. Or the padded undertunic. A small concession to comfort seemed right. Walking toward the fire, she could make out Adam and Jinaari, but didn't see Alesso.

Someone had placed a few rocks around the fire, giving them a place to sit. Both tents were up, as well. "Pick one," Jinaari told her, "and put your gear inside. Food will be ready in a couple of minutes."

Thia ducked into one, tossing her pack down. If she put out her bedroll now, it'd be ready when she was. As she untied the thin pad from her pack, she heard Adam whispering, "Do you really think he'll do that?"

"This is Alesso, Adam. What do you think?" Jinaari answered.

"I think he's still a paladin. Of your Order. And he's got some severe prejudices. I know you two have never gotten along, my friend, but I don't think he'd go that far."

"You think too much."

"As you have told me many times over the years. That's also why you keep me around."

"Althir. We need to talk." Alesso's voice was insistent, and too close to her tent.

"I'm listening."

"You can't do this, not alone. Stay here a few days, let me get Ashynn to Almair. I'll come back, rejoin you. Together, we'll keep Thia safe and take down Drogon. You need another sword down here."

"I'm not sitting here for weeks, Alesso." Jinaari paused. "You've got someone else to take care of. Your sister's going to need you for a long time. Deserting her as soon as you get to the surface isn't a good idea, and you know it."

"She's being hunted by all Byd Cudd. You can't take them all on. You're not that good."

"I've got Adam and Caelynn. Neither of them will let anyone get to her. She's not defenseless, either." Jinaari's voice had a finality to it.

"I owe her a life debt. I have to repay that," Alesso replied.

Adam cleared his throat. "She's not here so you'll feel better about your life, Alesso. What you want has nothing to do with anything. This isn't your fight. It's his. It's Thia's. Caelynn and I are just here to make sure they survive. Thia's tougher than she knows, but your sister isn't. Take care of her. Thia's not your problem. Not anymore."

"I'm her champion."

Thia stormed out of the tent, "Not any longer. I release

you of your vow to me. Take your sister and go home, Alesso. I don't want you near me."

He looked at her, glancing at Jinaari for a second before meeting her gaze. His blue eyes sent chills down her spine. "Fine. I'll go, for now. I'll repay the debt, though."

"Pay me back by taking care of Ashynn. She needs you more than I ever will."

He stormed away from them. Thia sank onto a rock between her friends, burying her head into her hands.

"Here, you need to eat. You're about to fall over." Jinaari waved a bowl of stew under her nose.

"Thank you," she muttered, taking it. It wasn't much, but it was hot. "I don't understand," she said. "He's never pretended to like me, or even tolerate my presence. But then he tells his sister she shouldn't be afraid of me. Says you're not worth trusting. And wants us to wait while he takes her to the surface and comes back. Why?"

"You saved his life, Thia. In doing so, you made him rethink how he sees the Fallen." Jinaari started to say.

She looked at him, "But I'm not Fallen! I'm human! The same as you!" Angrily, she stabbed at a piece of meat in her bowl. "That's how I was raised. That's all that should matter!"

"To us, sure. The three of us don't see you as he does. Like he did. You've challenged the foundation he's built his life on. Drakkus has been trying to teach him that for years. You cut away every one of his arguments, made him realize that maybe he was wrong. Alesso spent the last thirteen years nurturing his hatred, Thia. It's been the driving force in his life. That, and trying to beat me. He's lost to me more times than I can count. To him, protecting you is more than paying back a debt he thinks he owes you. It's another way to try and beat me."

She shook her head. "I still don't understand. I mean, yeah, you're arrogant and insufferable," she stopped as Adam broke out in laughter, "but there's a reason for it. You're good at what you do. I've seen both of you fight, Jinaari. He's not half as good as you are."

"I wouldn't worry about it, Thia," he said. "They're heading to the surface in the morning, and we're hunting down Drogon. Or at least find out how he's creating the storm and destroy that. You've got enough to worry about with your mother and Lolc Aon."

"My mother?" She heard him mutter something under his breath. "Jinaari, if you know something I should know, please tell me."

He took a deep breath and then looked at her. "The Fallen mentioned someone by name, remember?"

"Herasta? So?" Fear gripped her stomach and she stared at him.

"That's your mother." He looked at her.

"How do you know?" Her mother was hunting her? Wanted to turn her over to Lolc Aon? What kind of monster did that? Her heart was racing, and she desperately tried to keep her breathing under control.

"The one I chased told me."

"The one whose eyes looked like mine? That called me 'sister'?"

He nodded. "His name was Aust. He was your brother."

Everything began to spin, and she closed her eyes. All illusions she'd held as a child about how her mother's family wasn't evil, would welcome her warmly if they ever met, evaporated. They'd turn her over to Lolc Aon; let the Scorpion Queen poison her mind and soul.

"Thia?"

She stood up quickly, not caring as the bowl and its

contents fell to the ground and dove for the solitude of the tent. Throwing herself onto the bedroll, she curled up into a ball and rode the waves of panic. At some point, exhaustion overtook her, and she slept.

It was the pounding headache that woke her up. *What am I doing here? Admit it. This was a mistake. I should've told Father Philip no. They're never going to trust me to keep them safe. Every time I'm faced with anything hard, I panic. I fall apart. Go out there, admit it, and leave with Alesso.* Resolutely, she threw her cloak aside and got up, walking out of the tent.

"Morning, Thia," Adam commented from the small fire.

"Where's Jinaari?"

He pointed toward the pool. "Cleaning up. Is everything okay?"

She didn't answer him. Walking over to the rocks, she knew better than to surprise him. "Jinaari?" she called out, "Can I talk to you? It won't take long."

He walked around the rock, rubbing a towel across his bare arms. "What's up?" he asked, leaning against a boulder.

"I'm going to leave with Alesso and his sister, head back to the cloister," she started to speak.

"No, you're not." He interrupted, putting the towel down and giving her a direct look.

"I'm not going to be of any use to you if I fall apart every time I hear bad news," the words tumbled out in a rush. "I'm not cut out for this sort of thing! You told me, back on the ship, that you needed to trust that I had your back in a fight. How can you when I'm running away?"

"First off, I've never seen you run. Panic? Sure. But you stayed put when you needed to. Even when Alesso was faced with trading you to the Fallen, you didn't run—"

"There wasn't anywhere to run," she insisted.

"Doesn't matter. Not to me. Or Adam and Caelynn. Your life's been different than ours, certainly. If you weren't meant to be here, capable of doing what you need to do, Alesso would've died from the scorpion. Instead, he's halfway to the surface with his sister." He shifted how he sat but kept his focus on her. "Thia, you adapt faster than anyone I've ever met. A fighter is trained to see openings and react to them, take advantage where we can. You weren't. But you've had things thrown at you that would make most people I know crawl into a ball and never come back out."

"Like last night," she said, her voice breaking. "I'm not exactly proud of that."

"You dealt with it. That's different than running. You don't want to leave, Thia. It's not in you to quit. Sure, life dealt you a bad hand. We all have family associations we're not proud of. If I didn't trust you to have my back, you never would've made it this far. I don't let my friends give up that easily."

"We're friends?"

He smiled. "For my part we are. I stopped thinking of you as someone I had to babysit some time ago."

"You're still arrogant," she laughed.

"But not without reason," he countered. "I'm going to grab my shirt, then we can pack up once Caelynn's awake and Adam's done making breakfast. Drogon knows we're coming, and I hate to make him wait."

CHAPTER
FOURTEEN

Thia watched as Jinaari slid carefully back down the slanted rock. "I think we found it."

"Drogon?" Adam asked. Thia saw his fingers flex around his staff. He was ready for the fight. They all seemed eager, whereas her stomach was tied in knots.

The paladin shook his head. "I didn't see anyone. There's something in there, though. Given the energy coming off it, I'm thinking it's what's powering the storm." He looked at each of them. "Caelynn, this is on you. There's some sort of locked box at the end of the center path. It's got to be the power source. I need you to get there, open it up. That's when Adam blasts it."

"It's not going to be that easy. He'll have warded it, put something there to guard the box," the elf countered. She eased her pack off her back, setting it on the ground. Jinaari and Adam had dropped theirs as soon as they entered the cave.

"That's my job. I'll draw their attention, clear a path for you. Adam, keep something in reserve to destroy whatever's in the chest, but some back up fire power would be helpful. Thia—"

"I know," she said. "Stay out of range and keep people alive."

"Well, yes, but do you know any offensive spells? Besides against undead?"

She nodded. "A few. I've never cast them before, though. Are you sure you want me to experiment now?"

His dark eyes lit up. He actually enjoyed this! "Now is the perfect time. Same rule as Adam. Keep enough that you can heal if it's needed, but don't be afraid to do something new."

"But what if—"

"I trust you. You need to start trusting yourself. Keroys wouldn't have given you the ability if he didn't want you to use it." He shifted his gaze back to Caelynn. "There are three walkways, one on each side, plus one straight up the middle. That leads to the bottom of the machine where the box is. Adam and I will take the side paths, create the diversion. You head whichever way you want. Be sneaky."

"Always," she grinned.

"Thia, wait for one of us to get started. I don't want you to be a target. Make sure whatever is down there is focused on one of us before you start moving."

"You done talking, old man?" Adam kept his tone light. "Because I'd like to get to work."

"Let's do this."

Thia watched as the two men moved around the rock. Caelynn edged forward, motioning for Thia to follow her. "Stay near me until you need to go down there. Jinaari would have my hide if something happened to you."

"I wish he'd stop acting like I needed a babysitter all the time," she grumbled.

"Him? Not likely. Two Gods told him to keep you safe from a third. He takes that shit pretty seriously. We all do."

Her curiosity got the better of her and she moved far enough forward to see what they were facing.

A pool of brackish water filled the bottom of the cavern. Two narrow pathways surrounded the black liquid, the third led out to a center island. The box Jinaari mentioned sat on the ground. Above it, floating, was a series of metal balls. Each one the size of a horse and crackling with white lightning. The surface shifted continually, occasionally showing a glimpse of the contents. Faces frozen in terror and pain, hands outstretched.

"He's trapped souls inside. That's how he's powering it," she breathed.

Caelynn came up beside her. "What happens when we turn it off?"

"They'll be set free, but not peacefully." The depth of the horror she was witnessing struck her soul. "I'll have to destroy them, all of them. Even the innocent ones," she breathed. *Keroys, take them all. Please.*

"You'll give them peace, Thia. Being in that," she pointed at the machine, "is anything but."

Tearing her eyes away from the sight, she nodded. An explosion echoed in the chamber as Adam sent a hail of fire down onto something. It had begun.

"Caelynn, I'm—" she started to speak, but stopped. The pink haired woman was already halfway down one of the pathways, heading for the center. She slid her pack off, leaving it on the pile with the others. The box was still in the pouch on her belt. Everything else was extra weight, something that would slow her down.

She looked around the room, trying to locate Adam and Jinaari. A bolt of lightning shot off to her left and illuminated the paladin. *His armor's going to draw the energy to him if it gets too close!* Skidding down the rock, she ran for the path leading to him.

When she got close enough, she drew the sigil and healed him. A line of a dozen or more Dangreth stretched out past Jinaari; more waded through the pool, trying to surround him. Drawing a deep breath, she sent out a wave of magic. When it hit the creatures, their gray skin fell off in chunks as they disintegrated.

"Thanks," Jinaari called to her. "Go help Adam." He turned away, heading toward a raised platform at the far end of the room.

She ran around the path, trying to spot Caelynn as she passed the center point. The elf was low to the ground but moving fast. Reaching the other side, she spied the warlock. Sweat glistened on his face, but he looked healthy enough. Whatever he was fighting, he was holding his own.

"Now, Adam!" Caelynn screamed.

Thia twisted her body, working the sigil she needed. She had to time this perfectly. A blast from Adam's staff illuminated the room in a bright blue light. She watched the orbs closely. Slowly, they began to collapse downward; each sphere engulfing the one from above. When it got to the final one, cracks formed on the surface and the tormented souls within began to fly out.

Pushing herself flat against the wall, she whispered the incantation and released the magic. A silence descended on the room, followed by a cacophony of screams and wails. Unable to withstand it, she dropped to her knees and covered her ears. Some of them thanked her; others blamed her. The assault ended as quickly as it started. "Thia," Adam's voice was quiet. "You okay?"

Opening her eyes, she saw him kneeling in front of her. "Is it done?"

"Done?" another voice called out, chilling her blood. She knew that voice. "My dear child, it's only just begun."

Rising, she looked for the source. Standing on a raised dais on the opposite end of the room was a man in a blood red robe. Drogon hadn't changed so much that she didn't recognize him. The sickly yellow hue of his eyes, though, told her enough. Even the Gods had turned him away. "He's Forsaken," she whispered.

"Tell me, Thia. How is your father these days?" Her heart raced at his question.

"He's dead. You know that."

The smile he leveled at her was malicious. "Are you certain? He was the first one I put into those orbs. It was his soul you just destroyed. I'm surprised you didn't sense him, try to save him. But that's what you do best, isn't it? Make sure those few people who actually care about you die."

A growl formed in her chest, and she started to charge at Drogon. Five feet down the path, she was flying in the air, her arms pinned to her side.

"You're no match for me, child. I know you still have the box he made you. It should've been mine. A place for me to store part of myself. Instead, he turned me away and refused me." She flew closer to him, unable to stop. "Come closer, child. That I am Forsaken is a result of your father's inaction. And now the Gods fear me. They send this . . . thing . . ." he shifted his foot and Thia looked down. Jinaari lay unmoving at the edge of the platform, "to try to stop me. Garret's best? Hardly." With a kick, he sent Jinaari's body tumbling into the water; his armor making him sink quickly beneath the surface. "And then Keroys sends you. A half breed witch that he Marked as his Daughter but couldn't bother to train."

Thia heard a splash behind her. *Please, let that be Adam or Caelynn getting Jinaari!* Drogon pulled her even closer. She could have touched him if she could move. He reached out and stroked her cheek with the tip of his finger, sending shivers down her spine.

"You didn't know, did you? The paladin did, as did the other two. They knew what you were capable of, what gifts Keroys bestowed on you. And yet you came against me in ignorance, cloaked in some strange ideal of what was right that your father instilled in you. You and I are not finished, Thia Bransdottir. Lolc Aon will have her turn with you, unlock everything you're capable of, and then we'll meet again. I recommend you rethink your loyalties carefully, child. We could have so much fun together, you and I."

An arrow flew past her ear, burying itself into Drogon's shoulder. As he screamed, she plummeted. Her body hit the water hard; the impact forcing air from her lungs. Reflexively, she tried to breathe and started to choke. An arm circled her waist and pulled her forward. Twisting her neck and saw Caelynn. The chain shirt made it hard to fight against the current and she felt herself sinking. The elf gestured for Thia to take off her armor, but she shook her head. The cloak clasp came loose, and she shrugged out of it. The heavy fabric floated down, and she knew she'd be able to keep swimming. Caelynn pointed past her, and she saw a tunnel. *It must be the way out!* Ignoring her protesting muscles, she swam for it.

Her lungs burned, desperate for oxygen. Spots began to swarm in front of her eyes. A few feet into the tunnel, she was able to raise her head above the surface. "We keep going," Caelynn shouted above the roar echoing through the chamber. "This leads to the ocean. Adam got Jinaari out this way. There's not much time." She dove back under the water. Thia took a deep breath, plunging down after her.

She kept Caelynn in sight, weaving her way through the tunnel. It opened and she swam for the surface. When her head emerged above the waves, she looked around for the others. She saw Adam, waving frantically, standing on a sheltered sand bar. Jinaari's body lay on the ground. He wasn't moving.

As fast as she could, she swam over to them and climbed out of the water. "Is he breathing?" she demanded.

"I got a pulse, but it's weak," Adam told her.

"Help me get his armor off," she said as she knelt at the paladin's side. His fingers still clutched his sword. "Can you get that away from him?" she nodded at the weapon. "If he wakes up, I don't want him to hit one of us with it." Her fingers, numb from the cold water, slipped as she tried to unbuckle his breastplate. Adam eased the sword out of Jinaari's hand and placed it next to his shield, out of their reach.

"What can I do?" Caelynn asked.

"Start a fire, get our tents out." The buckle came loose, and she moved to the next one.

"I'll see what I can find. The packs are still back in the cave."

"Help me roll him over, Adam." Thia pushed against Jinaari's back, and they started on the other side. Once the armor was free, she threw it off to one side. "His shirt, too," she told him. "It's going to work best if I can touch his skin, see what's wrong."

Adam drew a dagger and started to slice at the fabric carefully. "He's turning blue."

Thia nodded, "I see it. We need that fire." She knelt

behind the paladin, studying his back. "I'm going to try and force the water out of his lungs. Make sure he doesn't choke." *Keroys, don't let me screw this up.* She placed a hand on his back; the skin was clammy and cold. His chest wasn't moving, but she could feel a faint heartbeat. It was growing weaker. Using her fingers, she began to trace the sigil she needed directly onto his skin. After the first time, his heartbeat began to strengthen. She dove deeper into her stores, drawing out more than she'd ever tried to use before, and did another casting.

His chest heaved and he started coughing. Water ran from his mouth, pouring onto the beach. The world began to spin. "He'll live," she whispered.

"Thia!" She heard Adam scream, saw him reach for her, as blackness overtook her.

CHAPTER
FIFTEEN

A gentle rocking motion surrounded her. She was warmer than she'd felt in days; a sense of comfort and safety enveloped her. Thia shifted, confused. The last thing she remembered was being on a beach, soaking wet, trying desperately to push the water out of Jinaari's lungs. Opening her eyes, she recognized the room. It was the captain's cabin on the Ninaa. She started to sit up, stopping when she realized she was naked.

A chair moved and she turned her head. Adam stood, watching her. "How'd we get here?" she asked.

"Captain was watching for us, found us on the beach once Caelynn got the fire going." He kept his voice low.

"Jinaari?"

"Alive, thanks to you. He's with Caelynn, on deck. How are you feeling?"

She couldn't describe the feeling. Physically, she was fine. The things Drogon had said to her, though. How much was true and how many were lies? "How long was I out?"

"Long enough that you scared us. There are some dry clothes in a cupboard under the bed. The captain told me to let you know you're welcome to anything that fits." He rose and headed to the door. "I've got to tell them you're awake. I recommend getting dressed quickly. They'll both want to see you." Turning the handle, he left, closing it behind him.

Throwing off the blankets, she scrambled out of the bunk. Her feet hit the wood floor and she knelt, searching the cupboards for something that she could wear. Pulling out the first things that looked like they'd fit, she rushed getting them on. She felt her cheeks grow warm. Which one of them had undressed her, put her in the bed?

Someone knocked at the door, "Thia?" Caelynn called out. "Can I come in?"

She sat back on the bed, crossing her legs in front of her. "Yes," she replied. The door opened and the elf came in, closing it behind her.

"How are you feeling?"

"Okay, I guess," she ran a hand through her hair. It was loose for the first time in weeks. Who knows where all the pins she'd used to hold it in place went. Probably onto the ocean floor. "Thank you. Your arrow was timely. Did it kill him?"

She shook her head. "No, I don't think so. As soon as you fell, I went after you. The shot wounded him, but it wasn't fatal. I thought about going back, after our packs, but Adam wouldn't let me. You scared us. The way you passed out after Jinaari started breathing . . . it was like your heart stopped at the same moment."

She shrugged. "It worked, that's what matters." She took a deep breath. "I have to know if something Drogon said is true."

"What part?"

"Am I Marked?"

The door opened again, and Thia shifted her attention

to the sound. Jinaari walked in, looking at her. "Caelynn, can you give us a few minutes?"

The elf looked between the two of them. "Sure," she said as she left the room.

Thia watched him as he sat in one of the chairs. His face was serious. "It's not a lie, is it? I'm Marked and you knew. You all knew," she whispered.

"Adam didn't, not until we got rescued. Caelynn only knew because I didn't want her to see it and say something when you were using the pool. And I wanted to make sure Ashynn didn't see it, either. Alesso doesn't need to know about it."

"What about me? It's on me!" She almost shouted the words. "Who Marked me? Keroys? Lolc Aon? Why can't I see it?"

He looked at her. "The Mark is from Keroys, not Lolc Aon. But that's why she's hunting you. She wants to harness what you'll be capable of one day, turn it to her own use. As to where, Caelynn said that it's on your back. Where few will ever see it."

She fell back onto the bed, her hands rubbing at her eyes. "How long have you known, Jinaari?"

"Keroys told me when I was training. He wanted me to keep it from you, but Garret intervened. Reminded him that I wasn't his follower, so he couldn't command me. When and how to tell you was left up to me."

She sat back up. "Yet you didn't. You waited for Drogon to do it. Don't you think that's a little late? You could've told me that morning, after Alesso left, when I wanted to quit!"

"I thought about it, yes. But I wasn't sure. I still had some doubts."

"Doubts? So, the whole bit about us being friends, you trusting me . . . that was a lie?"

He shook his head. "No. I haven't lied to you, Thia. I may not have told you everything I know, but that's not the same as a lie." He leaned back, running a hand through his dark hair, "I've had two Gods put restrictions on me. Or try to. I'm doing a balancing act between what they allow and what I think is best. I didn't tell you because I wasn't sure if you were ready to hear it. Just the idea of bearing the Mark of a God . . . part of me feels like I'm talking with a friend, another part knows that you have access to enough magic to level Almair without blinking." He paused. "As you're so good to remind me, I'm arrogant. And now I'm looking at someone who has the potential to do more damage with one finger than I can in my lifetime."

"I didn't ask for this," she muttered. "I don't know how to tap into it, what he wants me to do with it, nothing."

"He's the only one that can answer those questions, Thia. When we get to Almair, go back to your cloister. Talk with Keroys, with Father Philip. Adam's got a place called The Green Frog. We'll be there. When you're ready, come find us. Then we'll go where we need to go and do what we need to do. This isn't over yet." He rose and moved closer to the door. He tilted his head but didn't look at her. "Thank you. Adam told me you saved my life. I won't forget that."

"You kept me from falling into the pit," she replied. "I figured I owed you." She took a deep breath, releasing it slowly. "When you say we'll do what we need to do, what do you mean?

He turned to look at her. "Lolc Aon is still hunting you, Thia. Us being on the surface won't change that. We have time for you to get things right in your mind, talk with Keroys, but there's only one way to make sure the Fallen leave you alone. And that's one promise that I'm keeping. She's not turning you."

The door shut behind him, and she fell back on the bed. *How many ways can I screw up?* she thought. *I finally get someone I can trust in my life, and then I push him away. All of them. He's right about one thing. I need to talk to Father Philip. And Keroys, if he'll answer me.*

But was she ready to hear any answers they'd give her?

"You sure about that, Thia?" Adam asked as they stood at the end of the pier. "It's not a problem for us to take you there."

"I'm sure," she replied. People stopped and stared at her. She was back in her clothes, but her cloak was at the bottom of the ocean somewhere. All she owned was on her; her father's box still wrapped in leather in the pouch on her belt. Without the hood, everyone could see who she was. What she was. "I know the way, and I won't get lost."

"My inn's not far from your cloister. That's where we'll be. When you're ready, let us know."

She smiled. "Thank you, Adam. Take care of yourselves, okay?" Turning from them, she took a deep breath before starting to walk toward the city. It felt as if every single person stopped and stared at her, but she kept going.

"You're too stubborn for your own good," Jinaari said as he came up alongside her. "Next time, wait for me. Or let Adam escort you."

"And you're insufferable," she muttered, her tone light. They hadn't spoken much since she'd confronted him about the Mark. Having him walking with her made her feel safer, though. He wasn't in armor, but his sword hung from his hip. Anyone who might come after her would think twice. "Do you think Alesso and Ashynn made it out okay?"

"I was going to check on that while we were here. This is the closest chapterhouse. I'm certain that's where he would've taken her." He paused. "I'm surprised you'd ask. I thought you hated him."

"He's not my favorite person, but she deserved better than what life gave her. And he did fulfill the vow he gave me." She shrugged. "I'm so used to being hated that I understand what it can be like. Ashynn's going to need help to adjust to life on the surface. For her sake, I hope he's able to be patient with her."

They walked in silence, winding their way through the streets toward what was home for her. The late summer heat shimmered in waves as they walked. As the main gate came into view, he stopped her. "I'll turn off here. My chapterhouse is that way," he pointed down a side street. "The Green Frog is one street over, in an alley. If you need us, you know where we'll be."

"Thank you." She turned and walked toward the side door.

"Hey, Thia," Jinaari called after her.

"What?"

"I hope you get the answers you need. We'll be ready when you are." He walked down the side street, disappearing into the crowd.

Sighing, she walked over to the door and twisted the handle. As soon as she crossed the threshold, she searched for the sense of peace the cloister often gave her. It wasn't there.

"May I help you?" a young woman in acolyte robes hurried her way.

"I'm fine, thank you. I'll check in with Father Philip,

then head into the chapel." She started to walk toward where his office was. The acolyte picked up her skirts, rushing to keep up.

"Are you familiar with our cloister?" she asked. "I've not seen anyone who, um, looks like you do around here. Are you from Dragonspire? Or somewhere else?"

Thia stopped, turning on the young woman. "This has been my home for the last fifteen years. I know my way around, without an escort." She started walking again, picking up the pace. *A new acolyte? It's possible. I've been gone for what, two months? Three?* Shaking her head, she kept walking. *Does it really matter how long I've been gone? If I bear Keroys's Mark, everything's changed.*

As she marched through the hallways leading to Father Philip's office, she scanned the faces. Many she knew; some were surprised to see her. Others were shocked. A few were openly hostile, but she kept her head high. *I faced down worse than a gaggle of gossiping noble women who can't get a basic sigil right. Jinaari was right. I need to stop hiding.*

Two guards flanked the door to his private office, both were men she recognized. "Priestess? You're back? We didn't... is he expecting you?" one stammered.

"Yes, I'm back. Otherwise, I wouldn't be standing here. Is he seeing anyone now?"

The other one shook his head. "No. A messenger went in about fifteen minutes ago but left right afterward."

That was about the time they got off the ship. Father Philip was well informed about who came into the city. Before she could say anything, the doors opened. Father Philip stood between them, smiling at her. "Welcome home, Thia. Please, join me." He stepped aside, giving her room to enter. "Would one of you please ask the kitchen to send us some tea? Possibly a light lunch? And let anyone else know that I'm busy until evening services."

As soon as she crossed the threshold, she started to relax. This, at least, felt right. The simple furnishings, the odd pieces of art given to him by rulers and other dignitaries. She heard the doors close behind her and turned around.

"It's good to have you back with us, Thia," he grasped both of her hands in his and looked at her face. "You had quite the adventure. I see it in your eyes. Rumor has it the cloud above Tanisal has dissipated. You were successful, then?" He gestured to the small seating area away from his desk.

Gratefully, she sat in one of the chairs. "Yes, though he's still alive. He's Forsaken, Father. The four of us weren't skilled enough to counteract the magic he can wield."

He nodded. "That will come, with time."

"Because I'm a Daughter of Keroys and I'll grow into it?" Try as she might, she couldn't keep the bitterness out of her voice.

"Ah, that. You found out, then?" He sat up a little straighter in his chair.

"Drogon told me. Jinaari confirmed it. I haven't seen the Mark for myself." She leaned forward, resting her arms on her legs. "Why didn't you tell me? I could've had years here to train, to become accustomed to what this meant. Instead, I find out from someone the Gods have turned their back on. Whose magic is inherently evil. And I had nothing to prepare me for that battle."

The doors opened and a maid came in pushing a small, wheeled cart. The teacups rattled softly as she pushed it between them. "Thank you, Maire. You can go, we'll serve ourselves." She curtsied and scurried back out, shooting a final glance at Thia as she closed the doors.

Philip reached for the teapot and started to pour out the contents into a cup. "I learned about it from your father. It was the reason why I taught you privately whenever I went to your village. I was trying to evaluate your intellect; what spell work you'd be best suited for. You amazed me, even when you were so young, as you mastered every task I gave you. And quickly. The last time I came back here, before his death, I prayed for hours. Meditated on how best to train you, teach you, mentor you so that you'd be ready for whatever it was Keroys needed from you. That night, he answered me. He forbade me from telling you, or anyone else. You were given a private room, with a bath, so the others wouldn't see the Mark." He handed her a cup, then settled back with his own. "Thia, I know it was hard for you here. Many cannot see beyond your appearance. Imagine how much worse it could've been if they knew you also bore the favor of the God they served?"

She lowered her head. He was right. "Thia, you're at a dangerous point. You've kept your own counsel for most of your life. I like to hope you've seen me as a friend, a second father even. This is your Path to walk, but you cannot do so alone. To be strong isn't simply about magic or stubbornness."

Laughing, she smiled. "You sound like Jinaari."

"I'm not at all surprised. Given what I know of his arrogance, I was fairly certain the two of you would either learn to trust, or kill, each other. As you're both alive, I'm thinking the former." He turned serious again. "Some see vulnerability as a weakness. It's not. If you trust someone, talk to them. Let them know what you're thinking and feeling. Let them share your fears, your doubts. Because they will lend you their strength when you need it most."

He placed his teacup on the table. "Come," he said, rising from his seat. Thia quickly followed suit. "You need to unburden your soul, find answers. Keroys will hear you, I have no doubt. He has Marked you as his Daughter, after all. Use my private chapel, take as long as you need. I'll have someone make sure your room is ready when you're done. Later, perhaps tomorrow, we'll talk about this more."

"Father Philip, there's something else." The words rushed out. "We found out that Lolc Aon is hunting me. She wants to convert me, force me to forsake Keroys for her, so that she has access to this . . . power . . . he gave me. There's been more than one attempt already. I cannot stay here and risk the lives of everyone in the cloister."

"Nonsense," he patted her hands. "You are the Daughter of Keroys. The walls of his church will always protect you. I'll make sure the gates are guarded, have everyone keep their eyes open. The Fallen rarely come into Almair, and even fewer approach us here. We will keep you safe." He put an arm around her, and she leaned into it. "All will be well. Of that, I am certain."

He stopped in front of a small door off the room. Twisting the knob, he pushed it open. A small altar sat with a single bench in front of it. On top of the altar rested a set of scales. Keroys would balance the good within her against the evil. The weight of her life versus the release that death would be, one day. Two massive candelabras sat on each side. Reverently, she lit the beeswax pillars set into each one and let the sweet aroma permeate the air before she sat down and began to pray.

CHAPTER
SIXTEEN

Jinaari kept his pace, trying not to rush. As soon as he could, he flattened himself against the closest building and looked back. Thia disappeared through the side door of the cloister. He stood there, watching, for a few more minutes. He had to be certain no one had followed them.

He moved through the crowd. Too many people stared on their way from the ship. What was worse was that he couldn't tell if they were looking at her, or him. He caught a few people instinctively bow. He wanted this to be a quiet visit; get in, let Thia talk things over with Keroys, get back out of town. The longer they stayed, the harder it would be for him to ignore a summons from the Duke.

And the easier it would be for the Fallen to find Thia.

He veered off the main street and headed for The Green Frog. The chapterhouse could wait for tomorrow. Right now, he wanted a bath, some good ale, and sleep.

The sign said closed, but he walked in anyway. Adam sat at the bar, going over some ledgers with his business partner. Wilim ran the day-to-day operations. Adam's part involved coin. And the chance for them to have a place where people wouldn't easily find them.

Wilim glanced at him, gathered the books, and disappeared through a side door. "Did I scare him?" Jinaari joked as he sat on a stool.

"Possibly. You can be intimidating. Though I think it's something else." He rounded the bar and grabbed a tankard. Filling it from a keg sitting on the back ledge, Adam continued, "Did Thia get to her cloister safely?" He placed the mug in front of Jinaari.

"Yeah, she's fine. For now." Picking up the drink, he took a swig. "That's the good stuff. What's the occasion?"

"Your elevation." He slapped a piece of paper onto the table.

Jinaari scanned it, the announcement of his grandfather's death, his mother's coronation. And naming him as heir. "Shit," he breathed. "How many did you find?"

"Enough that the entire city likely knows. Have you made it to your chapterhouse yet?"

He shook his head. "No, I decided to come here. Something didn't feel right. Too many people stared at us as we walked." He grabbed the paper and wadded it up in a ball. "It's just my first name, no description. I might get lucky." Looking up at Adam, he grew serious. "Caelynn?"

"She won't care. She might tease you mercilessly, ask for the chance to play at your coronation, but that's it." Adam grew serious. "Thia's a different matter."

"She trusts me, Adam. I don't know that she'll trust the Crown Prince of Avoch."

Adam picked up a candlestick. He put a fresh candle in it and lit the wick. "They're the same person, Jinaari. She'll get used to the idea." Moving it over to the bar, he put it between them.

"I don't know," Jinaari said, reaching for the tankard. "My grandfather had his prejudices. They were worse than Alesso's. And he acted on them. A lot of the problems between Avoch and Byd Cudd began when he started to reign."

"It's no more important than who her mother is. The question isn't if you think she will still trust you. It's if you're afraid she won't."

"You think too much, Adam."

The warlock smiled. "So you've told me, many times. But that's what makes us friends. I do the thinking; you do the fighting." He paused. "You haven't answered my question."

"Let's keep it quiet, for now. I'll tell her myself when we're done with Lolc Aon. That's the priority. That's likely to cause her enough problems without adding this to the mix."

Adam nodded. "I'll talk to Caelynn, make sure she doesn't let anything slip out. I'll do the asking about Alesso for you. If you want to keep things quiet, you'll have to stay out of sight."

The door swung open and both men turned to look at the newcomer. Jinaari's hand instinctively flew to his sword. A thin man, dressed in a courtier's uniform, walked toward them. He bowed, holding out a sealed envelope. "Too late," Jinaari muttered as he took the note. The seal of the Duke of Almair was imprinted in the silver wax. Breaking it, he read the contents.

"His Grace requested that I wait for a reply, Your Royal Highness."

Jinaari placed the letter on the table. "Please let His Grace know that my visit to his city is not an official one or expected to be lengthy. While I appreciate his invitation, I must respectfully decline."

The courtier blinked rapidly, "I will, um, let His Grace know." He bowed again before turning around and leaving.

"Was that wise?" Adam asked.

"It's the truth. I'm still on a task that two Gods gave me. I don't have time," he picked up the letter and touched the edge to the flame, "to have dinner with a bunch of sycophants and schemers who don't understand what honor is." Once the paper began to burn, he dropped it into a dish and watched the edges blacken.

Rising, he glanced at Adam. "I'm heading upstairs. If anyone asks..."

"I haven't seen you."

Climbing the staircase, he reached the second landing and stopped. He placed his left hand against the wall and waited. The wall before him shifted slightly and he stepped through into the hidden area.

This was why Adam bought into the inn to begin with. Few beyond the group knew how to access this part of the property. Five suites, plus a common room. The idea was to give them a place to rest, decide what to do next. Two of the rooms were to be for Flink and Kathra. One was dead, the other sequestered from the world. *Thia should have one, but that's Adam's call to make*, he thought as he headed to his room. He glanced back at the exit. *No, she needs to be where she's at. It was my idea anyway. She'll be safe. There's no way the Fallen would try to come for her in the middle of the cloister.*

His room was simply furnished: a bed, with a chest at the end. A table with a pair of chairs. The rack for his armor. Two bags containing his gear sat on the floor, waiting. *At least I still have my armor*, he thought. Unbuckling his sword, he leaned it against the wall near the rack. Grabbing the first bag, he tossed it on the bed and began to unpack.

Two hours later, he sat in one of the chairs and carefully worked the oil into the sword. He'd paused long enough to bathe and start a fire, but the weapon needed his attention. There was something different about it, to be certain. Two Gods had touched it, imbued it with their will. The edge had not lost its sharpness, either. It was a weapon meant to slay a Goddess.

I won't use it on Thia, though. She's stronger than she thinks, than Keroys gives her credit for. As long as I keep her away from Herasta and Lolc Aon, she'll be fine.

"Jinaari?" Adam called through the door.

"It's open." He finished polishing the weapon and slid it back into the scabbard.

The warlock opened the door, leaning against the frame. "You've got a visitor." Moving aside, another figure stepped forward. His hands reached up, pulling the hood off his head.

"You gave my courtier quite the fright, Althir." Duke Tomil looked at him, smiling. "I think that was the first time anyone had dared tell him no."

"I meant it, Tomil. I don't have time for dinner parties. This isn't an official visit."

The other man nodded. "Mind if I sit down?" Easing into the chair, he looked at Adam.

"It's fine, Adam. Thanks," Jinaari said, waiting for his friend to leave. If it was something he needed to know, he'd fill both Adam and Caelynn in later. "So," he looked at the Duke, "what's so important that my future brother-in-law had to leave his home in secret to come find me? I know it's not because you'll miss my charming personality at dinner tomorrow."

"What really happened in Tanisal?"

"We found the problem, dealt with it. For now, anyway.

Drogon's Forsaken, and we weren't prepared for that. Next time, we will be."

"Because the Fallen priestess is Marked?"

Jinaari narrowed his eyes, "How'd you hear about that? And she's more human than Fallen."

"One of the maids has a sister who works in the cloister. She served them tea, overheard part of a conversation. I know Father Philip's trying to keep her out of sight, let her use his private chapel, but the word's spreading fast. There's a lot of people who don't think she's real; they want to see the Mark themselves. They can't believe he'd let one of the Fallen be his Daughter."

"She's half human. Her father raised her, on the surface. Tomil, I know her. She fears the Fallen part of her heritage. And she didn't even learn about the Mark herself until recently."

"Why bring her back here, Jinaari?"

"She needed to find answers. Ones I couldn't give her. She's a Daughter of Keroys and all that it entails. I've seen her work spells that would make most drop from exhaustion without blinking. And she's not even close to reaching her limit." He paused. "And that's part of the problem. Lolc Aon knows she's Marked, too."

Tomil let out a low whistle. "That's not good."

"No. That's where we're going, once Thia's ready. We're heading into Byd Cudd and dealing with the Scorpion Queen once and for all."

"Your mother wouldn't approve."

Jinaari stared at him. "I don't care. I've got two Gods who asked me to do a job. That trumps anything Her Majesty might think I need to do."

"Ouch." Tomil cringed at his tone. "What do you need from me? Besides trying to squelch any rumors about your priestess friend and not telling your mother what you just said?"

"Gear. We lost ours underneath Tanisal. Stuff we can use on the road to Byd Cudd. And information. Another paladin from my Order, Alesso Potiri, would've come through here a week or so ago. His sister was held captive by the Fallen and we managed to free her. Thia's concerned about her."

"I'll ask around, send you anything I can find out. The gear will be here by morning. When are you heading out?"

"As soon as Thia's ready."

Tomil rose, and Jinaari followed suit. "I'd like to meet her. Do you think she'd mind a visit from me?"

"She's spent fifteen years in that cloister, Tomil. And then got sent off to deal with things she'd never even read about. Only to discover she bears a Mark from Keroys. She's got enough to deal with. Meeting a Duke could make her panic."

The other man smiled. "And running around with the Crown Prince doesn't?"

Jinaari crossed his arms and leaned against the table. "I haven't told her. And I won't, not for a while. She trusts me. With where we're going, what we have to do, I can't risk losing that."

"And that's why you won't come to dinner." Tomil nodded. "That I can understand." He held out his hand to the paladin. "Take care of what you need to do. I won't ask how long it'll take. I know better. But try to be back by the wedding. Amara will be crushed if you're not there to walk her down the aisle."

He smiled. His sister was the one person in his family with whom he got along. "I'll do my best."

Raising the hood on his cloak, Tomil turned serious

again. "I'll do what I can to make sure you have peace here in the inn. I can't guarantee that if you leave, though."

"Are you putting me under house arrest, Your Grace?"

"Never," he shook his head. "I know better. Even if I deny the rumors, they're going to spread. It's best for both of you to keep out of sight as much as possible." He walked out of the room, closing the door behind him.

Jinaari stared at the closed door. He didn't want to rush, but Tomil's words concerned him. Shaking his head, he headed to the common room downstairs. Another ale or two while Caelynn performed would help pass the time.

It wouldn't guarantee he'd relax instead of watching everyone else in the bar, but it'd be a start.

CHAPTER
SEVENTEEN

Thia rose from the copper tub; the water was still warm, but her mind was restless. Grabbing a towel, she wrapped it around her body and sat in a chair close to the fire.

Keroys had spoken to her, but his answers left her with more questions. *How will I know when I'm ready to tap into everything he's given me? And what did he mean by I have to reject one life and accept another?* Sighing, she stared into the flames. She'd come here, hoping to find her balance with all of this. Instead, she felt more lost than ever.

Staring down at her hands, she examined them closely. They were the same as they'd been yesterday and the day before. A few callouses, broken and torn nails. A fresh scar or two. They weren't the hands of a priestess that stayed in a temple, praying.

They were now hands that didn't mind getting dirty.

I have to see it. I have to know.

Her fingers flew through the sigil while she muttered the incantation under her breath. Few ever learned the spell; even less dared to cast it. The air in front of her shimmered and an identical version of herself appeared. The spell was designed to confuse an attacker, allowing her to create multiple images. For this, though, she only needed the one. *I'll need to remember this one*, she thought. *It might come in handy ... down there.*

"Turn around," she commanded. The image obeyed.

She reached out, intent on moving the towel, and her hand went through the duplicate. *Damn it*. Standing up, she unwrapped the towel around her and watched the illusionary one fall away. There, centered on her spine, was a set of golden yellow balanced scales.

Keroys's Mark.

She bit back tears as the realization crashed down on her. It didn't matter if she wanted this or not, she was a Daughter of Keroys. As soon as the news spread, her life would change. Daughters and Sons of Gods, the mortals they put a Mark on, were seen as heroes, sages. Advisors to crowns, courted by royalty.

All Thia wanted was to feel like she belonged somewhere, anywhere. She'd not felt that way since the day her father died.

Swiping at the tears, she dismissed the illusion. *Get up,* she told herself, *get dressed. Go back to the chapel, talk to Keroys. This isn't right. It's a mistake. There's no way anyone will come to me for advice. They see only my Fallen side.*

She walked over to the chest that contained her clothes. Grabbing at what she could find, she got dressed.

"Thia? What's wrong?" Father Philip's voice came from the doorway.

She glanced at him as she shoved her feet into some soft shoes. "It's a mistake. I know it is. May I use your chapel again? I must convince Keroys to remove the Mark." She stood up and looked at him again. "Please?" Her voice quivered.

He entered the room and closed the door behind her. "Thia, sit down. There is something you need to hear."

Her heart sank. Something was wrong, she could see it on his face. "What's happened?"

"First, Keroys doesn't make mistakes. He gave you this power, made you his Daughter, for a purpose. You and I may not know what it is, but he does. Trust in that."

"Did something happen to Jinaari or Adam?" she stared at him. "Tell me, Father."

"As far as I know, your friends are safe. Earlier today, while you were in the chapel, an acolyte was caught trying to pour something into one of the water vats in the kitchen." He reached into a pocket of his robe and pulled out a small, glass vial. The wax seal around the cork stopper was broken, and the bottle was empty. In the firelight of her room, she could see small green drops that clung to the sides. "She was stopped, and we spoke with her." He paused, placing the bottle on the table, then reached out and took her hands into his. "She said it was supposed to be a love potion."

"Why are you telling me this?"

"She said she was in the market and a Fallen woman approached her. Gave her the bottle, told her how to use it, and refused coin. The apothecary master examined the contents. It was a sleeping draught, Thia. Strong enough that this small amount would've made every single person in the cloister fall into a deep slumber."

She closed her eyes. The Fallen had found her? Here? Her heart began to race.

"I have no problem risking whatever I must to keep you safe. It's the promise I gave to your father, before he died.

The rest of the people here," he paused, "they should be given the chance to decide for themselves."

"You're asking me to leave, aren't you?" she whispered. "This is the only home I've known for fifteen years. I don't know where to go."

"You said your friends are staying at an inn nearby, yes? Take whatever you need. I'll escort you myself. Keroys has set your Path before you, Thia Bransdottir. It is time that you begin to walk it."

"I'll . . ." she stammered. "I don't need you to escort me. I can find it on my own." She rose, glancing at the chest. She had an older cloak. It was worn but would still hide her face. The rest she could wear or bundle up within a blanket. Her eyes landed on the bottle. "May I have this? My friends may know more about it."

"Whatever you need, Thia." He rose, but she stayed on the bed. "We will see each other again. I believe that. And, when we do, I know you will have grown into your power." Without another word, he left, closing the door behind him.

Don't think, just act. Quickly, she put the chain shirt on over her tunic before winding the belt around her waist. The rest of her clothing she wrapped into a blanket and tied the corners to secure everything. Grabbing the bottle, she slipped it into the pouch with her box. She raised the hood of her cloak, draping it over her head, before picking up the bundle.

As she put her hand on the door, she hesitated. For the second time, she was leaving. This time felt different though.

When I walk out the gate this time, I won't be coming back. Not to stay. This isn't home anymore, and everyone but me knew it. Don't think. Just go.

She ran through the courtyard to a side door. The sentry didn't talk to her; he opened the door and closed it behind her. The sound of the latch falling into place echoed in her soul. Turning, she looked down the street, trying to remember which way Jinaari had said to go. Once she had her bearings, she ran down the dark street, one hand raised to keep the hood over her head. He had said the inn wasn't far. She should find it easily enough. The fear made it feel like forever, but she kept moving.

Glancing down an alley, she caught sight of the sign. A green frog, standing on two legs with overflowing mugs in both hands. Warm, inviting light beckoned from the windows. The sound of music drifted out as two men stumbled through the door and into the street. She glanced back, checking to see if she was followed. *Like I would know*, she chided herself. *If there were any Fallen out there, they'd have tried something by now.* Running up the cobblestone alley, she pulled open the door and stepped inside.

A long, polished wood bar ran the length of one wall. At the far end, Caelynn was on a stage, playing and singing. Thia looked around the room. Adam and Jinaari sat at a table, watching. She moved around the rest of the patrons and fell into a seat between them, making sure her back was against the wall. The bundle she carried slid from her fingers and fell to the floor. She then buried her head in her hands.

"Thia?" Adam asked. He sounded surprised. "Is everything okay?"

"I thought you were staying at the cloister," Jinaari said.

Raising her head, she noticed both men had moved closer to her. She wouldn't have to speak loudly to be heard by either of them. At the same time, no one else was close enough to eavesdrop.

"There was an . . . incident." Her voice trembled. It was impossible to keep the terror out of it.

"What sort of incident?" Jinaari's voice was low but insistent.

"They caught an acolyte pouring something into a barrel in the kitchen. When they tested the water, it'd been poisoned."

Adam let out a low whistle. "With what?"

"It was some sort of sleeping draught. Potent enough to put the entire cloister out for hours." Absently, she picked at a worn spot on the surface of the table. "It wasn't even magical. They questioned the acolyte. She said it was supposed to be a love potion. She's been pining for someone, I guess. She got it in an alley from a Fallen." She dug into the pouch and brought out the vial. Placing it on the table, she continued. "I didn't find out until tonight, after they figured everything out. She didn't try to do this until after I was there. Father Philip brought this to me and told me to leave. He didn't think they could protect me any longer." She paused again. "His exact words were, 'I have no problem risking whatever I must to keep you safe. The rest of the people here, they should be given the chance to decide for themselves'."

Jinaari reached out and picked up the vial. Thia watched him turn it over in his hand while she took some deep breaths. The panic and fear were subsiding. This was as close to safe as she could be. Both men had saved her life before. She trusted them.

"Damn," the paladin swore.

"What?" Adam slid a mug of mead over to Thia.

"Thank you," she muttered before raising it to her lips. The honeyed liquid slid down her throat. She rarely drank, but tonight would be the exception.

"See this mark here?" Jinaari held the bottle out to Adam. "That's a guild marking."

"So? The bottle was made by a glassmaker's guild member. What's wrong with that?" Adam asked.

Jinaari shook his head. "It's not a glassmaker mark. That's the seal of the Barren. They're master assassins," he looked at Thia, "trained by Lolc Aon herself."

"Why can't they just leave me alone," she whispered. "I'm nobody. I don't know Herasta. I've never been in Byd Cudd. I'm not a threat to anybody."

"It's not what you are now, Thia. It's what they know you'll become. The Gods have seen your future and are making sure the power you'll wield one day isn't misused." Jinaari paused. "I told you we'd have to take the fight to Lolc Aon. It's time."

"You're suggesting we go down to Byd Cudd?" Adam asked.

He nodded. "This isn't going to stop until Lolc Aon is dead. She's not going to come to us, so we need to go to her."

"What if," she drew a shuddering breath, "what if she gets to me and I change into something evil?"

"It's not going to happen." Jinaari took a drink from his tankard.

"But what if –"

Jinaari reached out and grasped her shoulder. "It's not going to. Stop thinking it will. The only way to get her to stop hunting you is to kill her. And I can't do that from here." He stared at her. "We'll keep you safe, Thia. Trust us."

A tray full of drinks dropped into the center of the table, the amber liquid within sloshing over the brim of the mugs. Grinning at them, a young man turned one of the empty chairs around and sat down. "Hey, you all look way too serious! Have a drink on me."

"This is a private conversation, friend. I suggest you find another table." Jinaari growled at the newcomer.

The man picked up one of the tankards and drank noisily. "This is where I need to be, though. You all need to lighten up, relax. I mean, sure, you're going down to Byd Cudd. You've got Fallen assassins trying to kidnap your friend there. But that's for tomorrow. Tonight, we need to get drunk and get to know each other better."

"You know quite a bit about us, friend. That could be a bad thing." Adam replied.

"Look, do you honestly think that only Garret and Keroys have a stake in all of this? Lolc Aon's pissed off most of her family with trying to poach that one," he pointed a finger at Thia. "And they're going to make sure she's chastised for it." He took another drink. "Name's Pan, by the way."

"Who sent you?" Thia asked.

A grin split his face. "I'm so glad you asked! Let me tell you about my Lord and Savior, Ash!"

Thia caught a look that passed between Adam and Jinaari. "Adam," the paladin said, "why don't you show Thia where her room is? Let her get settled. I'll talk with this one," he nodded at the brown-haired man.

"Good idea," he said. "Grab your stuff, Thia." He rose from the table, and she followed suit, picking up the bundle. As they reached the bottom of the staircase, she glanced back. The newcomer was talking, his hands gesturing toward her. Jinaari's face was a mask.

"It's this way," Adam's voice broke through her thoughts. Looking toward him, she saw him waiting on a small landing.

"Sorry," she muttered. "I'm coming." She followed him up the staircase.

When they got to the next landing, he stopped. "First things first. I have to key this to admit you." He placed his hand against the wall. Pulling back, he stepped aside. "Your turn. Just place your palm on the same spot I did."

Reaching out, she did as he instructed. The wood beneath her hand warmed up briefly. "Is that it?" she asked.

"Almost." He repeated the motion with his own hand again. "It should work now. Try it."

She placed her palm back on the spot, and the wall in front of them shimmered.

"Let's go," he said, smiling. "Ladies first."

Thia walked through the doorway, amazed. A circular common room, with an assortment of couches and chairs. Five doors led off the room. "This is amazing," she breathed.

"My room's here," he pointed toward the closest door on the left. "Caelynn's next to me, then Jinaari. I'd recommend this one," he walked to the end of the right wall. "If Pan does join us, that keeps someone between you and the entry. If they manage to find it." Adam opened the door.

She entered and stopped short. The room held a good-sized fireplace, a bed that was twice the size of the one she'd had at the cloister, and a pair of chests. Two chairs and a small table sat near the fireplace. "What's behind that?" she asked, pointing to an archway on the same wall as the bed.

"My favorite part!" Adam exclaimed. "Especially if we've been on the road for a while." He gestured at the bed. "Might as well put your stuff down there," he suggested as he led her to the door. He pushed it open, flattening against the frame so Thia could look past him easily. "I gave us each our own bath chamber."

The room was small, dominated by a large copper tub. "If you touch the sides, it'll fill with hot water. Took some work to get the spells right, but it's easier than hauling water up by the bucket."

"There's no windows anywhere," she commented. "How do we know if it's morning?"

His face grew serious. "That was on purpose. We didn't want to be spied on, have people try to see if we were here, etc. This wall here," he pointed to the one across from the entry to the room, "can be whatever you want me to make it. Just tell me and I'll do the spell work. It'll be an illusion, but you'll be able to control it."

Staring at the blank wood, she asked, "Anything?"

"Sure."

"When I was young, Papa took me to the ocean. We sat on top of a cliff and watched the stars fall from the sky all night long. It was so beautiful, peaceful." She paused. "Byd Cudd is underground, isn't it?

"Yes."

"And it's likely to take several weeks to get there, and back out?"

He nodded. "What about it?"

"I'm thinking," she sighed, "that I'd love to be able to have something open. Where I can see the sun rise, the tide come in, watch stars fall as the day fades into night. Does that make sense?"

"It does." He smiled at her. "I'm going to head over to my room, let you get settled. Jinaari will figure out who this Pan is, let us know in the morning. Get some rest, Thia. The bed will be more comfortable here than we're likely to get on the way. There aren't any inns we'll want to stop at. I anticipate a lot of sleeping on the ground, like we did under Tanisal."

Without another word, he left. She unhooked her cloak, draping it across one of the chairs, before pulling off the chain shirt and unpacking the few possessions she had. Her box she set on top of a chest, near the head of her bed.

Sitting on the bed, she tested the mattress. Adam was right. It was comfortable. A wave of exhaustion washed over her. She slipped off her shoes and curled up under the blankets. She was safe here. At least for tonight.

CHAPTER EIGHTEEN

"I don't know, Jinaari. We're not running a tour here. Are you sure he should be coming?" Adam's voice drifted into her room, waking Thia up.

"It wasn't my decision to make," the paladin's deep voice responded. "He's supposed to be here, same as you, me, and Caelynn. There's something Pan has to do, some way he'll help Thia. That's all I need to know."

She rose, shivering slightly. She'd not bothered to light the fire before going to bed. Grabbing the old cloak, she pulled it close around her as she went out to see what was going on.

"Who's coming with us?" she asked.

Both men looked her way. "Morning," Jinaari said. "How'd you sleep?"

Shrugging, she moved further into the common room and sat near them. "Good. I was tired." She gave him a direct look. "You didn't answer my question."

"His name's Pan Beckenburg. He's sleeping. He drank a lot last night, trying to convince me to let him join us."

Something tugged at her mind. Where had she heard that name before?

"Thia?"

Blinking, she looked at Jinaari. "What?"

"You looked like something was wrong."

"No," she said, shaking her head. "It's just that I remembered hearing that name before. But I don't remember where."

"The family's got a Barony somewhere. Maybe that's why?" Adam commented.

Thia sighed. "No. That's not it. I never paid attention to any of that. I don't even know who the ruler of Avoch is. It's probably nothing." She pulled her feet under her on the seat of the chair, trying to warm them underneath the cloak. "Does that mean we're leaving today? If Pan's coming with us, why should we wait?"

"Tomorrow. I'm waiting on some information and supplies to come in." Jinaari broke off a piece of bread from a loaf that sat on the table. He looked at her. "Is that the only cloak you have?"

"My other one got left in the cave. Most of what I owned was in that pack. I never had the inclination, or coin, to have a lot of clothes. When you spend your day in prayer or lessons, there's not a big need."

"Talk with Caelynn. She knows some shops. You'll need clothes that'll let you move and keep you warm," Adam said. "We won't have to worry about things like snow or rain, but it's going to be cooler than you're used to."

"I don't have any coin," she stammered. "It was in my pack. I'll make do with what I have."

"That's not a problem," Jinaari said.

She stared at him. "I won't take coin I can't repay."

"It's in our best interest," he pointed to Adam, then

back at himself, "to make sure you're comfortable, Thia. You can't draw the sigils if your hands are stiff from being cold. Or run, if it's necessary, in long skirts or boots that have no sole left. The chain shirt I gave you before was good, but you need better."

"Just let them do it, Thia." Caelynn came out of her room and grabbed an apple off the table before sitting down. "You belong with us. That means you get a share of anything we find. And, like he said, we've got an interest in making sure you're able to move." She bit into the fruit. "Am I taking her with me, or do you want me to just get stuff and bring it back here?'

"You can move easier in the city than she can," Jinaari said, "even with that hair of yours. She'd be remembered."

"Because I'm half Fallen?" She couldn't keep the bitterness out of her voice.

His fingers drummed against the arm of the chair. It was obvious to Thia that he was choosing his words carefully. "Because your eyes give you away. That's it. The rest of your features could pass as having ties to Caelynn's race." He gave her a direct look. "My job is to keep you safe. That means I get to decide where you go and what you do. Until we leave Almair, you stay up here or down in the common room. And you don't go down there unless one of us is with you."

"Calm down, old man," Adam joked. "You make her mad, she may decide to make your armor chafe you all the way to Byd Cudd."

Caelynn smiled at her. "Come on, Thia. Let's see what you have so I know what to get you. Besides, that one," she shot a glare at Jinaari, "needs to remember that bullying people that are capable of healing him isn't a great move on his part."

She rose, grabbing some food off the table, and led Caelynn to her room. She didn't fully trust her, not yet, but the others did. And the bard had been doing this sort of thing for a while. Certainly longer than Thia had. While she'd rather do her own shopping, she needed Caelynn's help. *Jinaari isn't going to let me leave the inn. My best chance at getting something that didn't fit like it was made for someone twice my size is to let her shop for me.*

"Jinaari's not nearly as bad as he sounds," Caelynn said as Thia closed the door. "He's a paladin, with a warrior's mentality. You'll get used to it."

"To which part? The arrogance or the insufferableness?" Thia asked.

Caelynn shrugged, "Both. The problem isn't that he's that way. It's that his swordsmanship and honor back it up. I've never seen him run from a fight or come close to losing. I don't know what Drogon did to knock him out but drowning almost killed him. You know that. So does he. It's not something Jinaari will forget, either." She went to the chest. "What are we working with?"

Thia opened it up, pulling out the few things she had and placing them on the bed. "Not much. I didn't pack anything I would've worn to perform rites or anything like that. From what it was like in Tanisal, I thought it wouldn't work to wear a floor-length robe." She sat on the bed, looking at what little she had. "It's not going to cost much, will it?"

"Pfft," she said, dismissing her concern with a wave of her hand. "Doesn't matter. We've been doing this long enough that we don't know how to spend the coin we have. Plus, Adam's got a stake in this place. He collects his portion every time we come back."

"The three of you have been doing this sort of thing for a while, then?"

"I've only been around for the last year. Those two," she nodded toward the common room, "have been working with each other for years. I think they met when Jinaari was still an initiate in his Order or something."

"Do you know why Adam calls him 'old man'? It looks like he's the older of the two."

"Oh, that," she laughed. "Adam told me the story. Jinaari and others were sent to escort him from Helmshouse to Dragonspire. They got delayed due to weather and Adam went out with some other warlocks to search for them. They were buried in the snow from an avalanche. Jinaari's hair and beard were white from the cold. Adam said it made him look like an old man. When he woke up and started giving orders, as he does, the nickname stuck in Adam's mind." She smiled. "Personally, I love it. Jinaari needs to be reminded that he's human."

"Has he ever been wrong? Made a mistake?"

"No," she sighed, "and that only adds to the arrogance. Anyway, enough about those two. You'll figure out how to work with them soon enough. They're not hard to read once you get to know them." Surveying the small pile on the bed, Caelynn nodded. "One more thing. Stand up and take off the cloak."

Thia did so, draping it on the open chest. Caelynn pulled a length of string with knots tied at regular intervals out of her belt pouch. "Raise your arms," the elf told her.

"What's that for?"

"It'll give me an idea of what size will fit you best when I get to the shop," she replied, wrapping the cord around her waist. Thia stood patiently as she measured a few more places. "That should do it." She stepped back, looking at her critically. "You're thin, but in okay shape. I'll get a few outfits, make sure they'll fit but also give you room to grow."

"Grow? We're going to be walking, fighting who knows what. Not feasting every night!"

"Yes, but your arm and leg muscles will get stronger, not shrink. I'm leaving the armor up to Jinaari. He knows that stuff better than I do." She winked. "Don't worry. He's not going to put you in plate armor like he wears. Probably the same sort of thing you wore before but better quality."

Thia sighed. "I wouldn't know what was good or bad, so it doesn't matter."

"It does, actually. We want you to live, Thia. Armor's the best way to do that." Caelynn wrapped the cord up and put it back in her pouch.

"Do you wear any? Or Adam?"

"Mine's hardened leather and I usually wear it under my clothes. I can't move as well, do what I need to do, in chain. The leather's quieter. As for Adam, no. Not that I know of. Warlocks have spells, though, that help protect them. And he stays out of direct combat. That staff of his has a nice range to it. Now, I'm going to go shopping. Try not to hurt Jinaari while I'm gone." Caelynn walked toward the door.

"I can't promise that," Thia laughed.

"Please? I mean, why should you get all the fun?" Both women laughed as they walked back into the common area.

The man from the night before sat with Adam, his face scrunching up in pain at the sound.

"Where's Jinaari?" Caelynn asked.

"Downstairs. He's expecting a delivery. Got everything you need?" Adam asked.

"Almost. Just need to get my coin."

"No need. I've got plenty, and he wanted me to go with you." Adam gestured at the other man as he rose. "Thia, I think you've met Pan. He's a little hung-over right now, so he probably won't be good company. Oh," he said, turning back around to face her, "one more thing. I worked on that illusion for your wall last night. Remind me when I get back and I'll show you where I'm at. I'd like to get your thoughts before I finalize it."

"I, ah, okay," she stammered. He remembered what she said and worked on the spell already?

"Great! If you need something, Jinaari's downstairs. But send Pan, okay?" He waited for her to nod in agreement, then followed Caelynn out the door.

She felt someone watching her and turned to face Pan. His face smiling.

"Hi," he croaked.

"Hello."

"I'm sorry if I gave you the wrong impression last night. You guys looked so serious, though. I thought buying a round would help lighten the mood."

She shrugged. "Things are . . . strange right now. We're all a bit on edge."

"Being hunted by a Goddess would do that to a person," Pan said.

"Look," she said, "I'm sure you're nice and all. If you weren't supposed to be here, Jinaari would've sent you away. Instead, he brought you up here. My life's been turned upside down recently, though, and I'm not in a talkative mood. I'm going to go back to my room for a while."

"Okay. Should I tell the big guy when he comes back where you went?"

"Only if he asks. He already knows more about me than

I do." She walked to her door and went inside, closing it behind her. She started to gather up what was on the bed, putting it back into the chest. *It doesn't make sense. Why did Keroys trust Jinaari enough to tell him about my Mark, but not me? What else does he know that I don't? And will he keep everything a secret from me like he did this?*

Closing the lid, she sat on the bed. *Stop thinking that way. He saved my life, more than once. And Keroys didn't want him to tell me. When he knew I knew, he didn't lie about it. I need to learn how to ask the right questions, that's all. This isn't a book; it's life. The answers aren't going to be easy to find.*

With a sigh, she flopped back on the mattress. The restlessness wouldn't go away, but she couldn't go anywhere, either. *Might as well test this magic bath Adam talked about. At least I'll be clean when Caelynn comes back.*

CHAPTER NINETEEN

The misty rain fell through the trees. The leaves, while mostly green, were beginning to turn. Every now and then, a larger drop would form, and Thia would feel it hit the top of her head. The hood of her coat kept her dry.

She tilted her neck, trying to work out the kinks. They'd left Almair days ago, and her body missed the bed back at The Green Frog. *This is what I need to do, where I need to be. Jinaari was right. It's time we brought the fight to Lolc Aon. He's arrogant, but he's also my best chance at having any sort of normal life.*

Her hands were encased in soft leather, supple enough for her to manipulate the magic but kept them warm and dry. The old cloak was replaced by a hooded coat made of dark gray wool. No more trying to keep folds of fabric around her, struggling to find the opening at the end of wide sleeves. This fit snugly against her body, even with the new chain shirt underneath her tunic.

And then there was her pack. She had no idea where it came from, or how it worked, but she'd been able to stuff everything Caelynn bought for her, including two pair of boots, and it wasn't full. There was no weight to it, either.

"We're almost there," Jinaari told them. "Stay close. This entrance isn't normally guarded but it wouldn't surprise me."

Thia swallowed, trying to keep the fear down. He'd said he knew a different route that led down to Byd Cudd, and she believed him. The plan was built on the idea that they'd get into the mountain and down to the city, without being found. Get in, take care of Lolc Aon, maybe Herasta, and get out. The whole time, making sure that she wasn't taken prisoner.

Don't go there, she thought. *It doesn't do me or anyone else any good to dwell on the 'what if' possibilities. Trust Jinaari and Adam. One's going to keep them from getting close enough, the other will get me out if they do.*

Jinaari's hand flew up, and she stopped. "Wait here," he said. As he walked forward, his back to the rocky cliff to her left, she noticed the others edging closer to her. Surrounding her. Her heart began to race. A series of whistled notes echoed in the forest, and she relaxed.

"Come forward," Jinaari called out. "They're friendly. Or so he says."

The tone of his voice was enough to warn her. Whoever he'd found wasn't going to be someone she wanted to see. Adam looked past her, nodding once to Caelynn. The elf silently retreated, blending into the surrounding trees. Thia quickly lost sight of her.

"Just in case," Adam said, his voice low.

Pan walked next to her. "Just in case what?"

Adam scowled at the young man. "Just in case whoever Jinaari found isn't as friendly as they say they are."

"Oh."

They rounded the bend and saw Jinaari standing in front of a crack in the rock, barely wide enough for him to pass through. Her heart skipped a beat as she stared at it. That had to be the entrance he talked about.

The paladin turned and looked at her. "We have company." Stepping aside, she saw Alesso leaning against the entrance.

"Priestess," he nodded at her. "I'm glad to see you're alive and well."

She looked at Jinaari. "What is he doing here? I thought you said he was seen heading back to Dragonspire?"

"Ask him." He crossed his arms, staring at the other paladin. "He won't answer me."

"I owe you my life, priestess," Alesso said. "Until that debt is repaid, I will stay by your side. You cannot stop me. I'll follow, or you can let me join you. The choice is yours."

"I don't want you here, Alesso. None of us do. You owe me *nothing*. Please," she said, exasperated, "just leave me alone. Your sister needs you more than I ever will."

"She's safe. A convent of nuns devoted to Hauk took her in. They specialize in caring for those who were brutalized by the Fallen, helping them reintegrate into the surface world." He stepped forward. Instinctively, Thia took a step back as Jinaari raised his arm in front of her protectively. "I can't leave. I tried," he hesitated, "I really did. I took Ashynn to the Sisters, was going to stay there, help her. But every single time I looked at her face, priestess, I felt ashamed. I almost traded you for her, after you healed me. After you brought me back from the brink of death. I considered repaying that kindness by handing you over to the Fallen. I never made it back to the chapterhouse. I cannot call myself a paladin of Garret until I repay this debt. I will keep you safe, trust me."

"You expect me to trust you?" she stared at him. "You just admitted you almost turned me over to the Fallen!"

"But I didn't."

"Was that because you thought better of it," Jinaari asked, "or because I showed up?"

Alesso's jaw tightened but he didn't answer.

"That's what I thought. Thia," he kept his attention on Alesso as he spoke to her, "We need to talk this over."

"Yeah," she breathed as she started to step back. Jinaari followed her, glancing over his shoulder at the other man. Alesso's gaze never left her, but he didn't try to approach them.

The four of them stood close together. "He's not going to respond to anyone but Thia. And that's limited, too, since he said he'd follow you no matter what. You won't be able to tell him to just go away. What do you want to do?"

"I don't know," she said, her voice low. "I don't trust him, especially after what he just said. I don't want him anywhere near me. Jinaari, you're the one that makes these decisions, not me. How can we get rid of him?" She looked past him as Caelynn joined them.

He shook his head. "I don't know that we can, not for a while anyway. If he's determined to do this, I'd rather have him traveling with us than causing problems I can't see. First things first. Thia, you're going to have to tell him he must listen and respond to all of us, not just you."

"Why me?" she asked, her eyes wide.

"Because you're the one he owes the debt to. He didn't even want to talk to me when I found him, only asked if you were nearby. I don't want him to sit out a fight, waiting for you to tell him to act."

She looked past the group at the brown-haired paladin.

Closing her eyes, she sighed. "Is there some way we can guarantee he won't be anywhere near me? He scares me."

"Definitely," Jinaari replied. "One of us stays with you at all times, even when we're sleeping. I'll put him on the watch rotation with one of us. He doesn't sit one by himself." He looked back at her. "You'll have to be firm. Spell it out for him. I've known him too long. If he can find any sort of loophole, he'll exploit it."

Thia took a deep breath and exhaled slowly. "I suppose I can always tell him new instructions as we go along. Let's get this over with." Nervously, she led the group back toward the cavern entrance. "The only way you can stay with us, Alesso, is if you listen to everyone, not just me. If Caelynn asks you a question, answer it. If Adam says it's your turn to make dinner, do it. Especially Jinaari. You fight when he does, follow every single order he gives you. Got it?"

Slowly, he nodded. "I understand, priestess."

"One more thing," she continued, looking him in the eyes. "You do not stand, sit, or sleep next to me. Ever. Once we go inside, I don't even want you talking to me. I don't trust you, Alesso."

"I will change that."

"Not likely," she muttered under her breath.

"Caelynn, you're up here with me. Pan, you and Thia follow. Adam and Alesso, you bring up the rear." Jinaari nodded at each of them in turn. "Adam, some light would be good."

"You've got it," he replied. The gauntlet on Jinaari's right hand began to glow. "Will that work?"

"It should. I'll let you know if I need more." He stared at Alesso. "We're going in now. Stand aside and wait for Adam to enter before you do. Got it?"

Alesso nodded, stepping away from the entrance.

Thia approached the crevice, her heart beating rapidly. She could make out Jinaari and Caelynn as they continued down into the darkness. Lolc Aon was in there, waiting. Swallowing her fear, she whispered, "This is what I have to do. Jinaari won't let them take me."

"Be careful where you place your trust, priestess," Alesso whispered. "His Royal Highness has more secrets than you could ever imagine."

She turned her head, glaring at him. "Thia? What's wrong?" Pan asked from behind her.

She shook her head, "Nothing," she replied. *I can do this*, she thought. *I need to do this*. Before she could back out, she walked into the cave.

The walls were rough, untouched by tools. She kept her eyes on Jinaari, watching as he turned when the passage narrowed. The vibration of small feet, thousands of them, echoed in the narrow walkway. "What's that sound?" she asked.

"Probably just centipedes, other bugs," Caelynn answered her. "We're disturbing their nests."

"No scorpions, though?"

"Not here. We're too close to the surface," Jinaari said. He turned around and looked her in the face. "Lolc Aon isn't called the Scorpion Queen without reason. We'll need to be careful, the closer we get." He smiled for a moment. "Just don't push on any loose bricks and you'll be fine."

Thia laughed. "You're the one who told us to check the wall."

He nodded, then turned around again. Her mood lightened. *I should've died that day. Everyone has secrets. Jinaari is no different. That doesn't mean I shouldn't trust him.*

After about two hours, the corridor opened. "Everyone,

take a break and eat something," Jinaari said. "We've got several hours of walking before we rest tonight."

Thia shrugged off her pack, dropping it on the floor. Kneeling next to it, she rummaged around inside, searching for the packets of food Adam had given everyone. Pan sat across from her, munching on an apple. "Where are you from, anyway?"

"A village called River Run. You've probably never heard of it. I think there were maybe thirty people who lived there. Outside of taking care of those who couldn't make it to Almair before the city gates closed, few stopped," she said.

"I think a small village would've been great to grow up in."

"What about you?" she asked.

"My family's from Cirrain. It's halfway between Almair and Dragonspire. It's not small, but not as big as either of those cities." He took another bite. "Your family's from there, then? River Run?"

"I guess. Papa didn't talk about where he was from. We didn't have any other family in the village. It was just us." She paused. "Why do you want to know?"

He shrugged. "Just making conversation. Ash told me I needed to help you, but not why. The more I know about you, the better chance I have to figure out what to do. You guys don't talk much when you walk, do you? I mean, I get why you put the one guy in the back. I don't think any of you liked him coming along. Why is that?"

"Ask Jinaari or Adam," she replied curtly. "Pan, do you always talk this much?"

"Not always. I don't talk in my sleep that I know of. And I actually talk more when I'm drunk. Jinaari wouldn't let me have any more ale until I'd convinced him to let me join you guys. He's scary, isn't he? I mean, all that armor and the sword and all. Is he really all that good at using it or is it just for show?"

"I'm that good," Jinaari replied.

Pan jumped, and Thia couldn't help but smile. She'd seen the paladin approach them and wanted to see what the newcomer did. "Oh, um, that's good to know," he stammered.

"We're moving again. Care to join us or did Ash tell you to wait for some reason?"

Thia stood up, trying hard not to laugh, as Pan scrambled to his feet. "Catch up with Caelynn," Jinaari instructed him. "I want to talk to Thia for a moment."

She waited for him to walk away before she looked at him. "What's wrong?"

"I was going to ask you that," he said, his voice low. "How are things with you? Adam told me that Alesso said something to you when we came inside."

"Some nonsense about how I shouldn't trust you. Said you had your share of secrets, called you 'His Royal Highness'. He must really hate you or something." His face shifted, becoming hard. "What is it?"

"Alesso's got a big mouth," he muttered. "He's playing mind games, trying to scare you. You know me well enough to trust me, right?"

She nodded.

"That's what matters. Anything else is a distraction, nothing more. He and I have competed against each other for over a decade. It looks like he thinks you're another prize he wants to win."

"What do you mean, 'a prize'? I'm terrified even being this close to Byd Cudd, and it's going to get worse the closer we get. How is protecting me a competition? I'm a nervous wreck!" She let out a sigh. "I don't need him trying to prove something to me . . . you . . . himself . . . whatever. I just need this to be over."

"Soon enough," he said. "I'll make sure the watch schedule's consistent so you know who's on when. Don't keep things bottled up. If you need to talk, we'll figure it out where the rest won't hear. The fight won't be easy. I need to know your mind is where it needs to be when it happens. Whatever you need to ask, I'll answer. Got it?"

"Okay. It's just . . . I didn't need the added stress of him watching every single move I make. It was bad enough when you were gone. There's no reason for him to be here this time. He's watching me, too. I can feel it." She leaned against the wall. "When he was around before, I knew where I stood. He hated me and didn't want to be there. Something's changed, and I don't believe his explanation one bit."

"Neither do I. Adam will stay in front of him, help maintain the distance. If you're okay with it, whoever's done with watch when Caelynn starts can sleep in the tent with you while she's up. That way, you won't be left alone."

"You don't think he'd try anything like that, do you?" she asked, horrified.

"I don't, no. But I promised I'd take care of you, Thia. Keep you safe. And I intend on doing just that."

CHAPTER TWENTY

Jinaari leaned against the wall of the cavern, alert for any sound beyond the others sleeping. The women were the only ones who set up a tent. He understood why. Caelynn didn't care; he'd traveled with her long enough to know that. Thia, though, needed that sense of privacy. That barrier between her and Alesso.

His gaze settled on his brother paladin. They'd been trained to rely on each other, trust that your brother had your back in both battle and life. That bond had never formed between himself and Potiri, though. Every other one of Garrett's Paladins, yes. There was a need to win that drove Alesso to be reckless and Jinaari couldn't be. Not when it came to Thia's safety.

He shifted his gaze to the tent. So far, Thia hadn't shown any signs of what Keroys feared. She was nervous and scared, yes. Alesso's presence wasn't helping her anxiety, but he was doing his best to keep them apart. Adam and Pan helped with that. He and Thia talked each night, once everyone else had settled down. Most of the time he only had to listen. So much of her life had been spent hiding from everyone, including herself. Discovering she bore Keroys's Mark, adjusting to what that implied, wasn't easy for her.

A movement caught his eye and he watched as Adam rose from his bedroll. Carefully, the warlock walked between Pan and Alesso and headed toward him. "All quiet?" he asked when he got closer.

Jinaari nodded, relaxing slightly. "Just some snoring. You're early. I've got another hour yet before you and Alesso take over."

Adam leaned against the wall next to him. "I woke up. Besides, we need to discuss something."

"What's on your mind?"

"I think we have a problem with Thia."

Jinaari stood up straight, looking at the blond man. "In what way?"

"If she woke up and found herself in front of Herasta or Lolc Aon, what do you think she'd do?"

"Not going to happen," Jinaari declared.

"Hear me out . . ."

"No, Adam. It's not going to happen. We are not going to let it happen."

Adam turned to him. "I know what you're saying. None of us want it to happen. I don't even think Alesso does. I'm talking hypothetically here."

"It's still not happening," Jinaari insisted. He looked over at the tent again. He had a job to do, damn it, and that included keeping her safe.

Adam sighed. "Just hear me out. Okay?" Jinaari nodded, and he continued. "Say there's a cave-in and we get separated. Or a trap is missed and she's on the wrong side of a door. There are dozens of ways it could happen. That's not the point."

"Keep talking."

"What do you think her first reaction will be?"

He stared at the tent, thinking. *Adam's right. If things went horribly wrong and that happened, Thia wouldn't react well at all. I've had the training to handle it; she wouldn't have a clue.* "She's going to panic."

"That's my point." Adam's voice had an urgency to it. "You know her better than I do. From what I know, her life hasn't been easy. But it's still been sheltered. Caelynn said she told her she didn't have friends back at the cloister. Her father's dead. Her mother's hunting her." He took a breath. "She barely has a handle on any sort of tactics during a fight. She's learning, I'll give her that. But there's nothing I've seen that makes me think she would have the slightest clue how to survive if she was being held hostage."

He nodded. "You're right. She doesn't. That's a problem." He paused. "What's your solution?"

"We need to work with her. I can teach her some meditation techniques that will help with the fear. If she can quiet her mind, she'd be able to assess a situation better."

"I like it. We'll start there. Talk with Caelynn when you wake her up. She could teach her how to pick locks, move quietly. I gave her those daggers; I should've taken the time to train her how to use them." Looking back at Adam, he said, "Wake up Alesso halfway through your shift, then Caelynn toward the end. Talk to her before you go back to sleep but keep Alesso out of it. Thia can barely handle him being here to begin with. She won't take any sort of instruction from him."

"Did she tell you what he said to her?"

"Yeah," he snorted, "he tried to warn her from trusting me. Called me a name I won't repeat, said I had secrets."

"What name? If it's creative enough, I may use it to get your attention sometime."

Jinaari glared at him. "He used my title," the last word came out as a hiss.

Adam drew back. "Oh, that's low. Did she catch on?"

"Not that I can tell. I think she thought it was a jab at my confidence—"

"You mean your arrogance?"

"Yeah, that. I don't think she realizes it's true. I had a chat with Alesso about it, made it clear that he wasn't to say those words again where she could hear them."

"She's going to find out, eventually. Why not just tell her?"

"Adam, you saw how hard it was for her to accept that she's Marked. She still hasn't completely realized what that means. Tomil's only going to be able to keep it quiet for so long. When we get back to the surface, she's going to be mobbed with people expecting miracles from her. And she hasn't even come into her abilities yet."

"Don't you think her knowing she's got the Crown Prince of Avoch watching her back will help?"

Jinaari glared at him. "It's my decision, Adam. I've got her trust. I earned that. I make that call, not you."

"Sorry," he said. "I'm just thinking of Thia."

"Yeah, I know." He stretched. "I'm heading to bed." He walked over near the front of the tent where he'd laid out his bedroll. Alesso would trip over him if he tried to get close to it. Laying down, his armor bit into his back. It wasn't comfortable, but he could sleep. Taking it off wasn't an option. Not down here.

Closing his eyes, his hand gripped the hilt of his blade as it rested on his chest. Adam had a point about telling Thia about his other life. *That's not me, though. Will she understand it's all a mask I have no choice but to wear? One that I'd gladly put aside and never pick up again?*

Exhaustion silenced the questions in his mind, and he drifted off.

He bolted awake as soon as someone tapped his foot. Caelynn looked at him, her face serious. "What time is it?"

"Time for us to get up," she replied.

Jinaari sat up, rolling his neck, trying to work out the kinks. "Any issues?"

"No," she said. "Adam talked to me before he crashed in the tent. I've got some extra picks, but we can't do that while we're moving. It'll have to wait until we stop. Adam's going to switch spots with Pan so he can work with her on the meditations." She gave him a serious look. "I know he thought there's a risk, but what about you? Is it really that serious?"

"Which part?" he asked as he rolled up the sleeping pad and stuck it in his bag. "We're not down here as tourists, Caelynn. I had two Gods tell me to kill a third. Before she can convert Thia. What part did you think wasn't serious?" He rose and looked at her.

"It's just," she sighed. "I like her, Jinaari. She's scared and desperate for something to hold onto. I've tried to make friends with her, but I can't seem to gain her trust. Not like you and Adam have. I don't want anything to happen to her."

"None of us do," he said.

"Not even Alesso?"

He picked up his helm and turned it over in his hands. "If he does anything to hurt her, he'll find out the hard way that I'm definitely the better swordsman." He looked around. Pan still slept, but the other paladin's bedroll was empty. "Where's he at?"

Caelynn pointed down the pathway they'd come from the night before. "Taking a piss, I believe."

"We've got company!" Alesso's voice rang out.

Jinaari shoved his helm on his head. "Get the rest up," he commanded Caelynn. "Now!" Turning, he picked up his sword from the ground where he'd placed it. Alesso came running into the small room. "What is it?" he demanded as he slid his arm into the grip on his shield.

"Spiders and a scorpion. And some Fallen wench that looks like the priestess." He stood next to Jinaari.

He heard the others moving behind him but didn't turn around. They knew the drill well enough now. If not, they'd remember once the fight started. He kept his attention on the wide opening. "How big?"

"Big enough."

The first creature came into view. The spider was easily as tall as he was; the pincers clicked together in a rhythmic pattern. "Adam!" Jinaari yelled. "I need more light!"

The opening was bathed in bright white light. The spider let loose a high-pitched scream and staggered back, trying to hide from Adam's spell.

It was replaced by a giant scorpion. Riding on its back was a Fallen woman. Jinaari stared at her. She could have been Thia's twin in another life. He glanced over his shoulder. Thia backed up against the cavern wall, her eyes wide in fear. Pan stood in front of her with his staff at the ready.

Turning his attention back to the woman, he whispered, "Try not to kill her. I want to ask some questions."

Alesso nodded. "I'll try, but I'm not pulling blows."

"This doesn't have to end in death, Thia," the woman called out. "Surrender to me, sister. Accept your fate and they will live."

Jinaari charged at the woman, slashing at the scorpion's claw when he got close enough. Alesso darted past him, driving his sword into the creature's head.

The woman leaped from its back, a short sword appearing in her hand. She smiled coldly at Jinaari. "Let's dance, shall we?"

Stepping forward, he swung at her, but she deftly dodged the blow. The scorpion's corpse blocked the entrance, and he sidestepped one of the legs. She was good. But he was better.

Jinaari caught her gaze shift behind him, but he refused to look. She smiled, tumbling away from him. That's when he heard Thia scream.

"Adam!" he bellowed.

"Damn thing has Thia!"

The Fallen woman was out of his reach, retreating. "Alesso!" he commanded, "Get her! Bring her back here!" As the other man moved after the woman, he turned around.

A spider sat high on the wall, peppered with arrows. Dangling about ten feet off the ground, Thia struggled against the cocoon of webbing. Pan and Adam stood underneath her. "Aim for the web!" Adam screamed at Caelynn.

Jinaari ran underneath Thia. "I'll catch her. Blast the damn thing!"

The warlock took a step back and raised his staff. A beam of red light shot from the tip, igniting the webbing. Thia began to fall, screaming hysterically, and Jinaari caught her. Glancing up, he saw the spider's corpse begin to break away from the ceiling. Without thinking, he tossed Thia to the ground and shielded her with his body. The creature landed with a sickening thud on top of the tent. Rising, he looked at Pan. "Help me get her free." With the younger man's help, they got her on her feet, facing him. "Thia, it's okay. We'll have you out in a minute."

She nodded, gasping for air. "I'm sorry," she stammered through her tears.

"You didn't do anything wrong," he replied as he cut at the strands. "Caelynn! Adam! Go help Alesso. I want that witch back here to answer questions."

"I've almost got through," Pan said calmly. "If you need to go help."

He looked at Thia, "I'm not leaving until you're free."

They kept sawing at the thick strands, gradually freeing her from them. As the last pieces fell away, Pan grabbed her by her arms and led her toward a large boulder.

Jinaari turned around. Adam, Caelynn, and Alesso walked back in. "She climbed on the large spider," Alesso said, "had it climb up a tunnel in the roof of the hallway. We lost her."

"Damn," he swore. He glanced at Adam, who nodded once, confirming Alesso's story. He looked over; the tent was crushed underneath the shriveled corpse. "Save the canvas, we can use that. Get the gear out, and break camp. We have to move fast, before she brings back reinforcements."

"I can help," Thia said, her voice shaky. She leaned past him, her eyes growing wide when she saw the carnage. "My box..." she whispered.

He blocked her view. "I'm sure it's fine. Caelynn or Adam will find it. You need to eat. Here," he grabbed his pack and pulled out some cheese.

"I'm fine."

"Eat," he told her, shoving the food into her hands. "You're about as stubborn as you claim I am arrogant."

"But you are arrogant. Insufferable. Demanding." She smiled.

"That makes you stubborn, annoying, and difficult. You're not going to win this fight. Eat."

She pulled a small corner off and ate it. "I shouldn't have reacted like that."

He leaned against the rock near her. "Why not? You weren't expecting to have a giant spider spit webbing at you. It's going to scare most people." He paused. "Your reaction was normal. Don't obsess over it."

"Do you know who she was?" her voice was barely above a whisper.

Jinaari shook his head. "No. She knew who you were, though. That's why I wanted to talk to her, get some answers."

"Maybe," she drew a deep breath, and he heard her voice shake. "Maybe I should've done what she said. I don't want any of you to die because of me."

"It's not happening, Thia. We knew the risks coming down here. Lolc Aon can't have you. Don't even think that way again."

Caelynn came over, Thia's belt in her hand. "Thought you'd like this," she said as she handed it to her.

"Thank you," she said. Jinaari saw her hands shake slightly as she found the leather wrapped box.

"Everything okay?"

She nodded, rewrapping it and putting it back in the pouch. "Yes. It's fine."

"I wasn't talking about the box."

She let out a long breath. "I don't think things are going

to be completely okay down here. But I'm calmer now, if that's what you mean."

"Good. Because I want to put some distance between us and that witch before she comes back." He walked over to his pack, shouldering it, and waited for everyone else to do the same. He'd expected an attack. *It's been too easy*, he thought. *Either they didn't know we were coming this way, or they were making sure we got through. They know now. The question is if they keep letting us come.*

CHAPTER
TWENTY-ONE

"It's not working, Adam," Thia said, exasperated. "I can't see what you're describing." Frustration built up in her. For the last hour, as they walked, he'd been trying to talk her through a basic exercise; something she could build off to stay calm whenever fear threatened to overtake her. "I have to close my eyes, but then I'm going to trip."

"We don't want that," he said. "What about your box?"

She looked at him. "My box? What about it?"

"Without unwrapping it, I want you to describe it to me."

"It's a rectangle. Small enough to rest in the palm of my hand. Tall enough that my fingers won't hide it when I'm holding it. The interior is steel. The compartments are lined with gold colored velvet. The outside is covered with an intricate gold filigree pattern of oak leaves and vines. Hidden within the pattern are three acorns, in copper, that are attuned to my touch."

"You can see it clearly, as we walk. The image is in your mind, yes?"

She nodded.

"Then use that as your focal point. Ignore everything else I've told you. Just see your box in your mind. Do you have it?'

A small sense of calm came over her. "Yes."

"Great. How do you feel?"

"Calm. I used to feel sad. I put it away for years, refusing to unwrap it. I only saw his death when I looked at it. Now, though, it reminds me of how much he loved me."

"This is the start of controlling fear, Thia. Finding something, anything, that you can picture in your mind that calms you down. What would he tell you when you were a child and got scared?"

"That, no matter what, he would protect me. Be there to chase away the nightmares. If not him, then Keroys. That I may feel lonely and sad, but I'd never truly be alone or abandoned." The constant fear she'd felt since they left Almair lessened enough that she felt her body relax a little.

"Whenever you start to feel anxious or afraid, try to bring the image into your mind. Things are going to get harder. You know this."

She nodded. The one Fallen had escaped, and who knew how many she'd bring back with her.

Adam continued, "You're stronger than you know, Thia. Jinaari and I both see it. Pretty sure Caelynn and Pan do as well. Your spell work doesn't make you exhausted any more, not like it did when we first met. You got used to that. You'll get used to the monsters, too."

"What did I do?" Pan interrupted them.

"I was telling Thia you think she's stronger than she knows. That's all."

"Oh, yeah. Totally!" he pushed his way between the two of them. Thia looked at Adam, who shrugged and stepped back. "I mean, you're a Daughter of Keroys! You can do magic that most of us can't imagine, let alone do!"

"Not yet, Pan. I haven't unlocked it."

He stared at her. "Why not?"

"I don't know," she said. "Keroys said I had to both reject one life and accept another. Until I understand what he meant by that, I can't begin to tap into what he gave me."

"Oh, that sucks. Guess we'll have to figure it out then. Do you think it has something to do with your mother? Wasn't she Fallen? Because you told me your dad was human, and you're only half human, so that means she had to be Fallen, right?" He kept talking, barely taking a breath between thoughts. "Maybe you have to reject the life she wants you to have, down in Byd Cudd. But you've lived your entire life on the surface, so haven't you already rejected that life?" He took a deep breath. "And what was that about a box? Was that something your father bought you? Can I see it?"

"Sure." She reached into her pouch, pulling it out as they walked. "He didn't buy it for me, though. He made it. He used to make them all the time, I guess. This was the last one he ever made." Unwrapping the leather that covered it, she held it out for him to see. "There's three copper acorns—"

"Hidden in the design. Each box was made with the acorns in different places, and only the owner could open it." The young man's face lit up. "Was his name Bran?"

Thia nodded. "Yes. Why?"

"What was his surname?"

"Tannersson. I figure his father's name was Tanner. That was the way things were in our village. Why?"

"I had an uncle named Bran who was an artisan. He

made boxes like that." He pointed to the one Thia held. "Mother has one, as do several others in my family. He left Cirrain, went to Almair. No one knows what happened to him after that. It was like he disappeared from the world. What happened to your father?"

"Fifteen years ago, Drogon came to the house, wanted him to make a box. But Papa refused, so he turned the village against us. Against me. Father Philip saved me and took me to the cloister in Almair." She rewrapped the box and put it away.

"Thia!" Pan practically screamed as he threw his arms around her. "My grandfather's name was Tanner. My uncle Bran was your father! When we finish this, I'll take you home so you can meet my family. Your family. We're cousins, Thia! Cousins!"

She blinked, trying to not let the young man's enthusiasm knock her off her feet. "I guess we are, if Papa really was your uncle."

"It all fits, Thia! Of course, he was my uncle! The boxes, his disappearance, it all makes sense! Mother is going to be so thrilled to meet you! Everyone will. You'll love Cirrain! Everyone but me follows Keroys, so you'll fit right in. I'm sure of it!" he practically danced with excitement.

Thia looked ahead and saw Jinaari watching them closely. "Pan, I think Jinaari needs me for something. Can you stay back here with Adam? Make sure Alesso doesn't get close enough to hear?"

His face grew serious. "I don't like him, Cousin. He stares at you too much. Don't worry. I'll talk to Adam; tell him we have to keep him away from you." Pan left her side and headed back toward the warlock. Breathing a sigh of relief, she walked toward the paladin.

"What was that all about?" he asked.

She shook her head, still trying to understand what happened. "I'm not certain, but Pan's convinced we're cousins. He says he had an uncle named Bran who made boxes like mine. He swears he's going to take me to his home when this is over."

"Do you believe him?"

"It makes more sense than other things in my life. Like Papa having a child with a Fallen woman. Being Marked by Keroys, hunted by Lolc Aon. In all honesty, being related to Pan is the least strange coincidence I've encountered since I met you." She looked around, "Where's Caelynn?"

"Scouting. I heard something up ahead. If we're walking into a fight, I'd like to know numbers ahead of time. How are things with you? Has Adam been helping you?"

"Better. We finally found something I could easily imagine and keep my eyes open at the same time." She paused, spotting Caelynn as she crept back toward them.

"Five Fallen, including the one that looks like Thia. They look like they're trying to pick their terrain for an ambush." She pushed back the hood on her jacket as she spoke.

"Any creatures with them?" Jinaari asked.

"No," she said, shaking her head. "They all look like warriors, too. No casters."

Alesso appeared at Thia's side. "I know you wanted me to stay quiet, but I have to ask. The area ahead of us, was part of it built instead of natural? And was there a blocked archway with three runes carved into the keystone?" His voice was insistent.

Thia looked at the other two, confused. Jinaari nodded at Caelynn, and she said, "On the other side of the room. I didn't get close enough to see the keystone, though. Why?"

The brown-haired paladin turned to Thia. "Priestess, I've tried to follow your instructions. On this, though, I cannot keep silent. Ashynn told me about a series of conduits down here that led directly to Lolc Aon's sanctuary. She built them as a way for the Barren to move about unseen, but even they don't know where every passage is. Ashynn's mistress told her about the network, how to recognize an entrance." He turned toward Jinaari. "If I'm right, we could get to her without the city knowing we're there. Would you rather fight just the Scorpion Queen or her and fifty thousand Fallen?"

She waited, trying to read Jinaari's face. *It sounds like a good plan, but I'm not a tactician.* "What do you think?"

"Why wait until now to tell us, Potiri? You could've said something a week ago." Jinaari crossed his arms, waiting.

"I wasn't sure we'd find one, honestly. And I trusted that you had a plan," he pointed at Jinaari, "that wouldn't get the priestess or the rest of us killed. She's having enough trouble simply being down here. Doesn't it make sense to get in faster? Get this done so we can take her back to the surface where she belongs? Use your head, Althir. Stop thinking you've got all the answers and listen for a damn change!"

"Thia? What do you think?" Jinaari turned to her.

She knew why he asked. Alesso wouldn't accept a decision unless it came from her. "The way you planned to go," she paused, "how long will it take? What's the chance of us being found?"

"It'd take longer if what he says is correct. And we'd be fighting our way there. It'd get us to the city walls, but not guarantee a way inside."

"If this is shorter, and the risk is less, I say we try it." Her voice was steady, though her stomach churned.

Jinaari nodded. "Then we go. First, though, we have to get past the patrol. Alesso, you and Caelynn are up front with me. Thia, you know what to do. Let's try and keep the one witch alive. If she's a relation, she'd likely to have information we need."

Alesso moved past her, whispering with Caelynn. "Jinaari?"

"What?" he asked as he put his helm on.

"I have an idea."

"I'm listening."

"Why not use me?" She held up a hand as he started to shake his head. "Hear me out. Send me out there, alone. The rest of you get into position. They're not going to hurt me. Lolc Aon wants me alive. It gives the five of you the advantage. They'll be distracted by me, not see you coming until it's too late."

"No," he told her emphatically. "You're not going to be bait. Ever. My job is to protect you, Thia. Not hand you over."

"You're not handing me over," she protested. "I'm a distraction, nothing more."

"Let's follow this out, then. You go out there, the first thing they'll do is disarm you. They'll find a way to restrain your hands, gag you, so you can't cast spells. They know what you're capable of, Thia. Even if this worked, which it won't, all it takes is for one of them to drag you away and you're screwed. When we caught up to you, your captor would threaten your life to get us to back down. We need you to fight with us, Thia. I need to know you're there, doing what you do. Your safety is my priority. I am not risking it."

Frustration rose in her. "Right now, I'm a liability. You've got to watch where I'm at while fighting. Doesn't it make more sense to turn that around? Make me an advantage instead?"

He shook his head. "You being near Adam and Pan is an advantage, Thia. I know where you are and trust you're safe. I also know I'm not going to die. You won't let me. You're too damn stubborn." His hand reached for the sword at his hip. "This discussion's over. I don't want you to even think about it again. Got it?"

She nodded, giving up for now, and watched as he drew his weapon before following Caelynn and Alesso. *If that's what needs to happen*, she thought, *it's going to happen. I just won't tell you ahead of time.*

Adam came up beside her. Shouting came from the passageway ahead of them and the clang of metal against metal. "Sounds like they started without us. That's rude."

"Let's go," she said. Jinaari was right about one thing. She wasn't about to let him die.

When she rounded the corner, the fight was in full swing. Two Fallen lay on the ground; blood staining the dirt beneath their bodies. Both paladins were fighting separate foes, and Caelynn alternated between them. "Adam!" Thia screamed, pointing at the woman that looked like her. She had stepped back and looked like she was ready to run.

"Oh, no you don't!" Pan said as he slammed the butt of his quarterstaff against the floor of the cavern. Thick roots erupted from the ground around her, winding around her legs and arms.

Thia drew a sigil, making sure the three in the thick of battle stayed healthy. The next thing she knew, her sight was restricted by a latticework of webbing.

"That's my cousin, bitch!" Pan roared.

Focus on the box! The panic began to subside, her hand sought out one of the daggers Jinaari had given her. The sticky fibers surrounded her but didn't touch her. It would take time, but she could cut her way out.

Why not burn them? She drew a deep breath, moved her hand off the weapon, and concentrated on drawing the sigil. A spark flew from her hands, igniting the threads. Sweat formed on her brow from the heat as the fire spread around her, hungrily devouring the cage. As the smoke cleared, she saw Jinaari and Alesso standing over the body of the Fallen woman who called her sister.

"Thia?" Jinaari called out. "Are you okay?"

"I'm fine," she said, pulling a bit of charred webbing off her sleeve. "What happened?"

Jinaari glared at Alesso. "I'm not sure yet." He inclined his head toward a wall, and Thia strode that way. Whatever he wanted to say, he didn't want the rest to hear. "Get something to eat," he told her as he approached. "They'll be busy for a while. I've never seen you burn things before. Is that something new?"

She dropped her pack and sat down next to it. Flipping open the top, she found some food. "It came to me, while I was surrounded by the webbing. That stuff's flammable. It was going to be faster to burn it away than cut through it. The words were a simple enough cantrip, but I changed something on the sigil. I don't know where the idea came from, but it worked." She munched on a bit of jerky. "What happened with her?"

"I'm not sure. Pan restrained her, kept her from running while we finished off the rest. He said the spell shouldn't have hurt her, and none of the vines were wrapped around places that would've killed her. Once we were done, though, she was gone." He sat down next to her. "You two could've been twins in a lot of ways. Aust said you had a sister with the same eye color. Think that was her?"

Thia shrugged. "Maybe. I'm not overly interested in finding out. Family down here means something different than it does on the surface. If Pan's right and we are cousins, I hope it's not as cutthroat." She smiled. "If they're anything like him, it'll be less death and more drinking. If we come out of this, I'd like to meet them."

"What is this 'if' stuff? We're going to take down Lolc Aon, and Herasta if she's nearby, and keep you safe. There's no 'if'. It's going to happen."

Jinaari's confidence was rooted in his arrogance, but it helped balance out her despair. "I'm not running off or anything like that if that's what you're thinking. I mean, yeah, the thought has crossed my mind a time or two. I thought it would keep all of you safer. But I also know you'd hunt me down. And Alesso wouldn't let me go, either."

"Why the hell would you even think that?" he demanded.

"Lolc Aon is a Goddess, Jinaari. I don't want your death, or any of theirs," she waved toward the rest of the group, "on my hands. If we don't take her down, she will slaughter all of you. At that point, I won't be able to fight back. If I surrendered, maybe you'd all live and I could find a way to resist."

"What about now? Are you still thinking that way?"

"No," she said. "I know it won't matter. Even if I agreed, she'd kill you while I watched. Or command me to do it. This sounds corny, but Pan's enthusiasm at us being cousins reminded me I've got a human side. That I'm not just half Fallen, susceptible to the darkness it implies. Papa believed I was good, as did Father Philip. Keroys put his Mark on me when I was born." She looked at him, smiling. "That has to mean something in me is good, right?"

Jinaari nodded. "It does indeed." He pointed at the rest

of the group. "Looks like they're done rummaging through pockets and packs. Alesso was right. The keystone does have runes on it." He rose and held out a hand to help her up. Once she stood in front of him, his face grew serious. "You trust me, right?"

"Yeah, I do."

"I know that's not easy for you to do. But none of us are going to hand you over without a fight."

"Not even Alesso?" she whispered.

"Not unless he wants to get my sword in his gut."

CHAPTER
TWENTY-TWO

"Well?" Jinaari said. "How do we open it?"

Thia watched as Alesso ran his hand over the archway. "Give me a minute," he growled. "Ashynn never went through one. She couldn't tell me everything about them, but I don't think it should be hard to figure out."

She shot a look at Jinaari. *Maybe we shouldn't go this way after all*, she thought. His face was calm, reassuring. *Even if this isn't the right way, he'll find a way.*

"Found it!" Alesso exclaimed, pushing against a brick in the archway. Instinctively, she stepped back. The pit trap seemed a lifetime ago, but the memory remained vivid.

The sound of long unused gears grinding against each other rumbled through the chamber. Thia glanced around nervously, noticing that Jinaari's hand went to his sword hilt. The solid rock wall behind the archway moved aside and she gasped.

The huge, translucent white exoskeleton of a giant scorpion sat about fifty feet ahead. Some other substance filled the gaps between the bones, making it into a tunnel. A thick band of what looked like webbing stretched between the archway and the entrance. The path was less than three feet wide and covered with a layer of dust.

"The conduits are made of calcified scorpion skeletons, with some webbing mixed in to make it easier to travel between them," Alesso said, looking back at her. "There's usually a room at the halfway point, where the Barren could rest if they needed to. But each one leads directly to Lolc Aon."

"You're the only one that knows the way," she said, trying desperately to keep her voice even. "You'll take lead position." Glancing at Jinaari, she saw him nod in agreement.

"I didn't say I knew the way," he began to protest.

"You knew about the conduit to begin with, said it was faster based on your information. You get us there, Jinaari will do what he does best, and then we'll get out. Got it?" she stared at him.

Alesso inclined his head slightly. "As you wish, priestess." Without another word, he turned and started to walk across the narrow bridge.

"You're next," Jinaari said from behind her. "I'll be right behind you, just in case."

"Just in case what?"

He looked past her at the inky darkness that surrounded the path ahead. "I caught you the last time you fell. I'll do it again." He paused. "Don't look down. I know you see better than I do. Neither of us wants to know how far it is. Just keep your eyes on the path, take your time. We're not in a hurry."

Thia took a deep breath and examined the path. Alesso's feet left distinct prints in the dust and dirt that covered it. "One step at a time," she said under her breath.

"No need to rush." Glancing up, she saw Alesso on the other side, leaning against the wall of the tunnel. The pointed end of the tail was suspended above his head. She focused her gaze on his chest. The armor had been repaired; a circle of copper marked where the strike had been.

I kept him alive. He owes me his life, and he knows it. That should mean he's not leading us into a trap. I hope. Then again, she'd only known two paladins of Garret in her life. One was in front of her, and the other behind her. She trusted Jinaari but couldn't shake the feeling that Alesso had other reasons for being here than what he'd told them.

They may have taken the same vow of service, but Thia suspected it meant more to Jinaari than it did Alesso.

She took her time. The sound of dirt crunching beneath her boots echoed slightly. The only other sound was the rest of the group following behind her. As she approached the other side, Alesso held his hand out to help her. "I got it," she said, moving quickly to stand just inside the exoskeleton. Jinaari nodded at her once, then turned around. She watched as Adam and Caelynn made it across and stood near her.

"Pan? What are you doing?" Jinaari asked.

"We gotta close it, right? I mean, we don't want them to follow us. That wouldn't be good." As he spoke, his hands ran across the archway on this side. "I'm thinking it's in the same area as the trigger on the other side. That's where I'd put it, anyway. Because then you don't have to have a second set of gears or anything."

"Adam," Jinaari's voice was barely above a whisper.

"Yeah?" Adam asked.

"Be ready to grab him, just in case."

Alesso snorted, "It's not going to collapse, Althir. Use

your head. If it did, the Barren would be potentially killing themselves. Those witches are smarter than that."

The dark-haired paladin didn't look at him. "It's too convenient, Potiri."

"What part?"

"All of it."

"Found it!" Pan called out. The grinding resumed and the entrance sealed itself. "I'll remember where it is, don't worry," he said as he ran across the pathway toward them. "Then we can get back out faster. And it makes a lot of noise! Did you hear the echo? We're going to know it if anyone comes at us from behind." He stopped, looking up at the scorpion's tail. "That looks pretty sharp. Do you think it's still poisonous?"

Thia shook her head. "I don't recommend trying to find out."

He smiled at her. "You'd keep me from dying, Cousin! I know it!" He walked into the area. "This is cool! It's like being in one of them but not where it's going to hurt!"

Thia bit her lip. The whole idea made her blood run cold. *I'm wanted by the Scorpion Queen and here I am, walking through who knows how many dead creatures and heading straight for her. There's nothing about this that I can say is cool.* The fear built in her stomach again, tying it into knots. "Alesso, get moving," she said, her voice shaking slightly.

"As you wish, priestess," he nodded at her and began to walk through the carcass.

"Thia?" Jinaari asked.

"What?"

"How are things with you? You don't look good."

"I'm walking through a calcified skeleton of Lolc Aon's favorite creature, heading toward her lair, which is exactly where she wants me. I'm terrified," she admitted.

Remembering what Adam taught her, she pictured her box in her mind and felt the anxiety fade. "But I can control it."

"Good. It looks like he was right about one thing. This passage hasn't been used in quite some time," he raised his hand and brushed aside a cobweb that dangled from the ceiling. "For now, that's a good thing."

"For now?"

Jinaari shrugged. "Things can change quickly down here. You know this. Just because it looks abandoned doesn't mean it'll stay that way. Remind me when we stop tonight, I'll teach you a few more moves with your daggers. Something tells me the odds of encountering others will increase as we get closer."

Thia nodded toward Alesso's back. "He said the Barren used them. I'm no match for a trained assassin. I can barely draw my blades without cutting myself."

"The two most dangerous fighters are the ones that are highly trained and the ones that have almost no training. Because you can't predict what either will do. The goal isn't for you to join a fight, Thia. The goal is for you to be able to defend yourself if someone slips past us somehow."

She nodded. "I know. You don't have to remind me all the time."

"It's just that you're so stubborn," he said, "that I'm not always sure you understand the importance of what I'm teaching you."

She opened her mouth, ready to argue with him, when she caught the small smile on his face. "Well," she replied, changing her mind, "if my teacher wasn't so arrogant..."

He laughed and she joined in. Alesso turned around, staring at her. Thia glared back. "I don't trust him, Jinaari." She kept her voice low. "I know there's no basis for it, but every time I see him, I think there's some other reason why he's here. One he hasn't told us."

"We've been over this, Thia," he chided her.

"I know. It's just . . ." she couldn't find the words. "I don't want to wake up and find out that he let the Fallen slaughter all of you or anything like that."

"We take our oaths very seriously within the Order. If he ever broke a vow or went against the one he swore to Garret, the consequences would be worse than you could imagine. He may have secrets, but he won't go against his oaths. The cost would be too huge."

"Have you ever known a paladin that broke that oath?"

"No," he answered. "We're taught about the few that have, as a lesson in what happens to those that do. It's been over a century since the last one did."

She let out a whistle. "That bad?"

"Worse, actually. It's not the banishment from the Order that's the messy part. They betrayed the trust we have in them as a brother. The oath breaker may leave the chapterhouse alive, but that never lasts long. We take it on ourselves to make sure they don't get the chance to make, or break, another oath. I don't think you want the details, do you?"

"No. I can't say there's been anyone within the church that I know of who was that bad. We have those who don't have an aptitude for magic or healing. Those who can barely summon enough energy to light a candle. They end up as bureaucrats someplace, secretaries or caretakers of relics. Those who can do the basic spells but don't have much personality end up in small churches in outlying villages. Someplace where they won't have a big congregation to look over, and the people will be happy just to have someone local. It's up to Keroys, ultimately, where a priest or priestess goes or what job they perform." She shrugged. "That's how I ended up with you guys, at least. He said I had to be here. And then there's the Mark, and that's a whole other mess to deal with."

"It's not a mess, Thia. It's there because Keroys saw potential in you to do his will. I know you're strong enough to do whatever it is he requires. It's not in you to shirk away from what's right or honorable."

"I hope you're right," she said.

"Of course, I'm right. I'm arrogant and insufferable, remember?"

CHAPTER
TWENTY-THREE

"Where are you going?"

Alesso paused and glanced at the pink haired bard. "I'm taking a piss. Would you prefer I do it in here and let you watch?"

Caelynn didn't move from where she sat near the opening, she just glared at him. He didn't bother to explain any further. Walking through the narrow opening, he headed down the corridor a short way. Not so far that Caelynn would be concerned, but far enough that he wouldn't be heard.

She doesn't trust me. None of them do. That Althir won't give me a slot on the watch schedule where I'm alone is a slap in the face. We're supposed to be brothers, yet what sort of trust has he ever shown me? None. He had a seat at the high table while I scrubbed floors! His mind drifted to Thia. *What's so special about the priestess, anyway? They all treat her like she's made of glass. She's a half-Fallen witch! She may pray to Keroys, but there's no way he'd give her the stores to cast the spells she does. She's a creature of Lolc Aon, through and through. There's nothing about her that's even remotely human.*

"You're late," a voice whispered behind his ear.

Turning, he met the Fallen woman's gaze. "It took longer to get to the archway than your note said it would. Some Fallen witch kept attacking us."

"It doesn't matter." The woman's stark white hair was cut short. "They're asleep?"

"All but one," he replied. "She's near the entrance. You should be able to knock her out without much fuss." He stared at her. "Nothing lethal, that was the agreement. On any of them."

"None will be harmed. They'll go into a deep sleep, and we'll liberate Herasta's daughter. If they choose to pursue us after they wake, I cannot promise what Lolc Aon will do to them."

"My payment?"

She stepped aside, revealing an older woman in a dirty dress. A chain around her waist led to the wrist of another Fallen. The slave raised her head, and his heart skipped a beat. "We are many things, paladin. Liars or oath breakers are not among them."

Ignoring the dig, he looked away from his mother and back to the Barren leader. "Give me her chain. You know where they're at."

"Not yet." The woman snapped her fingers, and several Fallen walked past him, carrying a wooden coffin. "When we have Lolc Aon's prize, your mother will be given over to you. And we will send you both someplace safe. Until that happens, the deal is not complete."

Nervously, he kept his eyes on his mother and tried to ignore the feeling he had about this being wrong. *I made a vow to free my family before I made any to Garret or my brother paladins. She's a witch, same as the rest of the Fallen, and has no business in the human world.*

He heard someone fall over. Caelynn? He pushed the guilt aside. This was what he needed to do to fulfill the promise he made to himself. For thirteen years, he'd held to it. No matter the cost, he would rescue his family.

Ashynn told him about their mother and how the Barren would trade her once he led Thia and the rest to the conduit. And how their father had died less than six months into their captivity. It was the one chance he'd had to gain her freedom. Althir would be pissed, yes. But he would be tied up down here, trying to rescue someone who probably wouldn't want to leave.

The calcified walls that created the chamber where they had camped turned a sickly dark purple. From the haze, the Fallen emerged with Thia's naked body and placed it in the coffin. Once sealed, they walked past him. The last one emerged, holding his pack and helm, and tossed them at him.

"She's all yours," the leader told him, handing over the bracelet that led to his mother. Something about the woman's cold smile chilled him. The moment he grasped the chain, the world around them spun violently.

"Alesso?" he heard his mother cry, confusion and fear in her voice.

The kaleidoscope of color and shapes subsided, and he blinked. They stood in the central courtyard of the chapterhouse in Dragonspire. He smiled. "It's fine, Mother," he reassured her. Placing his pack and helm on the ground, he embraced her. "We're safe now. See the men running toward us? They're my brothers in arms. There's a blacksmith here that can get you out of the chain."

Turning, he raised a hand in greeting as the commander strode their way. He said, "Drakkus, it's me."

"I know who it is," he growled. "Timon," he turned his

attention to the young boy next to him, "take Lady Potiri to Henry, ask him nicely to help free her. Words need to be said that she shouldn't hear."

Alesso blinked in confusion as the page led his mother away. "Drakkus, I don't understand..."

The fist came out of nowhere, connecting hard against his jaw and almost knocking him to the ground. "You're lucky that's all I was allowed to do. Someone else claimed the right to punish you for this."

The bitter iron taste of blood filled his mouth and he spat onto the ground. "I haven't done anything wrong, Drakkus. Who thinks I did?"

"That would be me, Potiri!" A deep voice rang through the courtyard.

A chill ran down his spine. The ring of armored knights surrounding him parted, and Garret walked toward him. Alesso dropped to his knee. "My Lord," he breathed. "How may I be of service?"

The polished boots stopped in front of him. "Stand up."

Rising, he kept his eyes off his God.

"If there is one thing I cannot abide, it's an oath breaker." The God stepped back, raising his voice. "When you enter my service, you give your word to serve me in all things. Who can recite these words to me?"

As one, the paladins surrounding him answered: "From this day onward, we are not just men. We are paladins of Garret. We follow his laws. We protect those who need it without hesitation. We draw our sword in need, not anger. We do not attack those who cannot defend themselves. Our lives are no longer our own, but his to command."

"Do you remember swearing this oath to me, Potiri?"

"Yes," he replied, "and I have kept to it."

"You lie to my FACE!" the God roared in anger. "I spoke

with your sister. I know where you were, and what you intended to do. That your mother is here is proof you carried through on it." He turned, gesturing toward Alesso. "Strip him of his sword and armor," he commanded.

Several paladins came forward. Alesso stood, stunned, as they began to unbuckle each piece. The sound of them clanging against each other as they were tossed into a single pile echoed through the courtyard.

"My paladins, he has turned over someone to the Fallen. A woman who has done him no harm. Indeed, she saved his life. And not just any woman. Thia Bransdottir is the Daughter of Keroys, Marked by him for a purpose. He has traded her life, handed over the power she possesses, to one who would twist it to something beyond evil. Something you will have to fight, and probably die, to protect Avoch from. This man who claimed to be your *brother* has sacrificed not just her body, but her soul. Sacrificed your lives. And for what? To bring his mother back from her enslavement.

"I'm not saying this is not a noble thing. But I told him, when I sent him to aid Thia before, that I would speak with my sister about his family. I would work to free them from Byd Cudd. He could not wait for me to fulfill my promise. In his impatience," Garret thrust a finger at Alesso, "he has given Lolc Aon the one thing she needs to return to your world and enslave everyone you know. He has traded the life of a woman he swore to *protect*, offered up the lives of each of you, in the process."

Alesso stared at his God; his eyes wide. Thia was Marked? A Daughter of Keroys? "No one told me," he whispered.

Garret turned on him. "You didn't need to be told, Potiri! As a paladin, you swore an oath to protect the innocent, not turn them over to Lolc Aon. You promised to follow my laws. Is not one of those to keep yourself separate from Byd Cudd and my sister unless I direct you to do differently?"

"Yes."

"Did I not give my word, as a God, to see to the release of your family?"

"Yes, but—"

"Did you sell out Althir, as well? Or the others that travel with him?"

"No," he replied. "The Barren promised that the rest would not be harmed unless they chose to chase after them."

"You'd better hope he can find Thia before she gets handed over to Lolc Aon." Garret stared at him intently. "Give me your medallion."

Alesso's heart sank, "My Lord, please," he begged.

"Give. Me. Your. Medallion. Now."

Wordlessly, Alesso reached under his tunic and grasped the chain. Raising it over his head, he handed it over.

Garret took it and stepped back. Alesso drew back from the look in his God's eyes. With a quick movement, the medallion was snapped in half. Garret dropped both pieces onto the ground, driving them into the dirt with his heel. "Hear me, my warriors. From this point forward, the name of Alesso Potiri is to be marked as Foresworn within your ranks. He is no longer a paladin of mine. None may give him aid or quarter. His family shall be sheltered and protected so long as they wish it. Let this shame be his alone to bear. Now," he pointed toward the gate. "Get out of my house."

The heavy wooden doors swung open. As the ring of knights shifted to give him passage, they all turned their backs to him. Stunned, he grabbed his pack from the ground. The armor he once proudly wore sat in a heap; the hilt of his sword dug into the dirt from the weight. His exit led past the smithy, and he caught sight of Henry working on the chains that bound his mother. Without a word, the blacksmith put down his tools and turned his back to him. His mother followed suit.

Anger rose in him, and he straightened his back. *I won't give them the satisfaction of seeing weakness. If the witch was as important as Garret claimed, I would've been told. Althir has a part in this. It stinks of privilege!*

He left the chapterhouse, not even turning around as the gates swung shut behind him. He had some coin, but it wouldn't last long. *At least Ashynn and Mother will be fine*, he thought. *I'll get some gear, find a job. Plenty of caravans that need mercenaries.*

If Althir comes out of this, I'll finally be able to prove to him I'm the better swordsman. No rules to keep me from killing his arrogant ass now.

He adjusted his pack as he looked at the road around him. Ahead, a few small groups were heading into the city itself. His chances of being hired and evading any of his former brothers who would revel in beating him to a pulp, would be better if he had a sword. Resolutely, he headed toward the gates leading into Dragonspire.

Halfway there, he spotted the wagon lumbering his way. The driver hid beneath a hooded cloak. Alesso stepped off the path, giving way to the team. "You look lost, friend," a male voice said as he stopped the horses.

"Not lost," he replied. "Just between jobs. Where are you from? I don't recognize your accent."

"Many places," he replied. "You have the look of someone who knows how to use a sword."

Alesso inclined his head. "I've had some training, yes."

"My Master is in need of someone to protect him in that way. You would be given food, shelter, and have access to armor and weaponry that most would never dream of. And paid, of course."

"Keep going."

"He would also give you the chance to enact your revenge against Prince Jinaari Althir."

Alesso narrowed his eyes, trying to see the face of the driver. "Who is your Master, that he would know of such things?"

The man turned his head, and the hood slid down. Gray skin covered the emaciated, bald head. An unnatural green light ringed his blue eyes. *A wraith?* "My Master is Drogon. He is Forsaken and in need of a sword. Your options are limited, Alesso Potiri. Few would hire a disgraced paladin of Garret. Even less will once the reason why your God deemed you Foresworn becomes known. If you believe this is all due to Althir and the Fallen witch, then climb into the wagon. If not, keep walking. You'll be dead in less than a week; your corpse lying in a broken heap in some alley after your former brothers find you. Drogon does not make offers lightly, nor does he repeat them."

Withered hands reached up, replacing the hood to its place as the wraith turned his focus back to the road ahead. *Althir knew she was Marked. He had to.* Alesso added it to the list of slights he believed Jinaari had directed at him over the years. It was bad enough he had been deployed as a backup when the rest went after Drogon initially. To be able to gain experience at the hands of a Forsaken mage ... the next time he met Althir, there would be a reckoning.

Without hesitating, he walked around to the back of the wagon. Tossing his pack onto a small box, he climbed in. The wraith shook the reins and the wagon jolted forward.

CHAPTER
TWENTY-FOUR

The ache went beyond normal levels, worming into Jinaari's consciousness. Something wasn't right. His mouth was dry, and his head felt like it had been stuffed with straw.

Pushing himself up, he heard someone crying quietly. Concerned, his eyes snapped open as he reached for his sword. Caelynn knelt with her back to him. Her shoulders shook as she sobbed.

"Caelynn?" he asked. His voice was raspy. Something was definitely wrong.

She straightened her shoulders and he saw her hands move to her face. But she didn't turn around. "It's my fault," she whispered.

He rose, surprised at how his body swayed. What had happened? His feet dragged, but he forced himself to walk to her. "What are you talking abo—" he stopped and stared.

Thia's bedroll, with her armor and clothing laid out neatly on top, lay empty before him. Even the pouch that held her box was there. But Thia wasn't.

"I was on watch with Alesso," Caelynn's voice broke. "He left, said he had to piss. I didn't think anything of it. I heard footsteps. I thought he was coming back. And then this hit me," she nodded at her lap. Resting on her knees was a small dart. "I couldn't move. That's when the Fallen came in. They covered the ground with some sort of fog and headed for Thia. Two of them stripped her of everything. I tried, Jinaari, but I couldn't move, couldn't even scream. They tied her hands, put a gag across her mouth, and took her away. One stayed behind, arranging her clothing. The gas got thicker, and I fell asleep."

Rage rose inside him. He thought Alesso was capable of a number of things, but not this! "Did you see him before you passed out?" The gas would explain how he felt.

She shook her head. "No. I don't remember him coming back. But his pack's gone, so I doubt he stayed around."

No, he ran. Did whatever unholy trade he entered into and left like a coward. Jinaari took a deep breath. *Stay calm. That's what they need from me.* "This isn't on you, Caelynn," he said, placing a reassuring hand on her shoulder. "Alesso would've found a way to do this, no matter who was on watch. Get some water. That should help flush the drug out of our system. We'll wake up Adam and Pan, pack up the gear. One of us will have to carry Thia's."

"What do you mean? Where is she?" Pan asked.

Jinaari raised his head and looked at the young man. "She's gone. Fallen got her, thanks to Alesso."

The young man bolted out of his bedroll and started to charge toward the entrance. "Bring back my cousin!" he screamed.

Jinaari reached out one arm and caught him, preventing him from leaving. "That's not going to help her," he said, his voice low but even. "We must be smart about this. Pack her gear, then yours. They got a head start, but we'll find her."

Pan looked at him, tears in his eyes. "Promise?"

"Absolutely." He felt Pan relax, then move toward Thia's pallet. Looking past him, Jinaari saw Adam standing up. His friend nodded. "Caelynn?"

She wiped at the tears on her face. "I've got this. Go talk with him. Pan, help me out. Let's try to get her stuff put away neatly."

Jinaari stepped around the other bedrolls and walked to the back of the room. Adam stood there, leaning against a wall, watching.

"Alesso?" he asked when Jinaari was close enough.

Nodding, he leaned against the wall next to his friend. "It was planned, too. This conduit wasn't accidental. If there's as many down here as he claimed, we must've passed several before we got to this one."

"Any idea how long ago it happened?"

"I'm assuming they've got several hours head start. Depending on how much farther until we hit Lolc Aon's sanctuary—"

"If he didn't lie to us about that, you mean." Adam interrupted.

"I don't think so. They knew we were coming. We would've heard them if they were behind us. That door made too much noise, and we're not that far from it. That tells me they came from the direction we're heading. I'll have Caelynn check the hallway. She should be able to know which way they went."

"If you know that, why ask Caelynn to check?"

"She's feeling guilty because she was on watch with him. We're going to need to give both of them things to do that make them feel like they're helping, no matter how small. Otherwise, they'll be consumed by guilt and not think straight when we find her."

"What about you?"

Jinaari looked at him. "What do you mean? I know what I'm doing."

Adam shrugged. "I've done this with you for how many years now? I know when it's a job and when it's personal."

"Alesso's mine, if that's what you mean. He's broken the vow he made when he took up the mantle of being a paladin of Garret's. What justice he hasn't already handed out, I will."

"I don't mean him, Jinaari."

"Stop beating around the bush, Adam. If you have something to say to me, say it."

"I think this particular job is more personal for you. I've seen you guard people before, my friend. I think there's more to it when it comes to Thia, that's all."

Jinaari looked around the room. "You think too much."

Adam laughed. "As you've told me on many occasions. What's the plan, then?"

"Chase them down, rescue Thia before she gets handed over. If not, find out where in the lair she's being held. Get her out, take down Lolc Aon, and leave."

"What if she's been turned?"

Jinaari stared at him. "It's not happening. We won't let it happen. If we have to, we knock her out and hogtie her to get her back to the surface. I'm not leaving her down here." He pushed away from the wall and headed to his pallet. Kneeling down, he packed up. *Hang on, Thia. You're stronger than you think. We'll find you. Don't let her find whatever weakness you have. You can't turn away from Keroys. It's not going to happen.*

Working in silence, they gathered up their belongings.

He kept focused on the task at hand, refusing to dwell on what happened. *I can't change it. It happened. All I can do now is find her.* Standing, he wrapped his belt around his waist and positioned the scabbard on his hip. Sliding the blade home, he thought, *Thia's life comes first. Then Lolc Aon. If I can find Herasta, we'll dispatch her as well. I don't want her coming after Thia again. Once all of that's done and she's safe, I'm coming for you, Potiri.*

CHAPTER
TWENTY-FIVE

Thia took a sharp breath as the black veil fell away from her brain. She was being carried. No. She was in a box that was moving.

She took a few deep breaths, trying to calm the panic that rose within her. What had Adam and Jinaari told her? Stay calm, learn your surroundings, observe. Evaluate everything so you're ready to act if opportunity comes. Focus on what happened before to find clues on what's happening now.

Her mind was fuzzy, but she remembered making camp. *They'd gone into the conduit; Alesso was leading them. He found the room, recommended they stop and rest. My feet were sore, and Jinaari didn't know if they'd find another place to camp. Or how far they were from Lolc Aon's sanctuary. Resting there was perfect.*

Too perfect.

Her breath was warm as it bounced off the lid and back onto her face. There was barely any space around her. Was she in a coffin, already dead?

Focus! She took a deep breath, gathering her thoughts. *What happened next?*

She'd gone to sleep. She was exhausted and didn't stay up and talk with Jinaari like she normally did. She'd curled up under her blanket and fell asleep without a fuss.

And now she was in a box of some kind. Her teeth bit into cloth. They'd gagged her. *Great.*

She went to move her hands. Nope. They were bound. She could feel the thin, sticky rope as it cut into her wrists when she moved. No, not rope. It was strong, but thin.

Like spider silk. Damn it!

Breathe . . . just breathe. Focus on the box. Find my center like Adam taught me.

She shifted, trying to gauge how much room she had, and felt her bare back scrape against the rough wood.

Okay. So, I'm tied up, naked, and in a coffin. This is not good!

She clenched her teeth. If she was here, where was everyone else? *Keroys, let them be safe!*

The crate shifted, tilting her forward. She winced as her body slid slightly, the skin cutting against the abrasive surface. The board beneath her feet vibrated as it landed on something solid. Wherever they were taking her, they'd arrived.

Fear rose in her, but she forced it down. Whatever she saw next, she'd face it head-on. *Think of my box!*

The lid to her prison opened, and she blinked against the dim light. Ten or more Fallen, all armed, surrounded the crate. Two of them reached out and grabbed her upper arms. Thia tried to pull free, but they held on. Without a word, they forced her forward.

A woman stood in front of the rest, lilac eyes evaluating

her. Thia felt her heart race. *Same hair, same eyes. This has to be Herasta. I'll never call her anything else.* There was no denying the relationship. Grasping onto the last thread of courage she had, Thia stared back. She wore a dress that barely covered her body. The center of the fabric was cut away, framing the red scorpion's tail that was tattooed on her abdomen.

"Leave us, Herasta. I wish to get acquainted with your daughter," a voice behind her ordered. Obediently, the Fallen began to fade into the shadows. *Keroys, I need you*, Thia prayed, her mouth working the phrase around the gag, as she slammed her eyes shut. She didn't want to see what was coming. Adrenaline coursed through her veins. *I'm sorry*, she thought. The last shreds of calm she had fell away as terror gripped her soul.

"Welcome, Thia. Do you not wish to see me? I've waited so long to meet you." The voice was seductive, calm, yet carried a note of command.

Keroys, I need you.

"You're in my realm, child. My brother cannot hear your pleas." Thia cringed as she felt something stroke the skin on her back. It wasn't a human finger. "I can feel your body tremble. But I wonder. Is it me you fear? Or the darkness within yourself? Shall we find out?"

Thia felt the tears as they fell from her eyes but kept them closed. *This is just a dream,* she told herself. *I'll wake up, and everyone will be nearby. We'll go down the passage, find the lair, and execute Jinaari's plan. I'll be close enough to keep him alive, but far enough away to stay out of Lolc Aon's reach. That's what's going to happen. This is a dream, nothing more.*

She winced as a needle pierced her wrist. Ice cold liquid began to flow through her veins as sticky, wet fibers began to spool around her legs. A single whimper escaped her throat as any hope that she was dreaming left her. "There,

there, Thia," Lolc Aon crooned in her ear. The sound was anything but soothing. "It's time for you to choose which side you will embrace. Time to find out what life in my service can be like. I give you one final gift, to help you when you make your decision."

Thia felt something slide into her hands, but terror refused to loosen its grip enough for her to know what it was. As the webbing wound up her body, something pulled the gag from her mouth. Unable to control herself, a single wail of desperation tore from her throat. The last strands covered her head, silencing her cries, as the drugs took over her mind.

The feeling of being restrained fell away, but she wouldn't open her eyes. *It's a dream, an illusion. Whatever's out there isn't real. I'm in a cocoon, somewhere. Jinaari and Adam are coming. Just stay calm until they get here. That's all I have to do. Breathe, fight back, and stay alive. That's what I have to do.*

"Open your eyes, Thia."

Her eyes flew open at the command. Before her was a hallway. Doors lined each side. Beneath her bare feet, the floor was carpeted in a thick rug of some kind. "Where is this?" she breathed.

"We're in your mind, child." The voice came from behind her. Soft and seductive, it sent chills down her spine. "How am I to get to know my newest priestess if I don't know what lurks in her head? I want to know everything. Your hopes, dreams, fears." Fingers ran through her hair, pulling it loose from the pins. "Your deepest desires live here, behind those doors. Even the ones you won't admit to yourself. It's all there. Let's open one."

Thia shook her head. "No. I won't let you use me like that. You can't force your way into my mind."

"I won't have to, child. By the time you're done confronting what you've done, you'll welcome me."

The door to her left flew open and she was shoved through. She landed in a puddle of thick, warm liquid. As the light of the hallway illuminated the room, she looked at her hands. Blood dripped off her fingers and ran down her arms. Around her were thousands of bodies. They were all dead.

Twisting in the pool, her eyes grew wide in horror as she began to make out the faces.

Pan.

Adam.

Caelynn.

Jinnaari.

Her father.

Father Philip.

In unison, the eyes on the corpses flew open.

"They died trying to protect you, child." Lolc Aon taunted her from the doorway. "You could've prevented their deaths, and you know it, simply by becoming mine. Explain it to them. Explain to them why your life was more important than any of theirs."

The mouths on her friends' faces began to move. The word began as a whisper, steadily rising in volume. "Why?"

Thia pressed her blood-soaked hands to her ears and screamed as the door was shut, plunging the room into darkness.

How long she sat in the blood, listening to the screams of her friends, she didn't know. It could have been an hour. It could have been ten. Without warning, the voices stopped. Thia took a deep breath. Something wet fell on her bare shoulder. Glancing up, she dove into a ball as the torrent of water pelted her, pushing the breath out of her lungs as it washed over her. The drops stung as they hit, driving her to the floor as light began to reflect off the stone beneath her. The blood washed off her skin; deep red lines that ran out in every direction. The blood of her friends, her family, shed in a fruitless attempt to save her. *I'm sorry! I didn't want any of you to die!* The rivulets began to run clear, and the shower ended. Her soul, though, was drenched with guilt.

Nothing would wash that away. And she knew it.

"Get up," a woman commanded her. A towel was thrown down near her hand.

Thia sat up, grasping at the rough fabric, and covered herself. Herasta stared at her. "Thank you," she muttered.

Her mother snorted. "For what? A towel? I knew you'd be weak when you came out of me. I should've kept you or made sure you died. Bran did nothing but make you even softer."

Thia hung her head, the wet strands of her hair falling around her face. "Then kill me now," she whispered. "Please."

"I won't allow that, child," Lolc Aon said.

Thia kept her head down. Tears mixed with the water that dripped from her head. *Keroys*, she begged, *please. I need you now more than ever.*

"Look at me."

She couldn't resist the command. Raising her head, she looked the Scorpion Queen in the face. Dark red hair fell down her back while green eyes locked on Thia's lilac ones. Voluptuous, sensual, and terrifying all at the same time, the Goddess regarded her with cool indifference.

"There," she said, a thin smile spreading across her face, "isn't this better than hiding from me? I'm not much different from you, child. All that time you wasted, being afraid of an image that isn't who I really am."

The water on the floor in front of her began to swirl together, drawn into a small pool by unseen magic. "You know what that is, don't you, Thia?"

She looked down. "It's a scrying mirror," her voice cracked with exhaustion.

"You know, then, that it will show the truth of the past. Thia, child," Lolc Aon's tone softened, "you must see this. You deserve to know the truth of what my brother, and your paladin friend, truly want."

The surface of the water shimmered. A scene came into focus. A circular room, with a portal in the center. Jinaari was handing Keroys his sword.

She watched as the God she'd dedicated her life to drew a single finger across the blade. "I ask that you use this weapon to end her life." Keroys said as he held the weapon out to Jinaari, "Do this for me, please."

"Do you understand now, child? Keroys Marked you because he fears what you'll become if you don't have his hand controlling you. He gave you this power, yet you're stronger than even he imagined. Strong enough that he asked Jinaari to kill you."

Thia stared at the image. Something wasn't right. *It's a partial truth. Jinaari would never agree to this.* Shaking her head, she took a deep breath. "No. I don't believe you. There's more to it. I know there is." She waived her hand over the image. Jinaari's voice come up from the water.

"You can't mean that?" he stared at Keroys; his eyes wide. "Why would you ask that I murder someone who's totally devoted to you? That makes no sense!"

"Tell him, brother," Garret's deep voice came from behind him.

Thia looked up, staring the Goddess in the face. "You're lying. He didn't agree to do that. Garret's there, too. More was said than you want me to know." She swallowed, trying to control her heartbeat. *Either she'll kill me now or try something else. Jinaari believes I'm stronger than I know. So does Adam. I have to stay alive until they get here.*

The water evaporated into a mist. "You're stronger than I thought, child." The Goddess knelt in front of her, grabbing her by the chin and forcing her to look at her. The smile on her face was full of malice. Thia's blood ran cold as she took in the calculating look in Lolc Aon's eyes. "But not strong enough. Let's find out what you're truly afraid of admitting to yourself."

The room spun and Thia succumbed to the blackness that surrounded her.

CHAPTER
TWENTY-SIX

"Well?" Jinaari asked Caelynn as she rushed toward him.

"It's the sanctuary. It has to be." She paused, catching her breath. "It's a huge room, but not many ways in or out. This opens behind a rock, so we'll have cover."

"Did you see anyone?"

Nodding, Caelynn stared at him. "Too many." She knelt and started to draw a crude map into the dust on the conduit floor. "There's a throne here. Lolc Aon's on it."

"You're sure it's her?" Adam asked.

"No one else would dare," Jinaari said. "What else?"

"There's someone or something wrapped up in a cocoon at her feet. It was moving, so if that's Thia, she's still alive. In front of the dais, you've got nine priestesses. This one," she tapped the center X she'd made. "From a distance, she looked like Thia."

Adam cleared his throat. "It's probably Herasta. I'll take care of her."

Caelynn marked off another eighteen figures in the dirt.

"Nine slaves, all male, guarded by Fallen warriors. They look drugged. And they're naked."

Pan shook his head. "That's not good."

"Why not?" Jinaari looked at him.

"When Lolc Aon raises someone to the priesthood, the first thing she has them do to prove their loyalty is give birth, establish a bloodline. The men are there for Thia to pick from." He looked at the paladin. "Those men are innocent. If she does anything to them, it means Lolc Aon has turned her. Keroys doesn't make exceptions if you do harm to someone who's innocent. If that's my cousin in the cocoon, we have to stop her before that happens."

"We will, Pan. I didn't come all this way to lose her," Jinaari reassured him, then looked at each of them. "Adam, stick to the perimeter. Try to get rid of the priestesses and the guards. Focus on Herasta but keep an eye out. You may need to seal the other entrances so reinforcements can't come in. Caelynn, I'm going to need your help with Lolc Aon. Distract her so I can get close enough." He tapped the drawing that Caelynn called the cocoon. "If that's Thia, we get her free. Pan, that's on you. I don't care if you have to knock her out, wrap her in vines, or what. But it's on you to restrain her until we know she's herself."

A series of rhythmic drumbeats drifted through the corridor. They were measured, as if anticipating something.

Jinaari stood up and shrugged off his pack, tossing it at Adam. "This time, let's try not to leave them behind."

Drawing his sword, he nodded to each of them. This was what he came here to do. Adrenaline surged through his veins as his heart began to beat in time with the drums.

Moving forward, he flattened himself against the rock Caelynn mentioned and waited for them to take up similar positions before looking around it. She'd described it almost perfectly. The path to his prey was straight. There were just close to three dozen people between him and Lolc Aon.

Everyone in the room focused on the writhing mass of webbing at the Goddess' feet. The tip of a dagger pierced it from the inside. Whatever it was, it was coming out. Raising his hand, he signaled the rest to wait. If this was Thia, he wanted to see what she did before they attacked.

He recognized her hair first as she emerged from the cocoon. Thia's face was blank, focused on the woman he thought was Herasta.

Pan started to rush past him, but he held out an arm, stopping him. "It's Thia," he whispered.

"Yes, but I want to see what she does. She's not herself."

"How can you tell?"

"Watch how she walks. It's not straight. The blade in her hand keeps turning, too. She's fighting against something, Pan. Give her time to win the battle."

Jinaari turned his attention back to the scene in front of him. Thia walked up to Herasta. Even from this distance, he could see the anger on her face. Without warning, the dagger she carried flew across her mother's neck, slashing her throat. As the body fell, she tore open the woman's chest and pulled out her heart.

"Cousin?" Pan whispered. Jinaari could hear the pain in his voice.

"Not yet," he cautioned. *Keroys would forgive this. I have to believe it.*

Thia had turned and walked toward Lolc Aon, presenting her with the heart. The Goddess told her something, but Jinaari couldn't make it out. All he saw was Thia walking toward the prisoners.

"Now!" he whispered the command. Leaping out from

behind the rock, he charged forward. "Prepare to meet your brother's justice!"

Pan was screaming Thia's name. As Jinaari ran, he saw her look up at him. The blank look disappeared from her face. Dropping the dagger, she fell to her knees. Raising her arms with her palms up, she screamed.

A bright yellow light radiated out from her body. He watched as she threw her head back, the light growing in strength until she was nothing more than a shadowy outline within the center. The earth beneath him began to shake. Pieces of the ceiling fell as the floor buckled and rose and he fought to keep his balance. When her scream died off, he looked around. The Fallen were dead, the prisoners dazed. Lolc Aon sat on her throne, her face frozen in shock.

Loud explosions echoed through the chamber. Jinaari glanced over his shoulder. Bolts of concentrated energy flew from Adam's staff, freeing the slaves of their bonds. The warlock gestured to the group, herding them toward an exit as Pan ran toward Thia.

Jinaari sprinted across the uneven floor, launching himself at the stunned Goddess. As he went to drive his sword into her, she parried the blow.

"You cannot kill me. No weapon can," she sneered at him.

He locked eyes with her. "Not even one that's touched by two Gods?"

Her eyes widened in fear as he twisted around, slicing his blade across her abdomen. His next blow shattered her knee. The ground shook violently as the Goddess fell to the ground. With a rage filled scream, Jinaari plunged his sword into her chest. Twisting it, he watched as life left her eyes. It was done.

Breathing heavily, he kept his eyes on the corpse at his

feet. "Where's Thia?" he asked. More blasts from Adam erupted as he sealed off some of the entrances.

"Over here," Caelynn answered. Her voice wasn't right.

Jinaari pulled his weapon from Lolc Aon's body and looked to his right. Pan knelt next to Thia. She was naked, her knees pulled up to her chest, and covered in blood. Cursing, he ran over the debris that littered the floor. As he moved, he sheathed his sword. "Adam," he called out, "Give me your cloak!"

The warlock ran to him, handing it over. Kneeling in front of her, Jinaari draped the red fabric over Thia's body. Her face was pale. Her lilac eyes weren't focusing on anything. "Thia," he asked quietly, "are you hurt?"

She stared back at him but didn't answer.

"She's in shock," he looked up at Caelynn and Pan. "Do you know if any of the blood is hers?"

The elf shook her head. "I don't think so. I think it came from . . . well, you saw it. What she did." Caelynn thrust her chin toward the corpse closest to them. Cold, lifeless eyes the same color as Thia's stared at the ceiling. "I'll grab the packs," she said as she left.

Jinaari nodded. "How much time do we have?"

"The priesthood's going to be in shock right now. We've got an hour at most. There's no way we can make it back up the conduit before they come after us," Pan answered. He knelt next to Thia. "Is she okay?"

Jinaari said, "She will be. But we can't stay here." He raised his head, surveying the chamber. "The way we came is too wide. We need a defensible position, someplace where we can force them to fight us one on one while she recovers."

"I have a better idea," Adam said.

"Let's hear it."

"Get Thia, then everyone grab onto me," the warlock commanded.

Scooping Thia into his arms, Jinaari rose. "You sure you're up to this? I saw how much you used during the fight."

Adam looked at the paladin. "It's necessary."

Keeping a firm grip on Thia, he grabbed Adam's tunic. Caelynn and Pan, shouldering the packs, followed suit. Adam drove his staff into the flagstones at their feet, and the crystal at the tip glowed even brighter. The cavern swirled around them, changing into a blur of color. When his vision cleared, they stood in their private common room in the Green Frog Inn.

Adam crumpled to the floor. His staff lay in pieces around him. The crystal at the tip no longer pulsed with magic. Instead, fine lines spread across its surface.

"Pan!" Jinaari called out, still cradling Thia. She was breathing, but it was shallow. Her entire body shivered.

"I've got him," Pan answered. "Take care of her." He began to help Adam to his feet.

"Caelynn, get her door open." Jinaari strode through the opening as soon as he could. "Draw a bath and wash the blood off her. We won't know if she's hurt until that's done. Put some clean clothes on her after that. When you can, get her in bed with some extra blankets. She needs to stay warm." He lowered Thia into a chair, then turned her head so she'd look at him. He still couldn't tell if her mind was intact. "Thia, listen to me," he kept his voice low, "Caelynn is going to take care of you. I've got to check on Adam. You're safe now. We're back at the Green Frog. Do you understand me?"

Slowly, her head moved. Her eyes were vacant, though, and he wasn't certain she heard him.

"I'll be back. I promise." Gently, he wiped at a large drop of congealed blood on her forehead. It smeared across her skin. Rising, he turned to Caelynn. "Once we get Adam settled, when I know he's okay, I'll watch her. You and Pan need to get some food and rest. You've earned it."

"Is she going to be okay?" she asked.

He glanced back at Thia. "She's stronger than she knows," he said before leaving the room. Closing the door behind him, he leaned against the wall. The rest looked to him for reassurance, leadership. They needed him to say she would pull through to believe it themselves. *Damn you, Drakkus. You'd better have been right when you said hope was enough!*

The door to Adam's room was open. He could hear someone retching as he got closer. Looking in the room, he saw Pan helping Adam into his bed.

"You didn't have to do that, Adam," he said.

The warlock sighed. "Yeah, I did. We needed to get out of there and didn't have time to wait. How's Thia?"

Jinaari glanced across the common area to her door. "She'll pull through." *Garret, I hope I'm right about that.* "How about you?"

"I've got a splitting headache that's likely to last a day or three. We aren't planning on going anywhere for a while, are we?"

"No," Jinaari said, his voice heavy with exhaustion. "I'd say we've earned a few days' rest."

"Good. You owe me a new staff," Adam's voice dropped off, and he started to snore softly.

Pan gestured out of the room. Jinaari left and waited as Pan closed the door behind him. "Okay, so what's wrong with Thia? Don't lie to me. I know she's not fine."

"She's in shock. She's covered in Herasta's blood. And

what she did was savage. She let loose a barrage of magic that I've never seen her do before. I've seen her kill things, but not like that. I hope she'll be fine once she gets some sleep." He looked at the door that led downstairs. "I've got to get a message to someone. At the cloister here in town, there's a Father Philip."

"I know the name. Thia told me he was the one that saved her when the villagers killed her father."

"I want him to see her. He may be able to strengthen her ties to Keroys. She's going to need that connection while she resolves her actions in her soul."

"I'll get it sent, grab us some food from the kitchen until he arrives. Adam will be fine once he wakes up. You need to clean up."

Jinaari stared at him, confused.

Pan continued, "You've been in a fight, my friend. Wash up, take care of your armor. Thia's likely going to be asleep for hours. It won't help her mental state if the first thing she sees is you drenched in blood." He paused. "I don't think we should leave her alone until we know if she's really okay. Can Caelynn stay with her for a while?"

"Yeah. I'll relieve her when the priest arrives. I want to talk with him first, so he knows what happened." Jinaari walked to his room and entered, closing the door behind him. Pan was right. He had time to clean himself up, get some food.

An hour later, a knock on his door sounded. Putting aside the rag he was using to clean his armor, he rose and opened it. Pan and Father Philip stood there. The priest's clothing was rumpled, as if he'd dressed in a hurry.

"I came as soon as I got the message, Prince. Is it true? Were you able to defeat Lolc Aon?" the priest asked.

Nodding, he replied, "Yes."

"And Thia?"

"She's alive, but I'd like you to see her. She was in a deep state of shock when we came back."

"Of course. I'll help her in any way I can."

"Pan, get some rest. I'll let you know if anything happens."

"I want to know when she wakes up, Jinaari," he insisted before disappearing into his room.

"This way, Father." He led the priest to Thia's door and twisted the handle, opening it slowly. Caelynn rose from a chair as they walked in. Thia was asleep on the bed. "How is she?"

"She fell asleep as soon as I got her in bed." Caelynn suppressed a yawn.

"This is Father Philip. He's a priest of Keroys, and one of Thia's oldest friends," he said by way of introduction. Walking closer to the elf, he whispered, "Did she say anything to you?"

She shook her head. "No. She stayed silent while I got the blood washed off. None of it was hers. She listened, did what I asked, but that was it. She fell asleep within minutes of me getting her in bed. How's Adam?"

"Sleeping. I just told Pan to get some rest, too."

Yawning again, she walked toward the door. "That sounds like a great idea."

Jinaari closed the door as she left, then sat in a chair. The priest sat on the edge of the bed and had taken one of Thia's hands in his.

"What happened to lead up to this?" he asked.

"Lolc Aon got a hold of her," Jinaari kept his voice low, "gave her some kind of drug. When we got there, she was coming out of a cocoon. Slashed the throat of someone we believe was her mother, tore out her heart, and presented it to the Goddess."

"Her mother was evil, yes?"

"Very much so."

A flicker of relief flashed through Father Philip's eyes. "Then what happened?"

"We interrupted the rite, before Thia could do anything else. At that point, she did ... something. I'm not sure what. The entire chamber exploded with a bright, yellow light. When it faded, all the Fallen in the chamber were dead except for Thia and Lolc Aon. It almost brought the ceiling down on us. I took out the Scorpion Queen. When I turned around, Thia sat on the ground, covered in blood, and in shock. Her eyes wouldn't focus, and she's not said a word to any of us."

"Does she hear you? If you talk to her, ask her to do something, does she do it?"

"Yes."

"That's a good sign." He reached out and touched her cheek. "Keroys hasn't deserted her. She's struggling with what she did, however. Taking a life is never easy. To do so with that much hatred and violence ... she faced what could've been her life, had her mother not abandoned her. It's a side of herself that Thia's feared for her entire life. When she's ready, she'll speak of what happened." Father Philip gently patted her hand before releasing it, then rose. "Who in your group is she likely to talk to?"

"Me."

He nodded. "Listen to her, without judgment or condemnation. She won't share what happened easily. But she must do so, or it'll eat at her soul for the rest of her life."

Jinaari nodded. "Thank you for coming."

The priest walked to the door. "She's stronger than she

knows. You may need to remind her of that. If either of you need me, I'll come." He left, closing the door softly behind him.

Jinaari shifted the position of the chair, making it where he could both see the door and Thia as she slept. Briskly, he rubbed his hands up his arms. The room was cool. Kneeling in front of the fireplace, he placed several logs onto the andirons. She hadn't said anything, but the cold of the caverns bothered her. *Maybe keeping the room warm will help you realize you're safe now.* Once it was lit, he went back to the chair and settled in for his turn on watch.

CHAPTER
TWENTY-SEVEN

Thia stirred as she began to wake up. *Where am I?* She forced herself to keep her breathing normal. *Think! If I'm still in Byd Cudd, I have to survive.* She was on a bed. She shifted her body, feeling fabric between her and the bedding. *At least I'm not naked this time.*

She kept her eyes closed, listening. A fire crackled and popped, but it wasn't loud. Another sound, the slow and even breathing of someone or something alive, reached her ears. The last bit of fog left her mind. She wasn't alone. If they were asleep, she had a chance to sneak out.

She took a deep breath, focusing her mind. *Think before acting. What's the last thing that happened?* Slivers of memories began to surface. She shoved aside anything dealing with Lolc Aon. *I can't deal with that and get out of here.* There had to be something more recent.

There'd been a fight. Something in her broke, and she'd screamed. But it was out of defiance, not pain. Herasta's body exploded, covering her with blood.

Faces and voices came into focus. Pan, Caelynn, Adam. Jinaari.

Someone put a cloak around her, carried her. She'd felt safe. Jinaari's face in front of her, telling her they were back at The Green Frog. Someone else gave her a bath, helped her change into clean clothes, and put her into bed.

She rolled over, opening her eyes. The paladin slept in a chair near the fireplace. Relief flooded her. *I'm at the inn. Maybe.* Fear crept into her mind. *Lolc Aon spent time in my mind. This could be another trick of hers. But how can I tell?* She moved the covers off her and swung her feet onto the floor. The linen shift she wore was clean and fell to just past her knees. Shivers ran through her body, making the hair on her arms stand up. The fire had died down, no longer heating the entire room. A shawl was draped across the chest closest to her. Reaching out, she settled it around her shoulders and walked toward the far wall. *Adam was here once when I woke up for a few minutes. He gave me some food; said they took turns taking care of me.* Her hand caressed the panel in the wall. *He finished the illusion.* Pressing lightly, the wall shimmered as the illusion activated. Thousands of stars filled the sky as waves crashed on the beach. On the horizon, the first rays of the sun began to show. A foot in front of her was a wrought iron fence. *He said I could touch the fence; it was real. But I wouldn't be able to actually go on the sand.* The breeze that moved her hair, the fresh, saltwater air, the roar of the waves were all an illusion. She walked to the edge, resting her elbows on the top rail. Inhaling deeply, she felt her body relax. *I'm at the inn. Nothing she made me see would match this. It's not just my memory, but Adam's interpretation of it. She can't duplicate something I hadn't seen yet.*

"That's impressive," Jinaari's deep voice was quiet, even.

Thia didn't move. "Adam and I talked about it before we

left for Byd Cudd. I wanted to have something open when we came back. I know it's not real, but it helps all the same." Her voice cracked. "How long was I out?"

"Almost a week. You'd wake up enough to eat a little, but you wouldn't talk," Jinaari replied. She heard the chair scrape across the floor as he stood up.

A week? No wonder her voice had cracked. She took a deep breath. *I need to know.* "Did we lose anyone?"

Out of the corner of her eye, she saw him. His hands grasped the rail, but he didn't look at her. "No. Adam slept for a day or so. He drained his magic stores to the bottom, shattered his staff pulling from it, to get us out of there. You weren't in any condition to help hold them off once the entire city realized what we'd done. Coming back here was the best option."

"Did we win?"

"Lolc Aon's dead, so yeah. I'd call that a win."

She felt the tension leave her body. So many weeks of being hunted by the Goddess, and it was over. Grasping the rail with both hands, she pushed away, bending at the waist, and let out a deep breath. It was over. All of it.

"So, Thia," he leaned against the rail and looked at her, "how are things with you?"

Straightening, she looked at him. "Why do you keep asking me that?"

"What do you mean?"

"You've asked me that same question before." She paused, looking out at the sea. The sunlight was growing. *This is so much more than I expected.* "The first time was when you came back from the time with the Gods. I've never heard you ask anyone else, just me. Why?" She turned her head his way, waiting.

He rested his forearms against the rail, looking at her.

She knew the look on his face. Either he'd tell her or avoid the question.

"If I answer, can I ask a question of you? And get an answer that's as truthful as the one I give you?"

She blinked, startled. *He's never asked that before. I need to know how much of what Lolc Aon showed me was true, and what was a lie.* "Yes."

He looked back at the stars, his face a mask. "I'd finished the training Garret insisted on, made it through the maze. There was a portal in the center, and Keroys was waiting for me. He asked to see my sword. I held it out to show him. He touched the blade, and then asked me for a favor. He was so afraid that Lolc Aon would turn you into something evil, he asked that I kill you if I thought you'd embraced the darkness." He turned and looked at her. "I asked that question, Thia, to make sure you were still yourself. Keroys said, if my sword was used, your soul would go back to him and not Lolc Aon. At least in death you'd be free of her taint. It was never something I wanted to do. I would stay awake at night, analyzing everything you said or did that day, to make sure evil hadn't taken you over."

What Lolc Aon had shown her was real, then. Keroys really did ask him to kill her. "I need to sit down," she muttered. She walked away from the illusionary wall and back into her room, sinking into the closest chair. She felt numb. *It was a scrying mirror, after all, and not some illusion I was able to manipulate.*

He followed her, pulling the other chair over and sitting down in front of her. "Talk to me, Thia. It tore me apart to think I'd have to do that."

She raised her head but didn't look at him. *If Lolc Aon had won, if I'd become what she wanted me to be, I would've deserved death.* "If that had happened," she drew a breath, trying to steady her voice, "I would've welcomed death by your hand." She swiped at a tear that fell down her cheek. "Whatever part of me that was still sane, anyway."

He reached out and took her hand in his. "It would've killed me to do it."

She nodded, understanding what he meant. He would have thought she was beyond saving, something he'd never doubted.

"Do I get to ask my question now?" His voice was low.

She closed her eyes, afraid of what it might be. "Yes," she whispered. Opening her eyes, Thia looked at him. "And I'll be as truthful as you have been." *Please, don't ask what happened,* she thought.

"What happened when Lolc Aon had you?"

Damn. She shifted her focus to her hands, trying to keep the tremors unnoticeable. "I was drugged, wrapped up in a cocoon of webbing. I tried," she choked, "I tried to stay calm. I really did. But the terror wouldn't let go. I lost it, like Adam was worried I would." She swiped angrily at the tears that were falling from her eyes. She couldn't look at him, not without stopping. Glancing at her hands, as she kept talking. "I blacked out. When I came to, I wasn't in the cocoon. I probably was, but the drugs were making me see things that weren't real. But Lolc Aon was there, in my mind. I stood in a hallway. She said that, behind the doors, were my own fears and desires. She opened one and shoved me inside. I saw hundreds of bodies, and they looked like all of you, Papa, even Father Philip. I was kneeling in blood. Everyone kept demanding to know why I let them die. A torrent of water fell on me at some point, washing away the blood, and Herasta was there. I begged her to kill me, but then Lolc Aon reappeared. She showed me part of the conversation between you and Keroys, where he asked you to kill me. But I pushed back, expanded the spell, and saw you appealing to Garret, arguing against making that promise." She drew a deep breath. "Part of me hoped it was another trick, not the truth, which is why I asked you what I did just now. I knew, if it really happened, you wouldn't lie to me. I kept praying to Keroys for strength. I knew you were trying to find me, get me back. I just had to stay alive until then.

"Then, Lolc Aon led me to another door. She had a smile that made my blood run cold. She thought that what she was about to show me would sway me to her side. The room had a bed, that was it. Someone was tied on it. I walked closer." Thia slammed her eyes closed, trying to get the words out. "Lolc Aon was right behind me, whispering about how she knew what I really wanted, even if I didn't, and that she had made it happen. All I had to do was take it, claim my place as her priestess. Her Daughter." She was sobbing. Her entire body shook at the memory.

"Thia, who was on the bed?"

She took a deep breath, "You were," she exhaled. The words began to tumble from her mouth. If she didn't say it quickly, she never would. "She told me to get on the bed, claim you as mine. Said that she'd turn you over to the slave market if I didn't. I reached out and touched your arm, scared that you were dead, and you opened your eyes. The look you gave me . . . it was full of anger, hatred, even fear. I stepped back, shaking. I started screaming, 'No,' over and over. 'Not like this'. She glared at me, said that it was too late. That's when I woke up in the cocoon and cut my way out." She paused. "When I saw Herasta, I saw a mirror image of myself. Of what I would become if I gave into Lolc Aon's demands. I hated her for abandoning me. She wasn't my mother; she was the embodiment of evil. If I killed her, I could kill that part of myself forever. I reasoned with myself that Keroys would understand my intent.

"Then, Lolc Aon told me to prove myself a leader and start my line. The drugs were making it hard for me to see the prisoners clearly. Their faces shifted constantly, and I wasn't sure who was in front of me. I," her voice shook, but she forced herself to keep talking, "kept seeing yours. And you were so angry at me for betraying you, for not staying strong. I saw the fear on your face. I thought that, if I just killed them, that it would be better for everyone. They'd be free... you'd be free... and I could take over the entire city. I could make them see that chaos wasn't a good path, teach them a better way. That's when I heard Pan screaming my name. I saw you running at me. Something inside me broke loose, and I saw what I would become if I did what she wanted. I screamed. When I stopped, the Fallen around me were dead and I was covered in blood. But I didn't know whose blood it was. I thought it might've been yours. Or Pan's... Adam's..." her breath caught in her throat. "I have a few memories of coming back here, but it's pretty sketchy."

She sat in her chair, her eyes closed and tears streaming down her cheeks. She felt his hand touch her face; his thumb gently wiped at the track left behind by her tears. "Thia, look at me. Please," he said, cradling her face in his hands.

Swallowing, she opened her eyes and met his. "Do you see any fear?" he asked, his voice barely above a whisper. "Any anger or hatred?"

His dark eyes locked with hers. There was something there, but it wasn't that. "No," she whispered back.

He leaned in closer to her. "Do you trust me?"

She nodded, unable to pull herself away from his gaze. Her body shook, but this was a different kind of fear. "Yes, but I'm not sure I trust myself."

"But I do," he whispered. Leaning even closer, his lips brushed against hers.

The door to her room flew open, and he moved away. "Jinaari..." Adam started to say, his voice trailing off.

His hands let go of her and he stood up. "What is it?"

"There's someone downstairs. He says he has a message from your mother," the warlock's voice was subdued.

Thia's cheeks grew hot, but she couldn't find her voice.

"We'll talk more when I get back," he whispered. Walking away from her, he said, "Let's go."

The door closed behind them. She sat, staring out at the rise and fall of the waves, waiting for the feeling of his kiss to fade.

Her stomach churned. Too many emotions clashed within her, and she couldn't make sense of any of them. Facing him when he came back terrified her more than the trip to Byd Cudd, but she didn't know why. *I'll leave, go to the cloister*, she thought, *ask Father Philip to use his chapel. I need to clear my mind.* Rising from the chair, she ran to one of the chests and pulled out some clothes. As she shoved her feet into a pair of short leather boots, she heard a knock at her door.

Turning as she rose, she headed for it and jerked it open. Pan stared at her; his brown eyes wide. "You're awake!" he exclaimed, throwing his arms around her.

"Pan," she said, trying to remove herself from his embrace. "I need to go to the cloister. Now."

"Okay," he said, "I'll come with you."

She moved around him, heading to the exit. "You don't have to do that, Pan. It's not far." Slamming her palm against the pressure point, she dove through the portal as soon as it opened and headed down the steps two at a time. The common room was quiet. Wilim was behind the bar, cleaning glasses. As she ran, she caught sight of Jinaari and Adam sitting at a table with a well-dressed man. Neither of her friends looked at her. They wouldn't have been able to stop her, anyway.

Her mind was blank; the driving need to be someplace where she felt she'd get some sense of peace overwhelmed everything else. "Thia," she heard Pan call out to her, "wait for me."

She didn't stop, though. The streets of Almair were quiet in the early morning hours. A few people moved about, pushing carts full of vegetables or bread. Deftly, she dodged around them, the sense of panic rising within her with every step. When the cloister finally came into view, she ran even faster.

The guard didn't ask her name, just opened the door to admit her. Dashing across the courtyard, she wove her way through the building to Father Philip's office. As she rounded the last corner, she saw him running her way. His robe was wrinkled as if he'd just thrown it on. "Thia?" he asked her, "What's wrong?"

Choking back tears, she stammered, "I need to use your private chapel. Please."

"Of course! Come with me," he draped a comforting arm around her and led her toward his office. "You brought a friend with you, I see."

"He invited himself. I just . . . I must talk to Keroys."

The older man led her through his office and toward the chapel door. "I anticipated as much, Thia, after your friends summoned me when you returned. You take as much time as you need."

As soon as she crossed the threshold, the panic began to subside and a calm replaced it. Tears still streamed down her face as she lit the candles, but her breathing was easier. This, at least, was familiar. She knew her place here, and what to expect. Settling onto the bench, she started to pray.

CHAPTER
TWENTY-EIGHT

"Well?" Adam asked him. "What do we do now?"

Jinaari watched as the messenger left. "Get horses, for one. I'm not walking all the way to Dragonspire." He rose from the table, his gaze going toward the staircase. "You can bring Pan and Caelynn up to speed. I'll talk to Thia."

"Is that what you were doing earlier?" The warlock teased him.

He glared at his friend, daring him to keep talking.

"I'm, ah, going to talk to Wilim, let him know I'm leaving again," Adam stammered, backing away from the table. "He can find horses for us, and an extra for the gear. I'll talk to the others when I'm done." He paused. "When do you want to leave?"

"If the horses can be here today, let's go. Otherwise, tomorrow." He turned and headed upstairs to their hidden area.

The first thing he noticed after crossing the threshold

was her open door. "Thia?" he called out as he walked toward it.

"She's not there." Caelynn replied.

Jinaari turned around and looked at her. "Where is she?"

The elf yawned, stretching as she stood in the doorway to her room. "Pan woke me up, said that Thia was going to her cloister and he was going with her." She looked at him, concerned. "Is everything okay?"

"Drogon's stirring again, near Dragonspire. Adam's arranging horses for us, but I need to talk to her before we leave."

"Damn it," she swore. "Jinaari, is she okay? Pan didn't tell me anything other than she'd woken up and needed to go see someone."

"She's fine. She woke up early this morning, and we had a long talk about what happened. She probably wanted to pray someplace familiar, that's all. How long ago did they leave?"

"Dunno, half an hour? Maybe an hour?"

Just after I left her, he thought. Nodding, he looked at her. "I'm going to find them, make sure she's okay." He walked toward the portal back to the inn.

"Hey, Jinaari," Caelynn called after him.

"Yeah?"

"When are we leaving?"

"Today, if possible. Tomorrow at the latest. We'll ride to Cirrain first, rest up there. It's going to take us a week by horseback before we get to Dragonspire. If we can see where he's at, we'll bypass the city entirely." If he could avoid court and all that went with it, he would.

"Is it that bad?"

He looked back at her. "Yeah, it is. It wasn't a random

message, Caelynn. The Queen summoned the Lord Defender."

"Shit," she breathed.

He didn't reply. Right now, he had to get to Thia and talk with her. *I can't hide the truth from her any longer. It's going to be better if she hears it from me. Maybe I can convince her that the titles don't matter. I'm still the person she knows.*

He kept a normal pace as he walked toward the cloister. *The more time I can give her, the better. Especially if Keroys answered her. She's wrestling with guilt, and it's going to take him to absolve her of it.*

The guard at the small side gate stood up straighter as he approached. "I'm looking for two friends of mine," he said, keeping his tone friendly. "A woman with blonde hair, and a younger man. She would've been looking for Father Philip."

"She's here, Milord." The guard opened the door. "Do you need me to find you an escort to his office?"

"No, that's fine," he said. "I can find it." He went inside, waiting for the guard to pull the gate shut behind him. He took a moment to orient himself. The only time he'd been here was with Drakkus when he first met Thia. The cloister's inner courtyard was ringed with arched walkways, most of which had classrooms or dormitories leading off them. At the far corner, not far from the entrance to the main church, was the hallway that led into the offices.

Robed acolytes stopped and watched him as he walked past, but none tried to talk to him. Two more turns and he found the correct room. Approaching the guards, he kept his voice low. "I need to speak with Father Philip."

"I'm sorry, Milord," one replied, "he gave us orders that he wasn't to be disturbed. He has guests right now."

"His guests are friends of mine. I'm sure it'll be fine if I join them." He reached out for the handle of the door, only to have the guards block it with their polearms.

"One of his guests is the Daughter of Keroys, Milord. I cannot allow you to enter unless Father Philip agrees."

He looked at them both. *I don't have time for this.* "Do you know who I am?"

"You're a paladin of Garret. I was here a few months back when you and your commander paid a visit."

"I'm more than that." He straightened his shoulders, staring at both of them. He didn't like what he was about to do, but he didn't have time to argue with them for an hour. "I'm Jinaari Althir, Lord Defender of Avoch and heir to Queen Agrana. I need to see the Daughter of Keroys. Now, you can either let me pass or have me bash your heads into the wall. It's your choice."

The two guards exchanged a nervous look. "I apologize, Your Highness. I'll let him know you're here." One opened the door enough to disappear into the room.

Within moments, the doors flew open, and the elder priest smiled at him. "Welcome, Prince. Please excuse my guards." He stood to one side, giving Jinaari room to move past him. "I didn't want anyone to disturb Thia," he said as he walked past, his voice barely above a whisper.

Pan sat in a chair on the far side of the room near a nondescript door. Leaping to his feet, the young man walked toward him.

"Where is she?" Jinaari asked.

"In there," Pan pointed to the door.

"Go back to the Green Frog. We're leaving for Dragonspire later today or tomorrow. I'll escort her back when she's ready."

"Why Dragonspire? Can we stop at Cirrain on the way?

My family lives there. We'd be able to let them meet Thia. I think it would help her to know she had family that accepted her as she is, you know? We don't care who her mother was."

"I planned to. Adam will fill you in on the rest." He looked at Pan. "I know she's your cousin, and you want to take care of her. The last thing she needs right now, though, is for any of us to hover over her. Go back to the inn. I won't leave her alone."

He nodded. "Okay." He glanced back at the chapel door. "She was really upset when we got here, Jinaari, but she wouldn't tell me why. Was it because of what she did in the sanctuary? Because I don't think she did anything bad. I really don't."

"Neither do I, Pan. Thia's had to do a lot of things over the last few months that she never thought she'd have to. And she learned that Keroys placed his Mark on her, too. She's dealt with it better than most people I know would've. I think she needed to hear from her God that her actions were justified is all." Jinaari watched as the young man left and the door closed behind him.

Turning to the priest, he asked, "Is she alone?"

"Unless Keroys is still with her, she should be. There's only one way in and out of that chapel. It was empty when she went in, and we made sure she wasn't disturbed." He tilted his head to one side. "Pan told me more details of what happened in Byd Cudd. I believe she's begun to access the power Keroys granted her. She's rejected one life, the one that she would've had with her mother and Lolc Aon. Now she has to accept a new one."

"Any idea what that would entail?"

Philip shrugged. "That's up to Keroys, not me. It could be accepting what being his Daughter means, embracing the role she would have. It could be something simpler, too. Considering he didn't tell her what the first part meant, I doubt he's going to be forthcoming on the rest of it." He sat down at his desk, resting his arm on the surface. "She's going to need friends around her for some time. Being a Daughter or Son of a God doesn't mean staying in a cloister or church, hiding from the world. It means being out in it, doing what is needed. Part of her has always believed she would come back here when her task was done. I know she's safe with you and your companions. It's where she belongs. You'll need to show her you want her around, though." He lowered his head and began to read a parchment on the desk.

Jinaari walked to the door leading to the chapel and listened. He could hear Thia talking, but no one answered. A prayer, perhaps? He hesitated, then twisted the knob slowly. They needed to talk about a number of things. Here she felt safe, and he wanted to take advantage of that.

She sat on the high-backed bench, her back to him. An eerie glow, shaped like a man, knelt in front of her. He looked at him, and Jinaari was struck by the ghost's similarities to both Thia and Pan. Her father?

The spirit stood up and placed a gentle kiss on the top of her head before dissipating. "I know you're there," she said.

Walking the few feet to the bench, he sat down next to her, "I wasn't trying to interrupt."

"It's okay," she didn't look at him. "Papa couldn't stay long. It was hard enough for him to manifest to begin with. Even with Keroys's blessing to do so." She fidgeted with her hands, picking at some piece of dirt he didn't see. "Where's Pan?"

"I sent him back to the inn, told him I'd walk back with

you when you were ready." He paused. "Has being here helped you?"

She nodded, her blonde curls hiding her face. "Keroys and I had a good talk. What happened down in Byd Cudd was necessary. I had to face the life I would've had down there, reject it completely. That was the first half of what's necessary for me to embrace all he's bestowed on me. Papa came to make sure I knew he didn't blame me for what I did to Herasta. There was no love between them, but he loved me the moment he learned I was to be born."

"I saw the resemblance. You may think you look like your mother, but there's a good deal of your father there. Enough that I think you can put to rest any question about being cousins with Pan."

She laughed. "Papa confirmed it, too. That was part of the pact he made with Herasta. He couldn't tell them where he was, or that I was alive. She may have given him the information to find me, but she made sure to isolate us both."

He took a deep breath. "You scared me. I came back upstairs, expecting you to be there, and you weren't." Reaching out, he took one of her hands in his, "Thia, I—"

"What did the messenger from your mother say?" Her tone shifted. She didn't remove her hand from his, but he could tell she wasn't ready to talk about what had happened between them.

"Drogon's resurfaced, near Dragonspire. She's requested that I come deal with it."

"Drogon?" She looked at him. "Are you certain?"

"She was. I was ordered to gather anyone and anything that I need to aid in dealing with the threat and take care of it. Adam's arranging horses for us." He looked at her. "I was hoping you'd come as well. We all do. The road will take us through Cirrain, Pan's home. You'd be able to meet your father's family."

She scrunched up her face, and he saw her confusion. "Who's your mother, Jinaari? And why would you obey an order like that? I thought your loyalties were with Garret."

"Do you remember when I told you that we all had family associations we weren't proud of?"

Nodding, she replied, "Yes."

"Althir is a fairly common surname, which has made it so I could live a relatively normal life. I have . . ." he paused, trying to get the words right so she'd understand his meaning, "relations that have some power within Avoch. As such, I was born with titles and privileges that I didn't earn." He took a deep breath. "My mother is Queen Agrana."

"You're a prince?!" She stared at him; her eyes wide.

"Not by choice," he told her. "You're part Fallen. That doesn't define you. It never has, not to me. Or Adam, Caelynn, or Pan. I didn't say anything before because I wanted you to know me. Jinaari. Not the title. The only ones I'm proud of are the ones I've earned. Paladin. Lord Defender. The stuff I was born with?" He shook his head. "If I have to spend five minutes at court, surrounded by the intrigues, it's too long." He stared at her, waiting for her to say something.

She blinked several times, stunned. "I don't know what to say."

"Would it have changed how you healed me?"

Thia shook her head. "No. Never."

"Around you, I'm who I was meant to be. I don't have to worry about backstabbing ambassadors or fussy manservants getting upset because I got too much mud on my boots. Adam and Caelynn accept this. I hope you can, as well."

She smiled. "Does this mean I can get away with saying you're a royal pain when you're being insufferable?"

He laughed. "Only if I can call you a stubborn witch."

She rose, finally taking her hand out of his. "When do we leave?" she asked, picking up some fabric that sat on the bench next to her.

"As soon as we can. If Adam was able to get horses, we'll go as soon as we can pack. Otherwise, first thing tomorrow morning."

He watched her look around the chapel. "Keroys told me this wasn't home anymore. He'll always be with me, but I can't rely on rituals, altars, and candles anymore. Whatever his plan for me is, it's not here. If Drogon's still out there, causing havoc, I can't help correct it from a temple."

Rising, he said, "That makes two of us." She turned and walked away from him. For a moment, he considered stopping her. There were still things they had to get straight between them. *Be patient*, he thought, *she just went through something that can only be described as terrifying. Make sure her mind is whole, ready to take on Drogon, before pushing anything else on her. No matter how right that kiss felt.*

Taking her arm, he led her from the chapel. "How's Adam?" she asked. "You said he broke his staff bringing us back to the inn."

"He's fine, outside of being worried about you. We all were." He stopped talking as she opened the door to the office. Father Philip rose from his desk as they entered.

"Are you feeling at peace now?" he asked, looking at Thia.

"As much as I can, yes. Thank you." She walked over to the older man, embracing him.

The priest returned the hug, stepping back after a moment. "I hear you're off on another adventure soon."

"I guess so. Keroys has work that needs doing, and I somehow was given the job."

Father Philip looked at Jinaari, then back at Thia. "You have companions you can trust, who will protect you as you do Keroys' work. With their aid, there's no task you can't finish."

"We need to go," Jinaari interrupted, touching Thia's arm.

"I'm ready," she said.

An uneasy silence settled between them as he escorted her across the complex and to the gate. *Once we're on the road, I'll get her to talk to me. There's time before we find Drogon.*

Halfway to the inn, she said, "Did he get a new one yet?"

"Who and what are you talking about?"

"Adam. You said his staff had shattered. Doesn't he need one to focus his magic? He doesn't do sigils like you or I do."

"I bought him a new one."

She smiled. "That was kind of you. They can't be cheap."

Jinaari shrugged. "It wasn't. Transportation's draining enough, as I understand it, when it's just one or two people. He put enough through that stick to get all five of us out. He saved our lives. The least I could do was buy him a new one."

Her laugh was light, even joyful. "What's so funny?" he asked.

"The way you two talk about each other. Neither of you have any fear of the other. There's nothing but trust between you two. It's not something I've experienced much in life."

"I trust you enough to agree when you call me arrogant."

"That's because you are. I'm being truthful."

They turned down the alley leading to the inn. "And you trust that, when I say you're stubborn, it's meant as a good thing. Same as my arrogance."

He opened the door, letting her go in first. Wilim nodded at them. "The horses will be here tomorrow. I've asked Elian to get some food packets ready tonight, put them aside for you to grab in the morning before you go."

"Thank you," Jinaari said as they headed toward the stairs. "Where's Adam and Pan?"

"They're both up there. Adam said he had something to show you."

He gently pushed Thia ahead of him. If Adam mentioned it to Wilim, it was important enough he didn't want Jinaari to get distracted. "Let's go."

Thia activated the portal when they reached the top of the stairs. Stepping through, he saw the others studying a long piece of parchment laid out on the center table. All three looked at them as they entered.

"Everything good, Thia?" Adam asked.

She nodded, finding a seat on a couch. "Yes, thank you. For everything."

Caelynn smiled at her as Jinaari sat down. "You're part of us, Thia. We take care of each other."

Jinaari cleared his throat, getting their attention. "What's this?" he asked, pointing to the parchment.

"When I recovered, I visited a friend of mine here in Almair. His name's Hamish," Adam began to explain.

"I remember you mentioning him," Thia interjected.

The blonde man nodded. "I wanted to talk to him before we went down to Byd Cudd, but we didn't have time. Thia was still asleep, so I paid him a visit. Drogon's a mage, he got some training in Helmshouse. I don't remember him, but that only means he didn't get any lessons from me. Thousands come there every year, and most leave long before they can take the trials.

"Anyway, Hamish is retired for the most part. His first love wasn't magic but tracking down why certain people made the choices they did. I told him about Drogon, Thia's history with him, all of that. Today, he sent this." Pointing to the table, he continued. "Hamish traced major things in Drogon's past, starting when he left Helmshouse."

Jinaari studied the timeline. "So, he was with Thia's father down in Byd Cudd?"

Adam nodded. "Yes. And he tried to convince Lolc Aon to give him immortality. She turned him down, probably rather brutally." He leaned over, putting his finger at various places on the scroll. "Over the next ten years, leading up to Bran's murder, he went to each of the other six Gods. Every time, he was rebuked, turned away. Foresworn. Finally, he went back to Lolc Aon. Hamish wasn't able to determine what deal he proposed to each one, but even she Foreswore him at that time. He became Forsaken."

"Then he wouldn't have any magic at all. But he did, under Tanisal." Caelynn said.

"It was the machine he built," Thia said. "He was able to trap souls, siphon power from them. My father was the first one he trapped."

Jinaari leaned back. "We destroyed that, though. How is he still doing anything, let alone enough to be a threat?"

"All Hamish could piece together was that Drogon can still wield magic, but he doesn't have stores like another mage would. If he's found a way to actually keep what he can channel, tap it at will like Thia or I can, he'll have abilities that would rival a Son or Daughter of any of the Gods." Adam looked at Thia. "Drogon was on this path when you were born, Thia. You're the only one I know in all of Avoch that's Marked. If anyone's going to stop him, it's you."

Jinaari turned his head toward her, studying her face. Her jaw was clenched, but she was calm. "You're not doing this alone. We'll be right there with you."

"There's more," Adam said.

Jinaari turned to him. "What else?"

"A paladin stopped by. Said to tell you that Garret has thrown Alesso out of the Order, in front of the entire chapterhouse at Dragonspire. Drakkus punched him in the jaw so hard he nearly fell over."

"I'd do more than that to him," Jinaari replied. "Did he say what happened after that?"

"He was last seen getting on a wagon with a stranger, leaving Dragonspire. The messenger said that several of your brothers were disappointed they didn't get to 'finish his banishment' first."

"Good."

Thia turned to him. "What's good about him being alive?"

"It means I still get to kill him."

CHAPTER
TWENTY-NINE

The city walls of Cirrain loomed in the distance. Sitting in the center of a patchwork of farms, the road wound through fields leading to the massive gates. Thia twisted in her saddle; she wasn't used to riding, and her body let her know it.

"Are you okay?" Jinaari asked as he rode next to her.

She nodded. "Just sore. I've spent more time on a horse over the last four days than I have in my entire life." Things weren't completely easy between them, and she knew that was on her. He'd tried several times to talk to her about what had happened when she woke, but she changed the subject each time. Until Lolc Aon had done what she did, Thia didn't admit to herself she cared for him in that way. *We have a job to do*, she thought. *I know I haven't done everything Keroys asked of me. Until I figure that out, unlock the magic he's given me, and we take down Drogon once and for all, it has to wait. Besides, his family's not known for being accepting of Fallen. He's not like them. At some point, though, his connection will make things difficult. I don't want to make him choose between duty and me.*

"You're going to love it, Cousin," Pan said as he moved his horse alongside hers. "Mother will welcome you for sure. If any of our aunts or uncles are home, they will as well. And you can meet the rest of our cousins!" His face lit up. "You're the oldest, but they're going to love you. I know it!"

"I hope they won't mind when it takes me time to get the names right," she said.

"They're really patient. I'm sure they'll remind you. I know Jinaari doesn't want to stay long. That's going to make everyone sad, just to warn you. I mean, you're finally coming home and all. They'll want you to stay for months so they can get to know you. But we're on a mission so it'll have to wait."

Thia sighed. Months? She wanted to meet Papa's family, yes, but she wasn't so sure about spending a lot of time getting to know them all at once. "One thing at a time, Pan. We really can't spend more than a night or two. We have to take care of Drogon."

He slumped a little. "I know. Mother will be disappointed, but she'll understand. She talks about duty all the time. We'll just have to make the most of the time we have." He looked up at the sky. "We'll get there before dark, which is good. Tomorrow will be when she'll want to introduce you to everyone. And we'll have to have the ceremony. There's no escaping that."

"Ceremony?" Jinaari asked.

"I mean, Mother's a Baroness and all her brothers and sisters have titles of some kind. Once Thia's officially welcomed into the family, she'll inherit her father's title." He paused, looking at her. "It's nothing to be afraid of, Cousin. Really. Nobody cares unless they go into Dragonspire and need to talk to the crown or anything."

She shot a glance at Jinaari. The paladin's hands clenched the reins of his horse slightly, but he seemed relaxed otherwise. Unconcerned. "It's not that I'm scared," she turned her attention back to Pan, "it's more that I'm still getting used to the idea that I'm the Daughter of Keroys. I'm not at all sure about adding to that. Do you think your mother would let this ceremony wait for another visit?"

Pan's face fell, and she instantly regretted her words. "Best to let it happen," Jinaari said quietly. "It's a formality, nothing else, but there's usually reasons to do it quickly. When we get settled, I can come by your room, give you some pointers on what to expect. It doesn't involve any blood oaths."

Her eyes went wide as she stared at him. "Blood oaths?"

"There's a few rites where it's required. Expected, even. This isn't one of them." He looked at her, a small smile on his face. "You trust me, right? That hasn't changed?"

She shook her head. "No, it hasn't."

"Good." He shifted his focus to the road ahead of them. Five riders were approaching, coming fast. "Pan?"

"It's normal this close to nightfall. They want to see who we are, escort us into the city before they close the gate. That's all. I'll talk to them, if you want me to."

"Probably a good idea, since they should recognize you."

As her cousin urged his horse forward to greet the escort, Adam moved up alongside her. "Jinaari's going to hang out in the back," he said. "There's a chance Pan's mother will recognize him, and he'd like to avoid that if he can."

"Why?" she asked.

The warlock grinned at her. "This isn't his

homecoming, Thia. It's yours. He doesn't want to take any focus away from you. Don't be surprised if you don't see much of him until we leave."

Pan was waiting for them, along with four of the guards. "Borin went back to let Mother know we're coming. I said you were friends, so I can surprise her when we get to the courtyard." He moved his horse alongside hers. "He's one of our cousins and will be mad at me later for not telling him. He's horrible at keeping secrets, though. There was this one time when he found me borrowing a cask of ale from the storeroom. He said he wouldn't say anything as long as I shared it with him. Then he got so drunk he got sick all over one of Mother's favorite benches and told her I made him drink that much. I wouldn't recommend telling him any secrets, Cousin. He's not trustworthy like I am."

The gates stood open, and four uniformed soldiers waited at the base as they passed through. Inside, the small city bustled with activity. Wide, clean roads were laid out in straight lines. Houses and shops lined each one. Some people stopped and watched them pass by, but most went about their business. Towering above everything at the center was a stately manor house, surrounded by a stone wall.

They were led to the front and entered the compound through an arched tunnel. It opened into a large courtyard. Several wide steps at the far end sat beneath double doors leading into the house itself. A woman stood, watching them, as they approached. Two others stood behind her.

Grooms came forward, grabbing the bridles of their horses. "Come on, Cousin!" Pan said with excitement as he dismounted.

She barely had her feet on the ground when he grabbed

her hand, pulling her forward. "Mother," he said, bowing at the woman on the steps.

"You didn't tell me you were coming home for a visit, Pan. Or that you would bring friends." Her voice was even.

Thia raised her head and took a closer look at her. This was her aunt? The woman's attention was on Pan, and she could see the resemblance.

"Mother, this is Thia," he pulled her forward and Thia awkwardly tried to curtsey. She was a Baroness, after all. "She's Uncle Bran's daughter!"

Thia felt the woman's gaze as she scrutinized her. "Truly?" The Baroness walked down the steps toward her.

"She is! Her name's Thia Bransdottir, for one. Her father's name was Bran, and he made the same boxes that you told me Uncle Bran used to make. She's even got one with her, the last one he ever made. And then, there's—" The woman's hand went up, and Pan stopped speaking.

Thia's heart raced as she moved closer. The woman placed both hands on her face and studied her. "I see my brother in you," she said. "Welcome home, Thia." Without another word, she embraced her.

Standing back, she smiled. "Forgive my son, he's excitable. But you know that already, don't you?" Her gaze shifted past Thia, and she started to walk away.

Thia turned around and saw the Baroness drop into a deep curtsey, one hand across her chest, at Jinaari's feet. "Welcome to our humble home, Your Royal Highness. How may the Beckenburg house serve the Crown?"

She watched Jinaari's jaw clench as the words hit her. He wasn't just a prince...he was *the prince*. "Please, Baroness, there's no need for formalities." He muttered something else that she couldn't hear as the Baroness rose.

"Rooms are being readied for you all. I'm sure you're

tired and wish to freshen up." She glanced at Jinaari. "I am anxious to hear of your journey. Please feel free to seek me out when you're rested. I will make myself available at any time." She gestured toward the open doors. "Allow me to lead you to your rooms." Picking up her skirts, she climbed up the steps.

"Thia." Pan put his hand on her arm. "I'm going to my room. If you need me, just ask around. Everyone knows where to find me." He smiled at her and followed the horses as they were being led away.

"Come on," Jinaari said, "we can't keep her waiting."

"I think you left out something when you told me you were related to the Queen," she whispered.

He gave her a direct look. "Maybe if you didn't keep making it impossible for us to talk to each other without being overheard I would've explained more."

The rebuke stung, but she deserved it.

"Thia?"

She glanced at the Baroness. "I'm sorry . . . I didn't . . ." she paused. "I'm not sure what the correct way to address you is."

Smiling, she replied. "Elizabeth is fine, if you're not comfortable with Aunt. I wouldn't worry about titles or anything. With the exception of visits like this one," she nodded at Jinaari, "we rarely use them publicly. Even less among family."

"Thank you, Elizabeth. I didn't hear your question, though."

"I asked how my brother was. We haven't heard from him since before you were born. Honestly, I don't remember getting any news about your arrival."

"He's dead," she said. "It happened fifteen years ago this past spring."

"Oh, no," Elizabeth breathed. "How old were you? Did you not know about us? Who took care of you?"

"I was ten. No, I didn't know about you. He never mentioned his family. A priest of Keroys took me to the cloister in Almair. I've spent most of my life there."

A maid came running toward them, a blue velvet box in her hands. Curtsying quickly, she handed it to Elizabeth before scurrying off. "Your Highness," Elizabeth stopped at a door, "the room isn't much, but it's one of the best ones we have. Your gear will be delivered shortly."

Jinaari glanced at Thia, his face unreadable, and walked into the room.

"Thia, please. This way." The Baroness stood with Pan two doors down the hallway. His face was calm, and he'd put on a clean tunic. "Alora, would you please show the other two to their chambers?"

A young woman gestured for Adam and Caelynn to follow her, and she led them farther down the hallway. Whatever Pan was here for, it wasn't something they were supposed to see.

"There's a tradition in this house," Elizabeth began, "when someone leaves us and we do not know their fate, we seal their room. A stasis field is placed within, to preserve everything as it was when they left. The room is then locked, and the key placed in storage, until they return." She handed Thia the box in her hands.

Opening it, she saw a single brass key resting on a cushion of satin. Looking up, she said, "I don't understand . . ."

"This was your father's room, Thia," Elizabeth placed a hand on the wood door. "As he is gone, the key belongs to you." She reached out and gently squeezed her hand. "Come, Pan. Your cousin needs to be alone."

Thia watched as the two walked down the hallway, disappearing around a corner. Glancing the other way, she saw Jinaari leaning in the doorway to his room, watching her. Removing the key from the box, she inserted it into the lock and twisted.

The tumblers moved freely. Turning the knob, she walked inside.

The room was plain and unassuming. So much so that it instantly brought a smile to her face. Their home had been much the same. Simple furniture without ornate decorations. A bed, with a padded bench sitting at the foot. A pair of comfortable looking chairs near the fireplace. An iron bound wood chest against a wall, with a table beneath the window. A second table, smaller than the first, sat next to the door. Removing the key, she put it down and closed the door. Something on the table drew her attention. Walking over, she stared at the small set of tools lying on top of a piece of soft leather. They were almost identical to a set he'd had when she was a child. The set he'd kept locked away. Small knives, tweezers, and a single magnifying glass meant to piece together intricate metal objects.

As her hand brushed across the tools, a knock sounded at her door. Turning, she saw someone enter. "Pardon, Milady. I was told this bag was yours?" The young man held up her pack.

"Yes," she stammered. "Thank you."

"Where would you like me to put it?"

"On the bench is fine, I suppose."

He crossed the room and put the bag down. "If you hear noises in there," he pointed to a door she hadn't noticed before, "it's just the maids. Baroness Elizabeth told them to bring hot water up in case any of you wanted to wash up.

Someone else will probably bring something to eat later." He bowed quickly and left.

She turned back around to the workspace. Her hands flew to her belt pouch, pulling out her box. She placed it on the desk. It felt right. "You told me you had a home once, Papa. But that your favorite one was in River Run with me. I don't know how long I'll stay, but it's nice knowing part of you is here."

The sound of feet in the next room, followed by water being poured, caught her attention. Walking to the door, she opened it and peered inside. A good-sized copper tub sat in front of a fireplace. Next to it was a small table. One woman was working on lighting a fire, while others flowed through a narrow door, carrying buckets of steaming water that they poured into the tub. Another woman watched the process closely. She raised her head, looking at Thia. "If you please, Miss. We're not quite ready for you." She walked over to her, gently guiding her back to the main room. "Once it's ready, I'll send Cinna in to fetch you. While you're bathing, she'll get the fire in here going. By the time you're done, you can let us know if you want any food. The Baroness said she didn't anticipate any of you dining with everyone else tonight."

"I don't want to add to your work," she said. "I can light the fire myself."

"Nonsense!" She insisted, forcing Thia to sit on the bed. "You wait right there, Miss." Turning around, she went through the door and closed it behind her.

"First rule you should learn, Thia, is never argue with the staff," Jinaari said from behind her.

Twisting, she saw him leaning against the doorframe. "I didn't hear you come in," she said.

"Second rule is to lock your door if you don't want

visitors. Can I come in? That's going on," he gestured toward her bath chamber, "in my room as well."

She nodded, leaning back against one of the bed posts and curling one leg underneath her. The mattress sank beneath his weight as he sat down. "Is it wrong to take care of myself somehow?"

"I don't think so. Being pampered and having someone constantly hovering just in case I needed something was one reason I left to begin with. Training as a paladin meant barracks at first. I have my own room now because I earned it. And Drakkus knows better than to try to assign an initiate to follow me everywhere."

"Please tell me that's not going to happen with this ceremony?"

He shrugged. "Doubtful. It's a formality, Thia, to protect the family and their claim to the land and titles. You just get to stand there, listen to the Baroness say publicly that you're her niece. Given that your father's title was probably His Lordship, you may get some token to represent the rank and that's it. Soon as the feasting is over, you can take it off and leave it here if you want. You'll be expected to wear it during dinner and the dancing, that's all."

"Dancing?" she stared at him, wide eyed. "Jinaari, can't I sit it out? Say I hurt my leg riding my horse or something?"

"First off, you're a healer. No one would believe you. Second, no, you can't sit it out. You and I will be the guests of honor. We need to be seen, Thia." His face changed, and she saw resignation in his eyes. "Like it or not, tomorrow night I have to be the one thing I've tried to avoid my entire life. I have to make everyone in that room think I'm ready to take over and rule Avoch if my mother passed away. And you'll need to make your first appearance as the Daughter of Keroys. This family, your family, needs to see the Mark. See you embrace what you are."

"It's a masquerade, then?"

"What do you mean?"

She sighed. "We have to pretend we're something we're not, put on a mask to make others happy." She looked at him. "How do you do it? Put yourself on display like that?"

"I take a deep breath and know it's only for a few hours at most. And I know I have my real friends to back me, remind me that the only arrogance out of me they'll tolerate is connected to my skill with a sword. Because I've proven myself with it, more than once." He paused and looked at her. "You won't be alone. I'll be there. So will Adam and Caelynn. Even Pan won't be able to escape the feast. If you need help, just ask. We care about you." His hand reached out for hers, and her heart skipped a beat when she saw the look in his eyes. "Some more than the others."

"Thia," a woman called out from the doorway.

Thia's head snapped toward the sound. The Baroness stood in the doorway. "Yes?"

"I hate to interrupt, Your Highness," she inclined her head at Jinaari.

He rose, but Thia caught the momentary shadow that crossed his face. "I'm not a formal person, Baroness, unless the situation calls for it. What's most important to me is protecting my companions. Your niece and son are among those. Please don't stand on ceremony around me."

She smiled. "I appreciate your candor. If possible, I need a moment with my niece."

Glancing back at her, Thia saw the unspoken question in his eyes. "It's fine," she said.

"I'm just down the hall if you need me," he replied.

Pointing at the key he said, "Don't forget rule number two," and closed the door.

Elizabeth waited for him to leave, then gave Thia a confused look. "You have rules?"

She chuckled. "I haven't been away from the cloister long. There's some things others understand that never crossed my mind, that's all. He swore an oath to both Garret and Keroys to keep me safe. In some cases, that includes rules I should follow."

"May I?" She gestured to a chair.

"Please," Thia said. She rose as her aunt walked across the room, settling on the bench at the end of the bed.

"I lied to you earlier, Thia. Not because I wanted to deceive you, but because too many were watching, listening." Elizabeth said as she sat down. Her back was straight, and her hands folded neatly in her lap.

"How so?" Thia asked.

"My brother – your father – did let me know he was going to be out of contact with us. And that there may be a child of his who would come here one day." She pulled a sealed letter out of a pocket hidden in her skirt. "He asked me to keep this until that happened."

Thia stared at the brown parchment. "What is it?" she asked.

Elizabeth shook her head. "I don't know. He asked that I keep it sealed until his child came home. Bran's letter to me only said he hoped it would answer questions he couldn't in life."

Thia stood and took the packet from the woman's outstretched hand. It wasn't thick, maybe two or three pages. A white ribbon wound around it, with a dark blue wax seal holding the edges together. "I thought he couldn't have contact with you," she whispered.

"That *geas* began when you were born. To the best of my knowledge, he wrote this before then, but not by much." She rose, wrapping an arm around Thia's shoulders. "If you need me, just ask someone and I'll come. If not, I'll see you at breakfast. I don't know what Bran tells you in there, and I don't need to. You are his child. That's enough for me." Thia felt her aunt's hand stroke her hair gently. "Welcome home."

Thia watched her leave, closing the door behind her.

She grabbed the key off the table and locked the door. Turning, she saw Cinna come in and kneel at the fireplace. "Is there some way to secure the other door?" she asked. "The one in there, where you came through?"

"Yes, Milady. There's a bolt you can throw on this side. But I recommend waiting until after your bath, so we're able to clean up." She dumped the contents of the dustpan into a small pail next to the fireplace. Deftly, she used a flint to light a small ball of wax and wool. Tossing it into the kindling, she continued to talk as the fire began to take hold. "Do you need me to help you get ready for your bath?" she asked as she picked up the pail. "Or I can wait and take your clothing to the washer if you like."

"No," Thia replied, shaking her head. "I'll take care of myself. It's what I'm used to."

"As you wish, Milady. If you leave them near the towels when you're done, we'll take care of everything." She did a small curtsey and left through the bath chamber.

Thia looked at the letter she held. Walking over to the door Cinna left through, she made sure the servants had left. She didn't want anyone else around when she read it.

She went back to the bench and sat down. Turning it over, her fingers brushed over the seal. There weren't any fancy designs in the wax, no crests or fancy script. Just two letters: B.B.

Why am I hesitating? Papa wrote this, to me. Taking a deep breath, she slid her finger under the wax and broke the seal.

Thia,

You're not in the world yet, but Keroys assures me you are my daughter. His Daughter, as well. If you have the intelligence and curiosity he tells me you will, you'll have questions. Ones I can't answer once you're born. I hope this will calm your soul in some way, even though I'm likely gone from this world.

There was no love between me and Herasta. What happened to bring you into the world was, to be frank, nothing more than what was necessary. I was there as part of a trade delegation; one of several artisans selected to show off the wealth and artistry that came from Almair. My boxes were well-received, and I was invited to present one to Herasta to commemorate her elevation.

I didn't know what this celebration meant among the Fallen, but the head of our delegation did. He warned me that it would be a mortal insult, one that could potentially put the negotiations at risk, as well as my own life, if I didn't accept the invitation. I was told to do whatever Herasta asked of me, without hesitation, for the good of everyone else. So, I did.

Six weeks later, as we began preparations to depart Byd Cudd, I learned she was with child. I went to her, asking if it was mine. She laughed at the idea, as she had spent the night with many men. However, I was the only human. Of that, she was certain.

I knew, if you were mine, what your life would be down there. I saw with my own eyes how they treated any child that wasn't purely Fallen. I also knew I would agree to anything to keep you from that fate. So, Herasta and I made a bargain. When her time was near, she would come to the surface for the birth. If the babe appeared human in any way, she would leave it there for me to find. If not, she'd take it back to Byd Cudd.

She made me swear to leave all I knew, raise you with no other family to lean on. And to never make another box. When I take over care of you, I will be permitted to make a living but not in a way that would bring notice.

And she insisted that we seal the pact by repeating the act that conceived you.

I started to think of a new trade on the way back. I have given away the few boxes I had left, though that angered one of the mages that traveled with us.

When I got back to Almair, I closed up my shop, paid the last of my rent, and left. Herasta told me where she'd go, and I found a small village within two days ride of the location. I have taken over an abandoned farm, set myself up as a shoemaker, and tried to make it ready to raise a babe.

Two months ago, by my reckoning, Keroys blessed me with a visit. He had me make a final box and added something to it when it was done. I don't know what, only that yours would do something no other box I created would. I do remember him saying, as I made it, that Herasta's child was mine. That I would have a daughter. And that he would put his Mark on you as soon as your lungs breathed air.

The box was finished last night. Keroys bade me write this letter, so you might know the truth of what happened. He will deliver it to our family in Cirrain somehow. I've packed a few things, prepared my horse, and will start off for the meeting place at dawn, as you're due any day now.

Thia, daughter, I already love you. I know your life will be full of trials, given your bloodline. But you are my child. Nothing will change that, or how excited I am to be your father.

Papa

Thia put the letter down, ignoring the tears that flowed.

"I love you too, Papa," she whispered. She took a deep breath, her body shuddering with silent grief. *I have to make him proud. No more hiding.* Resolutely, she stood and went to her pack. Opening the flap, she rummaged around for one dress. Keroys gave it to her, back at the cloister. He said it would be necessary to wear at some point, to show the world she bore his Mark.

Laying it across the chest, she sighed. Tomorrow night, she had to wear it. There wasn't a choice to hide any longer.

Jinaari was right. The Daughter of Keroys needed to start showing the world who she was. And that included herself.

CHAPTER
THIRTY

Thia kept a death grip on the dark blue fabric of her cloak as she followed Pan through the corridor to the main hall. Nervous energy filled every inch of her body. She still wasn't sure she could pull this off, but she knew she had to try.

"I hope we didn't overwhelm you today, Cousin," he said as they walked. "Mother did try to keep things low key."

"It was fine, Pan," she said. "I'm grateful she put so much thought into everything." Breakfast had been small; just her, the Baroness, and the aunts and uncles. All seven of them. She'd been presented with the medallion she now wore, a symbol of both her relationship to the family and a title of some kind. That was still a blur.

At lunch, the cousins were introduced. There were so many! Pan's sister, Valerie, was the closest to her own age. Though blind, the young woman was remarkably aware of everything that happened around her. When one of the youngest ones began to trip, she reached out and caught him before he fell.

One of them, Alba, had sat in a chair away from everyone else. Valerie said she had a disease that none of the healers could cure. She'd come because she wanted to meet Thia but feared infecting her at the same time. As soon as lunch was over, she'd gone back to her room to do research. There had to be a way to take away the girl's pain.

"We're here," Pan said, interrupting her thoughts. He'd stopped at a pair of plain doors. "I've got to leave you and Cinna here. Mother insists that we all be at the high table tonight, waiting, when you both come in." He smiled. "Don't worry, Cousin. The food's great and I'm betting that Jinaari's going to be almost as uncomfortable with all of this as you are."

"Does it show?" she asked nervously.

"I can see it, but I know you. I'm betting there's only three other people that will. None of which will make it harder for you." He smiled again and walked away.

Cinna opened the door. "I'll stay with you, Milady. You want your dress to be perfect when you enter, after all. And I'll make sure to take your cloak back to your room."

"It's not mine," she stammered. "It was loaned to me. Would you find out who it belongs to and return it? There wasn't a note or anything with it." The lightweight, finely woven fabric was obviously expensive, and Thia almost refused to wear it. Then Cinna pointed out it would cover her dress completely, making her entrance even grander.

"I can't do that, Milady. Baroness Elizabeth told me it was yours, and that no matter what you said I wasn't allowed to return it to her." Cinna moved to one side, giving Thia room to enter. Five steps in, she stopped.

Jinaari rose from his seat, and her heart began to race. She figured he'd wear something different than what she was used to seeing him in, but she wasn't prepared for this.

Black pants and a white shirt, neither of which were embellished but still finely made. A silver circlet, inlaid with gemstones, rested on his head. "What's wrong?" he asked.

"Nothing," she stammered. "It's just . . . I'm not used to seeing you out of armor, I guess."

"You're still hiding under a cloak. Or are you eating with that on?"

Cinna rushed in front of her, tugging at the wide strips of fabric that kept it tied together, "Of course she's not, Your Highness!" Before Thia could stop her, she'd removed the cloak and taken it away.

The heather gray dress fit her perfectly. When she'd first put it on, she'd stared at her reflection in shock. There was not an inch of leeway. The design accentuated every curve she had, and a few she didn't know about.

He let out a low whistle and moved closer to her. "I'm not used to seeing you in something like this, either." He glanced past her, lowering his voice enough that no one else would hear but her. "We need to talk, you and I. Tonight."

Trumpets blared, and she took a deep breath. "Tonight, you are the Crown Prince and I am the Daughter of Keroys."

He moved alongside her and held out his arm. "You can't avoid me forever."

Two tall doors at the far end of the room opened. Thia swallowed, trying to picture her box in her mind.

"Ready?" Jinaari asked her.

"No, but I can't stop now."

He covered her hand with his as it rested on his arm. "If anyone tries to harm you, Daughter, I will make them pay for it."

"Is that the word of the Lord Defender or my friend?"

"Which do you think?" He started to walk, keeping a steady pace. "Try smiling a little," he told her, "or nod to different people. It makes you seem approachable. Like it or not, we're on display right now."

They stopped at the doorway. The hall was full of close to two hundred people. Tables and benches filled most of the space. Ahead of them, a long table sat on a raised platform. Steps on each side led to the chairs behind it. Baroness Elizabeth stood at the center. The chairs to her left and right were both empty, waiting for them to join her. Pan smiled at her, and Valerie stood next to him. The rest of the seats were filled by her aunts and uncles.

"His Royal Highness, Prince Jinaari Althir," the herald began to speak, and the room went silent. "Lord Defender of Avoch, and Heir of Queen Agrana. Long may she reign!"

"Long may she reign," the populace recited the phrase in a single voice.

"Her Ladyship Thia Beckenburg, daughter of Bran, and Daughter of Keroys."

Thia curtseyed, glad for Jinaari's steadying arm.

"We are honored to break bread with you this night, Prince Jinaari. It is not often we have royal visitors. Or that we have family returned to us," Baroness Elizabeth greeted them. "Please, join us." She gestured to the empty seats on each side of her.

"Gladly, Your Excellency. Know that Her Majesty will be told of your kindness and hospitality." Jinaari led Thia toward the bottom of the dais. As they walked, she heard the shocked whispers behind them. "What's that all about?" he muttered.

"Keroys gave me this dress," she replied, keeping her voice low. "He said there would come a time where I would need to show to the world that I was, indeed, Marked."

Out of the corner of her eye, she saw his head move as he glanced behind her. The fabric was cut away, framing the Mark in a way that it couldn't be missed. "You certainly got their attention."

They stopped in front of the platform, and he let go of her arm. She didn't move away, though. "Your Excellency, if I may speak?"

Jinaari stopped and turned around, his head cocked slightly to one side. She knew the look. He hated surprises and she just handed him one.

Her aunt nodded, and Thia took a deep breath. It was one thing to show everyone the Mark. She knew the only way some would accept her was to demonstrate of the type of power she had. They didn't have to know she couldn't access it all, not yet. "You have shown me more kindness and acceptance in the last day than I have seen from many in my entire life. I wish to give something back to my family, if you will permit me to do so."

"What are you asking for, Thia?"

She turned, looking at one of her uncles. "Your daughter, Alba. Is she nearby? May I see her?"

He blinked. "Of course."

Thia stood in place, waiting, as the young woman was found. Within minutes, a cloaked figure began to walk toward her. She smiled at her. "You are my cousin, Alba. I know I can help you. Keroys has made it so I can. Are you willing to accept healing from me?"

The figure shook her head. "It's not possible. Others have already tried." The pain in her voice broke Thia's heart.

"They were wrong," she said. Reaching up, she removed the hood from Alba's head. Her face was full of oozing sores and flaking skin. "Trust me," she whispered. Thia drew the sigil, not worrying if anyone saw it. They'd never be able to duplicate it. As the spell left her hands and settled on Alba, a yellow light engulfed her. Slowly, the pus-filled sores began to dissipate. Alba's face was the first to clear away, followed by her hands. Thia knew it was working on her cousin's entire body. Within minutes, all sign of the infection evaporated, leaving smooth skin.

Alba raised her hands, staring at them in amazement. The girl then turned toward the high table, smiling at her parents.

They rushed to her, embracing their daughter, as the crowd began to talk rapidly. Thia ignored the noise and headed up to take her place next to her aunt. "That was, unexpected, Thia. But appreciated. Alba's been isolated due to the disease for over a year. It does my heart good to see her and her parents able to hold each other again."

"As I said, I wanted to repay the family in some way." Thia replied, reaching for her goblet.

Dinner began, and she kept her attention on her plate. So many pieces of silverware to keep track of! "It's okay, Cousin," Pan said. "No one's going to leave in a huff if you use the wrong fork."

She laughed. "Good." Looking up, she searched the crowd for Adam and Caelynn. She found the warlock easily. But she couldn't find Caelynn's pink head anywhere.

"She's up there," Pan motioned with his knife to the balcony that sat high on one of the walls. Several musicians were setting up, and the bard was among them.

As the dishes disappeared, she watched as the tables below were removed from the room and the benches moved to the side. Everyone looked at the high table expectantly.

"Thia?" Jinaari appeared at her elbow.

She took a moment to fold the cloth napkin and place it on the table. He'd warned her that it was expected for them to start the dancing. Rising, she took his hand and let him lead her back down to the floor.

As the music began, she whispered, "I'm not any good at this."

"You don't have to be perfect. Just don't step on my feet." Several other couples joined them, and they began the intricate movements of changing partners.

When she got back to him, he whispered, "We have to talk, you and I."

"About what?" she asked.

"I told you, back in Almair, that you and I needed to talk more once I finished with the messenger. You've been avoiding that conversation ever since."

"We're talking now, aren't we?"

"This isn't something I think you want to discuss in front of everyone else. Unless you're fine with me kissing you in front of your entire family?"

She felt her cheeks grow hot. He moved away from her, and she found herself dancing with Pan.

"What's wrong? You're blushing. Did you have too much mead? Are you sick?" The questions rushed out of his mouth.

"I'm fine," she said. "It's been a long day is all." They moved again, and she struggled to regain her composure. She knew he was watching her, waiting for the steps to bring them together again.

"Well?" he asked as they came together again.

"What is it that the crown requires of the Daughter of Keroys?" She tried to keep her voice light. Instead, it cracked.

"The crown? Nothing. This is between you and me, Thia. The rest of the world doesn't need to get involved."

"As long as you wear that circlet and I have on this dress, we aren't Thia and Jinaari. You know this better than I do." She spun away, grateful for the steps of the dance switching up.

The last notes died off, and the two lines of dancers bowed at each other. As the musicians took up a new tune, the crowd began to fill the dance floor. Taking advantage of the distraction, she slipped out a side door and headed back to her room. If anyone asked, she'd say the day's events were overwhelming.

It wasn't a lie.

Once in her room, she sat on the bench and buried her head in her hands. *Damn it*, she swore at herself. *Why am I so afraid of talking to him?* She'd let fear take over again. Taking several deep breaths, she tried to quell the nervousness. *I don't know what's worse. Being afraid he doesn't care, or terrified that he does.*

Glancing over, she saw the letter where she'd left it. "I'm sorry, Papa," she whispered. "I wish you were here, telling me not to be afraid of everything."

"You forgot the second rule," Jinaari said.

Her head jerked toward the sound of his voice. He leaned against the door jamb, one hand resting on the knob. "I guess it's habit," she stammered, looking away. "The doors at the cloister didn't have locks, and I've always felt safe at The Green Frog." Her voice trailed off as she heard him close the door, cutting off her escape. Whatever he was going to say, she'd have to hear it now.

"I told the Baroness you were tired," his tone was conversational, and that made her even more nervous. "She understood. But it was bad form to disappear like you did.

You'll have to work on that." He brought one of the chairs over and placed it in front of her before sitting down.

"I don't anticipate being invited to many feasts," she said.

"You should. That dress, what you did for your cousin . . . word is going to spread about who you are, what you can do. When we're done taking down Drogon, you'll have more invitations than you'll know what to do with." He pointed at the letter. "Who's that from?"

She took a deep breath. "My father. He wrote it before I was born. Somehow, he knew I'd come here." She looked back at her hands, her stomach in knots. *If I don't look at him, I won't see anything.* "When do we leave to take care of Drogon, anyway?" she asked, trying to steer the conversation around anything else he might bring up. "We've been here for two days already, and it's, what, a week until we get to Dragonspire from here?"

"Thia . . ." he said.

"I mean," she kept going. She knew she was rambling but didn't care. "It's got to be dealt with. We know what he is and having a Forsaken wandering about is never a good thing."

"Thia . . ." his voice was more insistent.

"You're the Lord Defender of the realm, right? If the crown summons you to deal with a problem, then you have to deal with it. Sitting around here for a week isn't what you need to do. I'm sure Adam and Caelynn are more than ready to get moving."

"Thia," Jinaari put his hands on the side of her face and forced her to look at him. "Take a breath. You sound like Pan."

She took a deep breath but wouldn't look at his face. *I trust him, he's saved my life countless times. So why am I so afraid of what he wants to say?*

"I need you to listen to me. Don't talk, just listen. Please."

She nodded, the knot in her stomach tightening even more.

Jinaari let go of her head and grasped her hands in his. "I've only truly trusted two people in my life. Even as a paladin, when we're trained to trust our brothers in a fight, it didn't extend past that training. Because of my position, I always wondered if any camaraderie they showed me was because of those connections. Adam is one of those people. You're the other one. I know that no matter what, you've got my back. I can relax around you in a way I still don't understand but never want to lose.

"When I woke up and discovered what Alesso had done, it was everything I could do not to punch holes in the wall. I had to stay calm. That's what the others needed from me, to see me stay focused. To be that arrogant prick you've rightly said I am. It was that confidence that kept them from falling apart. Kept me from doing the same. I'd made a promise to protect you and failed at it." She drew a deep breath but didn't speak as he squeezed her hand. "Don't tell me you don't blame me. I know this already. That doesn't mean I didn't feel like I had.

"At that moment, the mission shifted. It wasn't just about killing Lolc Aon. It was finding you, getting you out of there no matter what. I knew you'd fight against anything she tried. I had no doubt about that. You're one of the strongest women I've ever known, Thia. I knew I wouldn't have to do what Keroys asked of me. The question I couldn't answer was how hurt you'd be when we found you.

"The level of shock you were in scared me. I've never

been that frightened in my life. We all took turns watching you, hoping you'd wake up. It was in those moments that I came to realize that the reason went beyond trusting you. It hurt my soul to think you wouldn't wake up, that you wouldn't be there to remind me I'm insufferable or demanding. I remember hoping that your stubbornness was enough to get you through it." He paused. "You were fighting for your soul, and I couldn't do a damn thing except watch you do it.

"Father Philip told me I should try to get you to talk about what happened when you woke up. He said it was necessary, or it'd eat away at you. Cut into your confidence. You don't have much of that to begin with, though it's getting better."

Thia chuckled. "I'm trying, but it's not easy."

"I know that," he said. "You've grown so much since we first met. I've felt honored to watch you come out of that shell you built around yourself. I see who you are, Thia, not just what you think everyone sees." He paused. "When you told me what Lolc Aon did to you, I know that wasn't easy. She forced you to see something you wouldn't admit to yourself. Something both of us couldn't. You were honest with me. I wanted to do the same for you, show you that I had started to care for you beyond that as a friend."

"I gave up on the idea anyone could see me that way before I went to the cloister," she whispered. "Besides," she continued, "you're the Crown Prince of Avoch. You and I both know your rank alone means you can't be involved with anyone like me."

"You're the Daughter of Keroys, Thia. After what you did tonight, the dress you're wearing, the world will know. Who your mother was won't matter. Look at me." His voice was soft, but insistent.

She raised her head and met his eyes.

"Whatever this is," he continued, "is between us. No one else has a say in it. Hide from the rest of the world if you must, but don't hide from me."

"You know that's not how this will play out, Jinaari. As long as you wear that crown, and I wear this dress, there will be demands on us."

"You're right. But that doesn't dictate everything in our lives." He took a deep breath, releasing it slowly. "What happens out there is one thing. What happens here, between you and me, isn't part of that."

"But..."

"No buts. I'm here because I know you. I don't care about who your parents were, or what God they worshipped. Even if you weren't Marked, if Garret hadn't told me to protect you, I would be here. Because I accept you for who you are, even when you're being incredibly stubborn."

She laughed. "That's only because you're arrogant."

"If I can accept you, see you for who you truly are, can't you do the same for me? Around you, I am who I want to be. Not a prince, not a warrior. Just a man who sees himself fortunate to know you." He gazed at her, a question in his eyes.

She closed her eyes, unwilling to believe what she saw. "I'm scared," she whispered.

"Of me?"

Shaking her head, she said, "No. Never you."

"Then what is it? Thia, talk to me."

"I'm part Fallen, Jinaari. I've heard the stories of how the women are since I reached the cloister. The abuse, the degradation. I'm scared," she drew a breath, "of hurting you."

She felt his lips on her forehead. "Look at me, Thia."

His face filled her vision. All she saw was trust, no fear. "You're as human as I am. More so, in some ways. You're not going to hurt me."

He leaned forward, kissing her gently, and she didn't pull away.

CHAPTER
THIRTY-ONE

Thia opened her eyes. It had to be close to dawn, but there was no light coming through her window. Sitting up, she kept the blanket against her chest. Jinaari knelt in front of the fireplace. "Is something wrong?" she asked.

"It was cold in here, so I thought I'd put another log on." He rose. He was dressed, the white shirt untucked. "How are you?" he asked as he came alongside the bed.

"I'm okay. Why?"

He sat down, picking up her free hand. "This doesn't look normal."

Glancing down, she saw faint gold sparks rise from her fingertips. "That's never happened before," she said, raising her hand closer to her face. She tucked the blanket under her arm and looked at her left hand. It was doing the same thing. "I don't understand," she stammered.

He frowned. "How are your magic stores? Does that feel different in any way?"

She reached into that part of her mind, and her heart

began to race. Any limitation she'd felt before was gone. "It's ... I can't describe it."

"Try."

"It's bottomless now. Every restriction I've ever felt is gone. I don't think I have to draw a sigil even." Looking over at the worktable, she imagined her box rising in the air. Before she could take another breath, it began to hover above the wood surface. She lowered it and looked at Jinaari. "When I renounced Lolc Aon, there was a shift within me. I felt the raw power Keroys gave me, but I couldn't tap into it. That's gone. Why? How?"

"When I was at the portal, before I came back, Keroys said something else. He said you'd have to renounce everything about the life you would've lived if you'd been raised by your mother."

"I know. That was one of the conditions. I had to renounce one life and accept another."

Jinaari smiled. "Maybe the other life you had to accept was that there's people who don't see your bloodline, and only care about you." He engulfed one of her hands in his. "I told you I wasn't afraid of you. Looks like I finally got you to understand that."

"Do you really think it's that simple?"

Standing up, he shrugged. "I'm a warrior, Thia. The magic I can do is basic, simple things that'll keep me or someone else alive. If you're not sure, talk to Adam. Tell him what happened, see if he agrees with you. He's studied all kinds of magic."

She felt her cheeks grow hot. "I thought you said this was between you and me."

He grinned. "I didn't say you have to tell him everything. Even if you did, it won't matter to him or

Caelynn. Those two have been keeping each other warm for months."

"Is that what you call last night? Keeping each other warm?" She giggled.

Leaning down, he kissed her. "I certainly wasn't cold," he whispered. "You can tell him you think it's a result of accepting the welcome of your family. It could be part of it, you know. There's not been a single person here that I've seen look at you as anything but one of them." He walked over to the door. "I'm going back to my room, get changed, pack up. You reminded me last night that Drogon's still out there. I'd hate to keep him waiting." Reaching down, he picked up his boots.

"Duty calls?"

"Something like that." Jinaari turned the key in the lock. "We've got a week of hard riding ahead of us. You'll have time to get used to this bottomless well Keroys gave you. It's yours, now. You are the Daughter of Keroys in every way, Thia. Drogon's not going to hold back this time, so be ready for him." She watched him open the door and leave, closing it behind him.

Sliding out of bed, she walked over and turned the key. "Rule number two," she muttered. *He's right. I've got to learn how to control this, and what exactly I can do. I may have bottomless stores, but there's spells Keroys won't let me do. Drogon won't have any limits.*

She walked over to where her pack sat and dug out some clothes. Once she was dressed, she folded the dress she'd worn the night before. It served a purpose, yes, but wasn't something she could wear while riding a horse. *We're leaving today. Get ready, say our goodbyes, and go. I'll need to tell them I can access everything, so they're not surprised when I start experimenting.*

Her hand smoothed the fabric of the dress. Memories of the night before filled her mind. Not just the dinner, but afterward. Was it really that simple to unlock Keroys's gift?

"Yes, Daughter. It really was that simple."

Turning, she faced her God. "Then why was it so terrifying?"

He sat in a chair and motioned her to do the same. "Trust is never something you've given easily, Thia. And with reason. To accept that someone cares means they went beyond just words. It's the deeds they do, the faith they show in you. Your family here, you don't trust them yet."

"No," she replied as she sat down. "They haven't done anything but be welcoming, accepting, yet . . ."

"Yet you have seen family whose deeds counteract the words."

Thia nodded.

"Jinaari earned your trust, on every level. If he hadn't, you wouldn't have dreaded the conversation last night. Your fear wasn't that you'd hurt him, Daughter. It was that he would reject you."

"What happens now? You gave me this Mark, this power. What is it you need me to do?"

Keroys smiled. "I could say I want you to be happy, but you wouldn't accept that. You're stubborn, like your father." He gestured to the box resting on the table. "Bran argued with me for three days over making that box for you. He was convinced, wrongly, that even unwrapping his tools would break the bargain he'd made with Herasta. I pointed out that nothing was set in stone until your birth, as Herasta wouldn't know until then that he was the father. I knew, but she didn't.

"To answer your question, you know part of it. Drogon

must be brought down, before he can do more damage to the world."

"The rest?"

"Jinaari did what none of my family could. My sister is gone, unlikely to return. The people who followed her, though, are not all evil. I believe most will seek to rejoin the surface world. Prejudices run deep between humans and the Fallen. You know this. By Marking someone who is of both races, it was my hope that you could show Avoch that tolerance and understanding are a better path over slavery and slaughter."

"What if they won't listen to me?"

He smiled. "Then make your voice be heard. You're meant to be visible in the world, someone others can call on for help. They'll hesitate at first, but you'll win them over. I have faith in you."

Thia opened her mouth, ready to object, but he disappeared as quickly as he'd appeared. *I rejected one life, accepted another. But I still don't know what I'm doing.*

The doorknob rattled, and she looked toward the sound. "Thia?" Pan's voice was worried. "Are you awake?"

Rising, she walked to the door and unlocked it. Swinging it open, she let him into the room. "I'm fine. Why?"

"You left so early last night. Mother said you were tired, but I was worried."

She smiled. "It was a lot to take in yesterday, that's all. How's Alba?"

"Good, thanks to you. Valerie is totally in awe of you. I told her you might be able to make her see again, but she won't hear of it. Says it's how Keroys made her, and she's never known anything else so why play with it." Pan kept talking, barely taking a breath. "She does want to talk to you again, though, before we leave. Is that okay? I don't know when we're leaving or anything like that."

"We're leaving as soon as everyone gets their gear packed," Jinaari said from the door. Thia looked his way. He'd changed into his traveling gear, though he hadn't put any armor on yet.

"Today?" Pan asked.

"Unless you want to stay longer. Thia's got to take care of Drogon, Pan. We've got to get her there. We can't do that from here."

"I'll get packed." The young man headed for the door.

"I've already woken up Adam and Caelynn. We're meeting in the stables. If you see your mother, let her know. I'd rather leave quietly over making it a ceremony, though."

"Oh, okay. She'll probably still want to come say goodbye. Especially to Thia."

"You know where we're going, Pan. If she wants to meet us there, I'd love to thank her for all she's done," Thia said.

Pan left, and she turned back to her pack. "I'm almost ready," she said. She pulled out the chain shirt and lifted it over her head before grabbing a clean tunic.

Jinaari closed the door. "One more thing," he said as he walked closer to her.

"What's that?" she asked as she pulled the hem of the tunic down to lay flat against her body.

His hand came under her chin, raising her head to look at him. "Are we good? You and me? No regrets this morning?"

"No regrets," she said. She felt her cheeks grow warm but didn't care. "Unless you count me wishing we could find an inn on the road where we can keep each other warm again."

He grinned at her. "I'll keep that in mind."

Stepping away from him, she wrapped up her box. "Keroys came here, after you left."

"That's a good thing?"

Nodding, she continued to pack the belt pouch. "I know what I have to do, once we've dealt with Drogon. I just don't know how to do it." She wound the belt around her waist. "Do you think I can talk you and the others into hanging around me a while longer? I'll need help."

"I'm sworn to protect you. I'm not going anywhere. Pretty sure the rest will feel the same way." He lifted her pack off the bench.

Slipping her arms into her coat, she shifted her body enough to let the chain mail settle into a comfortable position. "Where's your bag?"

"In my room. I need to get my armor on."

"What stopped you?"

"I heard Pan pounding at your door. I was concerned he'd talk you into a goodbye that lasted half the day if I didn't motivate him." He pointed to the key in the lock. "You need that?"

Thia pulled it out, tapping it in her hand while he walked through the opening. "I'm not sure how often I'll be back. Maybe I should leave it here, for safekeeping."

"Take it, Thia. Even if you only visit once a year. I overheard what your aunt said about sealing the room after someone dies. Leaving the key would imply you didn't think you'd ever return."

That makes sense, she thought. *And I do want to come back, some day.* She followed Jinaari into the hallway, closing the door and locking it behind them. Heading down the hallway to his room, she said, "Give my pack. You've got to get your metal suit on."

Caelynn and Adam came into the hallway as Jinaari

opened the door to his room. "We're ready when you two are." Adam said as they got closer.

"Soon as he's done getting his armor on, we're heading to the stables," Thia explained. "Drogon's not going to wait patiently, and we have to stop him for good." Kneeling down, she pulled her gloves out of her pack. Between the cold temperatures outside and the yellow sparks that still flew off her fingers, she wanted to cover her hands before anyone asked questions.

"Thia, what's that?" Adam's voice was low.

"What's what?" She straightened up, pulling the glove onto one hand.

"There's sparks flying off your hands," Caelynn whispered. "That's not normal."

"The short version is I came into everything Keroys gave me."

Adam's head shifted to one side, and he gave her a curious look. "The long version?"

"Will wait until we're on the road," she replied. "I don't want anyone here to see this and ask questions." Lacing her fingers together, she made sure the gloves were on all the way. "I promise I'll tell you once we're alone. Pan's going to want to know, too."

"Does he know?" Caelynn pointed to Jinaari's door.

"Do I know what?" he asked as he stepped through.

"Thia's unlocked her power!"

Jinaari looked at her. "Really? Care to explain that one to me?"

Biting her lip, she kept the smile off her face. *He knows, but he's giving me the chance to tell the story I want them to know. One he'll never contradict.* "As I told them, it'll wait for the road. I don't want to explain everything three times."

He nodded. "Let's get going, then."

The four of them headed to the stables. Pan was there, talking with one of the grooms who was saddling his horse. Their horses were led out to the courtyard. Without a word, Thia secured her pack to her saddle.

"Will you be coming back, niece?" Elizabeth asked from behind her.

Thia turned around. "I hope so, one day. I can't say when that'll be, but I have my key."

Elizabeth reached out and took one of her hands. "Knowing you're alive, that Bran lives in you, makes me happy. Be safe." She looked at Jinaari. "You'll keep them all that way, won't you?"

"I will."

The Baroness smiled and stepped back. "Keroys is with you, Thia. Trust in him, in your companions, and do what you must. We'll wait your return, whenever it is." She walked away and headed to where Pan stood with the groom.

Thia mounted her horse, settling into the saddle. Around her, the others did the same. Jinaari looked at her, a question on his face. "I'm ready," she said.

"Then let's go. Drogon's waiting." He put his heels to his horse, urging it forward. Thia followed him.

As they went under the archway that left the keep, she looked over her shoulder. Elizabeth and the groom stood in the courtyard, watching them leave.

Turning around, she saw a man running at Jinaari. He stopped, and she moved closer. "Are you certain?" she heard him ask the man.

"The commander had it confirmed by three others. We went to the merchant who supplied the wraith. Everything suggests he's become a sell-sword, and Drogon was the highest bidder." The man glanced at Thia before continuing. "I'm sorry, brother. We weren't permitted to leave the chapterhouse until after he'd accepted the offer. If we'd gotten away sooner, he'd be dead in a ditch."

"That's fine. I know where to find him now. Are you heading back today?"

"Tomorrow. The entire chapterhouse got ordered to move with the army toward the valley. The camp should be established by now. You can't miss it."

Thia waited for the man to leave, then moved her horse up next to Jinaari. "What was that about?"

"Alesso managed to get himself a job before any of my brothers could educate him on his poor life choices." He spat at the ground. "He'll regret that decision, among others."

"What job?"

He looked at her, his face serious. "He's become Drogon's sell-sword."

CHAPTER
THIRTY-TWO

Five days later, the first evidence of Drogon's location came into view. In the distance, settled over the Dragonspire mountains, was something all too familiar. The storm cloud, illuminated by flashes of lightning, sat as if anchored. Thia shivered, grateful for the soft leather gloves she wore. There was more *wrongness* to the cloud than the one that'd been over Tanisal.

"Relax," Jinaari told her. "Distances here are deceiving. That's a full days' ride yet just to get to the foothills. We rest up, find a way in the next day."

"At least we won't have to go into the city," Adam said. "Unless it's necessary for the Lord Defender to talk about a problem before he solves it."

Jinaari snorted. "I'm a simple man. I'd rather take care of something over talk about the necessity of dealing with it." He sighed. "She's not there, anyway. I got news that the army and my brothers got ordered to march here. Her Majesty decided to watch me take care of the problem personally. We can't avoid her that easily."

Thia caught the disdain in his voice. "I can say Keroys needs me elsewhere and we can't delay. Would that help?"

"It might." His voice was curt. "Any guesses at what we're in for when we get into the valley?" Jinaari asked Adam.

"He's got to be in a tower of some kind," the blond man replied. "I've been in there. There are no caves to speak of, outside of the ones leading into or out of the area. Those aren't anything you'd want to hide in. They're too narrow and well known. The grassland's flat, and it wouldn't be difficult to build. I've thought of doing that myself a time or two."

"What's the terrain like? Will we be able to find cover?"

Adam shook his head. "I doubt it. There's nothing but a field rimmed by the mountains. We can get to the valley unseen, but not any closer. Unless he was stupid and put it against the rock instead of in the center."

"It won't matter," Thia said. "He's expecting us. He knows that I'm the only one that can stop him."

Jinaari nodded. "She's right. He wants something from her."

"What he wants," she said, raising her head, "is a rematch. I didn't know what I was when we met before. He did, though. He's the one that told me I was Marked. This is by design. Drogon knew Lolc Aon was after me, stayed quiet until Jinaari took care of her. He thinks my box should've been his. It's not, but truth doesn't matter to him."

"He's Forsaken, Thia," Pan said.

"I know," she replied. "Keroys made me his Daughter for a reason. Dealing with Drogon was part of it."

"What about Alesso?" Caelynn asked.

"Thia gets Drogon. Jinaari gets Alesso. We three just

make sure they can do their jobs." Adam looked over his shoulder at Thia. "I'm just wondering if you're going to leave the rest of us anything to play with."

Thia kept her eyes on the cloud as they talked. It was full of rage but contained in some way. It wouldn't take much to unleash it, though.

That's what he's drawing his magic from, she realized. *The cloud over Tanisal, the machine . . . it was him trying to find a way to store magic until he needed it. He's Forsaken. He has to draw his power from somewhere, a place it can stay until he calls on it. Drogon doesn't have the stores I do. It was taken from him.* "That's it."

"What is?" Jinaari's voice broke through her thoughts.

"I know why he wants me, wants my box," she breathed.

"Let's hear it."

She shook her head and took a deep breath, trying to find the words to explain it. "When we fought him underneath Tanisal, he said something to me. I didn't understand it at the time, but I do now."

"He said a lot of things, Thia," Caelynn pointed out. "Lies are part of what he is. I wouldn't put stock in anything that came out of his mouth."

"But he didn't lie to me, that's the thing. He's the one that told me I was Marked by Keroys. He knew Lolc Aon was coming after me. There's nothing he said that was a lie."

"What about the crap about your father being in that machine?" The elf asked.

"Even that was true. Papa came to me at the cloister, after I came out of my coma. His soul had been trapped in there. I didn't destroy it. I set it free, same as the rest of them."

"What did he tell you?" Adam asked. "I was trying to save the old man, so didn't hear it."

Thia smiled as Jinaari snorted at the nickname. "He said, 'It should've been mine. A place for me to store part of myself.' He was talking about the box that Papa made me. It's the last one he ever made. He couldn't make them again because of the agreement he made with Herasta." She twisted in her saddle, fumbling with the pouch with one hand. "I thought it would only hold spell components. But then I looked at the cloud and put the pieces together. Drogon doesn't have stores in him for magic, not like the rest of us do. He has to create things to put the magic into until he uses it."

"Like the storms or the machine," Jinaari finished her thought, nodding his head.

"Exactly. Since my box makes it so whatever I put in it never runs out—"

"He could put a small bit of magic in there and never run out. Damn." Adam shook his head. "If he gets that box, he'd be unstoppable."

Jinaari looked at her. "It's keyed to you, though. No one can open it but you. He needs you alive to gain access to it."

Slowly, she nodded her head. "Unless he can get me to transfer the attunement to him, that is."

"Can't we just destroy the box?" Pan asked.

Thia cradled the leather wrapped box in her hand, staring at it. "As a last resort, yes," she said. "But I'm not sure what will happen when we do."

"I don't like how you said that, Cousin," he said.

"The box is the last one Papa made. From what I've learned, the others that exist don't do what this one does. Yes, they're all made where the owner is the only one that can open them. That was part of the reason they were in demand. There's no lock for a thief to pick. I talked with your mother about it. None of the ones the family have work like mine does. Those are all normal boxes, nothing magical about them. Keroys did something to mine after Papa made it. It's the only one that keeps whatever you put into it."

"And, since it's attuned to you, that could rebound on you once it's destroyed," Adam shook his head. "It could make the headache I got when my staff cracked look like nothing more than a bruise."

"We don't destroy the box." Jinaari's voice cut off any argument.

She put the box back into the pouch and looked at him. "If it's the only way to keep him from having it, I will do exactly that. You stay out of my fight, Jinaari, and I'll stay out of yours."

"Speaking of a fight," Adam said.

Thia looked up, following where the warlock was pointing. Ahead of them, spread out across the foothills of the mountain range, was an army. Thousands of tents sat in neat rows around a series of larger tents in the middle. Banners fluttered in the breeze, emblazoned with both the symbol of Avoch and the royal seal.

"Looks like we found your mother, old man."

Thia caught the dark shadow that passed over Jinaari's face before he straightened in his saddle.

"Let's go, then," he said. "Her Majesty has been informed we're coming, and she doesn't like to be kept waiting."

Thia straightened in her saddle, her shoulders tensing up. She rode next to him but stayed silent. *This is his world, even if he doesn't like it. He'll keep me from screwing up.* Once they hit the sentries, they both would have to play the role that others expected of them. *If I'm lucky, they won't recognize me. I won't need to be the Daughter of Keroys until after we leave.*

"Pull down your hood, Thia," Jinaari told her.

Reaching up, she pushed it back. "Why?"

"You need to be seen. The Queen will have been told who you are, what you are, and given a description of you by now. She'll know everyone that travels with me. Duke Tomil would've informed her when we got back from Byd Cudd."

"The Duke knew who I was?" she asked, shocked.

He nodded. "He'd heard rumors before we went to take care of Lolc Aon. Someone on his staff has a sister who works for Father Philip. They overheard you talking to him about being Marked." He paused. "Be careful around her, Thia. My mother comes across as if she wants to be your ally, but she can play politics better than anyone I've ever met. Whatever she asks you to do, there's usually five reasons beyond what she tells you. Never give her a promise that's not clear and concise in what it encompasses. She'll twist it to fit what she needs before you realize that you've been trapped."

"I'd say that's a horrible thing to say about your own mother, but mine wasn't a paragon of virtue either." They rode in silence for a few minutes. "Would it be wrong if I insisted on one of you being present any time she and I talked?"

"If Her Royal Majesty says she will talk with someone alone, then everyone clears the room. Even her guards and attendants. She's in command and knows it. The power you wield should be enough that she'll treat you with respect."

"I heard a 'but' at the end of that, Jinaari."

He shifted in his saddle before looking at her. "My

family's not known for embracing the Fallen. Even ambassadors and trade delegations went to Almair over Dragonspire because of it. Tomil would negotiate and send the goods to the capital."

"Then why did you have me put my hood down?" she asked.

"She knows you're part Fallen already. I *hope* that she's done enough research to learn your full history. And that you're more human than anything else." He looked at her, his face softening. "She won't hurt you, Thia. She wouldn't dare. But her prejudices run deep. If I thought we had time, and it wasn't as cold, I'd have you pull that dress out and wear it. It may be necessary, if she insists on holding a formal meal or requires you to join her in court. For now, though, you need to put your mask on. Don't let her think you're not sure of yourself. She'll take advantage of it if she can."

She nodded, mulling over his words in her mind. Their conversations at night had helped her prepare for this. *The world only knows the Daughter, not me. I don't have to show them the person Jinaari knows, or even Adam and Caelynn. Time to put it to the test*, she thought. Closing her eyes, she took a few deep breaths. The image she saw in her mind was a confident, sure woman. Someone who was prepared to do what was necessary and wouldn't take no for an answer. Opening her eyes, she glanced at him. "And how does the Crown Prince of Avoch wish to introduce me?"

He nodded. "Hold onto that as long as you can. The camp needs to see that strength as much as my mother does."

The rest of the group moved behind the two of them, letting them take the lead. As soon as they came into view of the forward sentries, one took off running. "We've been recognized," Jinaari muttered.

"That's what we wanted, right?"

He nodded but stayed silent. One of the guards walked toward them, kneeling as they brought their horses to a stop. "Your Royal Highness," he said. "Her Majesty told us to expect you and your companions. May I have the honor of escorting you? Your friends will be shown to tents."

"Escort all of us or none of us," Jinaari said. "My companions will stay with me unless Her Majesty tells me directly herself."

The sentry rose, nodding. "Of course, I'm sorry," he stammered, "I didn't mean to give offense."

"None was taken. I'm certain that Her Majesty is anxious to greet us. Lead on."

Turning crisply, the soldier walked down the wide path between tents that served as a road. It was barely wide enough for them to ride side by side. Soldiers stopped what they were doing and watched as they passed. Many stared at her, their faces openly hostile. Thia kept her eyes on their escort, sitting as straight in her saddle as she dared. "You're doing fine," Jinaari whispered. "None of them would dare touch you right now."

"It's not now that worries me. It's later when I'm asleep. Canvas can be cut with a knife."

He moved his head slightly. "There's a contingent from my chapterhouse here. I'll get word to Drakkus, have him send some of my brothers to stand as your bodyguard when I'm not with you. After what happened with Alesso, none of them would dare let anyone near you."

She nodded. "Thank you."

Six groomsmen came running toward them as they approached the central pavilion and grabbed the reins of the horses. Dismounting, she took a moment to let her legs get used to being on the ground. They'd been riding for most of the day and her body ached. She felt a hand on her elbow. Raising her head, she looked at Jinaari.

"This way, Daughter."

She glanced back at the others. Adam and Caelynn's faces were stony and reserved. Pan's lit up with excitement. "I've never met the Queen," he said, smiling at her.

"Try not to show your disappointment," Jinaari told him quietly. "It's considered rude."

The horses were led away. Two armed guards stood at attention on either side of the wide awning leading into the pavilion. Thia stopped and Jinaari turned around, his face questioning her with a look. She took a deep breath to try to quiet the butterflies in her stomach. Nodding once, she said, "I'm ready."

He put her arm through his. "Remember who you are. You've got more power than she ever will. That doesn't mean you have to let her control you. You are beholden to Keroys and no one else, Daughter." mm

They stopped in front of a decorated wall. A courtier bowed, then moved aside the flap, and stepped through. A voice broke through the silence. "Your Majesty, Prince Jinaari and his companions have arrived."

CHAPTER
THIRTY-THREE

Jinaari waited for the herald to stop speaking, knowing what would happen next. "When we get to her, don't try to curtsy. Just follow what I do. You're not dressed for anything else," he kept his voice low.

Thia nodded her understanding. She was getting better at using a public face, but he knew her tells. Her nerves were pulled tight. "Drakkus is probably in there," he whispered. "Stay with Adam if I wander off. I need to talk to him about your guards."

The tent flap parted, and he led her into the makeshift great hall. Braziers filled with hot coals hung from the half dozen wooden posts that held up the roof. Candles burned at regular intervals. Between the two, the room was warm and well lit. A score of dignitaries turned to watch them enter. His attention though, was focused on the end of the room.

Queen Agrana sat regally in a chair, the back of it carved with a shield, scepter, and crown. The three symbols of rule within Avoch. Her brown hair pinned up, partially supporting her crown. Behind her, Amara and Stijyn stood.

His sister smiled at him warmly. His brother, though, watched Thia closely.

When they were within a few feet of his mother, he moved Thia's arm off his and knelt. Out of the corner of his eye, he saw her do the same.

"The Lord Defender has answered the summons of the Crown of Avoch," he kept his voice neutral. "How may I be of service?" *I know what needs to happen, damn it. Sitting in court talking about isn't going to get it done!*

"Rise and welcome, my son." His mother moved in front of him as he stood, embracing him. "I recognize some of your companions, but not all. Who travels with the Lord Defender to aid him on his task?"

"I am honored to introduce you to Her Ladyship Thia Bransdottir, the Daughter of Keroys." He stepped back slightly as Thia rose.

"Bransdottir? I don't recognize the surname," Agrana said.

"My father was Bran Beckenburg, Your Majesty. Part of the agreement he had to make in order to raise me was to cut all ties to his family," Thia spoke quietly, but she kept her voice even.

"That's a name I know. I will speak with you, privately, Daughter of Keroys. Yours is a story I've heard, but I think many details have been embellished at each retelling."

"If we have time, I will gladly do so. Our mission is such that long delays could have disastrous results to all Avoch. I am certain that is not what Your Majesty wishes to happen."

Jinaari kept a straight face, but it was hard to do. Thia had just single handedly made it so his mother couldn't keep them beyond tonight. In front of her entire court, too.

His mother moved toward Pan, and Adam started the

introduction. Looking past the warlock, Jinaari spotted Drakkus at the far side of the pavilion. Once he caught the commander's eye, he inclined his head to one side. With a nod, the other man began to move in that direction.

"Thia," he whispered, "I've found Drakkus. Stay with Adam until I get back." She nodded, and he began to weave his way through the courtiers.

"Jinaari!" Amara's happy squeal rang in his ear as she threw her arms around his neck from behind him. "Don't tell me you're running off without talking with your favorite sister?"

"You're our only sister," Stijyn replied.

Jinaari stopped and gave his sister a quick hug. "I have to talk to someone, then we'll catch up. I promise."

Stijyn reached out and stopped him from moving. "One condition."

"What?"

Inclining his head back to where Thia and the rest stood, Stijyn smiled. "You gotta introduce me to the blonde. She's stunning."

"Her name is Thia, Stijyn. I can introduce you, but I don't recommend trying any of your moves on her. She's not what you think." He walked away, hunting down Drakkus. His brother had a roving eye and collected women like trophies. Part of him wanted to watch her shoot him down, the other wanted to warn Thia.

"You look well," Drakkus said when Jinaari got close enough.

"I'm alive, and that means Potiri won't be long after I find him. Did Garret really Foreswear him in front of the entire chapterhouse?"

"Garret snapped his medallion in half, Jinaari. Had him stripped of his armor, allowed me to punch him in the jaw once. His mother even heard what happened." Drakkus's voice was thick with shock.

"Markus found me in Cirrain, before we left. He brought me up to speed. I'll be honest. I'm glad he got away before any of my brothers could find him. It means I can take care of the problem myself."

"What can we do to help?"

"I need some brothers you trust to guard Thia. I won't be able to watch her as closely as I normally can while we're here, and there were openly hostile faces among the army as we rode in." He glanced back toward his friends. Amara and Stijyn were heading toward them. "I have to get back there. The guards?"

"Will be nearby within an hour. I'll select them myself."

Jinaari smiled. "One more thing. How'd the punch feel?"

Drakkus grinned. "Too good. He deserved it."

He wove his way through the crowd and back to Thia. Amara was talking to her, laughing as she was prone to do. Stijyn, though, kept his focus on her. She had her hands folded in front of her, and he could see one finger twitching.

"I see you've met my siblings," he said as he came up behind her.

"Don't worry, Jinaari," Amara teased him. "We're saving the best, most embarrassing stories about you for later on."

"Mother's decided to invite your friends to dine with the four of us tonight. I hope to speak with you again soon, Milady." Stijyn bowed with a flourish, grabbing her hand and pressing his lips to it.

Thia's posture shifted, and he put a hand briefly on her back to remind her he was there. "Then I guess we should go get ready. We've been riding for several days, and

Mother won't like it if we all smell like our horses." He pointedly looked at his brother. "I'm looking forward to catching up." Grabbing Thia by the elbow, he led her away.

"What was that all about?" she muttered.

"Later. Stijyn can read lips." They walked over to the others. "We need to find out where our gear went, clean up. If this dinner is happening, I can't go in my armor."

Adam pointed at a uniformed man standing to one side. "I was told that one would lead us when we were ready to go."

"We're ready," Jinaari replied.

He let Adam take the lead, staying at Thia's side. "I talked with Drakkus. You'll be kept safe."

"Thank you."

"Be careful with Stijyn."

"Why?" she turned her head, looking at him.

They followed the attendant through some narrow passages. "It's hard to explain."

"Try," she replied. "There was something about how he looked at me that made me nervous."

"He sees a beautiful woman and he starts hunting. You're in his sights."

"The ladies are to be in here," the courtier stopped, moving aside a tent flap. "Your Highness has a place across the passage. The rest will need to follow me."

Jinaari exchanged a look with Adam as the two followed their guide. At least he was close to Thia, and Caelynn would be with her.

His chamber was luxurious by camp standards. Someone had set up a large bed, covered in furs. His pack rested on the carpeted floor near a single chair. A basin of steaming water sat on a simple wooden table, with a towel and soap nearby. It wasn't a full bath, but he'd make do.

It took a few minutes to get the armor off. He washed up, changed his clothes, and contemplated laying down. "If you do, you might sleep through dinner," his mother said from behind him.

Lowering himself onto the bed, he stared at her. "What do you need from me?"

She sat in the chair. "A mother always wants her children's love. I realized some time ago that I would not receive that from you." Resting her arms on the chair, she looked at him. "You have such a sense of honor and duty about you that Avoch would do well with you as its King, should enough of humanity still live."

"I hear a 'but' in there."

Her face turned serious. "I heard about your friend before you arrived. Knew who her father was, and that's a problem."

"Baroness Elizabeth and the rest of the family welcomed her without question. You see a problem where one doesn't exist."

"But it does," she insisted. "Years ago, before you were born, a marriage contract was drawn up. It would make the first-born daughter of the eldest Beckenburg son Queen of Avoch, once she was married to my first-born son."

He stared at her, stunned. "When did you plan to tell me?"

"Grow up. You were going to rule one day, simply because of who I am. Protecting the family line, keeping an Althir on the throne, is necessary." She inhaled. "As to when, it was a moot point for so long. Bran had disappeared, with no child that anyone knew of." She stared at him, and he drew back from the intense hatred in her eyes. "I will not allow a Fallen witch to share the throne with you, Jinaari. I've already written to Baroness

Elizabeth, ordering the nullification of the contract. I had planned to talk with several nobles at your sister's wedding. See if there was one who had a suitable replacement."

His mind shrank from her words. It wasn't the contracted marriage. He expected that. The ignorance and prejudice she showed now disgusted him. She dismissed Thia based on something she had no control over. "I'm done. I'll renounce every single title, decline any salary, whatever it takes. I will not be part of any family that thinks the way you do." Shaking his head, he kept on. "I used to hope you were different than Grandfather. That his prejudices hadn't wormed their way into your soul. Thia is as human as I am. Her mother was Fallen, yes. I watched as she," he pointed toward the canvas wall, "gutted her, turned her back on every single thing that was offered to her by Lolc Aon. She was Marked, at birth, by Keroys. He wouldn't have done that if she had the smallest inclination toward the evil her mother was. She saved my life more than once. Without her, I would not be here. And you're going to take one look at her and judge her like that? At least you could've waited until after dinner, until you talked with her and got an idea of who she is."

"Avoch cannot stand with the Fallen," she insisted. "That her father raised her is, I admit, admirable. Better that she had died with him than infiltrate the church. Have you ever seen this 'Mark' she claims to have? How can you be sure it's real and not some tattoo she had done to fool you? If she's the Daughter of Keroys, why hide it? I should've seen it when she walked into the room! If she's as human as you claim, then I am her Queen!"

"First, she has nothing to prove to you. The only one that can command her is Keroys. Second, it's on her back.

No one will see it unless Thia chooses to show it to them. It's not fake. Don't ever come to me with that bullshit again. She *is* the Daughter of Keroys, even if you'd rather she wasn't."

Agrana narrowed her eyes, staring at him. "It's on her back, you say? Where the only way someone sees it is if she decides they can? And you're certain it's not fake? Don't tell me you've shared your bed with that Fallen witch! Even Stijyn wouldn't be that stupid!"

Jinaari leaped to his feet. "Get out," he growled. "I'm leaving, and my friends will be going with me. Give Amara my best, tell her I'll still walk her down the aisle if she wants, but I am *done* with the rest of you." Rage filled his veins, and his fingers flexed. He wouldn't hurt her; she was still his mother.

Well done, my paladin. It's about time she learned that you cannot serve two masters. Garret's voice sounded in his mind.

Agrana rose, her face the same mask he'd grown up seeing. The one of a Queen, not a mother. "Is this your final decision? You choose a Fallen witch over your own blood?"

"I have always chosen friendship and trust over a crown."

"I give you and your friends an hour to leave this camp. After that, I will have her arrested and brought before me. I recommend you move quickly."

"On what charge?"

Agrana stopped at the canvas wall, one hand resting on the edge. "Impersonating a Daughter of Keroys, murder, insurrection. I'm sure I'll come up with something. Given her heritage, there's a high probability she'll get hurt before she's brought before me. An hour, no more." Without another word, she disappeared between the folds of the tent wall.

Jinaari didn't waste time. Removing his heavy cloak from the pack, he began to shove his armor inside. Tomil didn't say how he got the bags, but he was immensely grateful for them now. Wrapping his sword belt around his waist, he threw the cloak over his shoulders as he picked up his pack. Running across the hall, he entered Caelynn and Thia's room. The bard stood up as he entered, her face concerned. "Where's Thia?"

"Getting cleaned up for dinner. What's wrong?"

"Tell her to stop. I'm getting Adam and Pan, then we're leaving."

Caelynn nodded. "Okay, but why?"

He dropped his pack on the floor. "I'll explain when we're on the road," he said, heading back out of the tent. Rushing down the hall, he located his other friends and urged them to get packed.

The three men headed back to the other room. Caelynn and Thia were both dressed and had their packs ready. Picking his back up, he looked at the four of them. "We have to leave. Now."

Thia looked at him. "Why?"

"I'll explain later. I promise. It's not safe for you to be here any longer." He opened the tent flap and caught sight of Drakkus leading two paladins down the corridor to them. "We're leaving. Tonight."

The commander nodded. "I won't ask." Turning to the other men, he said, "We're escorts now. Stables first, then we ride with them until they're out of the encampment."

"Thia, keep your hood up. Same with the rest of you. We don't want to be recognized if we can help it."

Drakkus stopped. "Wait here while we clear it." He disappeared around the corner.

Thia stood at his side. "Jinaari, what's going on?"

He glanced at her, debating how much to tell her now. "I've renounced my titles, for starters. My mother wasn't pleased with my decision."

He saw the fear cross her face. "It's because of me, isn't it?"

"I'll tell everyone the details later, after we're far enough from here that I think we're safe. Adam?"

"What?" the warlock stepped forward.

"You said you've been in the valley where Drogon's hiding. Are there any caves we can hole up in? Tunnels that lead through the mountain?"

Adam nodded. "Yes. It might take me a few minutes to find the landmarks in the dark, but I'll get us there."

Jinaari nodded. "Good. You take point. Pan, you and Caelynn ride next to Thia. I'll bring up the rear. If I tell you to get her out, do it."

"You're scaring me," she whispered. "What's going on?"

He looked back at her, his voice low. "The Queen took issue with your parentage and doesn't believe your Mark is real. She gave us an hour to get out. If we're still around at that point, she plans to have you arrested."

Drakkus came back around the corner, and he looked at the commander. "The way's clear, and your horses are being saddled now. Morrisy and I will ride with you, help if needed until you get to safety. Exeter is staying here to delay pursuit if he can."

"Good. Let's go." Jinaari put his hand on Thia's back, moving her forward. The clock ticked faster than he wanted it to. They'd get out of the camp in time, but not where they could rest.

Moving quickly, they mounted their horses. Pan took the reins of the pack horse, and then moved closer to Thia. "We're ready," he said.

"Let's go," Jinaari replied. "Go as fast as you can, Adam, but try not to trample anyone."

"Only if they try to do something stupid," he said.

Exeter swung open the gate and they rode out. Caelynn moved alongside Thia, while Pan dropped back. The streets were barely wide enough to ride side by side. Three or four abreast wasn't going to happen until they got clear of the encampment.

He kept his focus on Thia as they rode. Drakkus and Morrisy stayed close enough to discourage pursuit. A number of soldiers came out of their tents or looked up from their fires as they thundered past. He grasped the reins of his horse with his left hand; his right was ready to draw his sword the moment someone got too close.

Finally, the edge of the encampment came into view. Adam sped up his horse, and the rest followed suit. They stayed at a full gallop until they were well beyond the sentry fires. Pulling his horse to a stop, Adam wheeled around. "Try not to get lost," he cautioned them. "I may have to change direction without much warning."

"Rest the horses for a few minutes," Jinaari said, "then we get going. Light up your staff." He looked at Drakkus, "I'll take care of them from here. Go back before you're missed. I don't want you to get in trouble for this."

"I told Exeter to head back to the encampment once we were clear, with instructions to start breaking camp. We were leaving as soon as you did tomorrow. This just speeds things up."

"She won't like that Garret's Paladins left."

"His will trumps that of Her Majesty. Althir, you're one of the best I've ever trained. And you've got the Daughter of Keroys with you. The rest aren't exactly sloppy. If the five of you can't take care of this problem, we need to be where we can help the populace of Avoch. Staying here and being slaughtered isn't part of the plan."

He reached out and grasped his friend's arm in parting. "Garret be with you," he said. "When this is over, I owe you a drink."

Drakkus smiled. "More than one. Keep them safe." He wheeled his horse around and the two rode off into the night.

"Adam?"

The staff the warlock carried emitted a dim light. "Getting my bearings now," he said, looking around. "Care to fill us in on why we're out here without our dinner?"

"Not until you've found that tunnel and I think we're safe enough to camp." Jinaari looked at Thia; her face still hidden under the folds of her hood. *Gods, I hope we find it before the mercenaries come hunting.*

CHAPTER
THIRTY-FOUR

Thia leaned against the tunnel wall near the opening, looking at the morning dew evaporate with the sun's rays. The steam rose in tendrils, blending into a single cloud that made the tower appear to float in the air. If it wasn't for what was inside the building, she'd have thought it was pretty.

"Nervous?" Jinaari said from behind her.

"No, actually," she replied. She didn't turn around but kept looking at the mist. "I thought I would be. I probably *should* be. Instead, I just want this to be over and done with."

"You've gained a warrior's mindset. Instead of dreading what's to come, you want it out of the way so you can enjoy life again."

She smiled at the pride she heard in his voice. "Still feel like you have to babysit me?" she teased him.

He wrapped his arms around her, and she leaned back. The breastplate he wore reassured her. "No. Not one bit. I will watch you, though. I know what you're capable of.

Drogon does, too. But it's your fight. I have my own to deal with."

"Alesso," she said, her voice tinged with sadness.

"Don't waste your pity on him, Thia. He's earned what I'm going to do to him."

"It's not him," she replied. "It's his sister and mother. He did what he did for them, and I think he always knew the price would be high. They didn't ask him to pay it, though."

"I'll feel better when he's dead."

"You can't just kill everyone who hates the Fallen, Jinaari. It's not going to change anyone's mind if we answer violence with more of the same." She took a deep breath, releasing it slowly. "The citizens of Byd Cudd are without a God now, unless Nannan raises someone up to replace Lolc Aon. Even then, not all the Fallen will instantly believe in them. Some may decide to worship one of the other Gods if they're welcomed. Others may become Forsaken. The need for power is strong among them. But more will want to come to the surface, want to rejoin humanity. I have to show Avoch that kindness, compassion, and honor are common among both races. Even if your mother doesn't believe it." Pausing, Thia remembered the look on his face when he told her what prompted their sudden flight. It hurt him to do what he did, and she knew it. "She'll come around. It'll take a few years, and I'll have to make sure that everything I say or do isn't directly a challenge to her rule. Eventually, though, the people will change their minds. It's when that happens, when the Fallen are no longer targeted for hatred and violence, that she'll realize she's wrong. I'll need to talk with Duke Tomil, when we get back to Almair, see where he's at. He's closer to our age, isn't he?"

"I hope so since Amara is engaged to him. Why?"

"It's easier to change the mind of someone younger. They want to challenge the status quo in a way someone who's older doesn't." Something changed in the mist, and she stood up straighter, trying to see the difference better.

"What is it?" he asked.

"Get everyone up," she told him. "Drogon knows we're here and he's sending out his welcoming committee."

The mist started to coalesce into skeletal figures. Their empty eye sockets glowed with an unnatural red light. She turned to Jinaari, pushing against his chest. "Go!" she commanded, "I'll take care of them."

He turned and ran back down the tunnel, yelling at their friends. She faced the oncoming army. Shuffling her feet, she steadied her stance before forming the sigil in her mind. A translucent shield formed in front of the cave. As the skeletons hit the barrier, their animated bones disintegrated into dust. *That should keep us safe until they're ready*, she thought.

She heard the others coming up behind her. "Wow," Pan breathed.

"How many are left?" Adam asked.

"Too many, but not for long," Thia replied. "Stay close to me," she instructed them. "I'm going to create a bubble around us with the shield. We'll be able to walk right up to the front door."

Caelynn chuckled. "You do promise to let us have some fun when we're inside, right?"

She altered the sigil for the spell enough to surround the group with the force field. "Don't run, Jinaari. I need a steady pace to keep this going."

"Got it." He held his sword in his hand and started to walk with even steps. "When we're inside, any resistance is on the three of you. Thia and I have to save our energy for later. This was ... unexpected."

Thia tried not to flinch as they walked across the field. *They're not real people*, she thought. *Just bones of ones long dead. I'm not hurting souls.* The skeletons threw themselves at the bubble without mercy, and she could hear the wails as they disintegrated. "Are we close?"

"Not much farther," Jinaari reassured her. "You're the one that told me to go slow."

He led them to the base of the tower. Red smoke ran through veins in the rock at regular intervals, making it look as if it was alive. "That's creepy," Pan muttered.

"No kidding," Thia replied. "Caelynn? Are you ready? I'm not dropping the shield over there until you are."

The elf fiddled with the lock picks in her hands. Kneeling, she positioned herself at eye level to the door's lock. "I'm ready," she said.

Thia altered her vision and the shield dropped in front of the door, allowing Caelynn to begin her work. A single bead of sweat ran down the side of her face. Jinaari looked at her, concerned. "I'm fine," she said. "It's just warm in this thing. I didn't think about us breathing for long."

"Got it!" Caelynn exclaimed. Glancing over, Thia watched the door swing inward. Caelynn disappeared through the opening.

"Adam, Pan, you two are next," Jinaari said.

"Go," she told him.

"Not until you're in there."

"I have to hold the shield until the last second," she snapped at him. "Get in there, be ready to close the door behind me."

He nodded at her once, then ran through. One step at a time, she walked toward the opening. The skeletons continued to mindlessly come after her, only to turn to ash and be replaced by more. "They're going to charge as soon as I drop this," she said.

"Do it," Jinaari commanded her.

She canceled the spell. As the swarm surged forward, someone grabbed her by the waist, pulling her into the tower, while Jinaari slammed the door shut. An unearthly wail of despair echoed into the chamber as bony fingers clawed at the wood and stone exterior.

Caelynn knelt in front of the lock, working with her picks. "There," she said, looking back over her shoulder. "The only way this door will open now is from this side."

Thia nodded. This was part of the plan. If things went as they hoped, they could take their time unlocking it. If it didn't, Adam was to get any survivors out. *That's not my path, though. Either I live, or Drogon does. One of us dies today.*

The inside of the room glowed with a reddish light from the stone around them. A single staircase wound up into the ceiling above them. "Caelynn, you're up." Jinaari said. She darted past him, taking the steps with caution.

"He knows we're coming," Thia reminded him. "I doubt there's any more locked doors."

"I'm thinking traps. He may try to separate us. And I don't know where Potiri will be in here."

She followed him, both trying to mimic Caelynn's steps. Pan and Adam trailed behind. Thia fought the urge to rush up the stairs. She understood the caution they took. She didn't want any of her friends to be hurt. *Is that realistic? We're going to fight a Forsaken, a Foresworn paladin, and whatever those two can throw at us. I know Jinaari's the better swordsman. And I know facing Drogon is part of what you need me to do, Keroys. But I don't want the price to be one of their lives.*

"It keeps going up," Caelynn said. "I'm not seeing anything but stairs. We've got to be halfway to the top by now."

"Adam," Thia said, "is there any way to tell if this is like your set up back at The Green Frog? Where there's hidden rooms and such?"

"Excellent suggestion," he replied. The tip of his staff glowed with a white light. A single finger of energy began to twist past Thia and Jinaari, hugging the outer edge of the stairs. It stopped between the paladin and bard, snaking around the stone to form the outline of a door and small landing. The illusion was shattered, and the light disappeared.

Caelynn knelt in front of it. "There's no lock," she said as she stood up. Grasping the knob, she twisted it. The door swung open without a sound. "Great," she said dryly, "it's another wall."

Jinaari walked up the few remaining steps and looked over Caelynn's shoulder. "This doesn't make sense," he said. "You said it was a wall, but I see stairs leading up. Thia?"

She started to walk toward them as Caelynn stretched out her arm, "It's a wall, Jinaari. See?"

As soon as her hand touched it, a beam of ice-cold air shot forward. Jinaari dove for Thia, pinning her against a wall. "You okay?" Jinaari asked her.

"Yeah," she said. Looking past him, she saw Caelynn lying on the floor; her skin turning blue as she watched. Dashing over to her friend, she knelt next to her. Her breathing was shallow as her entire body shivered. Thia focused on healing her. Her heartbeat and breathing became normal, but the color didn't fade. "It's not working," she said, panicking.

Pan's arms lifted her up. "Go. I'll take care of her. Adam will keep us safe. You and Jinaari have things to do."

"He's right, Thia. Tell me what you see through that opening."

Twisting, she stared at the doorway. "A single set of stairs, heading up."

"Adam? Pan?"

"It's a wall, like Caelynn said," the warlock answered. Pan nodded in agreement.

Jinaari said, "That's what I thought. You and I are the only ones who can pass safely, Thia. The rest stay here."

Pointing at Caelynn, she protested, "But she's hurt!"

"More will be hurt or killed if we don't do this. Pan and Adam will take care of her. You and I have appointments to keep." He glanced at Caelynn's body. "She'd want you to finish the job first."

Her heart was breaking, but Thia knew he was right. *She's stable. As long as Pan can get her warm, keep the frost from damaging her body, Caelynn will pull through.* "Let's go," she said.

Jinaari looked at Adam. "You know what to do."

"Good luck, old man."

She followed him up the stairs. Two steps up, she glanced back, hoping to see Caelynn one more time. The door had closed behind them.

"Hey," Jinaari said. "You need to focus, find that calm you had this morning. She'll be fine until you get back. If your mind isn't in the fight—"

"It won't matter anyway because I'll be dead." She nodded. He was right. The only thing she could do now for Caelynn was beat Drogon.

The staircase was steep, with handrails on each side. The same red smoke ran through the rocks here as it did elsewhere, illuminating the passage with a deathly light. There was enough of it to reflect off Jinaari's armor. The effect chilled her to the bone. *If I believed in omens, it would mean one of two things. Either one would include him being covered in blood. Whether it's his or someone else's is the question.*

He glanced back at her. "Everything okay?"

"Yeah. The light in here is crazy."

"It changes up ahead. I think we're near the top," he said.

"And then what?"

"Either we find what we're after, who we're after, or we keep looking."

Twenty steps later, she waited as he disappeared. "It's clear," he said. "Come up."

She ascended the last of the stairs and crawled out of a hole into a well-lit chamber. The reflection of a half dozen lit braziers on pedestals bounced off the polished marble walls, illuminating the room. Drogon sat on a high-backed chair across the chamber from them. The sickly yellow hue of his eyes stood out even more than it was the last time she saw him. Thia spotted a rune carved into the base of the throne. That had to be hit first.

"Welcome, Thia. How's your friend?" he smiled coldly.

"She'll be fine," she replied, keeping the tone conversational. She knew Jinaari was behind her, but she pushed him from her mind and focused everything on Drogon. His fingers flickered briefly, and she saw the threads of his spell in her mind as they headed her way. With a small smile, she waived a hand and dismissed them when they were close enough. "Did you really think a simple binding spell would hold me now, Drogon? I'm not the same person I was the last time we met."

The weathered face grew stern. "No, you're not. I can see that. You've come here to destroy me. Why?"

"The Forsaken have no place in this world. The Gods do not disavow even one follower easily. To have every single one of them turn away from someone means there is no hope, no redemption. Your madness led you down a dark path, one even they won't walk. I cannot allow you to unleash that upon Avoch."

As she spoke, an image formed in her mind. *Just see it, Daughter, and it will happen,* Keroys voice echoed in her soul.

The sigil he showed her solidified and magic shot out from her hands.

It hit the base of the throne between his shoes. "Sloppy," he chided her. "You may have the capacity, but your aim leaves much to be desired!"

As the words left his mouth, the chair collapsed beneath his weight, and he fell into the heap of rubble. "On the contrary," she said. "I know exactly where I'm aiming."

He pushed himself up, one hand raised to his face in disbelief. Blood ran in a thin line from the palm. Recovering quickly, he snapped his fingers.

Thia heard the sound of metal on metal as a pair of swords met behind her. Had Jinaari found Alesso? *Don't look!* She forced herself to keep her eyes on her opponent. *Jinaari's the better swordsman. He's doing his task so I can do mine.*

"You have no idea what you carry, witch!" Drogon screamed as he stood up. "Give me what is mine! That Mark on your back gives you everything you'll ever need. You will never know the pain of being cut off from magic. Give it to me and I'll let you and your friends go."

"And then what, Drogon? We walk out of here and live our lives while you enslave the rest of the world? While you destroy every person you believe slighted you? Drink at a tavern and tell stories while Avoch burns around us? No," she shook her head. "I will die a thousand deaths before that happens."

The bolt came at her fast, and she barely deflected it. The hair on her arms rose as the air around her became charged with electricity. Without thinking, she threw a ball of fire at him. When the air cleared in front of him, he still stood but the edges of his robe were singed.

They continued to throw spell after spell at each other; neither willing to back down. "He's dying, Thia," Drogon hissed at her. For a moment, she hesitated. "Go ahead and look. You let your friend down below die and brought this one up here to meet his doom. The other two won't last until the moon rises. You've lost, Daughter of Keroys. Give me what I want and live."

She heard the exhaustion in his voice. The strength of his spells had started to lessen. Her chest heaved from the effort, but she hadn't even begun to reach the bottom of her stores. *If Jinaari's dying, so be it. I can't help him by giving up.* Ignoring the sweat that trickled down her face, she gathered up more magic than she'd ever handled before and, with a scream that came from the depths of her soul, sent the bolt of energy toward Drogon.

The backlash of the spell hurled her away from her foe. Her body crashed against the marble wall. As she fell to the ground, she saw the Forsaken burst in flames the color of the sun. His screams were the last things she heard.

Thia's body flew past Jinaari, slamming into the wall not far from where he fought Alesso. *Thia!* He glanced her way. Her body lay still, unmoving.

Alesso's blade crashed down on his left shoulder. The edge slicing through a gap in the plates and biting into his skin. Jinaari sucked in his breath from the pain; his arm hung useless at his side.

"Your witch may have beat Drogon, Althir, but you haven't beaten me." Alesso mocked him. "She's dead. When I'm done with you, I'll make sure the rest of them are, as well."

Jinaari let a small smile form on his face. "You think you've beaten me? I'm not even winded yet." Ignoring the pain and blood that flowed from the wound, he swung his sword toward Potiri's legs. His opponent jumped backward to avoid the blow, stumbling on a small rock on the floor and falling prone.

He walked the few feet and stood over the man who was once his brother. "I'll tell your mother and sister you died quickly." Before Alesso could react, Jinaari plunged his sword through his chest.

The room began to spin. He was losing blood, and fast. Yanking his blade from Potiri's body, he stumbled toward Thia, the tip of his sword dragging across the floor. *Please be alive*, he prayed silently. Falling to his knees, he saw the faint rise and fall of her chest. Dropping the weapon, he reached out and touched her hand. What little magic he had left went to strengthen her. If he was going to die, at least she would survive.

As blackness overtook him, he heard Adam scream his name.

CHAPTER
THIRTY-FIVE

Pain woke her. An intense, burning sensation that told Thia she was still alive and made her wish she was dead at the same time.

Carefully, she opened her eyes. The illusionary wall had been activated, letting her see the waves crash upon the rocky shore. Her room, then, at The Green Frog. *But how did I get here?*

"Cousin?" Pan's voice was barely audible. "Are you awake?"

Thia tried to push herself up, but pain seared through her spine. Giving up, she sunk back into the mattress. "I think so," she said.

She heard him walk across the room toward her; his face coming into view as he sat on the bed beside her. "I don't recommend moving yet. I was able to fuse the broken bones, but they're awfully weak still. I'm not nearly as good at healing as you are."

"How'd we get back here?" she asked. *Maybe if I start with the easy questions, the hard ones won't be as bad.*

"Adam brought us. He didn't break his staff this time, either."

"How long ago?"

"Only a day or two. You've been asleep since we found you and Jinaari upstairs. There was a huge explosion, and the door you both went through opened again. Only this time it led right to where you guys were. We put Caelynn where we could hold onto all three of you and Adam did that thing he did to get us out of Byd Cudd."

"Did we," she took a deep breath, cringing at the pain. "Did we lose anyone?"

"Caelynn's alive, but her skin's strange. I did my best to get her warm. Adam helped, too, but that blast did something to her. She was the first one that woke up when we got back, but she hasn't said much to me. Adam's been spending a lot of time in her room, talking with her."

Thia nodded. "What about Jinaari?" Her soul hurt thinking about the answer.

"He woke up yesterday. He wanted to come in here, but Adam put a force field around his bed so he couldn't move. Something about he needed to calm down before he did something stupid."

"Like what?" she asked.

"Like punch holes in the wall until you woke up from the noise."

Thia and Pan both turned their heads toward the door. Jinaari stood there, leaning against the frame, with one arm in a sling. "Pan, can you give us a few minutes?" he asked.

"Um, yeah," he said, rising from the bed. "Don't let her get up, though. Her bones are likely to break again if she moves too much." The young man brushed past the paladin and left.

Jinaari closed the door and started to walk toward her.

"You look horrible," he said, his voice light. "I knew your stubbornness would be a problem. If you're going to use that much magic, didn't it occur to you to brace yourself somehow?"

"No. I mean, there was this other fight between a jerk and an arrogant prick going on behind me. I thought I could help you out if my path took me through Alesso." She smiled at him as he sat down on the bed. Nodding at the sling, she said, "He got one good shot in, at least. Does that mean you're some old man now?"

He laughed. "Adam gets away with calling me that, but you shouldn't even start." Reaching out with his good hand, he pushed some hair off her face. "I saw you flying across the room, heard your body hit the wall. That's when he got the shot in. It was the last one he ever got. On anyone."

"Good." She sighed. "Drogon?"

"Was becoming a pile of ash when I passed out." He pointed to his shoulder. "Potiri almost severed my arm, and I was losing blood. Pan patched me up before we came back here."

She frowned. "Show me."

"No."

"Excuse me?"

"You need to take care of yourself right now. You broke your back, ribs, and a few other things. Pan and Adam were able to put the bones back together, but they need to get stronger. Which means the only magic you're allowed to do for the foreseeable future is on yourself. Caelynn and I can wait."

"How is she?" Thia asked. "Pan said something was wrong with her skin." She imagined a healing sigil in her mind, let it settle over her body. The pain lessened considerably, and the weakness left her. She didn't feel perfect, but she wouldn't break when she tried to walk.

"It's blue now. The cold settled into her enough to change it. She's adjusting because her body is more sensitive to heat. Adam's been working in her room, getting the temperature comfortable so she can move around easier. I honestly don't know if she'll ever be the same."

"What happens now?"

"What do you mean?"

"Your mother threatened to have me arrested if I remember correctly. Does that still stand? Or did taking out a Forsaken redeem me in her eyes?" she said bitterly.

"Once I convinced Adam to let me get up, I got word to Tomil. He's looking into it. Even if she followed through on the threat, he won't enforce it. He's going to announce that the Daughter of Keroys has taken up residence in Almair. That, once she is ready, she will welcome any who wish to speak with her. But that any attempts at violence against her will be met with retribution from him. You'll be safe. He's working with the cloister on giving you a space where people can seek your wisdom without you being in any sort of danger. And has taken steps to make sure no one bothers you when you're here at the inn."

"Seek my wisdom?" She laughed. "I can't remember to brace myself when casting a spell."

"Doesn't matter. You've been hiding who you are, what you are, your entire life. When you walked out for the feast in Cirrain, that changed. You showed the world what I've seen for months. Most of the questions are going to be easy. People know what they need to do, but they're scared. They don't want to make the choice, so they'll come to you. You've made some tough decisions, Thia. I've seen you do it. Wisdom isn't telling someone what they should do, it's showing them the support they need to make the decision themselves."

"What about you? You've renounced your titles. You're as much a fugitive from the crown as I am."

He shifted. "Garret's ordered the chapterhouse near Dragonspire to be abandoned. They're coming here, siding with Tomil and you. If I'm needed, Drakkus knows where to find me." He gently picked up one of her hands and kissed it. "I made a promise to protect you, Thia. That hasn't changed. The only way it does is if Garret tells me to stop. Or you do."

"I suppose it's proper for the Daughter of Keroys to have a champion. Someone that stays by her side at all times." She smiled at him. "Someone suitably arrogant, insufferable, and demanding, of course."

"Of course," he whispered as he leaned down and kissed her.

SHIELD AND SCEPTER
NOVEMBER 2023

Acknowledgments

If you've followed me on social media, you know that I'm a big Dungeons & Dragons player. I've played the game since the late 1970's/early 1980's. It's been a constant source of inspiration for books, stories, and a way for me to explore the possibilities of life. Sometimes it takes playing a character who's strong for us to find that strength in ourselves.

Since 2015, I've been playing with one group of friends. We've kept characters around while players had to leave the table for months on end and found a way to stay connected during the pandemic. These people, for the most part, are my chosen family. We call ourselves The Murder Hobos.

I cannot let this book end without acknowledging the members. While not all appear in this one, I think it's important to let the world know who they were, and which character they brought to life at the table.

> Ed Brabant – Jinaari Althir
> Dale Collins – Helix Yarnchaser
> Joshua Collins – Pan Beckenburg
> Jillian Morgan – Caelynn
> Matt Morgan – Adam
> Rob Rowland – Gnat
> KM Warfield – Thia Bransdottir

ABOUT THE AUTHOR

Born in the late 1960's, K. M. has lived most of her life in the Pacific NW. While she's always been creative, she didn't turn towards writing until 2008. Writing under the name of KateMarie Collins, she released several titles. In 2019, the decision was made to forge a new path with her books. The Heroes of Avoch series, along with a new pen name, are the end result.

When she's not writing, she loves playing Dungeons & Dragons with friends, watching movies, and cuddling up with her cat. K. M. resides with her family in what she likes to refer to as "Seattle Suburbia".

You can find K. M. at the following sites:

Twitter: @KMWarfieldbooks
Her website: http://kmwarfield.com
Via email: kmwarfieldbooks@gmail.com

www.ingramcontent.com/pod-product-compliance
Lightning Source LLC
LaVergne TN
LVHW040038080526
838202LV00045B/3389